ECHOES OF THE SERPENT

A H JORDANE

HONEYWOOD HOUSE

First Edition
ISBN: 978-1-968183-02-8
Printed in the United States
Published by Honeywood House LLC
www.honeywoodhousepublishing.com
For permissions, contact:
info@honeywoodhousepublishing.com

Contents

CHAPTER ONE

Normal Is a Temporary Condition

They may think their secrets are safe, but her eyes are always on them. Not that anyone would notice. Few ever sense the quiet ones watching from the dark.

From her shadowy office, Ophira kept vigil. The city beyond her windows was bustling with activity, and her systems recorded it all. She tracked movements and flagged anomalies before anyone even noticed. If something tried to slip past her network, she would catch it. She always did.

At 4:17 a.m., the city lingered between darkness and dawn. Behind her, the coffee machine hissed as she reached for her hand-painted mug. A chill pressed against the windows. Outside the glass, the skyline stayed shrouded in darkness, a city stuck in stillness before waking.

Wall-to-wall feeds flickered in silent sync: a luxury penthouse in Dubai, an underground vault in Prague, and a long corridor lined with priceless treasures. The museum slept behind thick doors. The desert compound remained still. The estate in Argentina had not stirred for hours. Each was a world behind locked doors, each under her quiet watch.

She liked it that way.

A single command sent diagnostics sweeping through her network, the keyboard cool beneath her fingers. Threads of code flashed on the central screen, showing signal integrity checks, intrusion scans, and anomaly logs. She leaned back, holding her mug as data streamed across the display.

Three misaligned sensors. Already flagged for recalibration.

A delayed camera reset in Tokyo. Logged and corrected.

Nothing out of place. Nothing to worry about. Not yet.

She made a note for Aric to follow up. Double-checking was integral to the rhythm. She spent several minutes reviewing overnight alerts.

The clock ticked forward. 4:23 a.m. Another ordinary day.

A cold tingle brushed the edge of her awareness, neither sharp nor sudden but familiar. The feeling of being watched lingered just beyond reach. She sipped her coffee as her instincts stirred, restless.

Nothing. Not yet.

Getting paranoid, she thought.

Ay, querida, you wound me, Valentina teased, her voice a sultry blend of Spanish and French. *It's too early for your drama.*

Honey, some of us were dreamin' of sunbeams and songbirds, Sunny murmured, warm and slow like a Southern breeze. *Let a girl rest, sugar.*

Ophira didn't respond to them as she focused on the feeds, her gaze sweeping across the screens in search of an answer to the unease curling beneath her skin. The shifting images showed clean hallways, empty vaults, and guards sipping coffee in quiet lobbies.

She reached for the clipboard near her keyboard and recorded her morning updates by hand. Ink flowed across the paper in the precise rhythm she had memorized.

Most people expected danger to announce itself with sound and fury. In her experience, it never did. Routines were disrupted, order was overturned, and the illusion of control was shattered. That was how danger usually announced itself.

Behind her, the monitors flickered as a camera briefly glitched and then stabilized. A minor hiccup.

She didn't notice. But something had changed in the digital landscape around her, a disturbance too subtle for screens to capture.

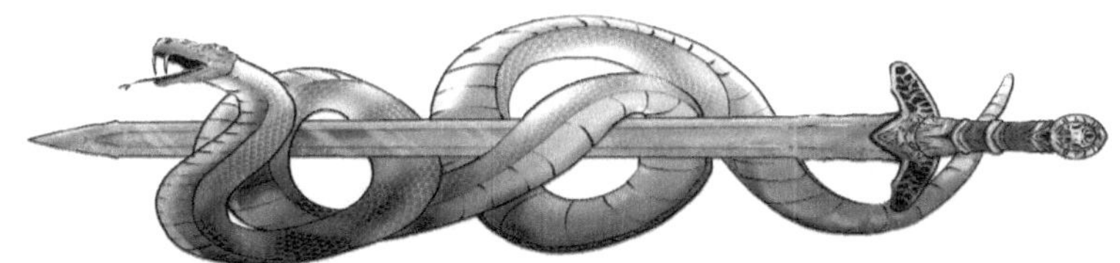

A feeling crept over Ophira as instinct tightened in her chest. The air in her office was too still, thick with charged tension, like the moment before lightning struck.

Something is wrong.

Stillness pressed in, quiet and expectant. The morning chill pressed against the windows behind her as the coffee aroma blended with the sterile warmth of the electronics. Across the room, shelves overflowed with case files and ancient research, straddling one foot in the modern world and the other rooted in history.

Everything was as she had left it. Normal.

But her instincts didn't trust normal.

The security feeds continued recording clean, empty corridors. A guard stretched, a paper cup in hand. The museum was quiet under the soft glow of automated exhibits. Outside, dawn peeled gold across glass and steel. The soft hum of electronics filled the quiet. The clock read 4:31 a.m.

Not a single detail was out of alignment.

Yet unease crept up her spine. She had built this fortress of routines on control. Nothing slipped through the cracks. But the stillness gnawed at her, a knot she couldn't untie.

What am I missing?

She leaned forward, her fingers gliding over the keyboard as she cycled through the feeds. Something had triggered her unease, somewhere between one frame and the next. She had to find it.

Ain't that a shady character sneakin' 'round Camera 5? Zeke interrupted her, his lazy cowboy drawl laced with dry amusement.

Ophira's lips twitched, but she stayed silent.

Ignore Zeke, Sage cut in crisply. *Check Camera 3. That's where your glitch came from.*

Her fingers hesitated over the keys. A glitch? *No.*

She hadn't noticed a glitch, but her companions always did.

They weren't new to her. They had always existed, woven into her thoughts as naturally as breathing. Not hallucinations. Not madness.

They were her. Different tones of the same chord.

Ophira adjusted the view, focusing on Camera 3. Initially, it displayed nothing unusual, the long, sterile hallway leading to the restricted vaults.

Then a flicker. A brief ripple distorted the image.

No, that's not right.

Bah! Camera feeds are beneath us! Valentina declared, a flash of shimmering gold flickering in Ophira's peripheral vision. *Let's do something worthy of legend!*

You've got this, sugar pie, Sunny murmured, her warm voice easing the edges of Ophira's focus.

Ophira gave a measured exhale, suppressing the urge to snap at them. *All of you, stop. I'm trying to concentrate.*

The glitch shouldn't have bothered her. She managed security for some of the world's most high-profile clients. Glitches were routine, and she was always in control of the situation.

And yet the unease in her chest whispered a familiar truth: control was an illusion, fragile and fleeting. In her line of work, routine could spiral into chaos in an instant.

She flagged the footage for review.

Aric could examine the backend later to determine if it was interference, feedback, or something less explainable.

She didn't have time to chase ghosts.

Her gaze drifted to her desk, where ancient fragments rested. Memories of another time. An ancient bronze medallion, its edges smoothed by centuries, was beside a shattered piece of pottery, its painted symbols still whispering of the gods who had made and abandoned it.

She picked up the medallion. It felt colder than she remembered, pressing into her palm like an echo of something she couldn't name. Her fingers tightened around it and then released.

Artifacts from another time.

Of another her.

Well, now, Sunny said, *that medallion sure does bring back some memories.*

Yeah, Zeke muttered, *like that one time it got us into a world of trouble. Pretty sure we almost died.*

Ah, but what is life without a bit of danger, Ophira? Valentina cooed, coiling in a grand flourish. *Live boldly! Seize ze day, as ze poets say!*

Val, honey, Sunny cut in, *some of us prefer a little peace 'fore we go invitin' trouble to sit down and stay a while.*

Ophira tightened her grip around the pen as she picked it up from her desk. *Boldness landed us in this mess in the first place.*

And caution kept us alive, Sage reminded her. *Don't forget that.*

She didn't. Not for a moment. The relics seemed to pulse with old memories, reminders of what she'd once been. The legend she used to be.

The world has forgotten you, Zeke murmured.

But you haven't, Sage said, his voice sharp and measured. *Look forward, not back. Don't let the past pull you in.*

Ophira closed her eyes for a moment, drawing a slow breath. *I'm not getting pulled in.* She knew better than most what happened when memory dictated the future.

But the unease lingered, echoing in her mind. The world knew her as Ophira, a top-tier security consultant and expert in systems, safeguards, and digital fortresses. They had no idea that beneath the sleek modern exterior, behind the sharp mind and steady hands, she was something ancient.

Something much deadlier.

The world may have forgotten Medusa.

But Medusa hadn't gone anywhere. She was just harder to find, living under a new name.

Her gaze returned to the polished surfaces of her monitors. Dark hair pulled into a neat bun, olive skin smooth and unmarked, and sharp hazel eyes scanned the world around her. *Normal.* Yet the past was never far behind.

Nor was the hunt.

And something told her that today wouldn't be an ordinary day.

Too quiet. Something's coming. Mark my words, Sage grumbled.

Let's not go lookin' for trouble, Sunny replied gently. *But Fee, honey, you do seem a little wound up. Take a deep breath.*

Why take a breath when you can take action? Valentina snickered, her golden highlights shimmering in the light as she swayed dramatically.

Ophira sighed and reclined in her chair. *You all sound like an anxiety support group gone rogue.*

The snakes closest to her face, which she affectionately referred to as her bang snakes, were always the most outspoken. They were more than decorations or reminders; they were part of her. A chorus of instincts she had come to live with, listen to, and at times ignore.

Valentina graced her left temple like the classic devil on her shoulder, her crimson scales with flame-like patterns befitting her role as the bold instigator who offered dramatic solutions with theatrical flair.

Sage crowned the center-top of her head like a living headpiece, his silver scales with circuit-like patterns symbolizing his role as her intellectual advisor, offering sharp tactical insights in his impatient New York accent.

Zeke, positioned at the front right of her head, served as her immediate advisor. His dark green scales, adorned with yellow lightning-bolt streaks, reflected his role as the first voice she heard in split second decisions, always ready with dry commentary delivered in his signature cowboy twang.

Sunny coiled comfortably near her right ear, where she could whisper reassurance directly, her golden scales with gentle wave patterns embodying her role as the group's calming presence with her warm Southern drawl.

Her human guise was merely a mask, a charming presentation crafted by a concealment charm. Underneath it all, she remained Medusa, and they were as integral to her being as the breath in her lungs.

Zeke chuckled. *Aw, darlin', if I had a heart, I'd be real touched right now.*

Ophira rolled her eyes at him, shaking her head as she sipped her coffee before getting back to work.

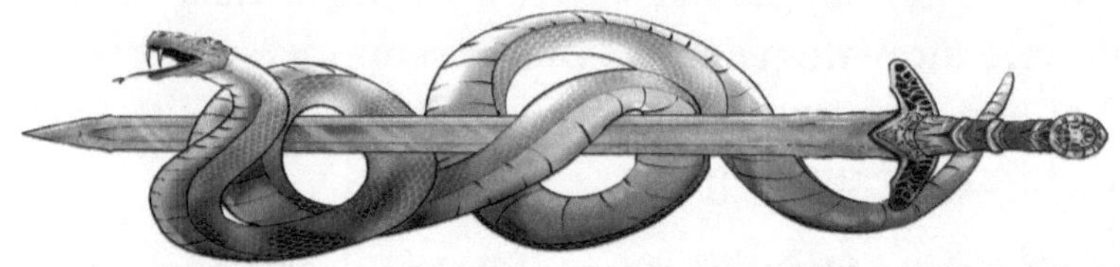

The shrill ring of her phone broke the morning stillness. Ophira glanced at the caller ID, registering the unknown number. Her fingers curled. Unknown callers rarely meant anything good. She sighed and picked up.

"Hello?"

The response flowed through the speaker like liquid smoke, warm, deep, and rich. A velvety undertone wrapped around her senses.

Each syllable laced with calm confidence that curled around her like incense. There was no rush, no demand. Just quiet, controlled power that made her sit straighter. This voice didn't ask for attention. It *commanded* it.

"Ophira Naga, I presume?" The air in the room shifted, becoming dense and charged, like the pressure before a storm.

Her grip on the receiver tightened. The way he said her name sent a slow shiver down her spine, an unsettling chill she didn't like. She was rarely caught off guard, and she hated it. Yet even now, she felt her defenses softening, slipping. That voice reminded her of ancient temples and sacred smoke. Of gods who spoke in riddles. It was the kind of voice that invited belief.

A trap.

Part of her didn't want to pull away. Zeke stirred uneasily near her collarbone, his coils tighter than usual. That alone told her to pay attention. She shook her head as if to clear the fog.

"Yes, this is Ophira. And you are?" She remained professional, neutral, even as her mind raced, trying to place the voice.

His soft laugh that followed was unhurried and refined, like a finely aged whiskey, leaving a lingering warmth that made her want to take another sip to savor the sensation. The hum of the monitors seemed louder now.

"My name is Marcus Templeson," he replied. "I've heard you're the best in the business at solving delicate matters."

Ophira found herself leaning into the phone, as if drawn closer by the sheer magnetism of his voice.

"I'm good at what I do." Her thoughts sharpened, weighing his words. There was a luxurious quality in his speech, like he savored the shape of every syllable. Not rushed. Not insistent. Just deeply certain that he would be heard. It was a voice built for persuasion. Or temptation. Her instincts flared, both intrigued and cautious.

"Oh, I believe it's more than that," Marcus replied, his tone deepening enough to feel intimate. "You solve problems most people wouldn't dare touch. That's exactly what I need."

A faint chill traced the back of her neck, raising the fine hairs at her nape.

There was a rhythm to this conversation. A pacing. Each pause was perfectly timed to let her lean in, just a little, before the next hook slid into place. She adjusted to the tempo before she even realized it.

"What kind of problem?" she asked, though she wasn't sure she wanted to know the answer.

"I have a proposition for you," Marcus continued. "A certain set of relics has gone missing. I believe you may be the only one capable of retrieving them."

Ophira raised an eyebrow, her mind immediately locking onto the word "relics." She felt a subtle shift in the atmosphere, as though the temperature in the room had dropped a few degrees. Relics weren't ordinary cases. They were dangerous, and far too often, they involved the divine.

Don't get reeled in, Zeke muttered. *His kind never bait the line unless they're sure you'll bite.*

"A set of relics, you say?" She kept her tone calm, but every sense was fully alert.

"Yes," Marcus replied. "A set of four ancient artifacts from a Mediterranean temple collection. Of great importance, I assure you. I can't share many details over an unsecured line, but I believe you're the right person for the job."

That voice curled into the edges of her mind, planting suggestions that sounded like her own.

Ophira narrowed her eyes at the screen in front of her, though her focus slipped from the security feeds. Something inside her stirred, an old instinct she hadn't felt in years. He wasn't merely a potential client. There was something more to Marcus, a presence she couldn't quite define.

You're being played, Sage warned sharply. *This is a masterclass in manipulation.*

She leaned back, calculating. "Why me?"

There was a brief silence on the other end, long enough for Ophira to feel the tension mount. When Marcus spoke again, his voice was lower. "Because you're known for solving the unsolvable. And this case needs someone with a particular set of skills."

The way he said *skills* sent another shiver down her spine, a word so perfectly placed in his velvety voice that it promised more than just a business transaction. For a moment, Ophira's thoughts strayed, imagining Marcus in person. She could see him, sharp and composed, carrying a presence that matched the authority in his voice. The image lingered, the fantasy drawing her in without her realizing.

They would be sitting across from each other, his voice softer, more intimate, the edges of their conversation blurred by a growing tension. His gaze would linger a little too long, his smile pulling her in without effort. She could almost feel the warmth of the moment—

She snapped herself back to reality, shaking her head slightly. A loose strand of dark hair slipped free from her bun, but she ignored it. *What the hell was that?*

"I see," she said. "I'll need more details before I make any decisions."

Marcus chuckled softly, a low, resonant sound that sent another chill down her spine. "Of course. I'd be happy to explain more in person. I think you'll find the case intriguing."

Ophira glanced at the ancient medallion on her desk, feeling a growing sense of unease. It seemed colder than it had a moment ago. Like it too was listening. The hairs on the back of her neck prickled, and yet she was indeed intrigued. The word relics hung in the air between them, charged with significance.

"And when would you like to meet?" she asked, already aware that she was agreeing.

"Today, if possible." Marcus's voice remained smooth and unhurried. "I'll be in your area this afternoon. We can meet at your office, if you'd like. I have the address."

Ophira felt her breath catch for a moment. He wasn't rushing her, but there was a quiet urgency beneath the surface, a subtle suggestion that this was a matter she couldn't afford to ignore.

She exhaled, fingers pressing against the smooth surface of her desk. *I could say no. I should say no. I should ask for more details first.* But the words slipped free before she could stop them.

"I can make time. My office is fine," she replied, tamping down the unexpected thrill humming beneath her skin.

"Excellent," Marcus said, his voice a rich, honeyed tone that made her spine tingle. "I look forward to meeting you in person, Ophira."

She could hear the satisfaction in his voice. And worse, she didn't hate the way it sounded when he said her name. "Until then," she replied, hanging up before she could dwell on how his voice seemed to linger. Even after she ended the call, her pulse raced, fingers still curled tightly around the phone. *It was just a voice. Just a man.* Yet his presence lingered, a whisper threading through her mind, impossible to shake. And that was a problem.

That was not normal, Sage muttered. *Something's not right here.*

He's got a voice like sin dipped in honey, Zeke drawled. *And you're actin' like you already licked the spoon.*

Ooh, Valentina purred from above her ear, *I like him.*

Ophira stared at the phone long after the call had ended, fingers still loosely gripping the receiver. The silence in the room felt heavier now, thick with tension she couldn't shake. She let out a gradual breath, forcing herself to release the phone and lean back in her chair. Her fingers tapped a steady beat against the desk, restless.

She rotated her neck, forcing the tension from her shoulders. No distractions. She had work to do.

A soft knock at the door pulled her from her musings. She blinked and squared her shoulders, pushing the last remnants of the call aside.

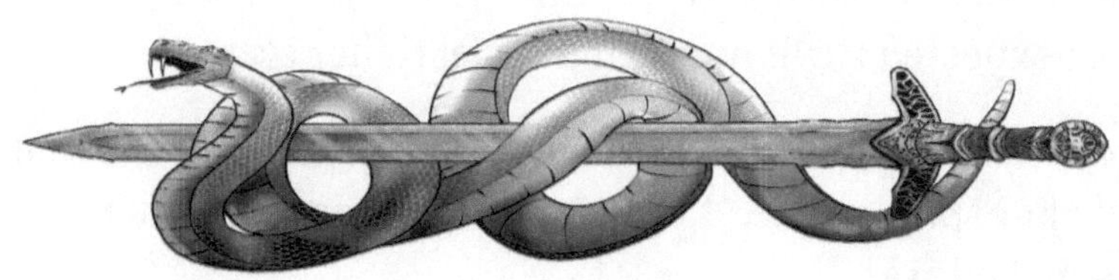

"Morning, Fee. Busy as usual, I see." Aric's voice sounded light and teasing as he stepped into the room. He tugged a knit beanie from his head, raking a hand through his windblown curls and shaking off the morning chill.

Well, if it ain't Mr. Sunshine himself. What's he grinning about? Zeke muttered, his dark green scales shifting near her right temple.

Now, don't be like that. He's a good man. Y'all play nice, Sunny said gently.

He distracts her from her true destiny! We are above such mundane ties! Valentina gasped in mock scandal.

Sage's tone remained flat. *His posture's relaxed, but he's scanning the room. He's perceptive. Don't underestimate him.*

Aric is not our enemy, and you know it. Cut the dramatics, Ophira chided them.

She didn't need to look to know it was Aric. Her body had already registered his presence, the shift in temperature, the slight easing in her shoulders. His energy always settled into the corners of her space like it belonged there. But comfort didn't dissolve caution.

He had been by her side for years now, her closest friend and the only partner she'd ever trusted fully. Since the day she hired him on a recommendation from someone who no longer existed in public record, he'd become the one constant in her carefully constructed life.

He was steady, brilliant, and intuitive. If she trusted anyone in this life, it was Aric Somner.

And still, trust had limits.

Ophira kept her expression neutral, though the snakes' banter pulled at her focus. "Same as always," she said. "I'm checking the overnight feeds. We had a few glitches I want to look into."

He stepped further in, leaning against the edge of her desk, arms folded in that easy, familiar way that always put her at ease. "And here I thought you'd finally learned how to relax."

Ophira allowed herself a faint smile. "You know me better than that."

He did, better than anyone. But even Aric didn't know everything.

He didn't know that Ophira Naga was merely the name she wore in this life, a mask hiding something else entirely. That the woman before him had been cursed by a goddess, hunted through history, and reborn in silence. He didn't know that the relics scattered across her desk weren't curiosities or collector's pieces.

They were memories.

She shot him a sidelong glance. His easy posture, the way he moved around her space without hesitation, spoke volumes about the depth of their partnership. But even with Aric, there were walls she couldn't let down. It wasn't the curse that kept her guarded. It was the danger, the threat that always loomed out of sight.

Aric moved to his desk, a second workstation across the room, cluttered with blueprints and half-dismantled surveillance gear. "Everything good?" he asked casually, slinging his coat over the back of the chair.

"Yeah," Ophira replied, her voice sharper than she intended. She shot him a glance, hoping he wouldn't notice the tension radiating from her.

He didn't seem to notice. "Good to hear. I swear, things are so quiet this morning I might fall asleep."

Ophira forced a smile, turning her attention back to the security feeds, though she wasn't really seeing them. "Quiet's better than trouble, right?"

Aric chuckled softly, leaning back in his chair. "True. Still, it'd be nice to have something to break up the monotony."

Monotony. Ophira nearly laughed. Excitement had already knocked, but she kept that to herself.

"Give it time," she said lightly, hoping to steer the conversation away from the growing turmoil in her head. The banter helped, but her thoughts kept circling the call.

Aric glanced at her, a teasing grin on his face. "You never let anything shake you, do you?" His grin faded slightly as his gaze lingered on her. "You say everything's fine, but your shoulders are saying something else."

If only he knew. The professional mask she wore had never felt heavier than it did now. And with Marcus's voice still echoing in her mind, control was the last thing she felt.

The snakes had gone quiet. All of them. Not out of disinterest but out of caution. That told her everything she needed to know.

"I'm fine," she replied a little too quickly.

He nodded and crossed the room to his desk, but she could feel his eyes on her a moment longer than necessary.

She managed a slight shrug, keeping her tone even. "It's a matter of focus."

"Yeah, well," Aric shot her a playful glance, "if anything interesting happens, let me know. Maybe I'll finally get a chance to prove I'm not just the pretty one."

Ophira smiled at his banter, the familiarity of it grounding her. Aric had no idea about the battle she was fighting internally, the way her attention kept straying back to Marcus. He didn't need to know.

"Any interesting cases come through?" he asked, reaching out to tap the edge of her desk, eyes scanning the assorted relics with curiosity.

Ophira shook her head. "Nothing out of the ordinary." But even as she said it, she felt the stirrings of something she couldn't quite place. It had been quiet lately. Her eyes flicked to the medallion Marcus had stirred into memory. It looked different now. Dimmer.

Aric sighed, overly dramatic. "Guess we'll have to make our own excitement."

She raised an eyebrow, watching as he moved toward the window, pulling the blinds open slightly to let in the morning light. "Excitement has a way of finding us whether we want it or not."

Aric shot her a grin, his usual easy charm lighting up the room. "Then I guess we'd better be ready."

Ophira chuckled softly but didn't respond. Her attention was back on the screens, where the live feeds flickered through images of offices, warehouses, and luxury estates.

She pressed a button, zooming in on one of the feeds. The corner of a warehouse, a place that had been flagged in her system for a security breach a few weeks ago, caught her attention.

"What's caught your eye?" Aric asked, watching her with mild interest.

Ophira didn't look up. "A routine check. Nothing to worry about."

He made a noncommittal sound, leaning against the wall now, arms crossed over his chest. "You're running on edge today."

"Today's an ordinary day," Ophira said more to herself than to him. But even as she spoke, a flicker of unease passed through her. She couldn't shake the feeling that something was coming, something she couldn't quite see yet.

Aric chuckled, his hands shoved into his pockets. "You know, you really ought to take it easy sometime. The city will survive without you watching over it every second."

Ophira allowed herself a faint smile. "Maybe, but I prefer to be sure."

He shook his head, his grin widening as he moved away from the wall and perched on the edge of her desk, spinning her favorite pen between his fingers like he owned the place. "You've got this place locked down tighter than Fort Knox. I'd say you're more than sure. You see anything unusual?"

"Not yet," Ophira replied, her fingers tapping lightly on the edge of her keyboard. "But it's early."

Aric flashed her a grin, a playful spark in his eyes. "Let's hope the day stays boring. We could use a break."

Ophira arched an eyebrow. "Says the man who was complaining about monotony five minutes ago."

He smirked. "Yeah, well, I am a deeply complex individual."

The only thing deep about him is his hero complex, Zeke chimed in.

She chuckled softly, watching as Aric made himself comfortable. Their partnership had always been easy, familiar, and light-hearted. Aric was the only person in her life who made her feel almost normal, but she had learned the cost of soft places and soft feelings the hard way.

As he picked up one of the ancient relics on her desk, inspecting it with casual curiosity, Ophira felt the familiar pull of the past. To Aric, they were odd decorations, curiosities she had collected over the years. But to her, they were reminders of the life she kept hidden, even from him.

"What's this one's story?" he asked, holding up the painted pottery shard that normally sat on her desk.

Ophira smiled faintly. "An old trinket. Nothing special."

He studied her for a moment before placing it back on the desk with a shrug. "If you say so. You've got enough of these things scattered around. Must be worth something to you."

"Sentimental value," she said, her tone light.

"Sentimental?" Aric raised an eyebrow, clearly amused. "I didn't know you were the sentimental type."

She offered him a noncommittal smile, but her thoughts were elsewhere. The relics held far more than sentimental value. They were part of her history, one she could never share.

"Anyway," Aric said, pushing away from the desk, "don't forget we've got a meeting later with that new client. I'll handle the preliminary stuff, but I'll need you there for the final sign-off."

"I'll be there," Ophira replied, her mind already shifting back to the tasks at hand.

As Aric moved toward the door, he paused, glancing back at her. "Fee, don't get buried in your work. You need a break once in a while."

She waved him off with a smile, watching as he left. The door clicked shut, leaving her alone with the quiet hum of the office. The silence returned, but it was altered now, heavier somehow. She felt the tension in the air. Something about the day felt different, though she couldn't quite put her finger on it.

The office, once her sanctuary, suddenly felt smaller and more like confinement. She rubbed at the back of her neck, fingers pausing on the delicate chain tucked beneath her collar. Still, it was hers. And in the silence, staying in control almost felt possible.

Chapter Two

Voices Carry (Especially the Dangerous Ones)

Ophira sat cross-legged on the couch, a half-empty mug balanced on the armrest beside her, laptop propped against her knees. The office hummed with its familiar blend of climate control and distant electronics, a quiet rhythm she'd absorbed over the years. But today, the stillness grated. Instead of settling into her bones, it crawled across her skin like a thread pulled too tight.

The anomaly report had come in ten minutes ago, logged with Aric's usual precision. Vault 3, Camera 3, one flicker. Minor, he'd noted. Probably firmware, he'd said. But Ophira knew better.

She wasn't convinced. Not yet.

She reached for her clipboard, flipping back to the line she'd jotted down after the flicker.

CAM3: Vault corridor | Static Pulse | 04:25 | Flagged for Review

Her pen hovered, then she checked it off.

She opened the playback feed, skipped to 04:25, and pressed play. The corridor appeared normal – clean, sterile, fluorescent-lit. First pass: smooth. Second pass: same. But on the third, slowed to half speed, her breath caught.

There.

A ripple. Not a glitch. A pulse, subtle as a held breath.

She leaned closer, pen tapping against her clipboard. Environmental logs showed nothing – no heat signatures, pressure dips, or breach alarms. Only the flicker.

She opened the backend logs. Aric had already pulled the last three days of data. Same time. Same camera. No other anomalies. Everything lined up. Today was the outlier. Everything pointed to a simple hardware hiccup. Still...

She tapped her pen against the desk, studying the frames with narrowed eyes. *What are you hiding?*

The footage held no answers. No shapes in the shadows. No unexplained reflections. No power surges, unscheduled access logs, or trip alarms. The system was clean. It was as if the corridor itself had exhaled for one brief second.

She exhaled quietly. It was probably nothing. But she didn't like relying on probably.

Zeke stirred faintly. *You already know it ain't nothin'. So why you still pokin' at that thing like it owes ya money?*

Because, Sage said coolly, *false negatives are dangerous. Especially the kind we deal with.*

"I'm aware," Ophira muttered, rubbing a thumb against the corner of her lip.

She hovered a moment longer before typing a brief internal note, "No replication of error. No correlating triggers. Logged for future reference."

Then she filed the anomaly report and closed the feed.

That should've been the end of it, but her hand hovered above the trackpad.

She pulled up the system's predictive failure modeling, her own proprietary algorithm, one Aric still hadn't managed to reverse-engineer. Two runs: normal tolerance thresholds. No cascading events. No hidden chains. Her spine refused to ease.

Move on. It's handled.

She should've felt settled, but her mind kept drifting.

Marcus's voice slid back into her mind like smoke under a door. That slow, unhurried cadence. The way he'd said her name. The weight of confidence he'd carried, like someone who knew exactly which levers to pull.

"Ophira Naga."

That voice didn't just haunt. It infiltrated. He had peeled back her focus like it was nothing. Unraveled her balance with nothing more than a name and a tone that shouldn't have carried so much weight.

She scowled, rubbing at her temple. *Not now.*

She opened a new note in the secure case file system, tabbed away from the anomaly logs. Not a formal file. Not yet. Only a heading:

Marcus Templeson - Contingencies

Her fingers paused above the keys. This wasn't background noise anymore. She was making space he hadn't earned.

She logged keywords. Cross-checked affiliations. Searched for mention of the name across client rosters and divine registry fragments from her offline archive. Nothing.

She scrolled through internal records. No client history. No flagged data. Still nothing. The man seemed to have materialized from suggestion, not fact.

Suspicious in itself.

She logged everything she had: name, voice timbre, phrasing, and request patterns. Search terms like relics, retrieval, and urgency.

Then she tapped her fingers against the desk. Her jaw tensed.

If this was real, it was already clean.

"All right," she muttered aloud, dragging the blank case file forward. "You've got my attention."

Not because she believed him.

Because she didn't.

And that meant she couldn't afford to be wrong.

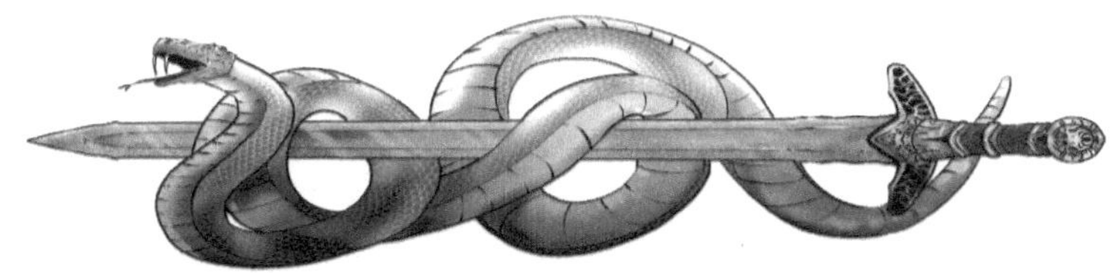

Over the next few hours, Ophira buried herself into her work, hoping the steady rhythm of tasks might drown the lingering tension Marcus had left behind. But no matter how many reports she combed through or logs she updated, his voice remained. It was a soft, insidious resonance, curling around her concentration.

Centuries of perfected control over herself, her environment, and her emotions. Now Marcus had breached those defenses with effortless ease, and the irritation cut deeper than she wanted to acknowledge.

She paused, the cursor blinking on the screen. Her half-eaten sandwich lay discarded, edges curling in the cool air. Her phone buzzed, the soft vibration cutting through the office stillness.

Her chest tightened at the sight of Marcus's name illuminating the screen, fingers freezing mid-motion.

Breathe, Ophira. Get a grip, she chided herself before answering.

"Mr. Templeson." She forced her voice into careful neutrality.

The velvet timbre of his voice slipped past her defenses instantly, unsettlingly intimate. "Ophira, I hope I'm not interrupting."

She straightened involuntarily. The warmth was there, but tinged with something else. Nervousness? Caution? The uncertainty sharpened her unease. "Not at all. Everything alright?"

He sighed. "Unfortunately, no," he responded, and though his tone was apologetic, the warmth remained, pulling her in despite herself. "Something has come up on my end, and I'm afraid I won't be able to make it to your office today as we planned."

Disappointment tugged at her unexpectedly, but the feeling fought against logic. This was good. More time, more distance. Yet her heartbeat betrayed that relief, fluttering against her ribs in faint protest.

"Unfortunate," she repeated softly. "Should we reschedule?"

"Yes, if you're available tomorrow morning." Marcus's voice held steady confidence, a smooth cadence that pulled her closer despite the instinct to retreat. "I can come by your office first thing. I apologize for the delay."

Ophira wanted to keep her distance, remain professional and focused. Yet the curiosity about the case and Marcus's subtle charm were undeniable. Even now, through the phone, his voice had a way of pulling her in, making her want to know more.

She didn't like how easily he affected her. That instinct to say yes couldn't be trusted. She needed to stay focused on the job, but the conflict churned beneath the surface.

It was a bad idea. She already knew that.

You're doing that thing again, sugar. Sunny's voice floated gently through her mind, a warm, honeyed caution. *Chasing shadows. Chasing trouble. Sometimes the best thing to do is just let sleepin' dogs lie.*

Don't pretend you're surprised, Zeke countered. *This guy's got her number. And she ain't exactly hangin' up.*

She clenched her jaw, irritated by the truth she couldn't deny. "Tomorrow morning works for me," she finally agreed. "I'll be here."

"Perfect." Marcus's voice resonated through the line like a well-practiced melody written solely with her in mind. "I look forward to it."

The call ended, and Ophira set the phone down with deliberate care, exhaling slowly. She leaned back in her chair, staring blankly at the monitors, tension building inside her. The light had shifted, a golden slant crawling up the far wall, and the room around her seemed quieter now, heavier in the aftermath of Marcus's voice.

She had only spoken to Marcus twice, but both times he had left her feeling unsettled, torn between her professional instincts and something far more personal.

I shouldn't let this get to me, she scolded herself, massaging her forehead as she tried to refocus. But the truth was, she was already in deeper than she had planned.

Valentina sighed, her tone dripping with exaggerated despair and a wavering French accent. *Such drama, Ophira. And so très magnifique orchestrated.*

Ophira rubbed her thumb lightly against the polished marble of the desk's surface, feeling the faint vibrations of equipment humming softly beneath her fingertips. Marcus represented far more than an ordinary client or case. He was a puzzle carefully crafted, a maze designed to trap her attention. He knew precisely which strings to pluck, each note resonating perfectly.

But more than that, he represented risk, the kind she had long trained herself to avoid.

This ain't a case. He's already inside your head, hoss, Zeke drawled irritably. *You're playin' a dangerous game.*

She exhaled softly, rubbing at the tension coiling at her temples. "I know exactly what I'm doing."

I sincerely doubt that, Sage observed dryly. *But you might find out soon enough.*

Her gaze drifted to the collection of relics that sat silently on the edge of her desk, fragments of her hidden past. They seemed heavier now, as if Marcus's presence, his very voice, had drawn them closer. Something about him tugged at those buried pieces of herself, whispered traces of memories she had long tried to silence.

Marcus Templeson was more than charming; he was enigmatic, careful, and deliberate. He'd given her enough to spark intrigue, withholding everything else until she stepped closer. A delicate balancing act, like hers.

He slipped past my defenses far too easily, she warned herself, her brow furrowing. Marcus had woven himself into her head without much effort, and that left her uneasy.

"I won't let my guard down again," she muttered softly.

Just another case, she told herself firmly. But the memory of his voice lingered like an unanswered challenge. As her thoughts began to spiral deeper, the door creaked open again. Aric poked his head in, flashing his usual mischievous grin.

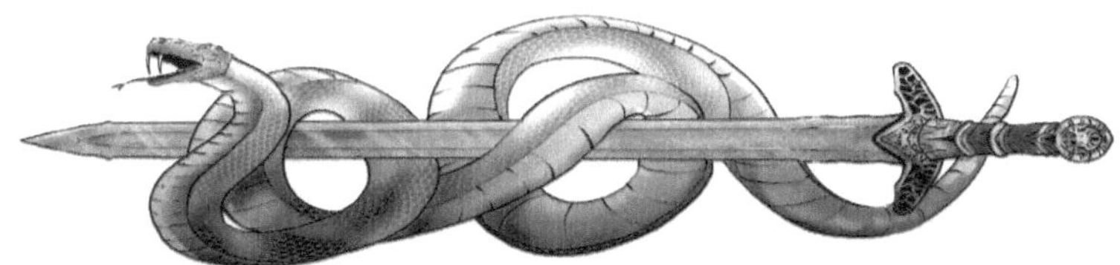

"All good here?" Aric asked, striding in without waiting for an answer. His energy was its own kind of weather, casual and bright, flooding the room with a confidence that made itself at home.

"Define 'good'," Ophira said, leaning back in her chair with a dry glance over at him.

Aric plopped down in the chair opposite her and kicked his boots up onto her desk. "I haven't heard any explosions or seen you throw anything at the walls yet, so I'm assuming you're not drowning in chaos. The usual 'I can handle everything' vibe."

Ophira folded her arms. "Explosions are bad for business. I try to keep things more...subtle."

"Right." He laughed. "Subtle. Like when you threw that guy out for getting handsy with you?"

"He deserved it."

"I didn't say he didn't. I was impressed by how subtle it was." He smirked, all sparkle and teeth, proud of her.

She rolled her eyes, but the gesture lacked heat. "You're jealous I handled it before you had a chance to flex your muscles."

Aric clutched his chest in mock offense. "Wounded. I live to flex." He dropped the act with a laugh. "But throwing people out is fun too."

A real smile broke through, catching her off guard. Aric had a talent for diffusing tension, keeping her from curling around her thoughts. And lately, those thoughts had been sharp.

"I take it you've got something on your mind?" His voice softened, though still wrapped in his usual charm.

"Nothing I can't handle," she said, careful and measured. "A new case."

His brow lifted. "Sounds like something more than a new case."

Ophira stood, moving to the window as if the change in position would give her a cleaner angle on the lies she was telling herself. "You know me. I like to be prepared."

Aric leaned back, arms crossed behind his head. "Classic Fee, always two steps ahead of a problem that hasn't even happened yet."

"Better than two steps behind."

Aric stretched his arms behind his back. "Remember, if you need backup, I work cheap. Mostly."

"I can handle one client meeting," she replied, but there was a faint hesitation she didn't manage to hide.

He caught it. Of course he did. Aric watched her with more care than most. That amused sparkle in his gaze didn't mask the awareness beneath.

"Noted," he said, standing and giving her a salute before starting for the door. "But if you end up throwing anyone out tomorrow, give me a heads-up. I'll bring popcorn."

Ophira laughed under her breath. "I'll try to rein in my subtlety."

He paused in the doorway, turning back to look at her with a knowing smile that faded as he tilted his head curiously, taking in her expression.

"Fee?"

"I want you to sit in on the meeting with Marcus Templeson," she said, breaking the silence.

Aric turned fully now, his brow lifting slightly in surprise. "You don't usually invite me to your meet-and-greets."

"This one feels different," Ophira replied, full of anticipation and unease.

He leaned against the doorframe, giving her the space to speak at her own pace.

"I need your read on him. Something about the case doesn't sit right with me," she went on.

Aric crossed his arms, studying her with a curious expression. "You think he's hiding something."

She gave a half-smile, though it didn't reach her eyes. "Aren't they always?"

"Fair point," Aric said. "You've got a hunch then?"

Ophira moved back to her desk, fingers ghosting over the files stacked at the edge. "Something about the way he described the relics, like a man who knew exactly what not to say. Vague enough to pique interest. Deliberate enough to avoid specifics. And that's what worries me. He's extremely careful."

Aric's playful posture straightened slightly. "You've dealt with vague clients before. What's different this time?"

Her hand drifted to the medallion near the corner of the desk. "It's not the case," she admitted, quieter now. "It's him. The way he speaks. Careful. Precise. Like he's always holding something back. There's more to Marcus than he's letting on, and I don't like being kept in the dark."

Aric followed her movement to the medallion but said nothing. That silence was one of the reasons she trusted him.

He pushed away from the wall and moved closer to her desk, his gaze locking onto hers. "So you want me there as backup? You think this is going to get messy?"

Ophira shook her head. "Not messy. I need your instincts, your gut read on him. I trust you to see what I might miss."

Careful now, Sage muttered. *Trust opens the door to more than help.*

Sunny's voice countered gently, *He's not a door, Sage. He's a window bringing in the light. Let her have it.*

Aric had always been able to ground her, to remind her that not everything had to be a battle. His calm demeanor helped her stay focused, even when the old memories threatened to pull her under.

"Alright," he said finally, "I'll be there."

The knot of tension in her chest loosened slightly. Marcus was unpredictable, and unpredictable people were dangerous. She couldn't afford to make any mistakes.

He turned back toward the doorway, getting ready to head home for the day. "I don't doubt you've got this under control, Fee. Don't forget to take a breath and get some rest. Tomorrow's another day."

She nodded once.

As the door shut with a soft click behind Aric, silence pressed in once again, heavier and more insistent. Tomorrow loomed in her mind, inevitable, uncertain. Marcus's voice lingered, a quiet melody she couldn't erase.

She would be ready. She had to be.

Yet even as she steeled herself, a quiet whisper slipped beneath her defenses. *You're already too late.*

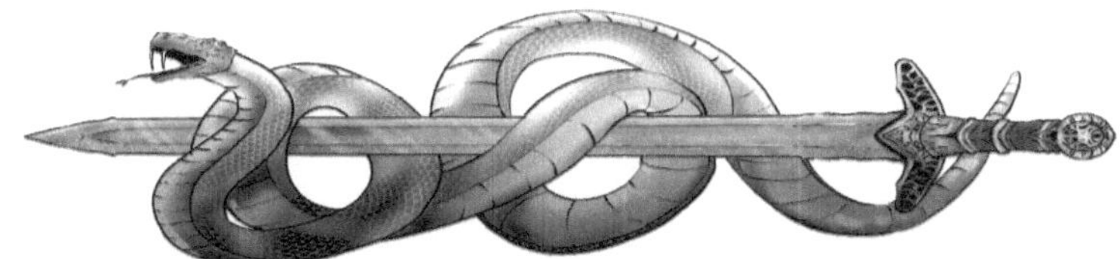

Ophira sat at her desk reviewing the preliminary research she'd compiled since yesterday's call with Marcus. Four ancient artifacts from a Mediterranean temple collection. She'd started building profiles on potential buyers, cross-referencing auction houses that specialized in ancient religious artifacts, flagging collectors known for acquiring temple pieces of questionable provenance.

But without photos, detailed descriptions, or specific provenance records, she was working blind. The lack of concrete specifics gnawed at her. She hated having so many unknowns.

Sounds like this guy's givin' us just enough info to hang ourselves with, Zeke drawled, his dark green head tilting lazily near her temple.

Deliberate omission, Sage intoned, his voice clipped and analytical. *Either he's hiding something, or he doesn't trust you yet.*

Ay, who cares about trust when zere are relics! We must retrieve them! Valentina hissed.

And if he's lying? Sage countered. *Are you so eager to walk into a trap?*

Now, let's not jump to conclusions, Sunny said. *Maybe he's just cautious. Not everyone's as bold as we are.*

Ophira's lips pressed into a thin line. *Whatever his reasons, it's not enough to go on.*

But that didn't mean she wouldn't find out.

The soft hum of her computer screens filled the office, the faint buzz of security monitors, and the steady drip of emails popping into her inbox provided a constant background rhythm. Yet despite the usual sounds of the day, there was an undeniable tension in the air.

The room was the same. Sleek, dark, sterile. Monitors and processors formed a symmetrical arc around her central desk, the black marble surface cool and polished under her palms. Today, it felt like glass underfoot.

Her eyes flicked to the bronze medallion resting at the desk's edge. The once-crisp etchings had been worn by centuries of touch. Her thumb drifted over it, muscle memory tracing a groove without thinking.

A relic of another life.

Her fingers tapped once, twice. The rhythm didn't soothe her. Marcus's voice still lingered – smooth and measured, the kind of cadence that stayed with her long after the conversation ended. The way he'd said her name hadn't just landed. It had settled.

A man with such a voice must be dangerous, Valentina purred, sliding into a sultry Spanish drawl. She curled tighter along Ophira's cheek, crimson scales catching the light like lacquer. *All the best ones are.*

Dangerous, sure, Zeke said with a short snort, his tongue flicking. *But also full of himself. Bet he practices that voice in the mirror. Probably throws in a smolder for good measure.*

Focus, Sage snapped. *His tone is irrelevant. We have a lead. We don't have trust. That's the variable.*

She clenched her jaw. Sage was right. Emotional distractions had no place here. She wasn't a teenager drawn in by a honeyed voice and clever phrasing. This was business. Strategy. Containment. She couldn't afford to get distracted by charm or charisma. There was too much at stake.

Still, her fingers drifted toward the medallion, brushing its cool surface. Relics had a way of drawing out the old world, the one she kept locked away, even from herself. Marcus had mentioned them as though they were part of the contract, a detail among many. But Ophira had lived through relics. She was one, in a sense. The way he spoke of them so lightly set her nerves alight.

Relics meant danger. They meant possible ties to the divine. And even though Ophira had distanced herself from that world, the shadows of it always loomed close.

She forced herself to glance at the wall of screens instead. Patterns. Traffic. Heat signatures. Something predictable.

Across the room, Aric stood with his arms crossed and his back half-turned, watching the monitors. He looked as calm as ever, but Ophira knew him well enough to sense his concern. He hadn't asked her directly about Marcus, but the tension between them wasn't lost on him. Aric always knew when something was off. And yet she felt his focus sharpen each time the tension in her body rose.

She studied him, letting her gaze linger on the strong line of his shoulders, the way he never needed to assert presence to own a room. She admired his ability to stay grounded, no matter the situation. He wasn't like the others who had come and gone from her life. He was steady, reliable.

And even though he didn't know her whole truth, he had always been there, never questioning her choices. Today, she needed him for more than his support. She needed his instincts, his read on Marcus. He was her ward against chaos.

Marcus's case might not even be a case at all.

She checked the time. He would be here soon.

She didn't know what to expect, only that she needed to stay sharp. This case could open doors she had long kept sealed, and she wasn't ready to face the consequences.

"More on edge than usual," Aric said, not turning. The low calm in his voice wrapped around her like a weighted blanket. "Want to tell me why?"

She considered lying. Deflecting. Something dismissive and professional. Instead, she exhaled and said, "Too many open doors. Not enough locks."

He turned then, dark eyes resting on her. "I can install some deadbolts if that would help."

She let out a soft laugh. "I wish the hardware store sold that kind of security."

"You don't have to stand guard alone."

Sunny whispered softly, curling her golden body just beneath Ophira's jaw. *You ain't never alone, sugar. Not even when the world forgets who you are.*

"Thanks," she said quietly.

He nodded, offering her a small smile. "Anytime, Fee. You know that."

Aric returned to the screens. The snakes fell silent.

And Ophira straightened in her seat.

Marcus was coming.

Whatever Marcus brought with him today, she would be ready. With Aric at her side, she had one more advantage in her corner. Still, no amount of preparation would be enough to hold the line if Marcus kept slipping past her defenses the way he already had. She hated how easily he lingered.

That wasn't who she was. Not what her world was about.

Control was everything.

And no matter what charm he wore or what secrets he carried, she promised herself that he would not catch her off guard again like he did during his phone calls.

Not here.

Not now.

CHAPTER THREE

CHARISMA IS A LOADED WEAPON

Marcus adjusted his cuffs outside Ophira's office, anticipation stirring in his chest. The moment before stepping into a room, before the balance of power subtly shifted, was always the sweetest. He could already feel tension rising, coiling beneath the surface like something living.

But today, it wasn't about power. It was about curiosity. About her.

He knocked twice, measured and purposeful. The sharp sound cut through the muted hum of the office beyond the door. A pause, a breath, then the faintest flicker of movement inside. *She heard me. She's waiting.*

Ophira Naga. Medusa. The woman behind the legend. She was hiding in plain sight, masquerading as a mortal, but Marcus could see the truth beneath the surface. He could barely suppress the smile that threatened to tug at his lips as he considered the irony. Here she was, sitting in a modern office, surrounded by technology and humans who had no idea what lurked beneath her polished exterior.

How seamlessly she had integrated herself into this world, keeping her secret for centuries. Secrets were his specialty, fragile things he'd always enjoyed uncovering, seeing beyond the masks people wore. He couldn't wait to find out how she had managed to fake her death so successfully.

It's fascinating to watch someone who used to be so powerful pretend to be ordinary. He observed the subtle ways she controlled her world, the careful mask she wore. How long would it take for that mask to slip? She might have been a force of nature once, but in this modern world, her power was subtler, hidden behind layers of careful constraints.

Two nights ago, he had tested that meticulous mask, slipping a probe toward her outer firewall to challenge its defenses. The system shut him out in four-tenths of a second, fast, elegant, almost taunting. He scrubbed the trace, but not perfectly. Today was about finally meeting her, about learning where that control might falter. Today, he would learn whether Medusa had noticed the phantom footsteps he left behind and whether that sharp mind was already sharpening its knives for him.

The handle gave beneath his palm, and as he stepped inside, he let the weight of the moment settle, just enough to remind her exactly who had entered the room. The office struck him immediately with its sleek surfaces, carefully controlled lighting, and everything positioned with considered precision. Even the air seemed managed, filtered and cool.

As always, he triggered that instant reaction. The air thickened, charged with an almost imperceptible tension, the kind that accompanied his entrance into any room. Eyes tracked him before he crossed the threshold, postures shifting subtly in unspoken acknowledgment of his presence. Marcus moved with a calm confidence, as if the very space around him bent slightly to accommodate his arrival.

But in this room, there was more than the usual awareness of his presence. He could feel it: an entity immeasurably older. *Medusa.*

She sat at her desk, her eyes meeting his with practiced neutrality, her posture carefully composed. To anyone else, she was simply a professional, perhaps even cold. But Marcus saw beyond that. He knew better.

Ophira, or rather Medusa, had been waiting for him. Not today, but for centuries, whether she knew it or not. His eyes drifted briefly to the relics scattered around her office. Artifacts from a time long past. She was living with the weight of her history all around her.

The room was cool and professional, much like its occupant. Sleek modernity mixed with carefully placed hints of antiquity. Ophira's office conveyed precision: polished steel and marble desks, high-end security equipment, and a wall of monitors displaying live feeds from her various clients. His eyes found the artifacts carefully scattered around the space. A bronze medallion resting near her laptop, fragments of pottery on a nearby shelf, and a glass case holding what appeared to be an ancient dagger.

He let his gaze drift to Ophira, taking her in fully now. She was every bit as striking as he'd expected: tall with an athletic build that spoke of strength and power. Her skin was a warm olive tone, smooth and unmarked, though Marcus knew the stories of the gorgon's cursed transformation.

Her eyes were the most captivating: sharp, dark, and unwavering, set beneath arched brows that gave her an air of quiet authority. Her hair was thick, dark, and pulled back into a sleek ponytail, revealing a sharp jawline and a face that held more authority in its stillness than most people could manage in words.

He was careful not to meet them directly – old habits from someone who knew the legends weren't just stories. Even with her powers held in check by what he could only imagine was centuries of careful discipline, even in this human guise, some instincts were worth maintaining.

She was poised, composed, her posture rigid but not stiff. She exuded precision, every motion measured, a performance she'd perfected over centuries. But she stilled her fingers intentionally over the desk's edge and caught herself before her jaw could tighten. *A practiced mask, nearly perfect.* She might have been Medusa once, but now she was fighting to remain Ophira.

And she was fighting him too, though she didn't even know it yet.

"Ms. Naga," Marcus greeted, his voice carrying the perfect blend of professionalism and charm. He allowed the faintest hint of a smile to cross his lips as he approached her desk, though his mind was already calculating the next steps. He wouldn't let on that he knew who she truly was, not yet. There was power in letting her believe she still had control of the situation.

Her eyes flickered. He could see the tension in her shoulders, the way her fingers stilled slightly on the desk as she regarded him. He hadn't said much yet, and already there was an undercurrent between them. Attraction, perhaps, or a cautious curiosity she instinctively felt. Either way, he had her attention.

Marcus let his gaze sweep the room, taking in the modern security equipment and the reminders of a long past. A medallion here, a shard of pottery there, each one a symbol of her past life as Medusa, carefully woven into her present as Ophira Naga. He knew what they were. He knew what they meant. But he wouldn't mention that yet.

"Thank you for agreeing to meet with me." His voice was smooth, unhurried, and calculated in its delivery. He made sure to sound respectful but with enough warmth to draw her in.

As he moved into the room, he let his gaze flicker briefly to the man standing nearby. Aric, her partner. Marcus had done his research. Aric was an integral part of Ophira's operation, but he was more than a business partner. He was tall, broad-shouldered, with the kind of casual confidence that came from years of experience. His hair was a sandy brown, slightly tousled, and his eyes were sharp, intelligent, though Marcus could see the skepticism there as well. Aric was watching him closely, though his posture remained relaxed, his arms crossed over his chest as he leaned against the wall.

Interesting. There was more between Ophira and Aric, more than colleagues. The way Aric positioned himself, the way he observed the room, spoke of a deeper connection, perhaps unspoken. It was subtle, but Marcus knew how to read these things. He made a mental note to keep an eye on that dynamic.

Marcus let his gaze drift back to Ophira, allowing himself to appreciate the complexity of her, this creature who had once been a myth, now reduced to a woman hiding behind an ordinary name.

"I've heard quite a bit about your work," Marcus continued, his voice calm but with a hint of warmth that seemed to fill the space. He didn't need to force charm – it came naturally. "Your reputation is impressive."

Ophira's eyes didn't waver, though Marcus could sense her trying to maintain her composure. "I'm sure you didn't come here to talk about my reputation," she replied, her voice cool, controlled.

Marcus's smile widened ever so slightly. She was sharp, no doubt about that. But he could feel the tension rising in her, the subtle pull his presence had on her, even if she wouldn't admit it. He had that effect on people, especially when he needed to.

Marcus extended his hand, movements unhurried. "I appreciate you taking the time to meet."

When their hands met, Ophira clasped it, her grip firm, professional, until she felt the pause, the way his thumb barely shifted, a near-imperceptible test of control.

A ripple of awareness flowed through her body, subtle but undeniable. She drew her hand back with disciplined restraint, though her jaw tightened before she could stop it. He didn't acknowledge it, if he noticed at all.

"Shall we?" she said, turning to the file. A deflection.

Marcus's eyes lingered on her. He let his hand drop slowly, his expression unreadable, though there was a faint gleam in his gaze. He allowed a slow smile. "Of course."

He's a client, girl. Get it together, she scolded herself as she retrieved the folder containing the details Marcus had provided. The stolen relics were the reason he was here, and she needed to remind herself of that. This was business. Nothing more.

Zeke stirred at her temple, amused. *Want me to keep an eye on Slick over there, boss? Or grab popcorn and watch the slow-mo heart spiral?*

As she began discussing the case, flipping through the documents with a calm, professional demeanor, she could feel Marcus's gaze on her. He was listening intently, but there was something in the way he watched her that stirred her unease. His focus wasn't solely on the case.

Her pulse quickened again, and she fought to keep her tone steady. "We've traced a few potential leads on the relics, but I'll need more details from you before we can proceed."

Marcus nodded, his eyes still lingering on her face, his smile ever so faint. "Of course," he said. "I'd be happy to provide whatever information you need." But his gaze didn't leave hers, and Ophira could feel the tension in the air thickening once again.

She forced herself to remain centered, fingers tightening on the file's edge. The slip in composure left her off balance in a way that rarely happened, her mind recalibrating to regain professional clarity.

Ophira shifted in her seat, her eyes flicking over the details of the file in front of her. The warmth of Marcus's handshake lingered, an odd sensation settling in the pit of her stomach. *Why was it still there?* It wasn't often that someone threw her off balance, especially not in a client meeting. Yet here she was, trying to shake the feeling.

Marcus settled across from her, relaxed to the point of arrogance. One arm draped easily, fingers tapping the polished surface in a tempo only he understood. His charcoal suit was a masterclass in precision, the fit intentional without feeling forced. A trace of cologne lingered.

He's deliberate. The thought surfaced unbidden. His sharp features, piercing blue eyes, and the way his dark hair was styled all pointed to a man who was calculated, crafted like a performance with no missteps. He gave the impression of a man who never made a move without considering the outcome first.

And it was working.

"I have to say," Marcus began, his voice pulling her attention back, "your reputation doesn't quite do you justice. It's one thing to hear about your skill, but seeing it in action... It's impressive."

Ophira felt a slight warmth creep into her cheeks, but she didn't let it show. There was an undertone, a careful shift in the way he spoke, as if he wasn't just discussing her skills as a consultant.

She tilted her head, assessing him. "I appreciate that, but I like to think results speak for themselves."

"They do," Marcus agreed, leaning forward slightly, his gaze never leaving hers. "But it's not only about results, is it? It's how you manage everything, how you stay in control of every situation."

There it was again, that slight shift. The way he said control, the way his voice softened enough to give the word more weight than it should have. He was testing her in some way, seeing how far he could push. The question now was why.

She met his gaze, unflinching. "Control isn't about holding on to everything. It's about knowing what to let go of." But she couldn't deny it. There was something undeniably suave about Marcus that made him hard to resist. He didn't push hard, didn't come across as overtly flirtatious, but the undertones were enough to make her question the dynamic of this meeting.

He knows exactly what he's doing. The idea lingered in her mind, not as a warning but as an observation. And that was the problem. She was used to being the one in control, the one who dictated the pace of these kinds of meetings. But Marcus was different. He had a way of shifting the balance without her even realizing it, and that left her feeling just a little off-kilter.

"That's the nature of this job," she said, her voice steady, though she couldn't quite keep the slight edge from it. "You don't last long if you don't know how to manage things properly."

"True," Marcus replied, his smile widening. "But not everyone manages it with as much…precision as you do."

Another subtle compliment, another slight shift that blurred the line between professional respect and personal relationship. Ophira felt her pulse quicken slightly, though she forced herself to remain calm. She was used to handling difficult situations, difficult people, but Marcus wasn't difficult in the traditional sense.

He wasn't trying to push her, not overtly. Instead, he was guiding the conversation with invisible threads, and she couldn't tell where they were meant to lead or where he wanted her to follow.

Zeke's voice curled in low from behind her ear, all grit and drawl. *That man's walkin' in here like he already knows how the story ends. And partner, I don't reckon we're the ones holdin' the pen.*

She offered Marcus a tight smile. "I like to be thorough."

Marcus leaned back in his chair, crossing his legs in one fluid motion. "I've noticed," he said, his tone casual but with that ever-present suggestion of more. His gaze drifted over her for a moment, brief enough to avoid impropriety but long enough for her to feel the weight of it. "It's rare to meet someone who manages their environment with such quiet precision. It's impressive."

Ophira felt her face warm again, but this time she didn't bother hiding it. There was no point. Marcus was clearly aware of the effect he was having, and trying to brush it off would only make things more awkward. Instead, she let out a small, quiet laugh, the sound surprising even her.

"I suppose that's one way to put it," she said, her tone lighter now. "But I'm sure you didn't come here to talk about my skills."

"No," Marcus agreed, though his smile didn't fade. "I'm here because I believe you're the only person who can help me with this case."

Ophira raised an eyebrow, feeling a slight shift in the atmosphere. Finally, the conversation was moving back toward more solid ground. She could handle cases, relics, mysteries, and solve problems. That was her comfort zone, not in the strange, flirtatious tension that had been building between them.

"Then let's focus on the case," she said, her voice firm but not unkind. "I'll need to know more about the relics you're trying to recover and any information you can provide on where they were last seen."

Marcus shifted back into professional mode. "They were taken from a private collector three weeks ago. Clean job – no alarms triggered, no signs of forced entry. Whoever did this knew exactly what they were looking for and how to get it. The collector is… discreet about his acquisitions, which limits our options for involving traditional law enforcement."

Ophira nodded, already shifting into investigative mode. The familiar territory of timelines, evidence, and methodology was precisely what she needed to regain her footing. She began laying out the next steps, grounding herself in the practical.

But even as she discussed timelines and evidence protocols, her mind kept drifting back to the warmth that still lingered on her palm.

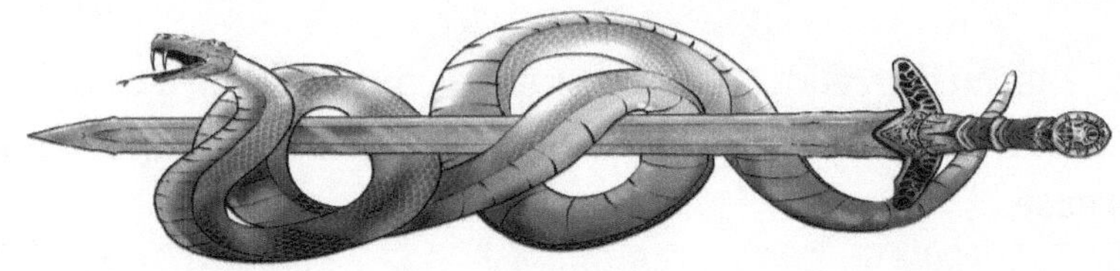

Aric leaned casually against the wall, arms crossed over his chest, his gaze flicking between Ophira and Marcus as they continued their conversation. On the surface, it all seemed perfectly normal, just two professionals discussing a case and trading information. But it felt wrong. Marcus felt off.

Aric had dealt with charming, persuasive men before, each one playing some angle. But Ophira's reaction made his gut twist.

She doesn't even realize it yet. But Aric did. Marcus wasn't smooth. He was calculated. An expert in slow, premeditated influence.

Aric tracked the subtle shifts: the slight tilt of her head, the brief hesitation. A barely there pause before responding to Marcus.

She's letting him in.

Aric knew it wasn't conscious. Ophira was too smart to trust a stranger this easily. But that was what made it worse. Marcus wasn't forcing his way in. He didn't have to. He was weaving himself into her space naturally, effortlessly.

He knows exactly what he's doing.

Aric clenched his jaw, arms tightening across his chest. Marcus wasn't overstepping, at least not in a way anyone else would notice. But the way he spoke?

Every word was just smooth enough to disarm, just careful enough to be unassuming, just suggestive enough to plant ideas without directly stating them. It wasn't overt. It was a subtle push, a slow unraveling.

And it was working.

Shit.

Aric had spent years by Ophira's side. He knew her moods, her tells. He'd watched her shut down men twice as charming as Marcus.

But this time? He could see the effect settling in, the way she was letting Marcus's words linger just a second too long before brushing them aside.

This isn't normal.

It wasn't attraction, at least not only that. It was subtler, more carefully managed. Marcus was unusually persuasive, intentional in a way that made Aric wary. He had seen Ophira handle war criminals and arms dealers without flinching. But Marcus was slipping through the cracks.

She has no idea it's happening.

This wasn't jealousy. This wasn't protectiveness for the sake of it. His gut twisted with warning, signaling danger he couldn't yet name.

She's letting her guard down, and he's making sure she doesn't even notice.

Aric exhaled slowly, forcing himself to stay composed. Something about Marcus felt off, and he wasn't letting it go.

As the conversation wrapped up, Marcus stood and gave Ophira a polite nod, his smile still in place, his charm effortless. *Very effortless.* Aric's eyes tracked his every movement, instincts tightening in his gut.

Marcus turned to leave, his steps smooth, unhurried – like a man who was always in control. I don't like this.

"Thank you for your time," Marcus said, his voice still rich, still measured. "I'll see you tomorrow to continue our discussion."

Ophira nodded, her expression unreadable, but Aric caught the small signs others would miss. The tension in her shoulders. The slight curl of her fingers against her desk. *She's affected, whether she realizes it or not.*

As the door clicked shut, the office felt different without Marcus's presence, as if the air itself had altered.

Ophira turned back to her desk, sorting through papers, but Aric saw the way she moved, the slight hesitation before setting the files down. *She's still thinking about him.*

Aric pushed away from the wall, walking over to stand beside her desk. He didn't say anything at first, letting the silence stretch between them for a beat longer than usual. "Well," he said, finally breaking the silence, "that was interesting."

Ophira looked up at him, a flicker passing over her face before she forced a smile. "Interesting? He seemed fairly straightforward to me."

Aric crossed his arms over his chest, his expression pensive. "He did," he agreed, though his tone carried the hint of doubt. "But he feels...off."

Ophira raised an eyebrow. "How?"

He exhaled through his nose, shaking his head slightly. "I don't know yet. Could be the way he carries himself. Or maybe it's the way you react to him."

She frowned. "And how did I react?"

Aric studied her for a moment, then offered a slight shrug. "Not like you usually do."

The words landed heavier than he'd intended.

Ophira raised an eyebrow, her gaze softening slightly as she studied him. She trusted Aric's instincts – he was one of the few people whose judgment she relied on. If he felt there was a problem, she wasn't going to dismiss it outright. But she wasn't ready to jump to conclusions either.

She gestured for him to sit down. "What do you think?"

Aric leaned forward slightly. "I don't know," he admitted, his hand raking through his hair in frustration. "I can't pinpoint it, but something about him doesn't sit right with me. He's very polished. Like he's rehearsed every word."

Ophira nodded slowly, her fingers tapping lightly on the edge of her desk. She couldn't deny that she had felt the subtle undercurrent that had run beneath the surface of their conversation.

Marcus had been professional, but there had been moments with an extra layer of meaning. Something personal. Something...elusive.

"I felt it too," she admitted. "He says all the right things, but there's something else underneath. I can't figure out what it is."

Aric leaned back in his chair, crossing his arms again. "Exactly. He's incredibly smooth. Nobody is that careful unless they're hiding something."

Ophira glanced down at the folder on her desk, her mind racing. Part of her wanted to dig deeper, to find out what Marcus might be hiding. But another part reminded her of the facts. Marcus had come to her for help with a legitimate case. He hadn't done anything overtly suspicious. Yet.

She let out a slow breath, weighing her options. "You think he's lying?"

"Not lying," Aric said after a beat. "But he's not telling us the whole story. There's more to this than what he's letting on."

Ophira looked up at him, her gaze steady. She trusted Aric more than anyone, but something about Marcus's case intrigued her, even if it did come with some misgivings. And at this point, she had no reason to turn him away. Not yet.

"I trust your instincts, Aric," she said, her voice soft but firm. "I do. But until we have something concrete, something more than a gut feeling, I'm willing to take him at his word. At least for now."

All they had was shared unease, an instinct warning of unnamed danger.

Still, Aric couldn't shake the lingering tension in his gut. "Promise me you'll keep your guard up with him," he said. "Don't let him get too close."

Ophira offered him a small smile, her eyes warm with gratitude. "You know me, Aric. I don't let anyone get too close."

He let out a soft chuckle, but the worry in his eyes remained. "I know. But something about this guy..." He shook his head. "Be careful, alright?"

Ophira nodded, the smile fading slightly as her uncertainty crept back in. She trusted Aric's judgment, and the fact that he was this anxious wasn't something she could easily dismiss.

But at the same time, she couldn't help feeling that Marcus's case was more important than they realized. And she wasn't about to walk away from it.

"I will," she promised, her voice soft but steady. "I'll be careful."

But as he stood and made his way toward the door, the knot of unease in his chest remained tight. If Marcus was already inside her defenses, Aric wasn't sure they'd see the next strike coming.

He paused at the threshold, glancing back at Ophira as she returned to her files. *Too late,* he thought. *It's already started.*

CHAPTER FOUR

BUSINESS CASUAL OR CASUAL BUSINESS?

As soon as the door closed behind Aric, the silence of the office returned, though now it felt charged with a new kind of energy. Ophira leaned back in her chair, letting out a slow breath. The meeting with Marcus hadn't gone exactly as she'd expected. She couldn't shake the strange feeling he left behind, the subtle tension that lingered in the room even after he'd gone.

Her attention drifted to her phone on the edge of her desk. There was no reason to expect anything more. The meeting was over, the case had been laid out, and tomorrow would bring the next step. Still, uneasy curiosity gnawed at her, even if she didn't want to admit it.

63

What is it about him that makes me second-guess things? Her hand reached out to tap the screen. No new messages. She shook her head, almost amused at herself. *Of course not, Fee. You're being ridiculous.*

Her phone buzzed in her hand.

Marcus
Looking forward to our next meeting. I think we're going to work well together.

Ophira's lips twitched. The words were all business, but she could still hear that voice in her head, calm and smooth, just amused enough to make her wonder what he really meant.

Ophira
We'll see about that. As long as we're both focused, it should go smoothly.

She hit send before she could overthink it. *It's a harmless client conversation. Nothing more.*

Her phone buzzed again almost immediately.

Marcus
Agreed, focus is key. Though I do believe a little flexibility can help us navigate un-expected opportunities. Tomorrow should be productive.

Ophira exhaled through her nose, shaking her head even as amusement curled in her chest. The reply felt flirtatious, but Marcus was careful. He knew exactly how to play this game.

> **Ophira**
> Flexibility's important, sure. But let's not
> get ahead of ourselves. It's still all about
> the results.

She sent the message, sitting back in her chair as the pressure in her chest eased. Marcus was playing a game, but she wasn't entirely opposed to playing along. The banter helped relieve the stress, even if it left her more unsettled than before.

Her phone buzzed one last time.

> **Marcus**
> Fair enough. Looking forward to seeing the
> results of our collaboration. Talk tomorrow.

Ophira set the phone down, amusement fading into something quieter. It wasn't just about the case anymore, and she knew it.

I know I should be cautious, she thought, pressing her lips together, but found herself hesitating, unsure why caution seemed more complicated than usual. Marcus seemed to have that effect.

She exhaled sharply and pushed back from the desk. The case was her focus. Not Marcus.

As she glanced at the phone one last time, quiet certainty settled beneath her curiosity. This wasn't going to stay simple. And it definitely wasn't over.

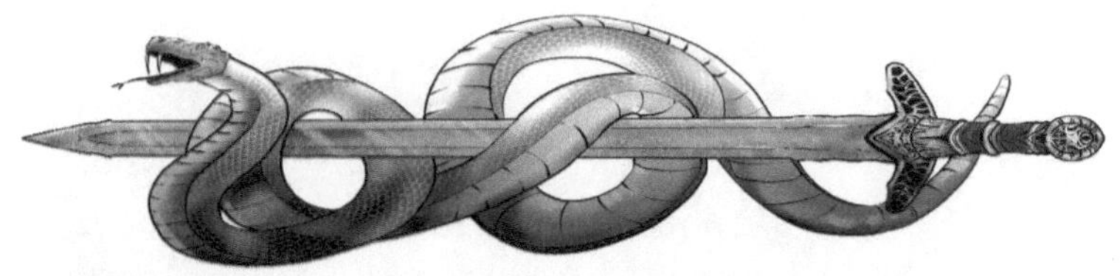

The next morning brought no relief from her restless thoughts. The soft glow of morning sun filtered through the blinds, casting streaks of pale light across Ophira's desk. Her fingers drummed absently on the armrest of her chair as she stared at the case files in front of her.

Marcus.

Her mind had wandered to him more times than she'd like to admit since their last meeting. He took up more space in her mind than he should.

I get it. The guy's got that whole tall, dark, and mysterious thing going on, Zeke quipped. *Doesn't mean you gotta moon over him like he's the last bronco in the canyon.*

Valentina declared, *You think too much with ze mind, querida. Follow your heart, your magnificent instincts! Dive in with passion and see what destiny brings, mi amor! That is what makes life fun and so deliciously unpredictable, no?*

It's only fun 'til someone loses an eye. Or gets cursed, Zeke muttered. *And guess who's gotta deal with it then? Us.*

No one's gettin' cursed, y'all, Sunny interjected softly. *It's a big case, and she's got enough on her plate without all this chatter.*

Ophira smiled faintly at their familiar bickering. They weren't wrong. She needed to stay sharp, especially now. *Sunny's right, we've got work to do.* She leaned back in her chair, glancing out the window to clear her mind. *I shouldn't be thinking about him like this. We have a case to focus on.*

Her gaze flicked over to the bronze medallion on her desk, a relic from another time, another life. It was a piece of the past she had locked away long ago, but Marcus's case had stirred something old within her. The fact that relics were involved in the case only made it harder to keep herself in check. There was too much riding on this – too much at stake for her to let her personal feelings get in the way.

Her phone buzzed. She glanced at the screen, half-expecting to see Marcus's name pop up, but it was a message about a different case.

She let out a small, almost disappointed sigh before shaking her head at herself. *You barely know him. Stop letting him take up so much space in your head.* She rubbed her temples, trying to ease the pressure building behind her eyes. She couldn't afford to let Marcus's charm distract her from the task at hand.

Across the room, Aric sat at his desk, his posture relaxed as he worked on something. His brow was furrowed in concentration, but his sharp look would occasionally flick over to her, as if sensing the shift in her demeanor. He hadn't said anything yet, but Ophira knew him well enough to know that he was picking up on the tension.

He's paying attention to every move you make. That's a good sign, Sage observed.

Or he's just tryin' to look useful. Jury's out, Zeke replied, his tongue flicking in amusement.

He wants to help, Sunny murmured with a warm tone. *You oughta let him.*

He will only slow us down, cara! Valentina declared dramatically. *Leave him behind and forge ahead with glory!*

Ophira shot them all a mental glare, her lips twitching despite herself. *If you all don't stop, I'll leave* **you** *behind.*

He's probably wondering what's gotten into me, she thought with a faint smile.

Finally, Aric spoke up, his voice cutting through the silence with a gentle ease. "You seem distracted today," he said, his tone casual, though his eyes were watchful as they flicked up from his work. "Everything alright?"

Ophira glanced over at him, the hint of a smile tugging at the corner of her lips. "I've got a lot on my mind," she replied, trying to sound more nonchalant than she felt.

Aric leaned back in his chair, crossing his arms as he studied her.

Ophira sighed softly, running a hand through her hair. "It's this case," she admitted after a beat. "It's different. That's all."

Aric raised an eyebrow, leaning forward slightly. "Different how?"

She debated whether to share what was bothering her. It wasn't the case itself, not entirely anyway. It was Marcus. But how could she explain that without sounding completely unprofessional?

"It's the relics," she said finally. "There's something about them that feels off. Like there's more to this than what we're seeing."

Aric's gaze sharpened slightly. He knew her well enough to know that when she had a gut feeling, it was usually worth paying attention to. But there was something else in her tone – something she wasn't saying.

He nodded, leaning back in his chair again. "We'll figure it out. We always do." He shot her a reassuring smile, but the worry hadn't left his expression.

As the minutes ticked by, she found herself staring at the clock, wondering when Marcus would show up. Wondering why she was even thinking about him at all.

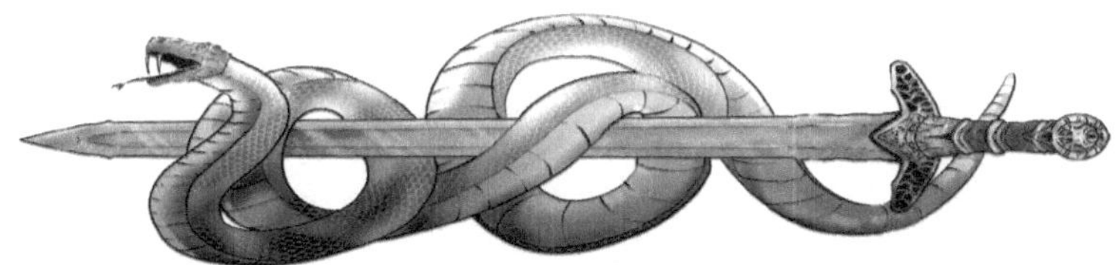

The steady hum of the office was interrupted by the soft click of the door. Ophira's head lifted as Marcus strode in, his entrance smooth and deliberate. The atmosphere shifted around him, quiet but undeniable.

That calm, collected presence seemed to settle over the room, drawing her attention before she could stop it. Something about him disrupted the normal rhythm, like a current running just beneath the surface.

Ophira swallowed, her professional mask slipping just slightly as her gaze tracked him. She wasn't used to feeling this unsettled, as if something in her had shifted off-center. Marcus had that effect.

It wasn't the polished exterior, though his professional confidence certainly helped. It was the careful way he observed, the attentive yet unobtrusive quality of his gaze. It left her sharp edges blunted and her breath tighter than it should be.

She straightened in her seat, pressing her palms flat against the desk like it could anchor her. *He's a client. Just like the thousands before him.* But the thought rang empty.

The case mattered, but the pull threading between them made it hard to stay focused. She could feel her control shifting beneath her, and it irritated her more than she cared to admit.

"I hope I'm not interrupting anything," Marcus said with enough charm to make her pulse quicken.

"No, not at all," Ophira replied, forcing herself to remain composed. Her tone was even, but inside, her mind was racing. *Why does the air feel different when he's here?* It wasn't a new question. Since their first meeting, she had felt this pull toward him, something magnetic that she couldn't quite shake, no matter how hard she tried.

Marcus's gaze swept over the room, pausing briefly on Aric, who stood near the security monitors, his posture casual but alert. Aric's sharp focus followed Marcus, and Ophira didn't miss the way Aric's arms crossed over his chest, the subtle tightening of his jaw. She could sense his reservations about Marcus. They were hanging in the air between them like an unaddressed issue.

"We were going over some preliminary details for the case," she continued, trying to shift her focus back to the task at hand. Her fingers absently traced the edge of the bronze medallion on her desk, its cool surface grounding her in a way that the conversation wasn't.

Marcus nodded with a faint smile. "Good," he said warmly, maintaining professional courtesy. "I wouldn't want to interrupt your flow."

Ophira felt her pulse skip. A pressure coiled in her chest, one that she couldn't quite explain.

Stop reacting to him, she scolded herself silently. The air between them felt charged, and no matter how she tried to stay professional, her body kept betraying her: shallow breath, warm skin, heightened awareness. She needed to pull herself together. She refused to be one of those women who got flustered over a smile and a suit.

"Let's get started," she said, gesturing toward the chair across from her. "We've got a lot to discuss."

As Marcus took his seat, his movements fluid and deliberate, Ophira could feel his eyes on her. She avoided his gaze for a moment, focusing instead on the file in front of her, trying to gather her thoughts. Her fingers flipped through the pages, but she wasn't reading them. It took everything in her to ignore the heat of his gaze.

Across the room, Aric's attention flicked between them, the tension unmistakable. He knew the situation felt wrong, even if he couldn't pinpoint exactly what. His instincts were razor-sharp, and Ophira had learned long ago to trust them. But even knowing that, she felt drawn to Marcus despite her better judgment.

"So," Marcus began, leaning forward slightly, "have you made any progress on tracking the stolen artifacts?"

Ophira cleared her throat, snapping her attention back to the conversation. "We've been looking into the collector theft," she replied, her voice steady, though inside, she was still tangled. "Checking auction houses, private dealers, anyone who might be moving Mediterranean antiquities. But there are still a lot of gaps in what we know about how they were taken."

Marcus nodded, his eyes never leaving hers. "That's to be expected. When you're dealing with high-quality classical antiquities from temple collections, they have a way of disappearing into private hands. But I have no doubt you'll find them."

There it was again. That subtle shift in his voice, that hint of something more beneath the surface of his words. It was like he was speaking in two layers, and she was caught somewhere in the middle.

Her gaze flickered briefly to Aric, who remained silent but watchful. His presence was steadying, but even he couldn't diffuse the pull that seemed to radiate from Marcus.

I need to stay focused, she reminded herself. Marcus wasn't making it easy. Every glance, every word seemed to draw her in further, until she wasn't sure if she was still talking about the case or something else entirely.

Marcus leaned back comfortably, his voice quietly respectful. "I'm impressed by how successfully you've built your business," he said, his tone casual, but there was an undeniable warmth in his voice. "Not many people can do what you do."

"It's all about the work," she said. "Results speak for themselves."

Marcus's smile widened ever so slightly. "Indeed, they do."

"So, where do we start with the next lead?" Ophira asked, keeping her voice steady and professional.

Marcus leaned back in his chair, his expression calm. "I think it's less about the next lead," he said slowly, his gaze finding hers, "and more about how we approach the situation as a whole."

There was something in the way he said it – a careful choice of words, delivered with that same quiet confidence that had piqued her curiosity from the moment they'd met. Ophira felt a flicker of something beneath the surface, but she wasn't about to let it distract her.

Before she could respond, Marcus shifted in his seat, his posture relaxed, but there was an undeniable intensity in his gaze. "You've created quite an operation here," he added, his voice steady, appreciative but professional. "It's even more impressive seeing it firsthand. This case is lucky to have you on it."

The compliment caught her off guard. It was nothing inappropriate, but the undertone was there, subtle and hard to ignore. She could feel a slight warmth creeping into her cheeks, but she quickly brushed it off, forcing a smile that she hoped remained professional.

"Thanks, but flattery doesn't solve cases," she replied. "Let's focus on the task at hand."

Aric, seated nearby, shifted in his chair, glancing between the two of them. Ophira could feel his eyes on her, but he remained silent for the moment, though she knew him well enough to sense his growing wariness. She stole a glance at him, and their eyes met briefly. His brow furrowed, but he didn't say anything.

Marcus seemed unfazed by the exchange. "Of course, I believe in giving credit where it's due."

Ophira nodded, turning her attention back to the files in front of her, but her mind kept circling back to Marcus. He was adept at striking a balance between charm and professionalism. He hadn't crossed any boundaries, but the way he spoke, the way he carried himself, made it hard to keep the conversation strictly business.

She concentrated on clearing her mind and then began to go over the information that they had uncovered so far about recent back-channel acquisitions, reviewing various items with Marcus. As the hours passed, discussing the details, she still found it hard to concentrate on anything but the man she was facing.

Aric cleared his throat suddenly, pushing himself up from his chair. "I've got a few things I need to check on," he said, his tone casual but with an underlying edge of protectiveness. He paused at the door, though his eyes lingered on Marcus for just a moment longer before he left the room.

The shift in the atmosphere was immediate. With Aric gone, the tension in the room seemed to intensify. Ophira straightened slightly in her seat, doing her best to maintain her professional demeanor, but it was becoming harder to ignore the pull between them.

Marcus's eyes followed Aric's departure, and a small, knowing smile tugged at the corners of his mouth. "Your colleague seems protective," he commented lightly.

Ophira shrugged, keeping her tone even. "We've worked together for a long time. He has my back, as I have his."

"I can see that," Marcus replied, his gaze settling back on her. "It's rare to find that kind of trust."

Marcus leaned back, his eyes skimming over the numerous pages of notes lying around him. "Why don't we take a break from the office?" he suggested. "We've been going over files for a while now, and I find it's easier to think when we're not surrounded by paperwork. There's a coffee shop down the street."

The suggestion was casual enough, but Ophira could feel the underlying invitation. Marcus was subtly opening the door to something more, testing the waters without being forward.

Coffee wasn't a big deal. Technically. But even small things carried weight when the lines were already blurring. This conversation had been dancing near something unspoken for too long, and she didn't know if she was ready to name it yet.

Marcus watched her carefully, his smile soft, patient, as if he could sense her hesitation but wasn't going to push.

"Coffee sounds good," Ophira said finally, offering a small smile in return. She pushed back the growing attraction she felt and forced herself to stay focused on the case, on the job, on everything except the way Marcus made her feel.

"Perfect," Marcus said, standing with the same fluidity as before. "Shall we?"

Ophira rose to her feet, keeping her composure as she moved to join him by the door. She could feel his presence beside her, his quiet confidence filling the space between them. Part of her wanted to remain guarded, to keep things strictly professional, but she couldn't help but feel intrigued.

As they walked toward the door, she allowed herself a brief glance at him. His posture was relaxed, his steps measured, and his expression remained composed. He was impossible to read, but something told her he knew exactly what he was doing.

One thing was becoming alarmingly clear: this case wasn't going to test her. It was already testing her.

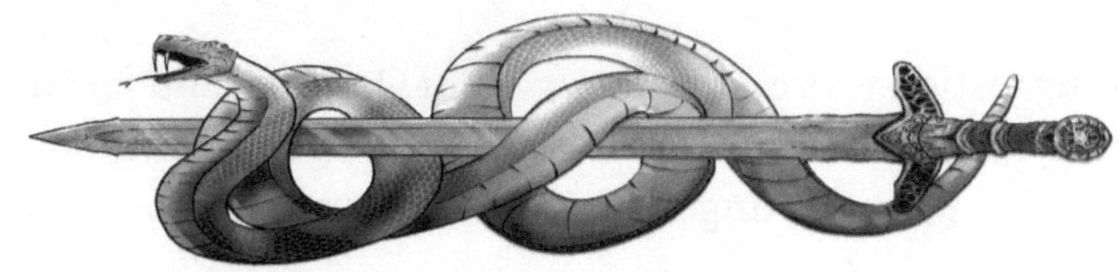

Before they stepped out, she called toward the back of the office, where Aric was sorting through some paperwork. "Hey, Aric! Marcus and I are heading out for a quick coffee run. You want anything?" Her tone was casual, but there was an unspoken message there, a subtle way of keeping Aric in the loop.

Aric glanced up briefly, casual yet observant. "I'm good, thanks. Take your time." He gave a small wave, though Ophira could feel his gaze lingering a little longer than usual. She nodded in return, feeling a strange mix of reassurance and slight apprehension from his watchful eyes. Aric always notices when things feel off.

She and Marcus stepped out of the office into the bustling mid-morning streets. The city had its usual hum, a mix of cars, conversations, and the distant sounds of street musicians setting up for the day. The café was only a few blocks away, and they fell into a comfortable rhythm as they walked.

Ophira couldn't help but notice how Marcus's presence beside her shifted the usual pace of her mornings. The energy between them was calm, yet charged, as if the city itself slowed to accommodate their conversation.

"Nice day for a coffee break," Marcus said, glancing up at the sky.

"Not bad," Ophira agreed. "Better than being stuck in the office all day."

He chuckled. "I imagine you don't get to do this often, step away from the job for a bit."

She smiled lightly. "Not as much as I should. Things tend to pile up when you run a business like mine."

"And when you're someone like you," Marcus added.

She shot him a sidelong glance. "Someone like me?"

Marcus gave a faint smile, his eyes warm and knowing. "Someone who's always in control. You can see it in how you carry yourself. But I'd bet there's more to you than the work."

She glanced at him, catching the glint of something in his eyes that wasn't professional admiration. There was warmth there, a quiet appreciation that made her feel seen. It was disarming, in a way she hadn't expected. Ophira chuckled, though something about his words lingered longer than she expected. *He's perceptive…probably more than is good for me.* But the compliment was gentle enough that it didn't feel like a tactic. It felt sincere.

As they approached the café, a small, quaint spot nestled between a bookstore and a bakery, Ophira felt the stiffness in her shoulders ease a bit.

She had always liked this place – its rustic charm, the smell of fresh pastries mixing with coffee beans. The café felt like a world apart from the high-stakes meetings and constant vigilance that came with her job.

Marcus held the door open for her, his hand brushing lightly past hers in the small space, leaving her quietly aware of his presence without dwelling on it. She told herself not to linger on it, but the feeling clung to her.

They stepped inside, and the soft hum of the espresso machine blended with the low murmur of conversations happening around them.

The décor was mismatched but welcoming, with wooden tables, mismatched chairs, and a few plants hanging from the ceiling in colorful pots. It was the kind of place where people lingered, taking their time, letting the rest of the world fall away for a while.

They ordered their drinks, Marcus choosing a cappuccino and Ophira sticking to her black coffee, and settled into a quiet corner table.

The café hummed with the soft clinking of cups and murmured conversations, a soothing background to the quiet between them.

Marcus asked, "Do you come here often?"

Ophira laughed softly. "I've been known to stop by now and then. It's a nice break from the chaos of the office. Why?"

"It suits you, this place. Quiet, peaceful…with the right amount of character."

She rolled her eyes playfully. "You've been throwing around a lot of compliments today. Are you always this charming?"

Marcus chuckled, his gaze steady. "Only when the company warrants it."

Ophira raised an eyebrow, unsure how to respond but feeling the warmth creep into her cheeks despite herself. *What's with this guy?* She tried to hide her smile by taking a long sip of coffee.

Their conversation shifted easily from work matters to lighter topics. He had an easy way about him that made her forget about the job, the relics, and the stress that always lingered in her world. She found herself laughing at his stories, feeling more relaxed than she had expected.

"What do you do when you're not tracking down dangerous artifacts?" Marcus asked, his tone light but with a hint of curiosity.

Ophira leaned back in her chair, smiling. "Not much these days. I read whenever I can, and I work out to clear my head. I try to keep things simple."

"Simple," Marcus repeated. "Somehow, I doubt anything about you is simple."

She tilted her head, smirking. "What's that supposed to mean?"

Marcus tilted his head. "You strike me as someone with layers. There's a lot more going on behind those eyes than you show the world."

Ophira felt a flutter in her chest, a mix of surprise and intrigue. *He's good, I'll give him that.* But the way he said it didn't feel like a line. It felt like he really saw her. And that was dangerous.

She shifted, trying to steer the conversation back toward safer ground. "You're not bad at reading people yourself, Marcus. Is that part of your business?"

"Could be," he said with a grin. "But I think it's more of a personal interest."

Ophira couldn't help but smile at that. "So you spend your free time psychoanalyzing people over coffee?"

"Only the interesting ones," he teased, his eyes twinkling with something unspoken.

She shook her head, biting back the laugh that threatened to escape. She found herself enjoying the back and forth. He had a way of making the conversation feel both playful and meaningful at the same time, and it was hard not to get pulled in.

Their conversation flowed effortlessly, the space between them growing smaller as they continued to talk. Marcus asked about her business, about the intricacies of what she did, but he also veered into more personal territory. Her favorite books, her travels, the things that mattered to her outside of work.

And somehow, without her realizing it, she was opening up more than she usually did, letting him see glimpses of her life she kept tightly guarded.

"There's something different about you," Marcus said softly, his voice warm and low. "It's rare to meet someone who's so in control yet so approachable."

Ophira felt the words sink in deeper than she expected. *I'm getting comfortable with him, aren't I?* But instead of feeling alarmed, she felt intrigued. She was starting to see more of Marcus, the man behind the smooth charm, the one who could make her feel at ease without even trying. And it was a feeling she hadn't realized she missed.

Their fingers brushed accidentally as they both reached for the sugar packet on the table. Ophira felt a jolt run through her, a brief but undeniable connection in that simple touch.

She pulled her hand back quickly, smiling to cover the sudden rush of warmth flooding her cheeks. *What's gotten into me? I'm acting like a teenager. This is entirely ridiculous.*

But Marcus didn't seem fazed. He smiled, his gaze lingering on her a moment longer before he spoke. "I'm glad we decided to meet outside the office. It's nice to see this side of you."

Ophira laughed softly, trying to shake the warmth still coursing through her. "This side? It's just coffee."

Marcus smiled gently. "Maybe. But it feels like a good step toward clearer thinking, doesn't it?"

She met his gaze, feeling the pull between them growing stronger. *Yeah, it's definitely more than coffee.*

As they left the café, the lingering friction from their coffee outing hadn't dissipated. Ophira felt a strange mix of excitement and hesitation building within her. The conversation had revealed more than she'd intended, and Marcus's probing questions still echoed in her mind.

The morning sun warmed the sidewalk as they walked in comfortable silence. Ophira found herself stealing glances at Marcus, noting the way he moved with quiet confidence, his hands tucked into his jacket pockets.

There was something reassuring about his presence, yet she couldn't shake the feeling that she was walking a tightrope between truth and deception.

They paused at the corner, waiting for the light to change. The street buzzed with typical city energy. People headed to work or errands, street vendors called out their wares, and the distant honk of impatient drivers punctuated the air. Ophira was beginning to relax into the rhythm of it all when movement caught her peripheral vision.

A man in a worn leather jacket hurried past, his stride purposeful but slightly too quick for the casual pace of the morning crowd. He collided with Marcus's shoulder with enough force to make Marcus step back slightly.

"Sorry, sorry," the stranger muttered, fumbling to collect the papers that had scattered from his briefcase like startled birds. The documents fluttered in the breeze, some landing at their feet, others dancing away down the sidewalk. He shot them an apologetic glance before crouching to gather his things.

But even as he appeared flustered, his movements remained economical and efficient. He knew exactly which papers to grab first, worked in a methodical pattern from nearest to farthest, and never once looked lost or confused about where anything had fallen.

Marcus barely registered the encounter, already stepping toward the crosswalk as the light turned green. "Some people are always in a rush," he said with a slight chuckle, brushing off his jacket where the man had bumped him.

But Ophira's eyes tracked the man's retreat, her training kicking in before she could suppress it. She noted how quickly he'd recovered his composure after the initial stumble, how his fingers hadn't trembled despite the apparent flustered state. His recovery had been too smooth, too practiced.

She filed the observation away, her hypervigilance automatically cataloguing details: average height, no distinguishing features, brown hair that needed a trim, movements that suggested he knew exactly where he was going despite the apparent confusion. The way he'd avoided eye contact after that first apologetic glance. How he'd managed to collect every single scattered paper despite the wind.

Probably nothing, she told herself, forcing her shoulders to relax as they crossed the street. But her instincts rarely dismissed coincidences so easily, and something about the perfectly imperfect stumble felt rehearsed. In her line of work, accidents were often anything but accidental.

Marcus was saying something about his afternoon appointments. Still, Ophira found herself scanning the crowd behind them, looking for a worn leather jacket that had already melted away into the urban landscape.

As they approached the building, Marcus paused slightly, turning toward her with a casual smile. "By the way, would you be open to discussing this more over dinner tonight?"

He said the words casually, but there was a deeper note beneath them. Ophira could feel it in the way his eyes met hers, full of unspoken possibilities.

She scanned his expression for any sign of ulterior motives but found only sincerity. *This is moving fast,* she thought, but a part of her wanted to say yes, to see where this could go.

"Dinner?" she asked, her tone light, though her pulse quickened at the suggestion.

Marcus had a smile that seemed utterly perfect. "I'd like to get to know you better, outside of the office."

Outside of the office... Ophira mulled it over before shaking her head. "I'm not free tonight."

Marcus offered a pleasant nod as they parted, showing no obvious disappointment. That neutrality should've been reassuring, but somehow it left her quietly uncertain.

As she walked back into her office, Ophira glanced around as if trying to ground herself in something solid. But the silence only left space for her thoughts to creep back in. The way Marcus had looked at her. The way her body had nearly said yes before her mouth said no.

You sure you said no loud enough? Sage muttered. *Because your hormones are still throwin' a parade.*

She pressed her lips together and turned toward her monitor, the familiar glow of case files offering a different kind of comfort.

Getting back to work was easy. Ignoring the part of her that hadn't wanted to say no was harder.

CHAPTER FIVE

GROUP PROJECTS NEVER END WELL (DOUBLY IF THEY'RE CURSED)

The photographs Marcus spread across her conference table the next morning should have been impossible to acquire. Yet there they were, four stolen relics that had vanished without a trace, captured in grainy black and white like evidence from a crime scene. The morning light filtered through her floor-to-ceiling windows, casting shadows across the photographs as he spread them out.

"I've managed to get my hands on some old photographs of the stolen artifacts," he said, his tone suggesting the acquisition hadn't been simple. "Took some convincing and a favor I'd rather not have called in, but these should give us our first real look at what we're hunting."

The photographs were blurry, but she could make out the details: a necklace, a sword, a chalice, and an urn.

Ophira leaned forward, taking control of the examination as her trained eyes swept across each black and white photograph methodically. Her gaze snagged on the sword's curved outline in the grainy photo, and unease curled in her chest.

Something about its shape, the way the blade curved. It reminded her of betrayal, the cold shock of discovering that the trusted ally who'd knelt at her feet in reverence had been cataloging her weaknesses, turning her secret into a weapon that nearly cost her everything.

She brushed her fingers along the cool marble edge of the table, the familiar texture grounding her in the present moment. *This isn't the same,* she told herself with the fierce determination of someone who'd survived by learning from past mistakes. Marcus had been nothing but helpful, professional, exactly what she needed.

But the weight of old wounds whispered otherwise, stirring the hypervigilance that had kept her alive through millennia of dangerous encounters. She'd learned to trust that whisper, which had saved her life more times than she could count.

"These are the relics that were stolen," Marcus explained, his fingers slowing as he turned each page, guiding the pace of revelation. "They've been floating between private collections for centuries. No verified origins, only rumors and stories about the damage they leave behind."

"We need to get in contact with anyone who might have an interest in buying these," Aric said, his voice sharp and focused. "Whether they know what these relics are or not, someone will want them. If the thieves are amateurs, they'll have a limited number of people they can sell to. That's our best shot at recovering them."

He glanced at Ophira. "Actually, a contact of mine mentioned something odd yesterday. Someone's been asking around about a chalice."

Ophira raised an eyebrow. "You think it's connected?"

"Could be. Could be nothing." Aric's voice carried a thoughtful weight, as if he were piecing together fragments of a larger puzzle. "If it is, we need to act fast."

"I agree," Marcus said. "But we need to keep this quiet. The moment this reaches the ultra-collectors, those obsessives with unlimited resources and no moral boundaries, it's over. They don't simply buy artifacts. They make them disappear completely. Private vaults, hidden collections, places where even governments can't reach. Once they're in those hands, it's as if the relics never existed."

Ophira's mind was already running through their next steps, patterns of investigation honed by centuries of surviving in the shadows between mortal and divine worlds. "We'll need to follow the money. These types of deals usually involve intermediaries, such as brokers, dealers, or individuals connected to the illegal markets. If we can track down the right people, we'll find the relics."

Marcus nodded, his gaze locking onto hers. "That's the key. The thieves don't know what they're sitting on, but the moment they realize it, they'll raise the price. We have to find them first."

Ophira nodded slowly. "We'll need more than this to go on. I can put a call out to my contacts, see if anyone knows about a collection fitting this description."

Aric chimed in, "I can reach out to some old friends in the underground trading scene, see if there's been any chatter about these relics changing hands. It's a long shot, but better than sitting on our hands."

Marcus studied them both, his relief evident. "Thanks. I've been running solo on this for too long. It's good to have some real help."

But Ophira wasn't entirely convinced yet. Marcus had been helpful, almost overly helpful. Information flowed from him fast and clean. *Unusually clean?* She filed the observation away, her gaze darting to his hands. No sign of nerves.

Warning signals flared in the back of her mind, urgent and insistent. *He's been useful so far,* she reasoned, but the doubts refused to quiet. The familiar question surfaced. *Am I being paranoid or finally being smart?*

He's making sense, but I can't afford to be careless, she thought, studying him with narrowed eyes. Marcus was charming, intelligent, and quick on his feet, but apprehension still gnawed at her.

I need to trust my instincts. I've been burned before.

As if sensing her hesitation, Marcus glanced over at her, his expression shifting to something softer, more vulnerable. "I know this sounds extreme, but we don't have the luxury of time here. The sooner we recover these relics, the sooner we can stop worrying about what might happen if they fall into the wrong hands."

Ophira nodded, though anxiety still tugged at her. *Never again.* The familiar vow echoed in her mind. Yet as Marcus leaned in closer, she caught his cologne again, woodsy and comforting, the warmth of his presence seeping into her. Her defenses, once ironclad, wavered, slipping with each look, each touch.

Marcus moved through her barriers effortlessly, a fact that set her pulse racing as much in excitement as in caution. She wanted to trust the ease of his presence, the way he made her job feel less lonely. But instincts whispered beneath the calm, an abundance of ease was its own kind of danger. That terrified her. *Truth? Or lies?*

Despite every instinct screaming caution, she pushed the unease aside for now. "I'll reach out to my contacts tonight," she said. "And we'll figure this out together."

Marcus smiled, but something in his gaze lingered. "I'm glad I can count on you."

As he turned back to the photographs, Ophira watched him closely, disquiet slipping under her skin again. He was giving her everything she asked for, so why did it still feel like a setup?

Ophira said nothing. But the weight of the folder in her hands felt heavier than it should have.

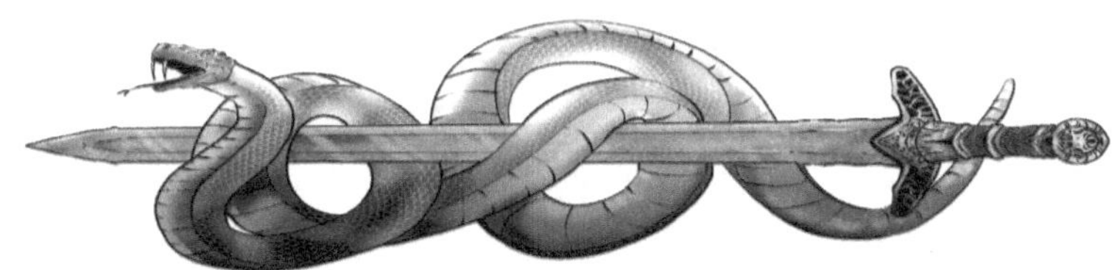

The moment the door clicked shut behind Marcus, a different kind of silence settled over the office, like the kind that follows the end of a performance.

Ophira remained seated for a beat longer, the folder still resting in front of her like evidence. She hadn't moved it since he'd placed it there, unwilling to disturb what felt like a crime scene. Her fingers traced the edge without touching, as if the weight of its contents might shift with the slightest touch.

Across the room, Aric leaned against the steel filing cabinet near the window, arms crossed loosely. He waited, reading her stillness. "That was a lot."

She didn't answer right away. The air still carried traces of Marcus's cologne, woodsy and reassuring, every note as measured as the man himself. She pushed the folder aside, finally breaking the spell.

"He knows too much," she said, her voice sharpening as the pieces clicked into place. "About the relics. About how this works. More than someone should who just stumbled into this case."

Aric raised an eyebrow. "You think he's lying?"

"No." She stood, slowly, stretching the tension from her shoulders. "I think he's leaving things out, offering enough to look helpful."

"Sounds like someone I know," Aric said quietly, something unreadable flickering in his eyes.

She shot him a look, half amusement, half warning, but didn't take the bait. "What do you make of the ultra-collector threat?"

"Real," he said immediately. "I've heard whispers about them before. Terrifying, if they're even half as obsessive as Marcus made them sound. But it doesn't really change the job. We still have to get there first."

Ophira nodded. "I agree, but we'll need more intel than this." She tapped the closed folder.

"Already working on it," Aric said. "I'll make some calls tonight. There's one guy I know from the Marrakesh circuit. If this is moving underground, he'll have heard something."

"Good. I'll send out a few of my own."

She walked back to her desk, needing the familiar ritual of work to ground herself, and called up the secure network.

You're doing the right thing, sugar, Sunny offered gently. *But that one's got charm that'll burrow right into your bones if you're not careful.*

He glides in like smoke and leaves you gasping for air, Valentina sighed dramatically. *Non! I do not trust zis one, mi amor. He smiles too much, and his teeth are too white, muy perfecto. Très dangereux!*

Ophira opened her encrypted messaging app and scrolled to a contact she hadn't used in months. Viktor had been reliable for years, specializing in Mediterranean antiquities that changed hands through less conventional means. If stolen temple relics were moving through back channels, he would know.

She typed quickly: *Four temple pieces. Mediterranean. Recent acquisition. Heard anything?*

The response came back within seconds, faster than Viktor's usual careful deliberation: No longer at this number.

Then the line went dead. Auto-disconnect.

Ophira stared at the screen, a chill settling in her chest. That wasn't Viktor's usual brush-off for sensitive topics. It was code. Either he was gone, or something had spooked him badly enough to burn his contact protocol.

She tried two more numbers from her network. Both bounced back with variations of the same message.

Someone's moving, she thought, fingers tightening around her phone. *And they're cleaning house as they go.*

Ophira's jaw tightened as she pulled up her backup contact list. The primary channels were compromised, but she had other options. Deeper ones. More dangerous ones. She typed out a message to a different kind of informant and hit send. A single, sharp ping echoed through the quiet office, confirming the dispatch.

She leaned back in her chair, exhaling through her nose. "This just got more complicated."

Aric looked up from his phone, catching the tension in her voice. "What happened?"

"Three of my best contacts just went dark. All at once." She set her phone down with deliberate care. "Either someone's cleaning house, or they're all running scared."

Aric nodded grimly, already understanding the implications. "Let me know if any of your backup contacts catch wind of something. Blood in the water draws sharks fast in this business."

Ophira didn't respond immediately. Her gaze settled on the folder again. Still paper. Still ink. But something in the weight of it had shifted, as if Marcus's touch had left more than fingerprints behind. Now it felt like the opening move in a game she didn't yet understand.

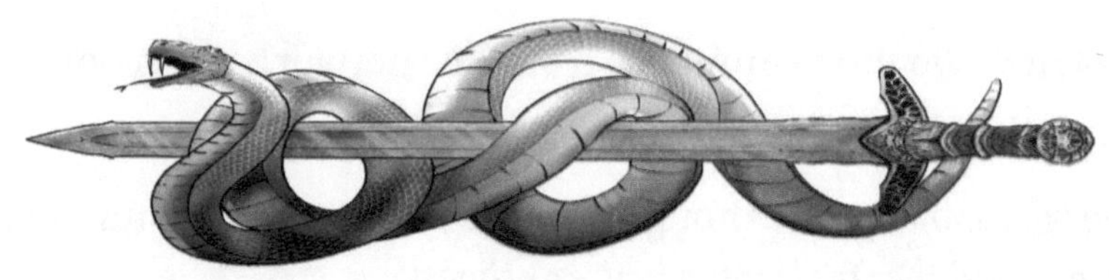

Back in her office the next afternoon, the grainy photographs blurred under Ophira's tired gaze, fragments of artifacts offering more questions than answers. She shifted in her seat, leaning closer to the images, but none stood out, worn pieces revealing nothing concrete. Beside her, Marcus leaned over the photographs, close enough that she caught his cologne again, his eyes scanning the pictures.

Hours had passed in silence, each photo pressing heavier on her chest. The apprehension hadn't left her since their meeting the day before. Something was off, not just in the pictures, but in the air between them.

"These relics are more than artifacts," Marcus said as he studied her reaction to the photographs. "I've heard the stories. Rumors about accidents, disappearances, even deaths. They say the relics carry a curse."

Cursed? Valentina hissed, her crimson head snapping up. *Of course it is! The best stories always are cursed, mi querida. It makes them so much more dangerous. Do you not feel it burning in your bones, Ophira?*

Or maybe it's a load of hooey to scare off competition, Zeke muttered. *People love a good ghost story when there's money on the line.*

Focus up, Sage said curtly. *Look, curses got basis in fact half the time. Worth checkin' out, ya know?*

Ophira resisted the urge to roll her eyes and sent them all a mental nudge. *I heard him. You don't all need to narrate this for me.*

Yeah, yeah, we get it, you think you've got it all handled, Sage muttered. *Guy talks about curses like he's got a PhD in 'em. That's what I'd call a red flag.*

Ophira glanced at Marcus, her curiosity edged with caution. "Cursed?" she asked, watching him closely. He met her gaze evenly, his expression unreadable, but something flickered in his eyes. Marcus spoke so knowingly, almost in passing, as if the curse were something he'd considered for much longer than he let on.

Marcus nodded, his expression serious. "That's one of the rumors, at least. No one seems to hold on to them for long; something always happens. Bad luck, strange disappearances, worse." His voice was steady, but Ophira caught the way his fingers stilled on the table.

She leaned back in her chair, absorbing the information. Cursed relics weren't a new concept to her, but Marcus's encyclopedic knowledge of artifact curses raised questions she wasn't ready to voice aloud. "So these thieves have no idea what they've stumbled into."

"They think it's another valuable collection. To them, it's gold, silver, and priceless artifacts to sell off to the highest bidder." He gestured toward the photographs. "But if word gets out about what these relics really are, we won't be dealing with ordinary artifact hunters anymore. We'll have ultra-collectors swooping in. Once they're in those hands, we'll never see them again."

Something's off, Zeke said quietly. *Call it instinct, but I've got a bad feeling about this guy.*

Your feelings are not fact, Sage countered. *Stick to the evidence. Speculation gets us nowhere.*

Sometimes, gut feelings matter, Sage, Sunny said warmly. *Ophira knows that better than anyone. Let her trust herself.*

Ophira rubbed the back of her neck, the weight of conflicting voices settling into familiar tension. The truth was, all of them had a point, and that was the problem. Her instincts, honed by millennia of hazardous encounters, whispered caution, but the evidence offered no clarity.

She wanted to trust the calm in his voice, the precision of his insight, but wanting to trust and being safe to trust were different lessons entirely, carved into her memory by betrayal.

The doubt curled tighter, quiet but insistent. An old warning, one she'd learned to heed the hard way.

Back when a god spoke her name with reverence and knelt at her feet in Athena's sacred hall. Back when she believed his presence was worship, not warning. She had trusted Poseidon's smile. She had trusted that the goddess who'd claimed her would intervene. But neither saved her. Not from the attack. Not from what followed.

She remembered the cold stone floor. The silence. The judgment. The unraveling of everything she thought she was.

And now Marcus sat beside her, voice soft, gaze steady, speaking of relics and curses with absolute certainty.

She wouldn't make the mistake of confusing charm with safety again.

But Marcus wasn't like them, her heart insisted. He hasn't done anything wrong.

Her grip on the desk tightened anyway. She couldn't shake Aric's warning, couldn't pretend the doubt wasn't there. Centuries of survival had taught her that ignored warnings often became fatal mistakes.

Trust is earned, not gifted, Sage said quietly. *Especially when the stakes are this high.*

The tension in the room thickened as Aric stepped away from the window, his movements slow and deliberate, eyes narrowing as they settled on Marcus at the conference table. "Ultra-collectors? Curses?" Aric's voice stayed even, but the pause between words was intentional. "You've clearly done your homework on this. How long have you been tracking these particular artifacts?"

Marcus leaned back slightly, his expression shifting to something cooler, more controlled, as if Aric's challenge had activated a different mode. "I'm simply sharing what I've learned through my research. Verification is part of your expertise, isn't it? And the ultra-collectors? Anyone involved in artifact recovery knows their reputation. These aren't amateurs. They're dangerous and always ahead of us. That's why we need to act fast."

Aric's eyes flicked to Ophira before returning to Marcus. "And you're here to help us stop them?" His tone was neutral, but an edge sharpened his words, a quiet challenge that hung in the air.

"Exactly," Marcus replied smoothly. "These relics belong in the museum. I'm making sure they don't disappear into the wrong hands."

Aric's fingers tapped once against his arm, the gesture casual, but his knuckles were white with tension. "Timing's interesting, though. You show up right when everything starts moving."

Marcus's smile never wavered. "Coincidences happen in this business more than you'd think."

"Maybe," Aric said, his tone neutral but watchful. "Seems like a lot of moving pieces aligning perfectly." He gestured to the photographs. "These relics, the timing, your expertise in exactly what we need to know."

Marcus spread his hands in an open gesture. "Sometimes the universe puts the right people in the right place. I'd rather think of it as fortunate than suspicious."

Ophira's stomach twisted at the escalating tension. Sunny hummed softly in response, a gentle melody that seemed to ease the sharp edges of the room's atmosphere.

Ophira made a quick choice, stepping between them with deliberate authority, her voice steady but firm. "Marcus has been invaluable so far, Aric. Let's not lose sight of the goal here."

But she began studying Marcus's responses with new attention. The way he answered Aric's questions without really answering them. The practiced ease of his explanations. It was all so polished.

"Exactly," Marcus agreed. "We need to recover these relics before they vanish into some billionaire's private collection." His voice grew more serious. "I convinced the original owner, a private collector in Switzerland, to donate them to the museum here once they're all recovered. That way, they'll be secure, and whatever curses or mysteries surround them will be properly contained. But we don't have much time. Once the thieves realize what they've got, the game changes."

Marcus paused, something shifting in his expression. "I should probably be more upfront about why this matters so much to me." He ran a hand through his hair, the first uncertain gesture Ophira had seen from him. "The person I'm working for… let's just say they're not someone you want to disappoint. This isn't about recovering stolen property, it's about proving I can deliver when it matters."

Now that feels real, Sunny said softly.

Or he's very good at comin' up with a likely story, Sage countered.

Ophira found herself leaning forward slightly, drawn by the apparent honesty. She tapped her fingers against the desk, absorbing both Marcus's words and the tension still humming between him and Aric. Marcus's explanation felt authentic, but Aric's caution felt warranted, too. She'd learned to trust both instinct and analysis, and right now they were pulling in different directions.

"So the thieves have no idea they're sitting on cursed relics. They're looking for a big payday?" she asked, steering the conversation back to safer ground.

Marcus nodded, visibly relieved to return to the case details. "Exactly. But once they realize what they have, everything changes. We need to find them before they understand the true value."

She leaned forward, curious now despite her swirling emotions. "What do we know about the relics themselves? Do we even have full descriptions?"

Marcus smiled, gathering his things back into his bag. "I'll reach out to a few contacts of my own tonight. Between all our networks, we should have some leads by morning."

As he stood to leave, Ophira felt the familiar pull of his presence, the way he seemed to fill the space around him with calm confidence. But underneath that attraction, something else stirred, an awareness she couldn't quite name.

The door clicked shut behind Marcus, and once again, the office felt different in his absence. Lighter, somehow. Less charged.

Ophira leaned back in her chair, the folder of photographs still resting on her desk. Tomorrow they'd begin the real hunt. Tonight, she had questions that had nothing to do with stolen relics and everything to do with the man who'd brought them to her attention.

The game was getting more complex by the hour.

<h1 style="text-align:center">CHAPTER SIX</h1>

<h1 style="text-align:center">RISK MANAGEMENT,
WHAT'S THAT?</h1>

The windows had gone dark, the city sinking into that heavy stillness between twilight and night. Inside Ophira's office, the only light came from the monitor glow, painting faint blues across the relics on her desk and the curve of Aric's jaw where he leaned against the far wall, watching her with the patience of someone who'd seen this obsession before.

The hum of electronics and the faint, distant thrum of the city below pressed in around them, mixing with the metallic scent of warm circuits and the ozone smell clinging to overworked monitors. The night itself seemed to be holding its breath.

He was watching her, not critically, waiting.

She remained silent as she worked. Her hands moved across the keys in clean, deliberate strokes, one monitor feeding into another as her custom filters combed through collector pings, trade alerts, and cross-referenced underground auctions.

"You really think this is the way to verify Marcus's claim?" Aric asked eventually, his voice low and skeptical. "Digging through rumor trails?"

Ophira didn't look up. "If relics are disappearing, there's chatter."

The photo Marcus had shown them was still open on her screen. Blurry. Grainy. Maybe even staged. But something about it wouldn't let go.

"It's been quiet," Aric said, glancing at his screen. "Nothing in the primary forums. No alerts from the usual trade bots. No chatter."

"That means no one's talking publicly." Ophira tapped a key, narrowing her search parameters. "The bigger the prize, the quieter the buzz."

"Or the more imaginary."

Ophira opened a back-channel database, a place they'd used before to track rumored acquisitions and illegal trade whispers. Most of the posts were junk: speculation, fake listings, troll bait.

But a few names stood out and made her pulse quicken. Known ultra-collectors, the kind who could buy and bury a piece of history in the time it took to finish a drink. One had attended an invite-only auction two weeks ago. Another had moved funds through three shells, ending with a museum in Cairo known for off-ledger artifacts.

As she scrolled through the database logs, a familiar signature caught her eye. An automated query from Dmitri's old network, but the routing was wrong. Instead of the usual Moscow servers, the request had bounced through Frankfurt, then Singapore, before landing in her system.

Ophira frowned, pulling up the trace data. The bot signature was legitimate, Dmitri's digital fingerprint, but the pathway was utterly foreign. Someone had either hijacked his network or was using his credentials to probe her system. The query itself was innocent enough, a standard verification ping, but the routing told a different story.

Someone's checking if I'm still active, she realized, her pulse quickening. *But who?*

She ran a quick analysis. The probe hadn't tried to breach anything, just knocked politely on her digital door and waited for a response. Almost like someone verifying she was who she claimed to be before making contact.

Or before making a move.

There wasn't a direct trail to Marcus's relics. Not really.

But there were echoes. Digital footprints. And now someone was quietly checking her credentials.

A thread of unease crawled beneath her ribs. Between the compromised contacts, the bot probe, and the suspicious silence around the stolen artifacts, everything felt orchestrated. If Marcus had been lying, there would have been noise. Angry posts. Competing rumors. Conflicting leads. But this silence was clean. Overly careful. Coordinated.

"It's too quiet," she muttered.

Aric leaned forward, arms folded. "That's a bad sign?"

"Sometimes quiet is worse than noise," she said. "No chatter means the people who know are keeping it close. Which means they know how to stay hidden." She gestured at her screen. "And someone just pinged my system to see if I'm real. Too many coincidences."

Aric's brow furrowed. "You think it's connected to Marcus?"

Her fingers paused over the keyboard, her eyes distant. The bot probe lingered in her mind, another piece of a puzzle she couldn't yet see. "Maybe. Or maybe Marcus isn't the only one interested in what I'm doing. Either way, someone's protecting a lead they don't want found, and someone else is trying to verify I'm real before they decide what to do about it."

You're not wrong, Sage said, his tone thoughtful. *That kind of silence usually means someone's moving.*

Zeke's voice followed, irreverent and sharp. *Like snakes in a henhouse, boss,* he drawled. *All it takes is one wrong step to spook the whole damn lot of 'em.*

Valentina sighed, *Ah, but chérie, if you push too hard, they might start sniffing around for the source. And that source is you, no?*

Her stomach twisted. Ultra-collectors were persistent, and a few of them had the resources to dig deep enough to find cracks in her story. Even one thread pulled too hard could unravel everything she'd built.

"I think he's telling the truth," she said quietly.

Aric turned toward her, brow creasing. "About all of it?"

"No. Maybe not even most of it." Her fingers hovered over the keys. "But something's happening. These pieces are moving. And if Marcus knew about it first…"

Aric shifted his weight, that guarded stance settling in. "You think it's worth the risk, following Marcus's lead?"

"I think," she said slowly, "someone's already in danger. We don't know who yet."

Aric studied her, the air between them thick with the weight of unspoken worries. When he finally spoke, his voice was softer.

"You sure this isn't just about Marcus?"

She inhaled, steadying herself. "He's not the only one who knows."

Aric shifted again, the faint creak of his jacket cutting through the hum of the monitors. "No active trades. No offers. Just noise."

"Noise is where movement starts."

He exhaled, rubbing his thumb across his palm. "Yeah. I know."

One thread caught her eye, coded language buried beneath a collector brag. It referenced a "return to stone" and "the guardian's heirloom." Two myth references layered into one. Sloppy, but still a thread to tug on.

"It's spreading," she said quietly.

Aric crossed to her desk, reading over her shoulder. "So people are talking."

"They're preparing."

This wasn't verification anymore. This was evidence that others were already chasing the trail. Quietly, carefully, but they were moving. Marcus had been right about that much.

"I don't like where this is going," Aric muttered, pulling back slightly.

Her mind had already shifted gears, thinking about routes, access points, and strategic chokeholds. The risk felt sharper now, like the chill of a blade resting against her skin. If the ultra-collectors realized she was on this trail, they'd want to know why.

Sunny's voice came gently. *Be careful now, darlin'. A plan ain't no good if it leaves you too deep in the briar patch to find your way out.*

Aric must have seen the change in her posture, the way her shoulders squared, the way her focus turned from the screen to something only she could see.

"Fee..."

"We're behind," she said, already opening a new tracker window.

"Or," he offered carefully, "we're not involved yet. We could still walk away."

She finally looked at him then, really looked. He wasn't wrong, but he was too late.

"I've already crossed that line."

Whatever this was, whatever Marcus had pulled her into, she was already calculating how to get ahead of it.

Valentina's voice drifted like smoke. *Mi amor, they will be watching you now. Every move you make.*

Aric stood there, watching her with that faint crease between his brows. The one he wore when he could see trouble coming but knew better than to stand between Ophira and whatever decision she'd made.

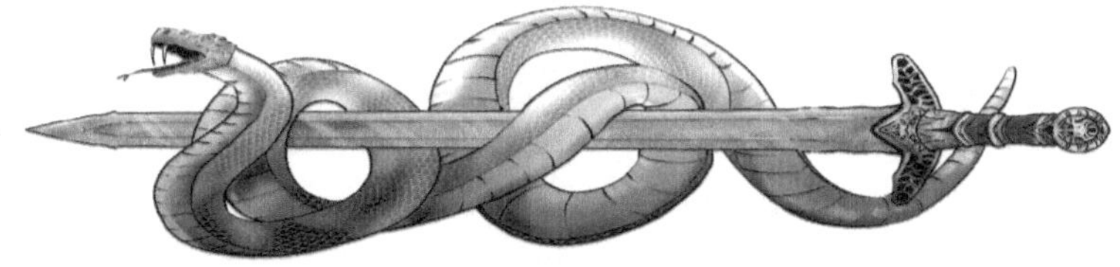

The screens were off, yet the room still hummed, softly familiar.

Ophira sat motionless, her spine curved forward, forearms resting on her knees. The tablet Marcus had given her lay beside the chair, closed and contained, yet not quiet. She could feel the memory of its glow behind her eyelids, an afterimage refusing to fade.

The last frame Marcus had sent remained etched in her mind: blurred, jagged, deliberate. Everything about it reeked of a setup. She could still sense the shape of the images inside her skull – the wrongness of them, the dissonance. And the fact that some part of her wanted to believe him.

Not *him*. The data.

She hadn't moved in ten minutes.

This is reckless, Sage snapped, his tone edged with frustration. *You know it. I know it. That slick bastard knows it.*

Reckless is when you act without a plan, Ophira replied, her words flat and certain.

This ain't a plan, Zeke drawled. *It's a gut decision dressed up in code, hoss. And you know what comes next: trouble in a five-gallon bucket.*

Sunny's voice was soft as she counseled, *It doesn't feel like recklessness to me. Feels more like the truth knocking at your door.*

Ophira flexed her jaw. Clarity should feel clean. Instead, this felt like pressure behind her eyes, like a slow-building tremor that wanted to shake her bones loose.

Valentina let out a wistful sigh, *Ahhh, mon ange, how thrilling it is, non? The heat before the plunge! The sting before the ruin!*

Not helpful, Sage snapped.

Ophira's gaze drifted toward the tablet, its black screen a mirror that reflected nothing but her hesitation. The pattern Marcus had hinted at was deliberate. Someone wasn't merely buying. They were curating, arranging the pieces like a puzzle only they could see.

She didn't have proof, not yet, but she knew how to recognize a setup when she saw one.

She didn't trust Marcus, not wholly. This wasn't about him. It wasn't even about proving him wrong. It was about what she noticed in the gaps – what he didn't say, what the others hadn't yet recognized.

The wall she had built to keep all of this out? It had already started to crack.

But he'd told her *enough.*

She closed her eyes for a moment. The cost of stepping in was clear: exposure, risk, and the weight of secrets too dangerous to name. But the cost of walking away carried its own kind of burden.

Zeke's voice cut through her thoughts. *You keep thinkin' like that, and you'll end up neck deep in this mess.*

Sunny countered, *Don't let the fear talk louder than your gut, sugar. You've never run from a fight when it mattered.*

Valentina gave a satisfied sigh. *Ahhh, the hunt begins, non? How delicious it will be to dance with shadows again!*

Sage added, *This is your call. But once you step in, you're all in.*

She opened her eyes, the weight of their voices pressing against her.

Her phone was silent on the table, its screen dark but expectant. She picked it up slowly, her thumb hovering over the message box. For a moment, she considered deleting the draft and walking away. But the urge vanished as quickly as it arrived.

She considered the pieces already in motion, the silence screaming of secrets, and the risk of letting others run the board while she remained on the sidelines.

Her thumb steadied.

Ophira
I'll take your case.

She hit send.

There was no confirmation, no response. Only the quiet hum of the room settling back around her, as if the shadows themselves were waiting for her to make the next move.

CHAPTER SEVEN

RED FLAGS MAKE GREAT BOOKMARKS

The office thrummed, monitors casting blue veins across Ophira's desk. Her fingers flew over keys, screens alive with collector networks weaving through dark-web threads, veiled aliases, and whispers of trades. The relics Marcus had described loomed like shadows, their blurred shapes seared behind her eyes: the necklace, sword, chalice, and urn.

She traced auction echoes. Flagged a Zurich wire tagged *chained relic*. A Macau whisper of *a blade that balances*. Her focus tightened, hunting patterns. Connections. Proof.

Ophira's jaw flexed. Marcus's warmth when she'd taken the case clung like dusk's heat, disarming and weighty. She didn't trust him, not entirely. But the data didn't lie. A Cairo shell fund had moved money days before the Zurich hit. Another reference: *stone's heirloom.*

Patterns.

She leaned back, considering her next move. The Cairo connection needed verification, and the Macau reference required deeper investigation. She could trace the wire transfers and cross-reference the auction timing with shipping manifests. Real detective work, the kind that took patience and methodical analysis.

These weren't coincidences.

Marcus had been vague about his sources, deflecting her questions with charm and promises. But she had real leads now. Real questions that demanded real answers.

She reached for her phone and dialed his number.

"Marcus? It's Ophira. I need to talk to you about what I've found. Can you meet me at The Grind in an hour?"

The Grind was a cluttered nook tucked between downtown's glass towers, its air thick with roasted beans and the musty scent of ink from old books lining the walls. The worn leather chair creaked beneath her as she settled in, and she could taste the bitter edge of espresso on her tongue before she'd even ordered.

Marcus sat by a window, navy blazer framing his relaxed confidence, eyes catching hers with an undertow she didn't yet recognize. "Ophira," he said, standing. "You sounded urgent on the phone."

She slid into the chair across from him, pulling out her tablet. "I've been digging into your relics. Zurich's humming with necklace chatter. Macau mentions a sword of mythic power, whatever that means. A Cairo shell fund moved money right before the Zurich hit." She met his eyes directly. "Want to tell me why those aren't coincidences?"

Marcus's laugh was soft, a brush of warmth. "You don't waste time. Most collectors dance around a find before they commit." He leaned forward, the steam from his espresso curling between them.

"I'm not a collector."

"No, you're no mere collector." His eyes glinted. "You're something more dangerous. The sword? Some say it cuts through lies. But myths are slippery things."

Ophira's latte warmed her palms, steadying her focus. "Myths don't find thieves. I need names, Marcus. Dealers, brokers, points of origin."

He tilted his head, unruffled. "Names don't come easy in this business." His hand shifted closer to hers. "But you? You'll find them first."

Her breath caught, tension sharp as a razor pressed to skin. She wanted facts, not his magnetism. But his gaze dismantled her defenses, one careful look at a time. "I find what's hidden. I start with the truth," she said.

"Truth takes time. It has to be given, not taken." His smile curved. "And I haven't earned yours yet."

She narrowed her eyes. "You haven't earned anything."

"But you're here."

A beat. Then: "I go where the trail leads."

"You have a way of spotting trails most of us miss," he said in a matter-of-fact tone. "Makes my job easier."

Her pulse tripped.

"And the chalice?"

Marcus shrugged. "Healing. Broken things made whole."

Vague. Useless. Frustration flared, yet his ease drew her deeper, a tide she fought and craved.

"Speaking of trails," Marcus said, leaning back with casual interest, "how does this work exactly? You and Aric make quite the team."

The shift caught her off guard. "We do. He's reliable, with a brilliant mind and fantastic instincts."

"How did you two meet? It's not every day you find someone who can keep up with your particular talents."

Despite herself, Ophira found the question disarming. "We worked a case together years ago. Art theft ring." She kept to the public version of their story. "He was private security then, I was freelance. We realized we made a good team."

"And now you run the whole operation together."

"Something like that." She examined his expression. "What about you? You seem awfully calm for someone whose reputation depends on recovering stolen relics."

Marcus's expression grew more serious. "When you're working for someone who doesn't accept failure, you learn to stay focused. Getting rattled doesn't help anyone."

His tone made her chest tighten. The weight he carried, the pressure he was under – it made her want to help him succeed.

They lingered over their drinks, the conversation drifting to easier topics. Marcus had a way of drawing her out, asking questions that made her forget she was supposed to be interrogating him. By the time she realized how much time had passed, her coffee was cold, and his charm had worked its way past her defenses.

"I should get back to work," she said, glancing at her watch.

As they rose to leave, Marcus stepped closer, pausing beside her.

"Dinner tonight?" he said, voice lower. "To celebrate your decision to join the hunt. Merlot on Fifth. Seven?"

His gaze held hers, a promise barely veiled.

Ophira wavered. Her usual sense of caution and self-preservation clashed with a reckless spark. Dig deeper or dive closer? "I'm in," she said, half-strategy, half-fall. Her heart tipped the scale. "Seven."

"Until then." Marcus's voice lingered, a velvet snare.

He walked out.

Ophira stood in his wake, heart steady but tilted, the edge of her instincts brushing against something she couldn't quite name.

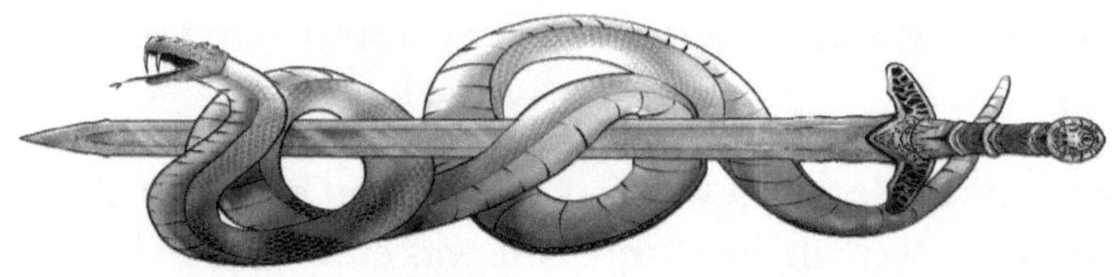

That evening, as she stood in front of the mirror, Ophira found herself fussing over her appearance in a way she hadn't done in a long time. Her wardrobe leaned toward practicality, but tonight she opted for something different. A sleek black dress that hugged her figure in all the right places, elegant but understated. Her hair, usually pulled back in a no-nonsense ponytail, was left loose, cascading in waves down her shoulders.

She looked polished and confident, but there was something in her eyes that she couldn't quite place. A spark of uncertainty. A flicker of excitement.

What am I doing? she thought. *This was supposed to be a simple case. Why am I even doing this?*

But her mind drifted back to Marcus. His effortless charm, the way he had made her laugh over something as simple as a cup of coffee. He had a way of making the world seem smaller. Like nothing else existed when they were talking. And now she couldn't deny that she was intrigued by him, drawn in by something she didn't fully understand yet.

By the time she arrived at Merlot on Fifth, the city was wrapped in the soft glow of twilight. The restaurant matched Marcus's description perfectly: elegant but not overly formal, a cozy space nestled between the evening's shadows and Fifth Avenue's pulse. Through floor-to-ceiling windows softened by burgundy drapes, candlelight danced across polished tables. Jazz whispered beneath the gentle clinking of wine glasses.

Marcus was already seated at a corner table near the window, a glass of wine in hand. When he saw her, he stood, his smile wide but not eager, each movement polished with a gentleman's grace.

He wore a charcoal-gray suit, tailored perfectly to his tall frame. The faintest hint of cologne lingered in the air as she approached, the soft fabric of her dress whispering against her legs as she walked. His dark hair was neatly styled, the sharp lines of his jaw softened by the warmth in his eyes.

"You look beautiful," Marcus said as he helped her into her seat. That left her momentarily breathless.

She offered a small smile, her pulse quickening. "Thank you. You don't look too bad yourself."

Marcus chuckled as he resumed his seat, fingers tracing the edge of his wine glass. "I'll take that as a compliment."

Ophira allowed herself a moment to take in the setting. The restaurant was unlike anywhere she usually went: quiet, intimate, but not pretentious. The kind of place where people come to lose themselves in conversation, enjoying the simple experience of being in each other's company. Tables were spaced far enough apart for privacy, the murmur of conversation blending with the soft music in the background.

The waiter approached with the menus. Marcus glanced at her, his smile warm. "Do you have a preference for wine? I did some research on this place, but I'd love to know what you actually enjoy."

Ophira felt the tension between them. "I'm partial to a good pinot noir. Something with complexity. But I'm open to suggestions."

Marcus nodded, approving. "Pinot noir it is then."

The conversation drifted naturally to lighter topics: travel, favorite restaurants, and their shared interest in history. Ophira found herself relaxing beyond what she'd expected. The quiet elegance of the restaurant, the dim lighting, and Marcus's easy charm made her feel transported, far from the stresses of her usual life.

When the wine arrived, Marcus raised his glass, his eyes catching hers in the candlelight. "To finding more than we expected."

Something in his tone made Ophira's heart skip, but she raised her glass and clinked it lightly against his. "To that."

The first sip of wine tasted smooth and rich, with hints of dark cherry and spice. It lingered on her palate, and Ophira couldn't help but smile as the warmth spread through her. It paired perfectly with the restaurant's atmosphere, its subtle luxury making everything feel more intimate, more personal.

As they began their meal, the conversation settled into a comfortable rhythm. Gradually, Marcus's questions, though still light, grew more personal. To her surprise, Ophira found herself opening up.

"So what do you do when you're not solving impossible cases?" Marcus asked, leaning back in his chair.

Ophira found herself smiling. "I collect things, actually. Ancient artifacts – not the valuable ones, just pieces that speak to me. Roman glass, pottery fragments. Things with their own stories."

"What kind of stories?"

"The human kind. Who held this cup? What did they think about while they drank from it?" She paused, surprised at how easily the words came. "I traveled to this dig site in Turkey once – found this small bronze mirror. Nothing special, but when I held it..." She shook her head. "Sorry, I'm rambling."

"Not at all. I understand that feeling." Marcus's voice grew quieter. "There's something about touching the past directly. History has always drawn me in that way – the ancient world, the forgotten places. It's like..." He searched for the words. "Like trying to solve a puzzle that's been scattered across centuries."

Something in his tone made her look up, catching a vulnerability in his expression that felt open, unguarded.

"What about when you're not working?" he asked. "How do you spend your free time?"

"Traveling, mostly. There's this monastery in Greece I visit sometimes – they have fragments from a Byzantine chapel. And there's a little market in Istanbul where this old man sells pieces he finds on his property." She found herself gesturing as she spoke. "Places that feel... untouched by the modern world."

"That sounds incredible. There's something about those for-gotten corners, isn't there?" Marcus's eyes brightened. "I was raised around history like that. Ancient places, old traditions. It teaches you to see the world differently."

He paused, seeming to choose his words carefully. "Some lessons stay with you no matter how far you travel from where you started."

There was something in the way he said it – a weight behind the words that suggested deeper meaning. Ophira caught her-self studying his face, seeing past the polished confidence to something more real underneath.

"You make it sound like a calling," she said softly.

"Maybe it is." His smile turned self-deprecating. "Though I'm probably not the first person to romanticize old stones and broken pottery."

There was a vulnerability in his words, something that made Ophira feel as if she were seeing a side of him that few others had. Ophira mused as she sipped her wine, the smooth taste lingering on her tongue, *There's something real here. Or at least I think there is.*

"You're not what I expected," she admitted as their entrees arrived, her voice soft as she met his gaze across the table.

Marcus raised an eyebrow, his lips curling into a small, amused smile. "Oh? And what exactly did you expect?"

Ophira hesitated, feeling the weight of his gaze. "I don't know. I guess I thought you'd be different. More reserved. But you're..."

"Open?" Marcus suggested, his tone teasing but with a hint of sincerity.

She smiled, shaking her head. "I guess that's one way to put it."

The dinner was exquisite, with grilled lamb, roasted vegetables, and delicate sauces that burst with flavor. The wine, the food, and Marcus's quiet attention all wrapped around her like a cocoon, making her forget, even for a little while, the weight she always carried.

As they finished their meal, the rich sauce still coating her tongue, and ordered dessert, the flirtation deepened. The wine had left a pleasant warmth in her chest, and she could smell the faint vanilla from the candle on their table mixing with Marcus's cologne.

His compliments, once subtle, became more personal. He spoke of her strength, her intelligence, the way she commanded a room without even trying. Ophira felt her defenses lowering, her smile widening, and laughter coming more easily.

By the time dessert arrived, a decadent chocolate tart that melted on her tongue, Ophira couldn't deny the pull between them. It was greater than attraction now.

Something beneath the surface made her question whether this connection was real or if the wine, candlelight, and Marcus's attention were weaving a spell she wanted to believe in.

They lingered over dessert, conversation drifting into quieter, more intimate territory. Ophira found herself leaning in, fingers brushing the rim of her wine glass as she listened to Marcus talk about his latest project, a mysterious artifact that had only recently come into his possession.

There was a passion in his voice that mirrored her own. For the first time in a long time, she felt like she was connecting with someone on a level that went beyond just work.

"I don't want the night to end," he said, his voice soft. "But I suppose we both have work tomorrow."

Ophira chuckled, the warmth of the wine and the evening making her feel more relaxed than she had in a long time. "Tomorrow's another day."

"I had a really great time tonight," Ophira said softly.

Marcus smiled, his eyes dark and intense. "So did I."

He stood, offering his hand to help her up. As they walked out together, the cool night air wrapped around them, refreshing after the warmth inside. Marcus walked her to her car, the silence between them comfortable but charged with unspoken tension.

Marcus had been attentive all evening, drawing her in without ever being overt. Ophira could feel it in the way he glanced at her out of the corner of his eye, the way his hand hovered near enough to hers without touching, teasing the idea of connection.

They arrived at her car. The world seemed to slow around them, the city's hum fading into the background as Marcus turned to face her fully.

His eyes held hers, and the tension that had been simmering between them all night reached its peak, like a wire stretched to its breaking point.

Ophira's heart fluttered in her chest, her pulse quickening as the moment stretched on. She could feel the warmth of his breath, the careful way he waited for her signal.

When she didn't step back, he moved closer.

She could feel the warmth of his arm brushing hers as they stood there, suspended in the quiet anticipation. This was the moment, wasn't it? The point of no return. She felt it in her bones.

Why am I hesitating? she wondered, though the answer was clear. She had spent so long keeping people at a distance, building walls around herself to protect her heart, her secrets.

But Marcus… Something about him threaded through her guard like smoke. She didn't invite him in. He was just there. He had a way of slipping past her defenses, making her feel seen in a way that both excited and unnerved her.

Am I ready for this?

He ain't just a man with nice shoes and smooth lies, Zeke muttered. *You let him in now, you better know where the exits are.*

Let her be, Sage replied with unusual gentleness. *She's already halfway gone.*

Marcus, sensing her hesitation, stepped closer. There was a quiet confidence in the way he carried himself, as though he knew exactly what he was doing – how to draw her in without ever pushing too far. His gaze softened, and in that moment, Ophira felt the world tilt slightly on its axis.

She could feel the tension crackling in the air between them, the way his presence seemed to fill the space, leaving little room for anything else. Her pulse thrummed in her ears as he took another step closer, their bodies now only inches apart. She could smell the faint scent of his cologne, woodsy and warm, and it sent a shiver down her spine.

Marcus's hand lifted, brushing a strand of her hair behind her ear. The touch was soft, barely there, but it set off a cascade of sensations in Ophira's chest – warmth, anticipation, and something else she couldn't quite name.

His fingers lingered near her jaw, his thumb grazing the edge of her cheek in a way that felt both intimate and restrained, as though he was holding back just enough to make her want more.

He's waiting, she realized, her breath catching in her throat. *He's waiting for me to make the next move.*

I shouldn't want this, but I do.

Before she could second-guess herself, she closed the distance between them.

Their lips met in a soft, tentative kiss, and the world seemed to fall away. It wasn't rushed, wasn't hurried. It was slow, deliberate, and filled with a quiet intensity that left her breathless.

His hand moved to the back of her neck, pulling her closer, and Ophira felt a jolt of electricity shoot through her, as though the kiss had unlocked something she had kept buried for far too long.

As the kiss deepened, she felt herself sinking into it, her body leaning into his as though it had always belonged there. His lips were soft but firm, his touch gentle yet commanding, and Ophira couldn't help but wonder how someone could feel both so familiar and so dangerous at the same time.

She couldn't know what the kiss meant to him.

For Marcus, the kiss began as a calculated move, another step in a plan he had rehearsed for weeks, yet the moment her lips touched his, the script wavered. The warmth of her mouth and the quiet trust sliding into her shoulders hooked something under his ribs that strategy could not explain.

I need her trust, he reminded himself, but it rang thinner than before, overtaken by an unexpected pull to stay in the kiss for its own sake, a pull that unsettled him beyond what any failure ever could. It wasn't a means to an end anymore. There was something about Ophira that made him want to see where this could lead. To see how far he could take it.

When they finally pulled apart, both of them were breathing harder than they had been a moment ago. The air between them felt charged, like the aftermath of a storm.

Ophira's lips tingled, still warm from the kiss, and a strange mix of emotions swirled inside her. Excitement. Confusion. A tiny seed of doubt.

Is this a horrible decision? she wondered, her heart still racing. *Or is this exactly what I've been missing?*

Marcus smiled down at her, his hand lingering on her arm, his grip just firm enough to keep her grounded. "Goodnight, Ophira," he said softly, his voice filled with a warmth that made her chest tighten.

She swallowed, trying to gather herself. "Goodnight, Marcus."

As she watched him walk away, disappearing into the night, Ophira leaned back against her car, her mind racing. The kiss had been deeper than anticipated, the connection stronger than she'd imagined.

And now, standing there alone in the quiet darkness, she couldn't shake the feeling that something significant had just shifted between them.

This just got more complicated.

CHAPTER EIGHT

WHEN YOUR WINGMAN CLIPS YOUR WINGS

The next morning, Ophira arrived at the office with a lightness in her step that hadn't been there for a while. The lingering warmth of the previous night with Marcus hadn't left her, and she could still feel the soft imprint of his kiss on her lips.

It had been a long time since she'd allowed herself to enjoy something like that. Something personal. Real. She had been so focused on keeping her life locked down, carefully managed, that she had almost forgotten what it felt like to let go, even just a little.

But as she stepped into her office, that lightness quickly met the cool hum of reality. The monitors blinked back at her with their usual precision, the warm office lighting casting everything in sharp focus.

Straighten up, Ophira. Time to get to work.

She set her bag down when Aric's voice broke the silence. "You're in early."

Ophira glanced over at him, surprised to see him already there, seated at his desk with a cup of coffee in hand. He watched her with a calm, steady gaze, but there was something different about the way he looked at her. Something that made her pause.

"Couldn't sleep," she said with a slight shrug. "Figured I'd get a head start on things."

Aric leaned back in his chair, his eyes fixed on her, searching for something beneath the surface. "You've seemed a little off lately," he said, his tone light but laced with unease. "Everything alright?"

The question caught Ophira off guard. She knew Aric well enough to recognize when he was worried. And he was worried now, though he was doing his best to keep it from showing.

She forced a smile, waving off his concern. "I'm fine. A lot on my mind."

Aric raised an eyebrow, unconvinced. "It's more than work, isn't it?"

Ophira flashed back to the dinner with Marcus, the kiss, the way her heart had raced in a way it hadn't in years. She told herself it was no big deal, just a moment. A date. But now, standing in front of Aric, uncertainty flickered through her. Was she getting caught up in this? Was Marcus really as straightforward as she wanted to believe?

He's being overprotective. I'm fine. There's nothing wrong with enjoying myself.

"I can handle this," she said aloud, her voice a touch firmer than she intended. "Everything's fine, Aric. You don't need to worry about me."

But a small part of her wondered if Aric had a point. He had always been there for her. He was her steady and reliable anchor when everything else shifted. He knew her better than anyone, and if he was alarmed, maybe there was something she wasn't seeing.

Aric didn't press the issue, but the look in his eyes told her he wasn't convinced. He leaned forward, resting his elbows on the desk, his expression serious but gentle. "Look, I know you don't want me to push, but if something's going on, you can tell me. You know that, right?"

Ophira's heart softened at the sincerity in his voice. But what she was feeling with Marcus wasn't something she could explain. It was new, exciting, and she felt like she was living for herself, not for the job or to hide her past.

"I appreciate it," she said. "I do. But there's nothing to worry about. I've got it handled."

Aric studied her for a moment longer, his jaw tightening slightly. He didn't like it. She could tell. But he wasn't going to push, at least not yet.

"If you say so," he said finally, though his tone made it clear he wasn't letting his guard down. "Be careful. That's all I'm saying."

Ophira nodded, offering him a reassuring smile. "Always."

But as she turned back to her desk, her smile faded. Aric's words lingered in her mind, even as she tried to brush them off. She knew he was looking out for her. He always had. But this was different. This was something she needed to figure out for herself.

He's worried. Wanting this doesn't make it wrong. But it doesn't make it smart either.

She pushed it aside, diving into the case files in front of her, forcing her mind to focus on the task at hand. But even as she worked, she couldn't shake the feeling that everything was shifting beyond her reach.

She closed her eyes for a moment, letting out a slow breath. Her professionalism and steady command had always been her strengths. She had built a career on keeping everything in perfect balance, never letting emotions interfere with her judgment.

But with Marcus, it was different. The lines were blurring. The case, the way Marcus had slipped so seamlessly into her life, the way she had allowed herself to open up to him.

She considered pulling back, putting some distance between herself and Marcus. But then she remembered the way he had looked at her last night, the warmth in his eyes, the way he had made her feel seen for the first time in what felt like centuries.

I'm getting in too deep, but I don't want to stop.

But even as she told herself that, the seed of doubt remained. There was still something about him she couldn't fully grasp. Something out of reach, like the missing pieces of a puzzle she wasn't sure she was ready to solve.

The pieces that could change everything.

Ophira glanced at the clock on her desk, realizing that the morning had slipped away from her in a haze of emotions. She needed to refocus, to push Marcus out of her mind, at least for now. The case still demanded her attention, and questions needed answering.

She pulled up the latest case files, forcing herself to concentrate on the patterns in the data. But before she could fully immerse herself in the work, the office door opened. Marcus stepped in with his usual confident smile. "Morning," he said, his eyes finding hers immediately. "Hope I'm not interrupting anything important."

Aric's posture shifted slightly, his expression becoming more guarded. "Just going over case files."

Before the tension could build, Aric's phone buzzed. He glanced at the screen, his expression sharpening. "I need to take this," he said, standing. "Been waiting for this call all morning – Alexandria contact." He moved toward the door, phone already pressed to his ear.

Marcus watched him go, then turned back to Ophira with a softer smile. He moved closer to her desk, settling into the chair Aric had vacated. "Busy morning?"

"Always." She studied his face, remembering the way he'd looked at her the night before.

"How are you feeling about last night?"

Ophira felt her cheeks warm slightly. "I had a really good time."

"So did I." He moved closer to her desk, his voice dropping to a more intimate tone. "I keep thinking about what you said – about artifacts having stories. I think this case has quite a story to tell."

She smiled despite her earlier resolve to stay focused. "Most of the interesting ones do."

"I'm looking forward to seeing how this one unfolds." His eyes held hers for a moment longer than necessary. "I'm confident we'll make good progress."

My feelings aren't clouding my judgment, she told herself. *This is exactly what I've been missing.*

But the doubt remained, waiting for the right moment to rise again.

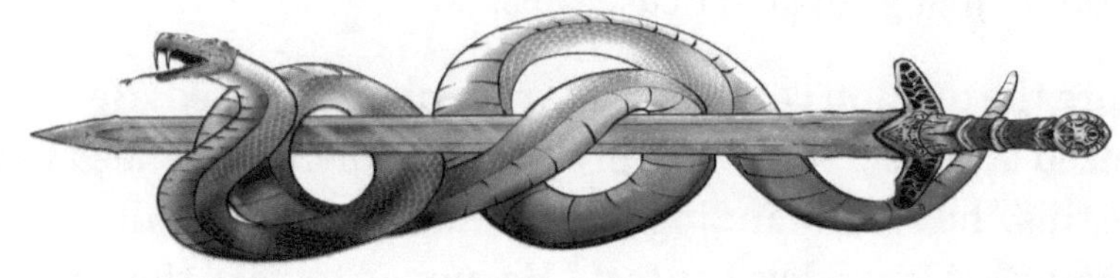

Marcus had claimed the chair beside Ophira's desk, a stack of dealer profiles spread between them, and the morning's personal moment had shifted into professional focus. However, the air still hummed with unspoken tension.

"The Zurich contact finally got back to me," Marcus said, sliding a printed email across to her. "Confirms the necklace surfaced there two weeks ago, but the seller used a proxy. No direct contact information."

Ophira scanned the message, making notes in the margins. "So we're still chasing shadows. What about the Macau lead?"

"Dead end. The sword mention was just marketplace gossip – no actual sighting." Marcus leaned back, frustration evident. "We're close to something, but every lead seems to evaporate when we get near it."

"So," Marcus said, his tone conversational as he set down one of the reports, "anything useful in those dealer profiles?"

Before Ophira could respond, Aric strode into the room with the kind of purposeful energy that meant he'd found something important. He didn't bother with pleasantries, his sharp gaze already scanning the papers spread across Marcus's lap.

"We need to move fast," he announced, setting his tablet down on Ophira's desk with more force than necessary. "I just got off the phone with a contact in Alexandria. There's intel on a private deal happening tomorrow in Izmir – someone's moving a ceremonial chalice through back channels."

Ophira leaned forward, immediately alert. "What are the details?"

"Ancient ceremonial piece, Mediterranean origin, matches the basic description we have of our stolen chalice. Temple-grade craftsmanship." Aric's finger traced across his tablet screen. "The timing's tight, though. The exchange is set for tomorrow afternoon, and if we're going to have any chance of intercepting it, we need to be in position by morning."

Marcus looked up from the reports, his expression brightening with interest. "Izmir? That's promising." He set the papers aside with deliberate calm. "I should come with you on this one. I've got established contacts in the Turkish antiquities market, and I understand how these back-channel deals work."

The change in Aric's posture was immediate and obvious. His shoulders stiffened, and when he spoke, his voice carried an edge that made Ophira's pen pause over her notes.

"Like you handled those shipping manifests from Rotterdam last week?" Aric's voice gained momentum. "Or the auction house contacts the week before that? You volunteered to reach out to your 'network' in London, remember? Said you'd have answers in two days."

"These investigations require finesse," Marcus replied, his tone remaining measured even as Aric's voice rose. "You can't just bulldoze through delicate relationships. It takes time to—"

"What it takes is actual work," Aric snapped, stepping closer to the desk. "We've been sitting here for weeks while you 'coordinate' and 'finesse' and our leads go cold. Every time we get a break in the case, you jump in with promises about your contacts and your expertise, then suddenly you're too busy to follow through."

Marcus held up a hand. "Look, I understand your frustration, but my contacts in Turkey will be crucial here. The language barrier alone, the cultural nuances of these transactions—"

"We're not tourists, Marcus," Aric cut him off. "We can handle ourselves."

"But the relationships I've built there took years to develop," Marcus pressed. "These dealers don't trust outsiders. Without the right introduction—"

"We'll figure it out," Aric said firmly.

Ophira glanced between them, sensing the tension escalating beyond what was productive. "Aric, he does have a point about the contacts."

Aric's jaw tightened, but before he could respond, Marcus raised both hands in a gesture of surrender.

"You know what? You're right," Marcus said, his voice taking on a tone of contrition. "I have been spread too thin, making promises I couldn't keep." He paused, seeming to consider. "Let me make this up to you properly. Take my plane – I'll arrange everything, handle all the logistics from here. You and Ophira can be in Izmir by dawn, positioned exactly where you need to be, without me getting in the way."

The offer seemed to catch Aric off guard, but his expression remained skeptical. "Just like that? You're suddenly willing to step back?"

Marcus spread his hands. "I'm trying to do the right thing here."

"The right thing would have been following through on the leads you promised to handle," Aric shot back. "Now you want us to trust you with transportation when you can't even manage basic follow-up?"

Ophira could see the tension wasn't dissipating. "Aric, what's the alternative? We need to get there tonight."

Aric's gaze flicked between them, his jaw still tight. "Fine. But I want departure times, flight plans, everything confirmed before we leave this office."

"Absolutely," Marcus said, already reaching for his phone. "I'll call the crew now, get everything arranged." He stood, gathering the reports he'd been reviewing. "I'll have all the details to you as soon as I can confirm everything."

He gave Ophira a brief smile of apology and made his way to the door. She watched as he left, the tension still thick in the air.

Ophira let out a slow breath and leaned back in her chair, casting a sidelong glance at Aric. His jaw was still tight, his posture rigid. It wasn't like him to be so openly hostile, especially toward a client, but she could see the tension between them had been brewing for weeks.

"Alright," she said, setting her pen down and turning to face him fully. "What's going on here, Aric?"

He crossed his arms, his brow furrowing. "You're telling me you don't see it? Something's off. I don't know what it is, and that's the problem. You usually notice this stuff before I do."

She raised an eyebrow, leaning back in her chair. "You think I haven't noticed things? I have. But it's not enough to assume he's up to something. I need more than…a bad feeling."

Aric grimaced. "Ophira, I've known you for years. We've been through situations that most people can't handle. And I'm telling you, there's danger here. You can't brush this off because you care about him."

She hesitated, biting her lip. "It's not that simple."

He exhaled sharply, stepped closer to her desk, and leaned down, his voice dropping to an urgent tone. "It's exactly that simple. You're too smart to ignore this. You've always trusted your instincts. Why is this different?"

Aric had always been the voice of reason when she needed it most, but this time was different. "I'm not ignoring it, Aric. But...I don't know. I can't walk away." She sighed, running a hand through her hair. "He hasn't done anything that proves he's lying."

Aric shook his head, his frustration bubbling over. "It's not about proving anything. It's about protecting yourself. You're getting too close, and I'm afraid that when it comes crashing down, you won't see it in time."

The weight of his words settled between them. Aric had been her anchor through every crisis, every late night, every dangerous case. His instincts had never failed her. He'd never been wrong before, but this time... "What if you're wrong, Aric? What if you're overreacting?"

He stared at her, his jaw working. "And what if I'm not?"

"I don't know." She looked away. "I can't ignore it, but I'm not ready to let go."

Aric sighed, the tension in his shoulders easing slightly. "I get it, Ophira. I do. But please… promise me you'll be careful. Don't let your feelings for him blind you to what's really going on."

Ophira nodded, but the gesture felt hollow. She looked at him, at the worry etched in his face, then back to the door Marcus had just exited.

She could feel the fracture forming between them, not in their friendship but in her faith in her instincts. The distance between them stretched like an invisible wall. For the first time, she felt truly alone.

She met his eyes, a flicker of vulnerability passing between them. "I promise I'll be careful, but I need more before I can…" She paused, the words catching. "Before I do anything."

Aric considered her for a moment longer then nodded, though she could see the worry still etched into his face. The leather of her chair squeaked as she shifted, and she could taste the metallic edge of anxiety on her tongue. "Alright, but don't wait too long, okay?"

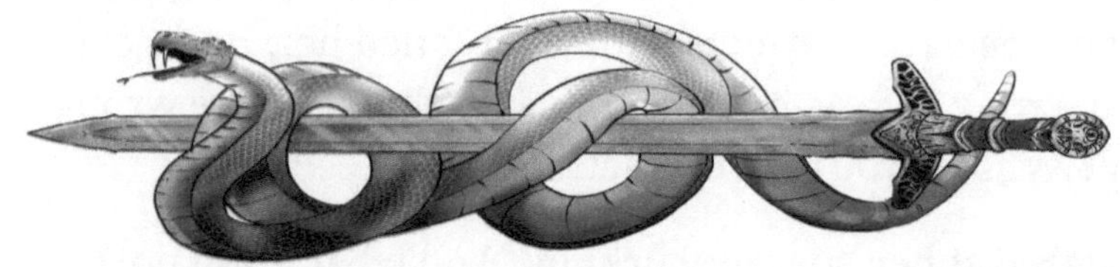

The late afternoon sun slanted through the office windows, casting long shadows across Ophira's desk as she gathered her notes from the day. She'd been checking her phone intermittently, waiting for Marcus's update about the flight arrangements. The Turkey lead felt promising, the kind of breakthrough they'd been waiting for.

The door opened, and Marcus stepped in, his usual confidence replaced by something that looked almost uneasy. His tie was loosened, his hair slightly disheveled, and the apologetic expression on his face made her stomach sink before he even spoke.

"Please tell me you have good news," she said, though his expression already told her otherwise.

Marcus ran a hand through his hair, a gesture she'd come to recognize as his tell when he was frustrated. He paused, seeming to gather himself before delivering the news.

"I'm afraid I don't have good news. The plane's grounded indefinitely." He met her eyes directly. "They discovered an issue with the avionics system during the pre-flight inspection – something about the GPS navigation module failing FAA compliance standards."

Ophira felt her shoulders drop. "How long will that take?"

"At least seventy-two hours, maybe more. They have to source parts from Germany, and with the weekend coming up..." He spread his hands in a helpless gesture. "I'm sorry, Ophira. I know how important this was."

Mierda, Valentina hissed in frustration. *Ze timing, it is so very convenient, no?*

Now, Val, Sunny chided gently, though her tone carried its own note of disappointment. *These things happen, sugar.*

Before Ophira could respond, Aric appeared in the doorway, his expression already dark with suspicion. "Let me guess," he said, his voice tight with barely controlled anger. "Something went wrong with your miraculous solution."

Marcus turned to face him, maintaining his apologetic demeanor. "Avionics failure. The plane's grounded until they can complete a full systems upgrade. I've already called around, but nothing's available on this short notice for an international flight."

"Of course not," Aric said, stepping fully into the room. "Funny how your grand gestures always seem to fall through at the worst possible moment."

"Aric," Ophira warned, though she couldn't entirely blame him for his frustration.

"No, seriously," Aric continued, his voice gaining momentum. "Rotterdam contacts that never materialized. London auction house leads that went nowhere. And now this. You offer your plane with such confidence, then oops, mechanical problems."

Marcus's jaw tightened slightly, but his voice remained measured. "I understand your frustration, but I can't control aircraft maintenance schedules. The FAA doesn't care about our timeline."

"Right. The FAA." Aric's laugh was bitter. "And I suppose there's no other way to get to Turkey by tomorrow morning?"

"Commercial flights are booked solid," Marcus replied. "That's what took me so long to get back. I checked every commercial flight around and every connecting flight that I could think of that would get you there in time. I even reached out to some private ownership contacts that I have to see if I could get you on with them. There's a conference in Istanbul this week, and everything's packed. The earliest I could get you there would be Saturday afternoon."

"Two days too late," Ophira said quietly, the weight of the missed opportunity settling over her.

Something's not right here, Zeke muttered, his voice darker than usual. *Too many coincidences, not enough luck.*

He seems genuinely upset about it, Sage observed neutrally. *But the pattern is troubling.*

Aric was pacing now, his hands clenched at his sides. "This is exactly what I'm talking about. Every time we get close to something real, something concrete, there's always a reason why we can't follow through. Always some excuse, some complication that happens to benefit whoever's trying to stay ahead of us."

"You think I'm sabotaging the case?" Marcus asked in surprise.

"I think you're remarkably good at making promises you can't keep," Aric shot back. "And I think our timing is shit because someone doesn't want us getting too close to the truth."

The tension in the room was thick enough to cut. Ophira looked between them, seeing the frustration in both their faces. Marcus seemed as disappointed as she felt, maybe more so. But Aric's suspicions weren't entirely unfounded. The pattern was starting to feel like more than just bad luck.

"Look," she said finally, "we're all frustrated. But standing here arguing isn't going to get us to Turkey any faster." She turned to Marcus. "Are you certain there's no other option?"

Marcus spread his hands. "I've exhausted every contact I have. If there were another way, I'd have found it."

Aric snorted. "Right. Because your network is so extensive and reliable."

"That's enough." Ophira's voice cut through their mutual antagonism. "We missed this one. It happens. We'll regroup and figure out our next move."

But as she watched Marcus gather his things and leave with another round of apologies, she couldn't shake the feeling that they'd just lost more than a lead. And judging by the look on Aric's face, he felt the same way.

CHAPTER NINE

TRADE SECRETS AND DEATH TRAPS

The call came in jagged shards. Compressed audio, low signal, someone speaking fast from somewhere they shouldn't have been.

"Moving it tonight…private transfer…warehouse off 9th, west loading. No paper trail. One buyer. High-tier piece."

Then static.

Ophira sat motionless at her desk, the blue glow of multiple monitors casting shadows across her face. She recognized the voice. Jimmy Lippmann was a fringe dealer she'd tagged three weeks ago during a routine sweep of black market chatter.

Not the kind that made waves, but sharp enough to know when something was worth passing up the chain. Jimmy specialized in moving pieces that weren't quite hot enough for the major players but too valuable for street-level dealers. If he was calling her secure line, it meant he'd already decided to disappear for a while.

She replayed the message twice, parsing every word for subtext. Jimmy's voice carried the kind of strain that came from watching over his shoulder, but there was also a touch of excitement – the kind that came from deals beyond his usual scope.

She tapped into her search filters, cross-referencing the warehouse identification codes with flagged shipping activity from the past seventy-two hours. The initial results showed standard industrial movement, but when she dug deeper into the metadata, patterns began to emerge. Several flagged aliases had surfaced in the shipping logs, each connected to different aspects of their investigation. One trail originated from Cairo, buried under three reroutes and tagged with a collector ID that had been marked inactive six months ago.

It wasn't proof, but it was a lead.

Feels like pressure, Sage said, his voice cutting through her concentration. *Like someone's tryin' to push us faster than we're ready to move.*

Or maybe it's time, sugar, Sunny offered gently. *Sometimes the right lead shows up when you need it most. But timing this tight... well, that does make me a mite nervous.*

Ophira expanded her query parameters, pulling in data from multiple intelligence feeds. Movement in collector chatter from the past week, including shipping manifests that had been modified after filing and locked listings under outdated pseudonyms. The warehouse district near 9th Street had seen a spike in activity, but most of it was buried under layers of legitimate commercial traffic.

One entry stood out. A shell purchase routed through Cairo, tagged with an encryption cipher that hadn't been used in over a year. She'd seen that particular signature before, attached to a shipment that had disappeared from Istanbul three weeks ago. The same timeframe as Marcus's initial contact about the missing relics.

She pulled up the warehouse's public records, cross-referencing ownership data with known shell corporations. The property had changed hands four times in the past two years, each transfer involving companies that existed only on paper. A classic laundering setup, designed to obscure real ownership while maintaining legal access.

The setup seemed orchestrated, but her investigative instincts told her it was real movement. After days of cold leads and dead ends, this had the weight of genuine activity behind it. The kind of activity that prompted people to take risks, which in turn created opportunities.

"Aric," she called.

"Did you say something?" Aric appeared in the doorway, arms crossed, still wearing the focused expression that meant he'd been working on his leads.

"I got a ping," she said, gesturing to her screens. "Warehouse near 9th. Private transport scheduled for tonight. High-grade object, no manifest, completely off-books shipment. Cairo-tagged purchase route buried under an old identification number."

He stepped in beside her, scanning the displays with practiced efficiency. "You think it's related to our case?"

"I think it's movement. Which is more than we've had in days." She pulled up a timeline showing their recent progress. "It's been a week since you heard about the Izmir connection, and everything's been completely silent since then. No chatter, no new intelligence, no shipping activity that matches our patterns."

"You think Marcus knows about this?"

She paused, considering the implications. "I doubt it. This came through my network, not his contacts. We'll call him on the way; he can meet us there if he's available."

Aric moved closer, eyes scanning her screen with the careful attention he brought to tactical planning. "Every lead, every mention we've gotten on this case came from overseas. Cairo, Istanbul, Izmir. Now we have a lead right here at home? This doesn't feel clean."

Ophira pulled up the shipping manifests side by side with the collector chatter logs, highlighting the connections she'd identified. "Look at the patterns," she said, tracing data flows across multiple screens. "The Cairo routing matches the cipher signature from the Istanbul contact Marcus mentioned. Same shell company structure we've been tracking, just with a local endpoint instead of another international transfer."

"But why surface here? Why now?" Aric leaned over her shoulder, studying the timestamps and geographic markers. "Everything's been carefully coordinated to stay overseas, maintain distance from any domestic jurisdiction. Suddenly, they're operating in our backyard?"

She traced the data flow with her finger, connecting points across a map overlay. "Because they need a final transfer point. You can't ship something this valuable internationally forever without eventually bringing it somewhere secure for handoff."

She switched to a detailed shipping route analysis. "Look – every trail we've followed has been building toward a single collection point. This warehouse fits the operational pattern."

"Or someone's finally gotten tired of playing games and decided to draw us out."

"Maybe." She pulled up additional intelligence, cross-referencing the warehouse location with known collector safe houses and auction points. "But it's a real lead either way. That's enough for tonight."

Zeke's voice cut through her thoughts, sharp with suspicion. *Someone's leadin' us around by the nose like prize bulls at a county fair. Question is, are we walkin' into the ring or the slaughterhouse?*

Good question, Sage agreed thoughtfully. *But look, if it is a setup, walkin' away means we lose our only active lead here. Sometimes you gotta take the risk.*

She was tired of empty circles and half-truths. Every lead that fizzled felt like another piece of herself she'd never get back, another step deeper into a world where nothing was what it seemed. Each dead end had worn at her patience, and the lack of progress only made it worse. *If someone's moving pieces, I need to know who. And why.*

He exhaled, jaw tightening as he processed the implications. "Then we go in controlled. Minimal team, no contact unless it turns solid."

She nodded, already pulling up the warehouse specifications and building a route overlay. "We'll sweep it first. Quiet entry, assess the situation before committing to anything."

The window would close fast – Jimmy's timeline suggested movement within hours, not days. Too fast to play it completely safe, but not so fast they'd walk into an obvious trap without preparation.

She locked in the location coordinates and reached for her jacket. Whatever was waiting in that warehouse, she was done letting opportunities slip through her fingers. It was time to call in her contractors and set up a plan.

She was already coordinating with her contractors as they prepared to leave. A quick call to Smith had him positioning surveillance teams in buildings overlooking the warehouse district. Jones would monitor digital traffic – any electronic chatter that might indicate a setup. Barber was coordinating vehicle deployment to nearby staging areas, ready to provide backup or extraction if needed.

"Contractors are in position," she told Aric as they headed for the exit. "Eyes on the area, backup protocols active."

The drive to the warehouse district took thirty minutes through empty streets. They maintained radio silence, using hand signals and predetermined routes. By the time they reached the staging area, the pre-dawn mist had settled over the industrial zone like a shroud.

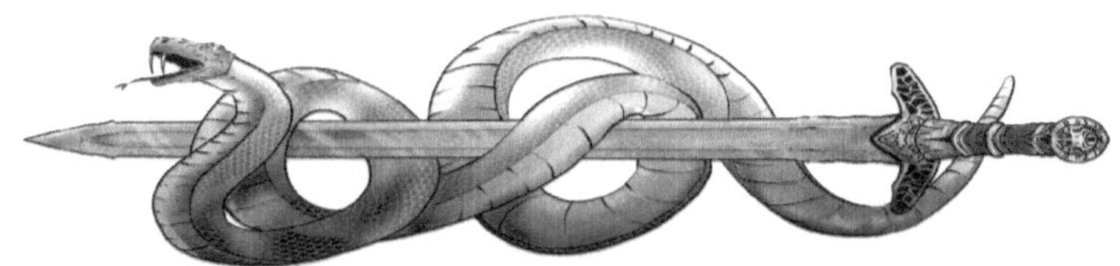

The warehouse loomed before them, its rusted corrugated walls and shattered upper windows belying the carefully organized interior within. What appeared abandoned from the street revealed itself as something far more deliberate once they slipped through the loading dock.

Two hours of surveillance from Aric's modified Ford Expedition had revealed the building's true nature. The SUV was a masterpiece of covert technology – outwardly resembling a standard luxury vehicle, but its interior had been converted into a comprehensive mobile operations center.

Multiple monitors displayed thermal imaging, signal intercepts, and communication feeds that would make government agencies envious. Aric had deployed two of his surveillance drones for aerial reconnaissance while monitoring electronic signatures from the Expedition's command console.

"Security sweep shows two guards," Aric reported, adjusting the thermal scanner mounted on the dashboard. "Both were stationed at the main entrance. No external cameras on the west side, but there's definitely electronic security on the loading dock."

Ophira studied the warehouse through military-grade binoculars. "Loading dock access?"

"Manageable. The electronic lock is standard commercial grade – nothing my gear can't handle." He packed his equipment into a compact tactical case, his movements precise and economical. "The interesting part is what the thermal shows inside. Climate-controlled sections, organized storage. This isn't some abandoned building being used for a quick handoff."

Marcus arrived ten minutes later, sliding into the back seat with practiced quiet. "Your warehouse lead matches intelligence I got from a freight broker in Istanbul," he said without preamble. "According to my contact, this place specializes in discreet transfers. Looks rough from the outside, but they keep immaculate records."

Ophira glanced at Aric, who gave a subtle nod. The information aligned with what they'd observed.

"Entry plan?" Marcus asked.

"West loading dock," Aric said, pulling on tactical gloves. "Ophira handles any electronic security, and I'll manage physical barriers. You watch our backs and signal if we get company."

They moved through the industrial district like shadows, using abandoned buildings and shipping containers for cover. The warehouse's deceptive exterior became more apparent as they approached – what looked like random rust patterns from a distance revealed themselves as carefully maintained camouflage. The broken windows were intact behind strategic grime, and the supposedly damaged loading dock operated on well-oiled hinges.

Aric worked on the electronic lock while Ophira kept watch. The mechanism clicked open with professional efficiency.

"Someone's spent money on this place," he murmured as they slipped inside.

The contrast hit them immediately. Where the exterior suggested decades of abandonment, the interior revealed sophisticated organization. Rows of climate-controlled storage units lined the outside walls, each secured with modern locks and environmental sensors. Professional lighting strips cast clean illumination across polished concrete floors, and the air carried the crisp scent of filtration systems rather than decay. The interior of the space was filled with a labyrinth of crates and packing materials.

Ophira stood at the threshold, the snakes whispering a familiar chorus of caution in her mind. The metallic tang of the air made her skin prickle. Something ancient pressed against her senses, awakening memories she'd spent years trying to bury.

Marcus's gaze tracked along the rows of crates. "Not your average storage facility," Marcus observed, his voice barely above a whisper.

They moved deeper into the space, past carefully labeled sections and inventory logs mounted on digital displays. Ophira's fingers brushed the hilt of the blade at her hip, her unease growing with every step closer to the center of the maze.

Well, ain't this cozier than a rattlesnake's den, Zeke muttered. *Betcha them crates are packin' skeletons and spiders.*

Sunny's voice was calm, her gentle drawl steadying. *Or it's just a warehouse, sugar. Let's not borrow trouble.*

Sage countered, *It's definitely a trap. Ten to one this whole setup's designed to lure someone specific. Namely, us.*

Ophira's focus narrowed as the weight in the air pressed closer. Something called to her, a magnetic pull she couldn't ignore. The sensation intensified with each step, drawing her toward the center of the room.

Her steps slowed as something drew her attention to the center of the room. That was when she saw it: the necklace, bathed in soft, almost reverent light.

"There," she said.

It was on a crimson velvet cushion inside a protective glass case. The necklace's chain caught the light, its craftsmanship appearing almost fluid, as though immortal hands had weaved the links themselves. The metal was bronze with an iridescent hue that shifted with the light. Hints of gold, blue, and violet flickered along its surface, as though it contained the colors of the heavens themselves.

¡Dios mío! What magnificence! Such beauty, such danger! Valentina sighed. *It sings with ze power of a thousand angels, non? Ma reine, you must have zis magnificent treasure!*

Flawless, Sage murmured, his tone filled with cautious appreciation. *The craftsmanship is impossibly advanced.*

Sunny's soft reassurance grounded Ophira. *Whatever it is, it's waitin'. Be careful, darlin'.*

A strange, prickling energy radiated from the artifact, and Ophira fought to keep her expression neutral. *Don't let it draw you in,* she told herself, stepping closer.

The pendant at its center was a circular disk, no larger than the palm of a hand, forged with divine precision. It bore intricate engravings. Symbols Ophira didn't immediately recognize but felt familiar, like whispers from an ancient past. Fine etchings of olive branches bordered the edges of the pendant, their delicate leaves catching the light. At the center of the disk was a single symbol, so faint it seemed to disappear if she looked directly at it: the head of an owl, barely discernible, its eyes narrowed in silent observation. The design stirred something in her, though she couldn't quite place why.

At the heart of the pendant, there was an almost imperceptible flicker, a sensation more than a sight, as if something within the metal beat with a hidden force, ancient and powerful. It wasn't a light, not in any visible sense, but a faint, rhythmic energy that Ophira could feel rather than see.

It seemed to respond to her presence, as though the pendant was aware of her, its silent power shifting in recognition. The sensation unsettled her, as if the necklace watched and waited.

Ophira paused, her breath catching as the necklace seemed to pull her closer. It wasn't its age or the delicate etchings on the metal; something palpable radiated from within, vibrating with whispers from somewhere beyond. The relic's pulse felt like a memory she'd never lived, stirring something deep within her. A longing she didn't understand.

The energy surged through her senses. It stirred half-formed memories, glimpses of temples bathed in golden light, shadows from her dreams. The sensation wrapped around her with a force that left her trembling. It felt alive, humming with something ancient and powerful, something that stirred unease deep within her. It made her skin tingle, and her instincts screamed at her to take a step back.

There's something about this necklace. It feels alive, connected to the gods.

The thought flashed unbidden, and she quickly pushed it aside.

Aric, who had been studying the case beside her, glanced over at Ophira, sensing her unease. "What are you thinking?" he asked quietly with trepidation.

Ophira's eyes were fixed on the necklace. She reached out cautiously, her hand hovering above the glass case, as though touching it would give her some answers. "It's strange," she murmured, "it feels charged, somehow. There's energy coming from it."

Aric stepped closer, leaning in to examine the symbols on the pendant more closely. "These markings… Do they look familiar?" he asked, his fingers brushing against the cool surface of the glass. Ophira could hear the subtle undercurrent of caution.

She shook her head slightly. "Not directly," she said, but her mind raced to connect the dots. The symbols were unfamiliar, yet they stirred something deep within her. She couldn't place it, but there was an undeniable connection between the necklace and the divine forces she had encountered before.

Marcus, who had been standing a few paces behind them, stepped forward. His gaze was fixed on the necklace. "It's certainly unique," he remarked.

Aric straightened up, his sharp eyes flicking between the necklace and Marcus. "There's a lot we don't know about this piece," he said. "Its origin, its purpose... It's all a mystery."

Ophira shot Aric a glance, grateful for his steady presence. He was always the practical one, grounded in facts and logic, which made him the perfect counterbalance to her sometimes impulsive instincts. In moments like this, his support was invaluable.

Reaching out, she hesitated before her fingers brushed the edge of the display case. Her heart pounded, an instinctual warning flashing in her mind. But she pushed it aside, letting her curiosity win out. This was the reason they were here, after all. Carefully, she opened the case and reached for the necklace.

As her fingertips grazed the cool metal, a surge of energy shot up her arm, sharp and electric. Ophira's breath caught in her throat, her vision blurring as the room tilted around her.

For a heartbeat, it felt like she was suspended in time, the ground beneath her dissolving. An image flooded her mind. Bright. Golden. Powerful. Like something plucked from another world.

Her fingers trembled, the sensation so visceral that it left her gasping as she instinctively pulled back. She saw flashes of something ancient: a temple bathed in golden light, the echo of whispered prayers, and the faint outline of figures she couldn't quite place. The sensation was so overwhelming, so intense, that she pulled back instinctively, her hand trembling.

Was that a vision? Or something else? Echoes of the image lingered in her mind. The power radiating from the necklace was undeniable, alive in a way that felt ancient and overwhelming. She couldn't shake the feeling that it was trying to communicate something vital yet out of reach.

"Ophira?" Aric's hand was suddenly on her shoulder, grounding her. "What happened?"

She blinked, her vision slowly clearing, though the echoes of the images lingered like an aftertaste. "It's powerful," she gasped. "I saw images, memories maybe. But they weren't mine."

Marcus stepped closer, his brow furrowing as he studied her. "It reacted to you. That's unusual. Artifacts like this sometimes carry residual energy, but it's rare to see them respond like that."

"Exactly," Aric said as he exchanged a glance with Marcus. "It's unexpected, but maybe your experience with artifacts explains it.

Marcus glanced at the necklace. "It's not unheard of for relics like this to carry traces of energy," he said. "Especially if they were once important or heavily used."

Ophira's eyes widened. *What exactly does he mean by that?* she wondered, trying to gauge how much Marcus truly understood. His insightful presence might be what they needed tonight.

As she pondered this, Aric's voice broke through her thoughts. "The craftsmanship is impressive, but there's something else going on here." He leaned in closer, his eyes narrowing as he inspected the symbols etched into the pendant. "I can't quite place it, but these markings are significant. There's meaning behind them."

Ophira nodded, her fingers itching to take the necklace back out of its case, to hold it in her hands again and see if it would reveal anything more. But she resisted the urge. The energy it emanated was intense, unpredictable. She couldn't risk it.

"There's something off about this," she said quietly, her eyes still locked on the necklace. "I can feel it."

Aric moved closer, his hand gently brushing her arm. "You don't have to push yourself," he said softly, though his gaze remained fixed on Marcus, sharp and assessing. "These things have a way of revealing themselves in time."

When Ophira didn't immediately respond, his focus shifted to the necklace, his brows furrowing as he leaned closer to examine the symbols etched into the pendant. He lowered his voice so only she could hear. "We still don't have Marcus's full measure."

She glanced at him, wary.

Aric's calm, steady voice had its usual effect, grounding her. She nodded again, appreciating his support even as the necklace's mystery continued to gnaw at her.

Why do I feel this connection to it? Ophira wondered, the vision from earlier still lingering in the back of her mind. The flashes of ancient times, of temples and whispered prayers, were too vivid to dismiss, but too fleeting to make sense of.

Marcus stood quietly, eyes fixed on the necklace. His expression was focused, contemplative, as if he were trying to make sense of what he was seeing. Ophira glanced at him, watching for any sign of reaction. She hoped she wasn't alone in her uncertainty.

After a few moments of tense silence, Aric stepped back, folding his arms across his chest. "We'll need to dig deeper into this," he said. "I'll cross-reference the symbols with some of the archives and see if we can find anything that matches."

Ophira nodded, preoccupied with the necklace's unsettling energy. She couldn't escape the conviction that this artifact was far more than it appeared on the surface.

As they stood there, the three of them were surrounded by ancient relics and the quiet hum of the warehouse's security system, and the weight of the moment pressed down on Ophira. The necklace was important, but its significance, its power, were unknowable, like a distant memory she couldn't quite recall.

What are we dealing with here? she thought, her instincts prickling at the edges of her mind. *This is no ordinary artifact.*

But for now, all they could do was gather more information, dig deeper into the mystery, and hope that the answers would reveal themselves before it was too late.

"I'll reach out to Dr. Ghestad at the museum and see whether she's logged anything on these symbols," Marcus said, giving them a brief nod. "I'll report back as soon as I have something solid. I need to move back towards the entrance. I'm not getting a cell signal here."

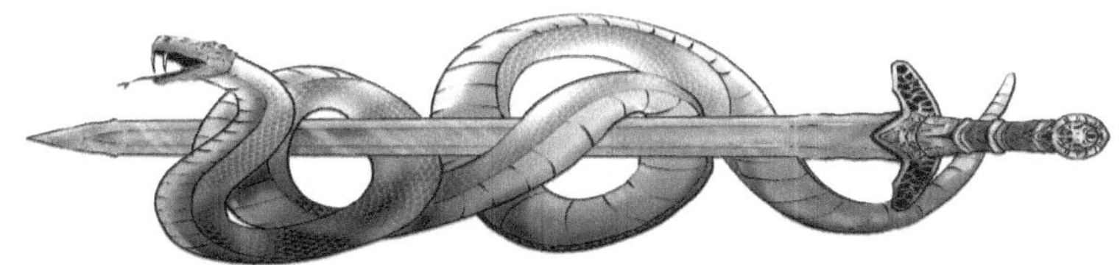

Ophira watched him disappear down the row of crates, his footsteps echoing until they faded entirely. Only the warehouse's ambient hum filled the space.

Then, as if Marcus had been holding back the tide, the atmosphere shifted between her and Aric, becoming heavier, more charged. The necklace's case seemed to pulse with softer light in the corner of her vision.

Aric shifted beside her, his gaze hardening as he glanced between the relic and her. Now, with the two of them alone again, the tension between them was undeniable.

Aric's suspicion had been simmering beneath the surface for days, but tonight it appeared ready to boil over. Ophira knew the coming conversation was inevitable, but a part of her still wanted to delay it.

Aric crossed his arms, exhaling sharply. "You don't find it strange how much he knows?"

Ophira frowned, feeling a familiar tug of defensiveness rise in her chest. "Marcus has been nothing but helpful," she said. "He's had access to the case notes for longer than we have, and his contacts run deep."

"That's not what I'm talking about," Aric said. "It's not his access. It's everything. His demeanor, the way he handles things like this." He nodded toward the necklace, his eyes darkening. "You felt it, didn't you? That power or whatever it is. But Marcus acts like it's nothing. That's what bothers me."

Ophira stared at the necklace for a moment, letting his words sink in. The relic, for all its beauty, gave off unsettling energy. She had felt it from the moment they laid eyes on it, and Marcus had remained unfazed.

But she'd seen how he approached problems in his methodical and analytical way. Perhaps he was so fascinated by the puzzle that he failed to notice the danger radiating from it.

"I trust Marcus, Aric," she said, but her confidence waned immediately. *Do I really?* She swallowed hard. "He's made connections we couldn't have made without him. We don't have time for doubts right now, not when we're this close. Besides, he brought us the case. Why would he do that if he didn't need the help?"

Ophira couldn't ignore the flicker of uncertainty in the back of her mind. *Am I missing something?* The doubt twisted in her chest, but she couldn't afford to acknowledge it.

"Maybe." Aric's voice was grim, his brow furrowing deeper. "But something about this feels off. Doesn't it bother you how much he knows? How unaffected he is by all of it? I've been doing this as long as you have, Ophira, and this guy is different. Something's not adding up."

Ophira opened her mouth to respond but found herself hesitating. Aric wasn't wrong. She'd noticed Marcus's unnatural composure, the way he'd studied the necklace with pure intellectual curiosity, like he was working out a historical riddle rather than standing before something that made her skin crawl. She could feel unease creeping in, wondering what it was about Marcus that made Aric view him with so much suspicion.

"I get that you're concerned, Aric. I do. But we need to keep moving forward, and he's given us no concrete reason not to trust him. I can handle this."

Aric sighed, his expression tightening. He ran a hand through his hair, clearly frustrated. "He's given us plenty of reason to be suspicious. You're emotionally involved with him. And I think it's clouding your judgment."

"That's not fair," Ophira shot back, irritation flaring. She was well aware of how complicated things had become between her and Marcus. The way he looked at her, the careful distance he maintained. It all suggested he saw something in her she wasn't ready to reveal. But that didn't mean she was compromising their work. *Did it?*

"It's not about being fair," Aric pressed, urgent. "It's about being smart. Look, I've got a bad feeling about this guy. And I've trusted my instincts for a long time."

Ophira bit her lip, torn between her trust in Marcus and her loyalty to Aric. She had always valued Aric's instincts, but her connection with Marcus had grown deeper.

Ophira said, "I know you're worried, but we've crossed the point of no return here. We can't turn back without risking everything. I need to see this through, for all of us."

Aric's jaw clenched, but he didn't press the issue further. His frustration was evident, but he knew when to let her make her own choices. Still, as he turned back toward the necklace, his gaze remained wary.

"I hope you're right about him," Aric muttered, voice low as he turned away.

Ophira found herself gravitating back to the glass case, her eyes locked onto the necklace. The pull was stronger now, without Marcus's presence to distract her. It wasn't the design or the shimmer beneath the lights. Something deeper called to her, something that had been waiting. It drew her in, even as it made her skin prickle with unease.

It feels alive, she thought, her fingers brushing the cool glass. *What's powering it?*

The symbols etched into the pendant seemed to shift under her gaze, each line holding meaning beyond her understanding. Part of her wondered if it connected to the power she'd kept suppressed for so long.

Whatever the case, Ophira couldn't tear her gaze away. Its presence vibrated at the edge of her awareness.

"Ophira."

Aric's voice pulled her back to the present, snapping her out of her reverie. She blinked, turning to face him.

"Are you alright?"

"Yeah, I'm fine," she replied, though her voice wavered slightly. "Just thinking."

Aric's eyes narrowed. "Thinking about Marcus?"

"No," Ophira said, her voice sharper than intended. She turned back to the necklace, her fingers still resting on the glass. "I'm thinking about the relic."

Aric's gaze followed hers, and they stood in silence for a moment, both contemplating the artifact before them.

"You're too close to this," Aric said quietly. "To him."

Despite everything Aric had said, she couldn't bring herself to doubt him entirely. He'd brought them the case, shown them the photographs, and connected the myths to the relics. When her research led them here, his Istanbul contact had confirmed what she'd found.

I have no reason not to trust him, she thought, even as doubt gnawed at her as fiercely as she warred against the irritation she felt at having this conversation again. *I've come this far. I'm not pulling back now.*

Her fingers slid off the glass, and she turned to face Aric. "We need to keep moving forward. We're close to something big. I can feel it."

Aric didn't respond, but the tension in his shoulders told her that he wasn't convinced. He gave her a brief nod. The wariness in his eyes was hard to miss.

Behind Aric, the necklace began to glow.

Not the soft illumination from the warehouse lights, but something else entirely. Ancient power pulsed through the pendant, and the owl symbol at its center opened ethereal eyes that fixed directly on Ophira.

You cannot hide from me, a voice pierced her mind, softly feminine yet cold and without mercy. ***I have been waiting for you.***

Ophira's breath caught, her heart hammering against her ribs. But before she could process what was happening, the supernatural light faded, leaving only the warehouse's ordinary illumination.

The voice was gone. But its promise lingered, wrapping around her like a chain she couldn't see.

CHAPTER TEN

UNLUCKY CHARMS: THEY'RE MAGICALLY UNSTABLE

Heavy silence stretched between them. As Ophira opened her mouth to speak, the door creaked open, and Marcus reappeared. His usual calm demeanor was in place, his steps confident, his gaze unwavering. But as he crossed the threshold, something about him seemed different. Something Ophira couldn't quite put her finger on.

"I spoke to Dr. Ghestad," he said, phone in hand. "She didn't have much in the way of actual documentation that references these symbols, but she thinks they look similar to a few items that she's seen before."

He continued walking towards them, his eyes on the necklace as he finished his updated. "Nothing remarkable. A few Greek vases, coins, that sort of thing. She'll continue digging and suggested we meet up tomorrow after the museum closes to review what she comes up with."

Ophira's mind buzzed with the implications. If the necklace was powerful, what did it have in common with such mundane items? It felt out of place, especially since she still reeled from the voice that had thundered through her consciousness moments before. The necklace sat innocuously in its case now, showing no signs of the supernatural display that had just occurred.

She glanced at Aric, who showed no indication he'd witnessed anything unusual. Good. The last thing she needed was questions about why the artifact had spoken directly to her.

That thing's got some serious attitude, Zeke muttered. *Talking like it owns the place.*

Ancient power recognizes ancient power, Valentina purred. *It knows what you are, querida.*

Which is precisely why we're keeping our mouths shut, Sage added grimly. *No need to advertise our connection to whatever that was.*

Marcus stepped beside her, his presence as steady as ever, though the weight of her conversation with Aric still lingered. "Any progress?" he asked as he glanced at the necklace in the glass case.

"We're getting there," she said, offering a small smile. Ophira absent-mindedly brushed her fingers against the edge of the display case again, her mind still racing from the strange voice she'd heard a few minutes ago. But this time, the pendant pulsed in answer. It was faint but discernible, like a heartbeat returning after stillness.

Did that thing just blink? Zeke muttered.

No, Sage said, low. *It remembered her.*

The room fell silent, a new tension heavy in the air, pressing down like an unseen weight. Ophira cast one last glance at the necklace, the faint shimmer now almost like an eye watching her, aware. She sensed something ancient lurking beyond the light, waiting.

She caught the way Aric's posture stiffened, his stance subtly angled as if positioning himself between her and Marcus. She could feel the weight of their silence, each of them holding back something unsaid, the tension coiling like a spring. For the first time, Ophira felt the urge to step back, to see if distance would reveal what she couldn't identify.

Before she could speak, the temperature in the room plummeted. A sudden, inexplicable chill swept over her, wrapping around her shoulders like cold fingers. Her breath caught, and for a brief moment, Ophira thought she saw an image, a flicker of light, or maybe a shadow at the edge of her vision.

It was brief, gone as soon as it appeared, but the sensation it left behind was undeniable. Something ancient and powerful had stirred, as if watching her from the dark corners of the room.

When she blinked, it vanished, leaving her questioning her senses.

"Are you seeing this?" Marcus's voice cut through the eerie silence. She blinked. The chill that had crept over her had thickened, turning the air heavy. The ground beneath their feet trembled, and her pulse quickened as the walls groaned, shifting like the stirrings of some ancient creature. A low creak echoed, a sound that sent cold sweat prickling across her skin. Whatever it was she'd sensed moments before was here, and it was waking.

Before she could fully process what was happening, thick vines erupted from the walls, snaking toward them with terrifying speed. Stone and moss-covered tendrils wrapped around her legs, tugging, pulling. It was as if the very air had turned against them.

Ophira gritted her teeth as she wrestled with the constricting vines. *Look for an answer. There has to be a way out.*

She gasped, pulling at the vines around her ankles, but they were too strong. The more she struggled, the closer they wound around her, climbing higher. Marcus and Aric weren't faring any better; both were trapped, tendrils slithering up their bodies, binding them in place.

Stop pullin', darlin', Sunny advised gently. *You're only makin' it worse.*

Sage's tone was sharp. *The vines are reacting to resistance. You need a different approach.*

Or you could just burn zem, Valentina suggested, her voice dripping with menace. *Such fire would be poetic, no?*

Think. There has to be something, Ophira told them as she scanned the room for options.

This isn't a relic, her mind raced. *This is something more dangerous.*

The vines twisted again, and pain shot up her legs. She yanked hard, desperate. It didn't work. The tendrils tautened, climbing higher. *Think faster. Move. Do something. Anything.*

"Marcus!" she cried, her voice strangled as she strained against the vines. "We need to—"

"I know." His voice was harsh, like he was concentrating fiercely on coming up with a plan to save them.

The vines continued their merciless ascent, now wrapping around her waist, their stone-like texture grating against her skin. Out of the corner of her eye, she saw Marcus struggling, his brow furrowed in concentration. The tendrils around him pressed in hard, constricting his torso. She flinched as she saw how compact they had gotten.

Then, as quickly as the vines had strengthened, they seemed to ease, their hold on him loosening by a fraction. Marcus exhaled sharply, his face still calm.

Oh, good, Ophira thought, trying to steady herself. *Marcus seems to be making headway.*

She tore her gaze from him, forcing herself to concentrate on their situation. *Think, Ophira, think.* She ran through every possible scenario in her mind. How to fight the vines. How to escape without revealing too much. Her mind was a chaotic mess of options, none of them good.

What about the relic? Her eyes darted to the necklace, still resting on its display pedestal. *Was it the source of this trap? Destroying it might help...or make things worse.* There was no way to know for sure.

Across from her, Aric struggled too, his face twisted in discomfort. His skin... Was it paler than usual? She blinked, momentarily unsure. *No, that's not right.* His skin flickered, shifting in color from tan to a strange, grayish hue for the briefest moment.

Oh my God. Her heart leapt into her throat. *He's suffocating. Look at him. He's not getting enough air.*

"Aric!" she shouted, panic rising. He coughed but forced a weak smile in her direction, his tone strained. "I'm fine. Really." He managed a shaky breath, trying to downplay the severity of the situation. "It's a little...constricting."

But Ophira wasn't convinced. His skin had flickered again. Was he suffocating? He looked like he was on the edge, struggling to breathe.

She bit her lip as panic clawed at her mind. *I can't let them die.*

Her alarm spiraled. *Act or wait? Expose herself or stay hidden?* She clenched her fists. The power under her skin simmered, coiling like a snake. She needed to act, but what would it cost her?

There has to be another way.

She scanned the room, desperate for any solution. Her mind spun through half-formed plans. Burn the vines. Destroy the relic. Maybe even cut herself free with something sharp nearby. But none of them would work. The vines grew too thick, moved too fast, and the relic posed too much danger to tamper with blindly.

Time was slipping away, and she was running out of options.

"Marcus," she called out, her voice wavering. "Are you—"

"I'm good," he replied, though his expression gave nothing away. The vines hadn't contracted again, and it almost looked as though they were loosening their grip on him.

Her mind snagged on the detail. Marcus wasn't struggling. He wasn't even tense. The vines should have crushed him by now. *Why hadn't they? Is that why he's not struggling? Will they relax if I do? Dammit, there's no time to think.* The vines around her squeezed, biting into her skin. Not while Aric was turning a shade too close to death for comfort.

Focus.

Her gaze darted to the necklace, the relic that had triggered this trap in the first place. Maybe it wasn't the vines she needed to fight. Perhaps the necklace itself was the key. Her mind worked at rapid speed, trying to fit the pieces together. *Could I destroy it? Would that stop this? Or is that what it wants me to do?*

Do it, Ophira, a new voice echoed in her mind, ancient and commanding. Deep and masculine, it rolled through her head like thunder, too powerful to be anything except divine. ***Stop thinking and act.***

Her grip increased on the vines while her heart raced. It wasn't doubt. It was pressure. Urgency. *Could she fight it? Could she find another way?* She ran through the scenarios again in her head. Attack the relic. Try to pull herself and the others free. Maybe there was something else in the room she could use to cut through the vines.

Each possibility felt weaker than the last. The pressure was building. Time was running out.

Do it. Stop thinking. Act now, Ophira!

Her heart pounded. The vines squeezed closer, digging into her skin. They dragged her down. Cold, unrelenting. She could feel their intent: *bury her alive*. Each breath became a struggle, the constriction creeping up her torso. *I have to act soon*, she thought, panic clawing at her mind. *If I don't, we're all dead.*

The walls groaned, stone grinding against stone as they closed in. The air seemed to shift, growing heavier. Ophira yanked again, her muscles burning. The vines tensed. Her legs buckled. She glanced at Marcus, who stood still, the vines pressing close. His face remained calm, as if he were waiting for something rather than fighting for his life. Something flickered in his eyes, but was gone again before she could name it. *What's going on over there?*

She shook her head, trying to clear her mind. There wasn't time to dwell on Marcus's behavior. She could barely move now, her legs nearly pinned together by the stone-like grip of the vines. Her fingers scrambled at her sides, searching for anything to cut them loose, but there was nothing. Not even a sharp edge to work with. She felt her pulse throb in her ears, her body trembling from the effort, but the vines were stronger. The more she fought, the more they seemed to intensify in retaliation.

Beside her, Aric grunted as he struggled to free himself, his face contorted in discomfort, but even in this, he managed a half-hearted smile. "These things really don't know when to quit, huh?"

Ophira tried to return the grin, but the pressure was too much. Her heart pounded, the weight of the vines constricting her chest. She couldn't breathe, couldn't think. Every second that passed brought them closer to death. *Do something,* her mind screamed. *Now.*

But what could she do without revealing herself? The power beneath her skin begged to be unleashed, yet using it meant destroying everything she'd built to stay hidden. *If I show them…*

She tried to pull free again, the vines digging deeper. A sharp pain shot up her leg. Her vision blurred for a moment, but she blinked it away. The others were depending on her, and the trap was increasing with each second. *We're out of time.* She gritted her teeth, feeling the familiar heat of her power simmer beneath the surface. She couldn't hold it back. The power clawed at her, begging to be used.

Just a little. Just enough.

Ophira closed her eyes, forcing a steady breath as panic clawed at her. She let the smallest pulse of power slip free, her gaze flicking briefly to the vines around her legs. Heat surged from her core, sharp and fierce, until the fibrous grip hardened to stone under her intense stare. She opened her eyes to see the transformation, her heart hammering as she prayed neither Marcus nor Aric had noticed exactly what happened.

Turning them to stone, Sage murmured. *Strips their flexibility. Smart. Effective.*

Effective? It is perfection, Valentina purred. *Such grace, mi amor. Such control.*

You did good, Fee, Sunny said gently. *But we ain't done. Help the others.*

Ophira exhaled, her focus shifting to Marcus and Aric. *This isn't over yet.*

Opening her eyes, she watched as the vines around her legs hardened into solid stone, their once-living form freezing in place. The tension in her chest loosened, but only for a heart-beat. *There, I'm free,* she thought, barely allowing herself the luxury of relief.

But the vines around Marcus and Aric were still narrowing, growing more relentless. She could feel the trap closing in, the air thick with ancient magic. She had to act again, this time more decisively, or none of them were getting out of here alive.

Do it, she urged herself. *A little more.*

She summoned the power again. Another pulse rippled out. The vines trembled, their stone-like forms quivering. Then they cracked. They hardened, just as before, but this time it wasn't only the ones wrapped around her. Marcus's tendrils stiffened too, turning from writhing plant life into solid stone.

Her heart pounded as the transformation took hold. The vines stiffened, the once-living tendrils growing brittle, cracking under their own weight. Stone crumbled, dust spilling to the floor, leaving Marcus and Aric standing amidst the debris.

Ophira's attention narrowed on Marcus, whose unsettling calmness sent unease prickling through her chest. *How are you not freaking out?* she wondered, suspicious.

She exhaled, her chest heaving with the effort. *I did it.* She'd managed to free them without giving too much away. *I hope.* When she glanced at Marcus, his gaze stayed on her a heartbeat longer than comfort allowed. No alarm showed on his face, only a level of attention that carried its own weight. A quick look at Aric showed him busy brushing off debris, seemingly absorbed with his recovery. A chill struck her. *Had either of them seen what she did?*

She forced her breathing to slow, masking the spike of panic while reminding herself that a calm look did not always mean comprehension. She held his look for half a heartbeat, then glanced aside as if busy assessing the damage.

He dusted off his jacket, glancing around the room as though to check that it was truly over. "Looks like you hit the trigger," he said with surprising calmness. "Good timing."

Ophira offered a stiff nod, the question still twisting in her gut: *What exactly had they seen?* Ophira blinked, her pulse still pounding in her ears. "Yeah, must have gotten lucky."

She forced a smile, but unease clung to her, cold and heavy. How could he be so calm? No one had that kind of composure after nearly being crushed. And yet Marcus stood there, like it had all been a mild inconvenience, his face a mask of composure. At least Aric was reacting normally, shaken but relieved to be alive.

Why aren't either of them freaking out? The question gnawed at her, but she buried it deep. This wasn't the time to let her suspicions run wild. They had gotten out, and that was all that mattered right now.

"Lucky?" Aric's voice pulled her back to the moment, light and humorous despite everything. He flashed a crooked grin, brushing the dust from his sleeves. "You've got ridiculously excellent timing, Fee. You've got better odds than most casinos."

Ophira let out a nervous laugh, playing along. "Yeah, remind me to buy a lottery ticket later." She shifted her weight, trying to seem casual, but the tension in her chest wouldn't entirely leave.

Aric clapped a hand on her shoulder. "Next time, how about we skip the whole 'being nearly crushed by vines' part? I've got a thing about breathing, you know?"

She chuckled again, though her mind remained elsewhere. Marcus was quiet. She risked a glance in his direction, but he was already turning away, examining the remnants of the trap as if he hadn't just been moments away from being crushed.

Does he know what I did? Her mind spun. She couldn't question him now. Not while everything hung by a thread.

"We should move," Marcus said suddenly, his voice steady. "No telling if there's another layer to this trap. Let's not test our luck further."

Ophira nodded, but her gaze drifted back to the necklace still sparkling behind its shattered glass case. "We need to secure the relic."

"Fee..." Aric's voice carried a warning. "What if touching it sets off another trap? We barely survived the first one."

Sunshine makes a damn good point, boss, Zeke muttered. *That thing nearly killed us all.*

But zis is what we came for, no? Valentina protested. *Such beautiful danger should not be left for lesser hands.*

Marcus moved closer to the display. "The trap was triggered by proximity, not contact. Now that it's been discharged, it might be safe." He gestured toward the stone debris and took another step toward the necklace.

Ophira studied the necklace, her instincts warring. Every logical part of her screamed that touching it was dangerous. But this was precisely what they'd come for, and she was able to withstand damage that the others couldn't. "I'll do it. Stand back. If something happens, you two get out."

"Like hell," Aric muttered. "I'll do it. You stay back."

"No way," Marcus said, stepping forward. "This is my case, my responsibility—"

"Both of you stop," Ophira cut them off. "Look at me, then look at yourselves. I'm half your size and a third your weight. If this thing is triggered by proximity or pressure, I'm the least likely to set it off again." She gestured at the stone debris around the case. "We don't know if the trap reset itself or if there are secondary triggers."

Aric's jaw tightened, but he stayed back, muscles coiled and ready to move. Marcus looked as if he wanted to argue further, but stepped away from the case, moving toward Aric.

"If anything happens—" Marcus started.

"You two get out," she finished firmly. "That's an order."

She reached through the broken glass, her fingers hovering just above the ancient metal. *Please don't kill us all,* she prayed, then grasped the necklace quickly.

Nothing happened.

The silence stretched for several long heartbeats before Aric let out a shaky laugh. "That was anticlimactic."

Ophira wrapped the necklace carefully in her jacket, the weight of it heavier than she'd expected. "I'll store this in the vault until we can figure out how to examine it properly. The last thing we need is this thing hurting someone else while we're trying to understand what we're dealing with."

They walked in silence, the warehouse settling around them with creaks and distant echoes. But inside Ophira's mind, the tension was far from quiet. She replayed everything, scrutinizing every detail, every movement, every word, watching them both as they moved toward the exit.

Did they not see what happened? The question gnawed at her.

Marcus walked ahead, examining debris with the same detached interest he might show ancient pottery, as if magical death traps were just another minor inconvenience. No tremor in his hands. No backward glances at where they'd nearly died. She couldn't tell if he was processing what happened, compartmentalizing it, or deliberately masking his reactions.

Aric, meanwhile, kept shaking dust from his jacket and muttering about needing a drink.

Aric didn't notice anything, she realized with relief. But Marcus was giving her nothing to read. Was he in shock, or that unflappable? Or was he carefully avoiding her eyes because he'd seen exactly what she'd done?

Keep it together, she scolded herself. *Act normal. Maybe you got lucky.*

She adjusted her grip on the jacket-wrapped necklace, the weight of it steady and silent in her hand. Whatever it was, it didn't belong out in the open. Not for one more minute.

"I'm taking this to the vault," she said, her voice low. "Let's all get some rest. We can debrief later."

Neither man argued. No one had the energy.

They followed her out into the soft light of early morning, the broken trap inside the warehouse creaking behind them like it was exhaling too.

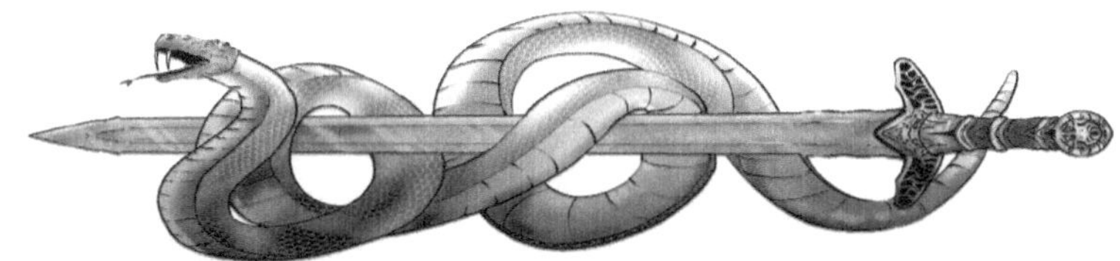

Hours later, Ophira moved through her apartment on auto-pilot. She set her bag down with more force than necessary, the thud echoing in the quiet space. Her hands shook slightly as she kicked off her boots, leaving them where they fell. The thought of eating felt absurd. Her entire body felt drained, every muscle aching from the energy she'd expended fighting the vines and the emotional toll of keeping so many secrets.

Boss, that was like playing hide-and-seek with a tornado, Zeke muttered, his usual nervous energy cranked up to eleven. *Except the tornado had an attitude problem and a personal vendetta.*

The necklace knew you, Sage said grimly. *The way it pulsed when you touched the case again. That wasn't a coincidence.*

Ophira sank into her couch, her head falling into her hands. The memory of that ancient voice still reverberated through her consciousness: **You cannot hide from me. I have been waiting.** What did it want from her? Why her specifically? And then during the trap, that other voice, different but equally commanding: **Do it, Ophira. Stop thinking and act.** Two separate voices, both speaking directly to her mind. What did that mean?

Ah, but of course they know you, chérie, Valentina purred. *You are magnifique, irresistible.*

Two different voices, though, sugar, Sunny added, her drawl warm but concerned. *That's what's got me puzzled. One from that trinket, another durin' the fight. What's that about?*

The quiet hum of her apartment's air conditioning felt deafening in contrast to the day's chaos. Every shadow seemed to hold the memory of those supernatural moments. The temperature dropping. The walls groaning. The vines with their stone-like grip, intent on burying them alive.

And Marcus. The memory of his composed face during the chaos kept replaying in her mind. She couldn't shake how calm he'd seemed when everything went supernatural. Most people would have been panicking.

I'm telling you, boss, that guy's smoother than a buttered penguin on ice, Zeke muttered. *Who stays that chill when death vines are doing their best impression of a python convention?*

His composure was... noteworthy, Sage said carefully. *Most people would have shown more distress.*

She couldn't quite shake Aric's earlier warnings, and her exhausted mind kept circling back to questions she couldn't answer.

Or unless he's just really, really good at keepin' his cool, Sunny suggested. *Some folks got nerves of steel, sugar. Seen it before.*

Oui, perhaps he is simply unflappable? Valentina added. *Some men, zey handle crisis very well.*

Ophira's phone buzzed on the coffee table, jolting her back to the present. She reached for it with trembling fingers, her heart rate spiking when she saw Marcus's name on the screen.

> **Marcus**
> I know it's late, but I wanted to check in. Are you okay?

She stared at the message for a long moment, her thumb hovering over the keyboard. How was she supposed to answer that? No, she wasn't okay. She'd just been threatened by an ancient artifact, nearly killed by a supernatural trap, and forced to use her powers in front of the two people she was trying hardest to hide them from.

Keep your cards close to your chest, boss, Zeke warned. *Something feels off, even if I can't put my finger on what.*

Wise advice, darlin', Sunny agreed. *When in doubt, say less.*

Her pulse quickened, uncertainty squeezing her chest like a vise. Maybe it was genuine concern. Maybe he was just being kind, checking on her after what they'd all been through.

> **Ophira**
> I'm fine.

The reply felt curt, but she wasn't in the mood for elaborate explanations. She couldn't afford to let her guard down, not when so much was at stake. She started to put the phone down when another buzz lit up the screen.

> **Marcus**
> You sure? That was pretty intense back there.
> I can swing by if you want company.

Nope, nuh uh, not happenin', Zeke said quickly. *Last thing we need is him poking around your personal space. Bad enough he's got you all twisted up emotionally.*

Sometimes solitude is the better choice, chérie, Valentina added. *Especially when one's thoughts are so... how you say... jumbled.*

Ophira's stomach twisted. She was too drained tonight for company, too emotionally raw. The comfort Marcus usually brought felt overwhelming right now when she needed space to process everything that had happened.

> **Ophira**
> It's been a long day. I need some rest. I'll
> see you tomorrow for the meeting with
> Dr. Ghestad.

She hit send before she could second-guess herself, then immediately wondered if she was being too distant. But she was too tired to analyze every word.

Something's got his attention, Sage pointed out. *The question remains whether that's good or bad for us.*

There was a longer pause this time before Marcus's reply appeared, and Ophira found herself holding her breath.

> **Marcus**
> Of course. Let me know if you need anything.

She set the phone down and sighed, shaking off the buzz of overstimulation. He was being considerate, but in her depleted state, every message felt weighted with hidden meaning. Too much had happened today. She felt stretched too thin, pulled in too many directions.

You handled yourself real well today, hun, Sunny said gently. *Saved everyone without making a fuss about it.*

Magnifique technique with ze stone transformation, Valentina added with satisfaction. *So elegant, so artistic, so...vengeful.*

Still gives me the shivers though, Zeke said with a nervous laugh. *Watching those vines turn to rock like that. Remind me never to get on your bad side, boss.*

Ophira appreciated the reassurance, even as exhaustion weighed on her. Tonight had been intense, and she needed time to process it all.

The weight of it all pressed down on her shoulders like a physical burden. The necklace's threatening voice. The trap that had nearly killed them. The questions she couldn't answer and the secrets she had to keep.

She thought about Aric, grateful for his steady presence through all of this. At least she had one person whose support she could count on, even if she couldn't tell him everything about herself.

Rest, sugar, Sunny urged softly. *Tomorrow's gonna bring its own troubles. No point borrowing more tonight.*

Drained beyond measure, Ophira forced herself to bed, hoping exhaustion would quiet the questions circling her mind like vultures. She stretched out, her body aching as the tension of the day finally began to catch up with her. Her muscles protested every movement, reminders of the power she'd channeled and the physical strain of the trap.

Her mind buzzed with fragments of the evening. The fight with the vines, their relentless grip. Marcus's calm acceptance of the supernatural chaos. Aric's shaky relief afterward. The necklace's pulse of recognition when she'd touched the case. That ancient, commanding voice roaring that it had been waiting for her.

What did it want from me? she wondered as sleep began to pull her under. *And why were there two different voices? Why did it sound like they both knew me?*

But exhaustion finally won out, pulling her into sleep that would bring unexpected peace.

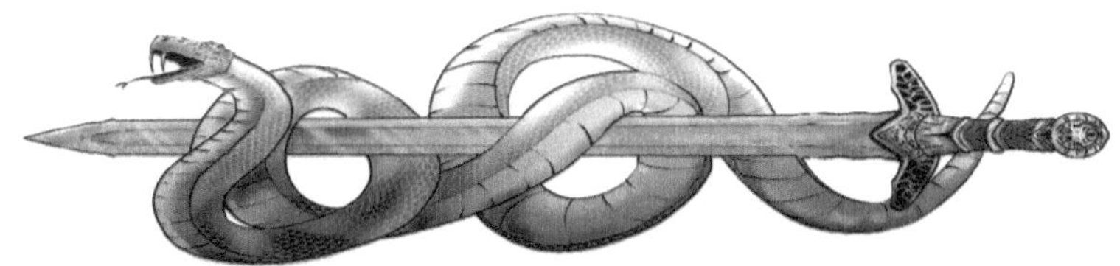

Ophira found herself in the midst of a lush, vibrant forest, the air redolent with moss and blooming flowers. The sunlight streamed through the canopy, dappling the ground in golden patches.

Everything seemed surreal yet soothing, like stepping into a forgotten memory. The chaos of the day felt distant here, muffled by the gentle sounds of rustling leaves and distant birdsong.

She wasn't alone. A figure stood in the distance, tall and statuesque, his silhouette exuding both strength and grace. As she approached, the details of his appearance sharpened, and Ophira felt a strange mix of familiarity and awe.

The man stood tall, his posture relaxed yet radiating control, as though the world around him bent to his will. His long, dark hair shimmered faintly, like starlight shifting in water. His pale skin, touched with a faint blue tint, seemed to absorb the moonlight filtering through the trees.

When their gazes met, she froze. His eyes, deep violet and swirling with an otherworldly energy, were captivating, filled with a dreamlike quality that seemed to pierce through her.

He wore robes dark as twilight, edged in silver and blue. They moved like mist and shimmered with quiet light. Though he didn't speak, his presence radiated reassurance, a quiet promise that she wasn't alone.

The air around him seemed to hum, and the forest responded to him. Branches shifted as if in deference, and the light softened around him.

"I don't understand what's happening to me," she found herself saying, the words tumbling out before she could stop them. The weight of the day's events pressed against her chest. "The voices, the necklace, the way everything keeps spiraling out of control."

He tilted his head slightly, listening with the patience of someone who had all the time in the world. His expression was gentle, understanding without judgment. When he moved closer, each step seemed to ease the knots of tension in her shoulders.

"I keep trying to hide what I am," she continued, surprised by her honesty. "But it feels like something is hunting me, calling to me. Two different voices now, and I don't know what either of them wants or why they both seem to know me."

The figure extended a hand, not to pull her forward but to anchor her in place, a silent reminder of the foundation she'd forgotten. His touch was warm, grounding, and suddenly the forest around them felt less like a dream and more like a sanctuary.

The tension in her chest eased as she stood before him. The questions that had been circling her mind like vultures began to quiet.

He studied her face with an expression of deep compassion, as if he could see every burden she carried and wanted to help her set them down.

"But what if I can't handle this?" she whispered. "What if whatever's calling to me is too powerful? What if I hurt the people I care about?"

His smile was gentle, sad, and infinitely kind. He reached out and touched her forehead with the lightest pressure, and suddenly the threatening voices from the day seemed distant, their promises muffled and unimportant.

The forest hummed with life around her, leaves rustling in a breeze she couldn't feel. He tilted his head slightly, as if listening to something just out of reach.

His expression softened, and when he spoke, his lips stayed still, but his words echoed in her mind.

Rest now. You are stronger than you know, and you are not as alone as you believe.

His voice was deep and melodic, the kind of sound that could unravel every knot of anxiety in her chest. It carried a weight she couldn't define, a hypnotic quality that wrapped around her like a warm embrace.

But more than that, it held wisdom, as if he understood the burden of secrets and the exhaustion that came with constantly looking over one's shoulder.

Tomorrow will bring its own guidance. Trust in your strength, and trust in those who stand beside you.

The words settled into her bones like a promise. The fear that had been gnawing at her since the warehouse began to recede, replaced by something she hadn't felt in a long time: peace. Not the absence of problems, but the profound certainty that she could face whatever came next.

As she relaxed into the dream, the figure began to fade, but his presence lingered like the warmth of sunlight on skin. The forest grew softer around the edges, the sounds becoming a gentle lullaby that seemed designed just for her.

The warmth of his presence enveloped her, the forest fading into a soft blur as the weight of the day melted away. Ophira let out a breath in relief, the tension unraveling as she sank deeper into the dream, the promise of peace finally within reach.

Birdsong pulled her from the dream, her eyes opening to dawn's faint glow filtering through her curtains. For the first time in days, she felt rested, the aches in her muscles dulled, her mind quiet.

The dream lingered at the edges of her mind, vivid yet elusive. She couldn't place the figure or explain the sense of calm he'd left behind. But as she sat up and stretched, the memory of his steady presence stayed with her, a quiet reassurance that carried her into the new day. Somehow, his words echoed faintly in her waking mind: she was stronger than she knew, and she wasn't as alone as she believed.

CHAPTER ELEVEN

THE FINE ART OF BLENDING IN (STILL LIFE WITH ANXIETY)

Ophira's BMW X5 purred to a stop in front of the museum, its sleek black exterior gleaming under the streetlights. Marcus sat in the passenger seat, while Aric settled in the back, tension crackling between them. As the engine quieted, Ophira glanced at Marcus. One hand rested on the armrest, the other drummed against his knee.

"Ready?" Marcus asked, turning toward her with that half-smile that always sent her heart skittering.

She gave a slight nod and opened the door, cool night air rushing in. Ophira stepped out of the car, crisp evening air brushing her skin as she took in the towering museum facade. The museum loomed ahead, its neoclassical columns casting elongated shadows. In the fading light, the grandeur seemed otherworldly, stone walls whispering of centuries-old secrets.

Love me a good ominous building, Zeke muttered dryly. *Really sets the mood for a casual evening stroll.*

It's not ominous, Sage countered. *It's architecturally significant. Show some respect.*

Ophira glanced briefly at the towering columns. Valentina stayed uncharacteristically silent, her attention fixed on the museum as if she too felt its weight.

Aric stepped out of the car last, his expression more guarded, his movements careful. She knew he was watching. He had been ever since Marcus entered their lives. Aric's wariness was a constant reminder to keep her distance, to stay focused on the case.

The reminder faded as she walked beside Marcus toward the entrance, and his hand brushed lightly across her back. She glanced up at him, catching his gaze as he turned his attention to the massive oak doors ahead of them. The warm glow of the museum's exterior lights illuminated his features, casting a soft, golden hue over his skin.

"Places like this always speak to me," Marcus said quietly. "So much hidden in the cracks of history. The trick is knowing how to listen."

Ophira glanced up at the entrance to the museum, the intricate carvings above the door telling their own tales. Figures from myth and history intertwined in a dance that had long since been forgotten by most. She felt the same pull toward the past, an almost instinctive awareness that this place held more than mere artifacts. It held power. And danger.

"It certainly has an atmosphere," she replied carefully, the words measured. Ophira kept her expression neutral, though her thoughts were alive with caution. Marcus's easy confidence mixed with the museum's hush, giving the air a gravity that set her nerves humming. She dismissed the feeling for now and stepped forward. Marcus's presence, the subtle touches, and the warmth of his smile pulled her attention elsewhere. She couldn't deny how quickly things between them had progressed, and how hard it was to resist.

The heavy oak doors creaked as they opened, revealing the dimly lit grandeur of the museum's entrance hall. The ceiling stretched high above them, a vaulted expanse that seemed to echo with the passage of time.

Marble statues of ancient gods and heroes lined the walls, their cold eyes watching as the trio entered the sacred space. The scent of old stone and polished wood filled the air, mingling with something ancient like dust from forgotten tombs and relics untouched for centuries.

This place is hummin' with somethin', Zeke muttered. *And it ain't just history.*

Sage responded, *Residual energy. Artifacts absorb it over time. You should know that by now.*

Ophira let their voices fade into the background as her gaze swept across the room. The grandeur was overwhelming, the details of the architecture pulling her deeper into the atmosphere.

The floors were a checkerboard of black and white marble, worn smooth from decades of visitors, yet still glossy under the warm light of the chandeliers above. It felt timeless, like stepping into a place where past and present coexisted, history's weight pressing down with every breath.

Stay sharp, she thought, her heels clicking softly against the marble as she stepped further into the space.

"This place is incredible," she murmured, her eyes drawn to the intricate frescoes that adorned the walls, depicting scenes of triumph, war, and conquest. She could almost hear the battles that had once been fought, the clang of swords and the cries of warriors.

"It's even more impressive when you realize how much of the world's history is housed here," Marcus said, glancing at her. His eyes lingered on her a moment before returning to the artifacts displayed in glass cases along the edges of the room. "So many stories waiting to be discovered."

The hallway stretched out ahead, dimly lit by the museum's sterile lighting, casting long shadows that seemed to cling to every corner. Ophira's footsteps echoed softly as she walked, but her mind was anything but quiet. She replayed the events over and over, the analytical part of her brain grasping for answers. Something didn't sit right. The trap, how had it been triggered?

She ran through the possibilities. The relic was ancient, dangerous, no doubt, but it had been held for years without incident. Traps like that wouldn't have been able to be kept a secret in this modern time of information. Rumors would have spread. Why now? What had changed? Her fingers brushed the fabric of her jacket absentmindedly, searching for clues she couldn't quite grasp. *Was it something we touched? Something we said?*

Her eyes narrowed as her mind went back to the moment when the vines had erupted from the walls. It hadn't been random. There was an order to it, a purpose. Traps like that didn't spring without reason. They were meant to protect something, to keep it hidden. But what exactly?

What was the purpose of that trap? The vines had come alive with a frightening speed, like they had been waiting, lying dormant, until we set them off. Her mind flashed to the necklace, safely locked in her secured, climate-controlled vault. Was that hidden treasure the source of the magic, or had the trap been meant to test anyone bold enough to pursue the relic before them?

Her brow furrowed. Her power had only flared up after the vines began to strangle her, but maybe it had been enough to change the course of events. The relic room had been filled with ancient magic, remnants of the past clinging to the artifact. Could her energy have interacted with that? Or was it something else?

Did the relic trigger it? Or did I?

Her worries shifted sharply to Marcus. *Did he see what I did?* The vines had come alive so suddenly, choking her, and her power had flared in response. She retraced the moment – the crushing vines, her desperate surge of energy, the stone spreading through organic matter. He was right there when it happened.

She stole a glance at Marcus as they walked. He seemed re-laxed, normal. *Maybe he was too focused on his survival to notice. Maybe the chaos masked what I did.* The hope offered some com-fort, but the fear lingered.

Ophira's footsteps slowed as she spiraled. Marcus had been steady through everything.

Marcus's voice broke through her thoughts, soft and steady. "You sure you're alright?" He offered a warm smile. "You handled that better than you think. Anyone else would have panicked. Let me shoulder some of this with you."

Ophira forced herself to meet his gaze. Her heart pounded beneath the surface, but her voice came out steady. "I needed to clear my head. Yesterday was intense." She wasn't ready to unravel, not here. Not in front of him.

Marcus studied her. A faint tremor ghosted across his knuck-les before he slid his hand into a pocket and offered a gentle smile. "Of course," he said, voice low with reassurance. The small slip of composure tugged at her heart more than any polished line could have.

The silence between them dragged on long enough to make her skin itch. She shifted her weight, and when Marcus finally turned to consult Aric, she seized the moment to breathe.

Needing space to clear her head, she angled down a side corridor that opened into the next exhibit hall.

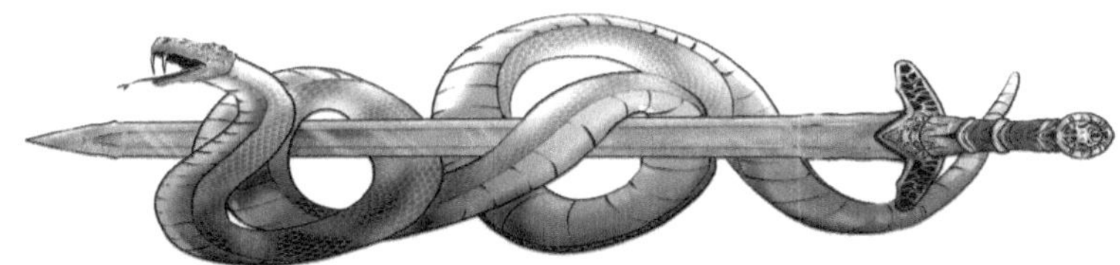

Ophira entered the dimly lit chamber, air heavy with the scent of aged stone and metal. The faint hum of the museum's climate control system underscored the silence, but it wasn't enough to mask the creak of distant footsteps. Too faint to place, but loud enough to set her on edge.

The centerpiece of the room loomed ahead: a glass case holding the latest artifact to arrive, a bronze helm etched with intricate runes. Overhead, the lights flickered faintly, casting shifting shadows across the walls and giving the statues an eerie sense of motion. Ophira adjusted her scarf instinctively, the sensation of the relic's proximity making her skin prickle.

She paused, her gaze sweeping the hall. For a moment, it felt as though the air thickened, the silence pressing in around her. She couldn't shake the feeling that she wasn't alone.

"Pretty piece, isn't it?" The guard standing by the case, a lanky man with sharp eyes, nodded toward the helm. "Came in last week. Some kind of Greek thing."

Ophira smiled politely. "Something like that." She forced her feet to remain still, though her instincts screamed to back away. The artifact felt alive, humming faintly in her bones.

The air turned icy, a chill so sharp it felt like ghostly fingers brushing along her spine. Ophira inhaled sharply, her breath forming a thin cloud in the suddenly frigid air. A faint hiss, low and insistent, coiled in her ears, as if the room itself had exhaled in warning. Her pulse raced, instincts screaming danger, as her eyes darted to her hand.

For the briefest, horrifying moment, the familiar illusion faltered. Her real skin snapped into view under the exhibit's harsh lights, pale with a faint greenish tint, shimmering like polished stone. She clenched her fist, the motion sharp and desperate, willing the charm to hold.

A strange, static-like buzz rippled through her veins as she fought to steady her breathing. The moment dragged, stretching into what felt like eternity, before the air warmed again and her olive-toned skin returned, smooth and unmarred.

She felt exposed, the curse bubbling close to the surface. When the guard's voice broke the silence, she nearly jumped. "You okay?" He seemed wary, though not unkind. "Looked a bit green for a moment there, like you saw a ghost."

Ophira forced a smile, her lips stiff. "I'm fine," she said, brushing her scarf. "Probably need some air." Her heart was still pounding, her fingers trembling as she tucked them out of sight. The helm's faint hum seemed to mock her, as though it had been waiting for the moment she let her guard down. *Whatever that thing was, it had no business being here.*

Hearing Aric call out to her, she returned to the other room. She didn't understand what had happened, but didn't have time to think about it with everything else going on. Her mind was a whirl of contradictions, the weight of everything pressing at once. Whatever had happened in that warehouse had changed things.

As they moved down the hallway, Ophira felt something shift. The composure she had once leaned on now felt fragile, strained under questions she could not yet answer. Marcus had not said or done anything outright, but the doubt had taken root, and her mind would not let it go.

Still, part of her did not want to force the issue if he truly hadn't seen anything. She held the line, quiet and cautious, choosing to wait and watch. She would keep her guard up, but clung to the hope that she would not have to run and start her life over again to remain safely hidden.

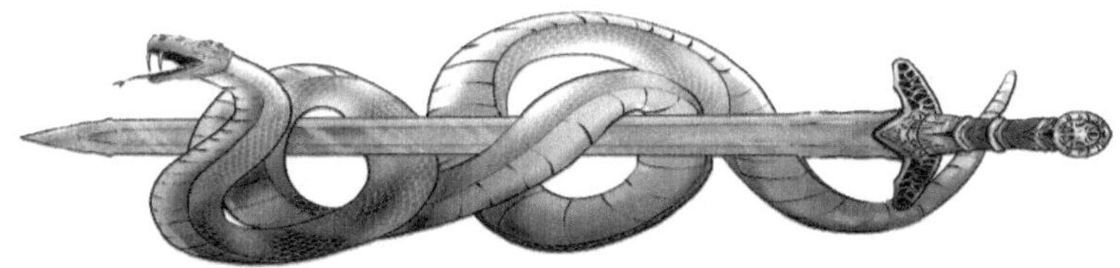

They walked further into the main hall, where towering glass cases held relics from ancient civilizations. Golden statues, worn scrolls, and intricately designed weapons were behind the glass, each piece a fragment of history. Ophira could feel the energy emanating from them: the stories, the emotions, the lives that had once been attached to these objects. It was as if the museum was alive, breathing with the ghosts of those long gone.

"This sword," Marcus said, pausing before one of the larger displays. "It belonged to a Macedonian general. Legend says it was forged in the fires of Hephaestus himself."

Ophira stepped closer, studying the polished blade. It was beautiful, the craftsmanship intricate, with ancient symbols etched into the hilt. But it wasn't the craftsmanship that caught her attention. There was something familiar about the energy radiating from it.

She leaned in slightly, her breath catching in her throat as the connection became clearer. This wasn't a relic of a bygone era. This sword had seen bloodshed, betrayal, and victory. It had been wielded by someone who had changed the course of history, and the echoes of those moments were still embedded in the metal.

"Interesting choice," Marcus commented, noticing her gaze. "You seem drawn to the ones with the most legendary stories."

She frowned, turning her attention back to the artifact. There was an underlying tension in his voice, one she couldn't quite interpret. It was as if he knew more than he was letting on, but wasn't ready to share it yet.

"This vase…" she said, her fingers brushing the glass. "It feels familiar, like I've seen it before."

Marcus's eyes darkened slightly. "Maybe it's the kind of artifact that speaks to you on a deeper level."

Ophira glanced at him, her brow furrowing as she considered his words. Maybe that's why the artifacts pulled at her. Not because they held power but because they understood what it meant to be forgotten and misremembered.

The sound of Aric clearing his throat behind them broke the moment, reminding her that they weren't alone. She turned away, focusing on the next display, but she could feel the tension hanging in the air between her and Marcus, thick and heavy.

The investigation was what mattered. The relics. The thieves. Yet every moment she spent in Marcus's presence, she found herself drawn deeper into the web he was spinning. His charm, his knowledge, his subtle touch: all too easy to get lost in.

"This place has seen a lot over the years," Marcus said as he stepped closer. "But none of it compares to what we're uncovering now. History remembers the conquerors but never forgets the ones who knew where to look."

She glanced at him, her pulse jumping. His words always carried layers – just enough shadow to make her wonder. The warmth in his eyes made it harder to resist, harder to stay grounded in what was real.

Before she could dwell on it any further, Aric's voice broke through the silence. "We should keep moving. We don't have time to get caught up in the exhibits."

Ophira gave a slight nod, though she was still contemplating Marcus's words as they continued through the hall. Each step they took brought them closer to their goal, but the undercurrent of tension between her and Marcus was making it increasingly difficult to concentrate.

As they moved deeper into the museum, the faint hum of ancient secrets seemed to grow louder around them, the artifacts watching with silent, unseen eyes.

A turn at the end of the corridor opened into another vaulted hall, older and quieter than the rest, where the air itself felt weighed down by centuries. Each step Ophira took echoed softly on the polished marble floor, the sound almost lost beneath the hum of the museum's climate control system. The exhibits they passed grew older, more obscure, as though each room they entered was taking them further back in time.

It was in this quiet, almost eerie atmosphere that they were greeted by a figure standing at the far end of the next hall. Dr. Sedona Ghestad, the museum's head curator, was a slender, elegant woman with shoulder-length brown hair pulled back in a precise style. Her light olive complexion and refined features gave her an air of Mediterranean sophistication, while her tailored blazer and crisp slacks spoke to her academic authority. She stood near a large display of relics, her posture perfectly composed and professional, but her dark brown eyes were anything but passive as they observed the trio with piercing intelligence.

Looks like she's sizing us up for dinner, Zeke muttered, wary.

She's analyzing patterns, not planning an ambush, Sage corrected.

I do not trust ze poised ones, Valentina hissed. *Such polish hides ze daggers underneath.*

Sunny's warmth slipped through the tension. *Now, y'all don't go rilin' her up after yesterday's scare. She can handle herself fine.*

Ophira stepped forward. *Keep calm. Watch her carefully.*

Marcus stepped forward with practiced ease. "Dr. Ghestad, allow me to introduce Ophira Naga and Aric Somner. Their insights have been invaluable in this recovery case."

Dr. Ghestad inclined her head slightly, her gaze lingering on Ophira for a fraction before shifting to Aric. "A pleasure to meet you both. Your reputations precede you."

Marcus turned slightly toward Ophira and Aric. "And this is Dr. Sedona Ghestad, leading scholar of Greek and Hellenic studies, currently serving as the museum's head curator during our cultural exchange ambassador program through our sister museum in Crete. She's one of the foremost voices in artifact preservation and has played a crucial role in safeguarding some of the world's rarest relics."

"Dr. Ghestad," she greeted, shaking the woman's outstretched hand, "thank you for meeting with us."

Dr. Ghestad smiled wanly. "Of course. I always have time for those who appreciate history. Marcus and I have spoken about you. It's always fascinating to meet those with a deep interest in the past."

Ophira's gaze flickered briefly to Marcus, then back to the curator. There was something disconcerting in the way Dr. Ghestad said that, but she let it slide. Instead, she tilted her head slightly, her instincts picking up on something else.

"Ghestad," she mused, "that doesn't sound Greek. More Germanic, maybe?"

Dr. Ghestad's expression didn't shift. If anything, the faintest ghost of amusement crossed her lips. "Names can be deceiving, Ms. Naga."

A chill curled at the base of Ophira's spine. There was an amusement in her voice, like an inside joke she wasn't sharing.

Before Ophira could analyze it further, Marcus said, "Dr. Ghestad has been instrumental in acquiring some of the museum's rarer pieces, including a few relics that might interest us."

The moment passed, but the uneasy flicker in Ophira's mind lingered beneath the surface.

The museum curator had been one of their key contacts in securing access to certain off-limits sections of the museum. She was helpful to their investigation, though Ophira couldn't shake the feeling that the woman was interested in more than their inquiries.

"I'm always fascinated when someone takes an interest in our more elusive collections." Dr. Ghestad's expression was neutral as she took a few steps toward them, her heels clicking against the floor. Ophira immediately noticed how poised she was.

There was something almost predatory in the way she moved, like a lioness calmly watching over her territory. She turned her gaze to Marcus, her eyes lingering on him a beat longer than necessary. There was something in her expression that Ophira couldn't quite read, as if Dr. Ghestad recognized something in Marcus that she hadn't yet revealed.

"It's always fascinating to see how much history is woven into these relics," Dr. Ghestad continued. "They carry so much power, don't they?"

Ophira caught the subtle shift in Dr. Ghestad's tone, a slight drop in pitch that made the hairs on the back of her neck stand up. She glanced at Marcus, who returned Dr. Ghestad's gaze with an unreadable expression of his own. A possessive unease stirred within her, an instinct she couldn't ignore. *Is she interested in him, too? Do they have a history? Or am I still off balance from yesterday?*

The possibility tightened her chest as Dr. Ghestad's gaze lingered on Marcus a moment, sparking something territorial and troubling within her. He remained calm, collected, every inch the charming and knowledgeable expert.

"Yes," Marcus replied smoothly, his tone matching the professionalism of their host. "That's why we're here, to understand the history and the significance of these artifacts before they vanish into private hands."

Dr. Ghestad's eyes gleamed at his response, and for a moment, Ophira caught something, sharpness, maybe curiosity. Or something else? It was gone in a blink, replaced by the smooth veneer of a woman used to playing host to museum visitors.

Ophira's unease deepened. There was something about Dr. Ghestad she couldn't place. The way her gaze lingered on Marcus, tracking their every move like a predator sizing up prey. Ophira tried to brush it off – this was a museum, after all, and Dr. Ghestad had every reason to be protective of her exhibits. But still… something felt off.

There's something about her…like she's watching us, waiting for something, Ophira thought, her instincts prickling at the edge of her mind. She brushed it off as curiosity about the relics and lingering unease from the vines. They were, after all, investigating a significant theft.

Dr. Ghestad turned her attention to the display beside her, gesturing to a series of artifacts arranged meticulously behind glass. "These pieces are part of a special collection we've been curating for years. Each item has a long and storied past, some more elusive than others." She paused, her gaze sliding back to Ophira. "I'm sure someone with your eye for detail can appreciate the complexity of these items."

Ophira gave a polite smile, trying to ignore the strange tension she felt building in the room. "I'm looking forward to learning more."

Dr. Ghestad turned back to the display. "These relics have passed through many hands, each leaving a mark. Some say they absorb power from their owners. Fascinating, isn't it?"

The way she said it made Ophira's skin prickle with unease. She felt Marcus shift slightly beside her, and a glance at Aric showed that even he seemed more guarded than usual. Ophira couldn't help but wonder how much of what Dr. Ghestad was saying was for their benefit and how much was for her own hidden purposes.

Marcus kept his calm demeanor. "That's what makes them so dangerous, doesn't it?" he said. "The more powerful the relics, the greater the risk of them falling into the wrong hands."

Dr. Ghestad's eyes flicked back to him, her smile returning with an edge of something sharper. "Indeed. That's why it's crucial to understand not just their history, but their potential. Only then can we ensure they are handled properly."

The conversation felt like a dance, each word carefully chosen, each response measured. Ophira couldn't shake the feeling that Dr. Ghestad was testing them, gauging their knowledge, their intentions. And though the curator remained outwardly pleasant, there was something predatory in her gaze that set Ophira's nerves on edge.

Strategist, Sage noted quietly.

Predator, Zeke added.

Ophira kept her nerves tightly reined in. *Chill out. Let her think she's in control.*

As they continued discussing the artifacts and the symbols that were reminiscent of the ones from the necklace, Ophira couldn't help but feel Dr. Ghestad's eyes on her, as though watching her every move with unnerving precision. It was as though the curator could see right through her, past the surface, past the walls Ophira had carefully constructed around herself.

The overhead lights flickered again, their glow dimming for just a moment before stabilizing. Shadows stretched unnaturally long along the marble floor, pooling at the edges of the room. Ophira caught the faintest sound and turned sharply, her heart racing. Nothing. The exhibits stood silent, unmoving, their polished cases glinting under the steady hum of the lights.

As they continued discussing the artifacts, Aric's voice cut through the tension. "You heard that, didn't you?" His sharp gaze flicked to Marcus, then back to the shadows.

Ophira nodded subtly, her senses on high alert. She couldn't help but feel Dr. Ghestad's eyes on her, as though watching her every move with unnerving precision. Even Marcus seemed unusually still, his gaze lingering on the necklace in the glass case.

Dr. Ghestad continued to speak as they moved through the gallery, her tone casual but her interest sharp. "It's always a challenge, preserving these relics, especially when there are so many who wish to possess them for reasons beyond their historical value."

Ophira narrowed her eyes slightly at the comment, sensing a hidden meaning behind the words. She couldn't shake the feeling that Dr. Ghestad knew more than she was letting on, that this wasn't merely another day at the museum for her. And yet, there was nothing overt in her behavior that would indicate suspicion.

She's doing her job, Ophira tried to reassure herself, but it was hard to ignore the unease gnawing at her. Dr. Ghestad's presence added a strange layer of tension that Ophira hadn't expected. She was supposed to be assisting with the investigation, but her observation of Marcus and Ophira felt more like an assessment. It was as if she was sizing them up for something.

As Dr. Ghestad reviewed a Phoenician torque with Marcus, she paused, eyes bright with scholarly interest. "Did you bring the recovered necklace? I would value a firsthand inspection."

Aric answered before Ophira could speak, "It's secured in our vault, Doctor. We never travel with high-risk pieces, but we have spectral scans and measurements if that helps."

The curator nodded appreciatively, but there was a brief flicker of something in her eyes, almost as though she were testing them, waiting for a reaction.

As Dr. Ghestad turned back to discuss the exhibit with Marcus, Ophira was grateful for the chance to step away, her mind buzzing. She exchanged a glance with Aric, who gave her a slight, reassuring nod. An aide approached Dr. Ghestad with a clipboard in hand, and she stepped to the side to discuss a museum matter.

As she and Aric moved on, Ophira couldn't shake the feeling that their encounter with Dr. Ghestad was more than a casual meeting. Ophira held her composure, nodding as Marcus stepped closer to rejoin them. She felt his presence beside her, calm and steady, but it didn't ease the growing discomfort she felt.

Ophira followed Marcus and Aric as they approached the curation hall, her mind still turning over the strange undercurrent of tension she had felt in Dr. Ghestad's presence. The click of their footsteps echoed in the hallway, the sterile scent of polished stone and curated history filling the air. The museum was quiet, the kind of quiet that suggested centuries of secrets lurking just beneath the surface. As they neared the hall, a heavy glass door slid open, revealing a dimly lit room filled with displays of rare and priceless relics.

The curation hall was dimly lit, designed to cast the relics on display in soft, reverent light. The air was thick with history, the walls lined with ancient artifacts encased in glass, each one telling a silent story.

They had no idea they were being watched.

Unseen and silent, a figure lingered in the shadows of the hallway, their presence hidden, yet their eyes were sharp. A faint shimmer at the edge of the darkness hinted at their presence, out of reach but there, watching. Calculating.

From the darkness, they tracked every movement. Ophira's careful steps. The flicker of doubt as she glanced at Marcus. The tension in the air, sharp and stretched like a live wire, was ready to snap. They remained silent, invisible, but their attention never wavered. They were watching.

Ophira, in particular, held their attention. There was something about her, a subtle display of power earlier, hidden beneath her calm exterior. *Interesting...her power exceeds my expectations. She must be watched carefully.*

A low, nearly inaudible hum of satisfaction stirred in the observer's mind. The trap had been effective, revealing not only the strength of the relic but the potential within Ophira herself. She was growing too quickly, perhaps. Her control over her abilities had been subtle, yet the pulse of power had resonated through the room, unmistakable.

Their gaze followed Ophira, taking in her tense posture, the flicker of uncertainty in her eyes as she glanced at Marcus. A crack had begun to form between them, one that could widen if not carefully managed. It was essential for Marcus to keep her close. He could not afford to let her pull away. Tension would not serve the greater plan.

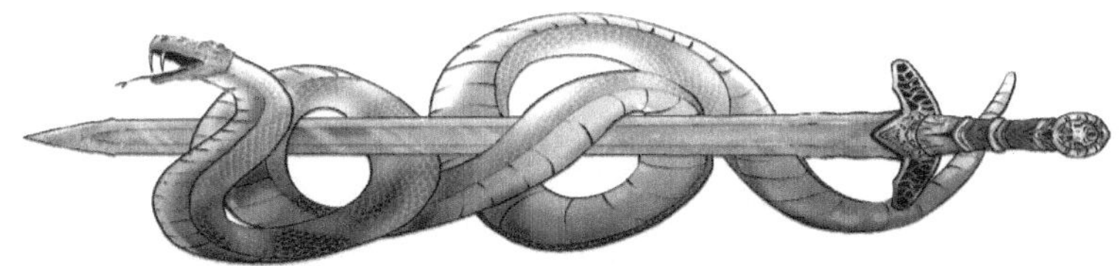

Late the following morning, Ophira sat at her desk, staring blankly at the papers scattered before her. The familiar comfort of her office, with its bookshelves full of ancient texts and relics carefully displayed behind glass, did little to ease her mind from worrying about the event earlier in the week. A place that once felt like her refuge now seemed more like a maze full of unsolved questions, with Marcus right at the center.

The supernatural trap had rattled her, the vines and panic seared into her memory. But more than that, the use of her power wasn't subtle. Stone-turning, life-ending power that she'd barely managed to control.

She glanced at the window, sunlight streaming through as if mocking her unease. He was right there when it happened. She frowned. *If he saw... If he knows what I am...*

Ophira rubbed her temples, trying to dispel the fears. *Get it together,* she told herself. *Maybe he was too focused on survival to notice anything else. Surely he'd have said something by now if he had. You're worrying yourself sick for no reason at all. You're better than this. Pull yourself together.*

As her internal monologue hit peak snark, a knock sounded at her office door, making her jump slightly. "Come in," she called, trying not to sound like she'd just been arguing with herself.

Marcus stepped in, a smile in place, carrying a cup of coffee. *Because he always knows,* she thought, already feeling her walls start to crack.

"I thought you could use this," he said, setting the coffee down in front of her with a warm, easy smile that softened her edge.

Ophira managed a smile, wrapping her fingers around the cup. She let the scent of the coffee ease some of her earlier tension.

"Thanks," she murmured, curling her hands around the cup. The warmth seeped into her fingers, the familiarity comforting, but her mind kept its careful watch.

He's considerate. He's steady. But the worried voice whispered, *What if he saw what I really am? What if he's being careful around me now because he knows?*

She gave a half-hearted shrug. "Yeah," she replied, raising the cup to her lips. "A lot to think about."

"I'm glad we made it out of there in one piece," Marcus said, his smile warm and sincere.

Ophira smiled back, but it felt forced. She knew it, and Marcus probably did too. *I must be more tired than I realized if I can't even fake a smile right.* She sighed inwardly, mentally swatting at the persistent apprehension. *Maybe I'm overreacting.*

Only maybe? Pretty sure you'd know by now if he'd seen anything, Sage said.

The silence in her office stretched on, the warmth of the coffee doing little to calm the storm brewing in her head. Marcus sat across from her, his presence usually an anchor, but today it only heightened her confusion. Before she could spiral further, Marcus broke the silence.

"You've been carrying too much on your own," Marcus said, his voice gentler now. "Even the strongest minds need time to reset. Let me take care of lunch today. Just an hour, you deserve that much."

Ophira blinked. "Lunch? Now?"

"Yes, now," he chuckled, standing and offering her his hand. "You look like you need a break."

Ophira smiled back, and this time it felt true. *He's acting completely normal,* she realized with relief as she took his hand. *If he'd seen what I did, he wouldn't be here offering lunch and being kind. My secret is safe. We're safe. We don't have to run. Thank god, I really didn't want to. I've built a good life here.*

She grabbed her bag and followed him out of the office, leaving her worries behind.

RESISTANCE IS FUTILE, BUT THE WINE IS EXCELLENT

Lunch had been everything she needed before a whole afternoon of research. As their discussion wound down, Marcus leaned back and ran a hand through his hair. "We've got a lot of work ahead of us," he said, weary, "but I think we're making progress."

Ophira nodded, the weight of the day's work settling into her muscles. They'd spent hours cross-referencing auction house records with the stolen artifacts list. The sword, the necklace, the chalice, the urn. Each piece carried whispers of divine power that made her skin prickle with recognition.

The research into their cursed properties had revealed disturbing patterns: unexplained deaths, sudden disappearances, and violent ends that followed each relic like a shadow.

And Marcus? She wanted to believe he was being honest, despite how smoothly the answers came, despite how easily they fell from his lips. During lunch, she'd felt relief that he didn't seem to recognize her true nature.

But now, watching him organize their findings with practiced efficiency, something nagged at her. The way he'd catalogued the divine symbols, the knowing look in his eyes when she'd mentioned the cursed artifacts. How much did he know? Ophira rubbed her temples as the day's questions ground against them, feeding a growing headache.

Marcus's voice came in softer than before. "You never give yourself a breather," he said, concern in his voice. "Let me handle the authentication research and the auction house contacts. I have connections that could speed things up, and you've been carrying too much of the burden. We can't afford to overlook anything because you're stretched too thin."

His tone made her pause. She studied his earnest expression, trying to pinpoint what felt off about his eagerness to help. *All their leads, all their sources,* she realized. *He'd have access to everything.* If she took him up on the offer, he'd have the keys to the kingdom. That kind of trust had only ever belonged to her and Aric.

She didn't think he realized what he was asking for. And maybe that's what unsettled her most.

"Maybe we should take a break, regroup with fresh eyes?" Her tone stayed light, but a small part of her noticed how easily he had offered to carry the weight.

Oh sure, let the handsome stranger handle the important stuff, Zeke said dryly.

He's being helpful, Sunny protested. *Sometimes people just want to help.*

Watch how quickly he volunteers, Sage observed quietly. *Always positioning himself as indispensable.*

Marcus raised an eyebrow. "Really? I thought you were the 'all-nighters until we crack it' type," he said, playfully.

"Even I know when to call it a night," she replied, leaning back in her chair, a half-smile on her lips. "Besides, no breakthrough comes from a burned-out brain."

He chuckled, the sound low and easy. "Fair point."

A pause lingered between them before Ophira broke the silence, her voice more tentative this time. "How about we continue this conversation over dinner at my place?"

His eyes flicked up, surprise melting into anticipation. "You'd like to have dinner with me?"

She shrugged casually, masking both the flutter that rose in her chest and her true motivation. "Why not? We've earned a break. Besides, I think we'd both benefit from a change of pace. We can still talk shop, but not under fluorescent lights."

Away from the office, with fewer distractions, maybe she could get a better read on what he truly understood. Not because she didn't trust him, but because trusting someone this much had always come with a cost.

His smile broadened, and her heart stuttered for a moment. Zent. "I'd like that."

"Great," she said, standing up to see him out. "I'll see you at eight?"

Marcus nodded, grabbing his jacket. "Looking forward to it."

The moment the door clicked shut behind him, Ophira reached for her phone. The warmth of his smile lingered longer than she liked, yet his offer to take over their most sensitive research kept echoing in her mind. She'd invited him to dinner not to interrogate him, but to get a clearer sense of what kind of trust he was asking for. And whether he even realized how much access that trust would give him.

But already, she could feel her resolve softening around the edges. That was precisely what worried her.

Focus on ze work, Valentina urged sharply. *Do not let pretty words cloud your judgment. His offer to 'handle ze details'? Non! Too convenient.*

But his worryin' seemed honest, Sunny said wistfully. *The way he looked at you when you rubbed your temples...*

The best predators always seem honest, darlin', Zeke drawled, his mental voice tight with warning. *That's what makes 'em dangerous. And did you see how quick he was to volunteer for the sensitive stuff?*

You're all being paranoid, Sunny protested. *Not everyone is a threat. I'm sure he doesn't even realize what it meant.*

She tapped out a message to Ronan, one of her most trusted contacts. One of the few who hadn't disappeared.

Ophira

Have you heard anything new about the sword? I need something to go on, we haven't found anything yet.

Ronan

Some chatter. Quiet inquiries, nothing big yet. Whoever's asking knows how to stay off the radar.

Ophira

Could they be connected to the theft?

Ronan

Too early to say, but it's possible. They're asking the right questions. I'll keep digging.

Ophira

What about Izmir? Any updates?

Ronan

Nothing at all out of that area. It's gone silent. Nobody's talking.

Ophira studied the message, thumb brushing the edge of the phone. Marcus's caution about "not blurring clues" wrestled with her hope that he truly had her best interests at heart.

He guides your thinking, Sage noted. *Subtle, but consistent. Always steering.*

You're all being paranoid, Sunny sighed. *He's trying to help us succeed.*

Maybe, Ophira thought, frustrated with the constant debate in her head. *Or maybe I'm losing my edge.*

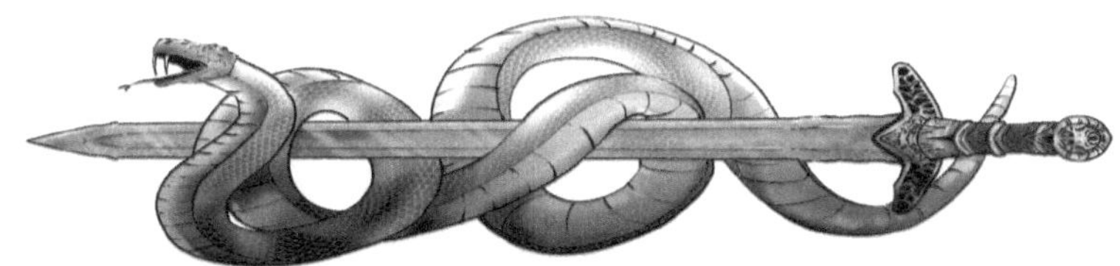

That evening, Ophira moved around her kitchen, stirring a pot of rich tomato sauce that filled the room with the scent of herbs and garlic. Steam rose from the pasta water, adding a bit of fragrant humidity to the air as she stole glances at the clock. She wasn't nervous. She kept repeating it to herself: this was strategic, an investigation disguised as dinner. She had her questions ready, her guard up. But there was a tension hanging in the air that she couldn't quite shake. Part anticipation, part dread that she might not get the answers she was looking for.

This wasn't just about the investigation anymore. When had she stopped thinking about extracting information and started anticipating his smile? Part of her relished how close they'd become, while another part of her wrestled with the familiar creeping doubt that refused to disappear.

Stay focused, she reminded herself, hands tightening around the spoon. *Pay attention. See what he knows. Don't let your guard down.*

You're overthinking this, Sunny said gently. *Maybe just enjoy the evening.*

Non! Valentina protested. *Stay sharp, chérie. Remember what we discussed.*

One night off from being suspicious won't kill us, Sunny countered.

Except when it can, Sage replied.

The doorbell pulled her from her musing. Ophira wiped her hands on a towel before answering. When she opened the door, Marcus stood there. He looked effortlessly handsome in a black button-down and jeans, his smile easy and confident.

Focus on the job, she reminded herself, even as her pulse quickened.

Hard to focus when he's all cleaned up like Sunday best, Zeke drawled. *Man's got the whole package, darlin'. I'll give him that.*

That's precisely the problem, Sage murmured.

"Right on time." She stepped aside to let him in.

"I wouldn't dare be late," he teased as he walked in, glancing around the entryway with curious appreciation. "Smells great, by the way."

She smiled, leading him to the kitchen. "I hope you like pasta."

Dinner flowed more easily than she had expected. The conversation started light, with casual remarks about the city, their work, even the weather. It moved with surprising ease.

She had meant to stay focused. This was supposed to be her chance to get a better read on him, to see if he even realized what he had asked for earlier and how much access it would give him.

Pay attention, she reminded herself. *Ask about the inconsistencies. Look for signs he understands the weight of it.*

But instead, she found herself slipping. Let the current pull her under, just a little. Letting the rhythm of conversation draw her in and laughing more easily than she meant to. Her resolve softened with every shared smile.

You're losin' the plot, Sage warned quietly.

Maybe that's not such a bad thing, Sunny whispered back.

The quiet clinking of silverware against plates filled the room as they ate, the silence settling comfortably between them rather than straining. Wine caught the candlelight in their glasses, casting warm shadows across the table. Eventually, Ophira realized they needed to revisit the real reason Marcus was there.

Pouring them both another glass of wine, she decided to dive in. "You've mentioned these relics might be cursed," she began, watching his reaction. "You seem to know quite a bit about that. Have you had any experience with cursed artifacts before?"

Marcus leaned back in his chair, swirling the wine in his glass, the dim lighting casting shadows across his face. "You know, working with you on this case has been…" He paused, seeming to search for the right words. "Different from what I expected. Better."

He met her eyes with what looked like vulnerability. "I've spent so many years just trying to prove myself, always looking over my shoulder, wondering if I'm making the right choices. But with you, I feel like I can actually breathe. Like maybe I don't have to carry all of this alone." His voice grew quieter, more intimate. "I know I told you about the pressure I'm under, but what I didn't say is how isolating it's been. Until now."

He's good, Sage whispered, barely audible now. *Look how he's makin' this about connection, about needing you.*

But Ophira found herself leaning forward, drawn in despite the warning. The way he'd said "until now." There was actual relief there, wasn't there? She took a sip of wine, letting the moment settle before gently steering back. "I appreciate you sharing that with me. But about these relics… if they're that dangerous, why would anyone risk stealing them without knowing what they're getting into?"

Marcus's expression darkened as he set the glass down. "Greed, most likely. The thieves probably thought they were just valuable artifacts, something they could flip for a fortune. They didn't realize the danger. But the stories I've come across suggest there's more to it. Old myths, warnings about people who got too close meeting violent, unexplained ends."

"Like what?" Ophira kept her voice light.

"Accidents. Mysterious deaths." His jaw tightened. "Every time these things change hands, people die. The history isn't pretty."

Ophira nodded along, but her mind churned with questions. Marcus's voice carried certainty, but doubt still gnawed at her. The pieces fit, yet the puzzle still felt incomplete.

He's making sense, but why does it feel like something is missing? Her thoughts swirled as she watched him, analyzing his every move. *I can't afford to overlook anything.*

And still, despite the unanswered questions, despite the persistent edge of doubt, she welcomed the silence that followed. It was comfortable, his presence in her home making everything feel quieter, closer.

This is your chance, some instinct warned. *Ask the hard questions. Find the cracks.* But as she watched him move through her sanctuary with such natural ease, that voice grew fainter, overwhelmed by a longing she'd suppressed for centuries. As they moved into the living room, wine glasses in hand, Ophira's resolve softened.

Her home reflected her in ways few people ever saw. It was tucked away in a quiet part of the city, a place she had carefully curated over the years to feel both timeless and modern, a sanctuary where she could escape the weight of her past.

The hallway off the dining area opened into a sleek living space. Ancient texts and modern thrillers lined floor-to-ceiling shelves under high ceilings, while dark wood floors caught the soft lighting's gleam. Artifacts and relics, remnants of her hidden history, were strategically placed around the room, not as trophies but as reminders of who she was beneath the surface.

This is who I am, Ophira thought, glancing at the relics that adorned her shelves. *Not the mask I wear for the world, but this. My sanctuary. And yet here he is, moving through it like he belongs. Why do I want him to stay?*

To anyone else, the space might have seemed cold or distant. But to Ophira, this was her stronghold. Here, she could control the narrative of her life and keep her past at bay.

Yet now, with Marcus stepping through the door, the air shifted, the space becoming something more vulnerable, more exposed. His presence in her sanctuary felt like a turning point, a crack in the armor she'd worn for centuries.

Why does it feel like he belongs here? She wondered, glancing at Marcus as he moved through her most personal space.

Marcus stepped in, his eyes sweeping over the room with an appreciative hum. His gaze lingered on an ancient bronze mirror, then moved to a carved stone fragment displayed like modern art.

"I knew there was more to you," he murmured, his fingers almost reaching toward a Celtic torque before stopping himself. "But this is something else."

He doesn't belong, Zeke muttered darkly. *This place is ours. He's an outsider.*

Maybe that's the point, Sunny countered gently. *Maybe she wants him to belong.*

Bah! Valentina exclaimed. *He belongs like a snake belongs in a henhouse. Beware ze smooth ones, Ophira. Zey bite ze hardest!*

Ophira shot them an amused mental glare. *Cut it out,* she commanded, then turned to Marcus with a faint smile. "It's not much, but it's mine."

She felt a slight flutter in her chest. Few had ever crossed this threshold. She had always kept her private life separate from the world, using her home as a shield.

But now, with Marcus standing in the heart of her domain away from the rest of the world, she felt something shift inside her.

This is moving fast, she thought, biting her lip as her gaze traced Marcus's figure. *But I can't deny how he makes me feel. It's as if the walls I've built for centuries are crumbling all at once. I've kept people out for centuries, so why am I letting him in now? Is it his presence? His charm? Or am I just tired of being alone?*

She turned toward him, watching as he took in the intricate details of the space. His gaze lingered on the artifacts, the old tomes, and the relics that held pieces of her long-forgotten past. He moved through the room with natural ease, like he belonged there, like he understood the weight of the things she carried.

It's like he sees through the walls I've built. That scares me, she admitted silently. *But at the same time, it's what I've been longing for.*

"Not many people get to see this side of me," she said softly.

Marcus turned toward her, his expression warm but tinged with curiosity. "I'm honored," he replied, closing the distance between them. His hand grazed hers, sending a shiver up her arm. "You're letting me in, Ophira. That means something, doesn't it?"

Does it? she wondered, her mind swirling with conflict. She had always kept people at arm's length, never allowing them to get close.

But with Marcus, it felt different. There was something about him that made her feel seen, truly seen, in a way she hadn't been in centuries.

She could sense the subtle manipulation, of course, she wasn't blind to it, but that didn't stop her from wanting more. There was an undeniable pull between them, something deeper than attraction.

Is this a game we're playing here? she questioned. *Or am I afraid to feel something real?*

She turned toward him, feeling the weight of the moment pressing down on her. "You're different," she said softly, her voice catching in her throat. "There's something about you, but I don't know what it is."

Marcus smiled, his hand reaching up to brush a strand of her hair behind her ear. The touch was soft, tender, but there was an intensity in his eyes that made her heart race. "Maybe it's because I see you for who you are," he said. "All of you."

Does he really see me? Or does he see what he wants to see?

Look how carefully he's touching her, Sunny observed, her voice softer than usual. *Like she's precious.*

Even Zeke's usual skepticism seemed muted. *Well... I suppose he ain't been wrong about anything yet.*

For a moment, all the doubts, all the fears, seemed to fade away, leaving only the two of them, standing in the quiet intimacy of her home.

She leaned in slightly, her breath hitching as his fingers traced the edge of her jaw, a featherlight touch that sent a shockwave through her.

Even if it is moving fast, I don't want it to stop. For once, I don't want to think about what's right or wrong. I want to feel.

Anticipation thickened between them. The room's edges blurred. Marcus leaned in, his lips grazing hers softly at first, testing the waters. Ophira's heart pounded in her chest as she closed the distance between them, deepening the kiss, letting herself get lost in the moment.

For Marcus, this was a calculated move, but as their kiss deepened, something shifted in him, too. *She's more than I imagined,* he realized, his mind flickering between strategy and attraction. *I need her trust. This is all part of the plan. But why does her touch make me question my intentions?*

This wasn't about winning her over or about securing her trust for the case. Part of him was drawn to her, captivated by her strength, her vulnerability, and the mystery that surrounded her.

He hadn't expected to feel this way, but as her lips moved against his, he felt a flicker of something more. Something that could complicate everything.

I'm in control, Marcus reminded himself, but the heat between them made him question his resolve.

His hands slid around her waist, pulling her closer, and Ophira felt herself melting into the moment. The kiss was slow, deliberate, but there was an intensity to it that left her breathless.

She could feel the warmth of his body against hers, the way his hands moved over her, gentle but firm, as though he was staking his claim.

Am I letting my guard down too quickly? she wondered, but the thought was fleeting, replaced by the rush of desire flooding through her. *I've been so alone for so long. Maybe it's time I let someone in.*

They broke apart, breathless. The silence hummed with possibility. Marcus's usual poise slipped for a heartbeat, and his eyes flickered with something raw, as if he was startled by the depth of his feelings.

"Tell me you feel it too," he whispered, breath hitching.

I've spent centuries behind these walls, Ophira's mind raced, *but he's as vulnerable as I am in this moment.* She met his gaze, voice catching, "I do."

The confession lingered between them as Marcus's hand softened on her waist. He closed his eyes briefly, as though centering himself.

Trust always carries a price, she reminded herself. But for once, her snakes weren't chiming in with warnings or doubts. The unusual quiet should have concerned her, but as she let the warmth of his touch anchor her, the silent warning in her chest dimmed into a longing she could no longer deny.

Chapter Thirteen

Total Eclipse of the Guard

Satisfaction curled in Marcus's chest, watching Ophira's defenses crumble. *I have her,* he thought. The plan called for emotional manipulation, for making her dependent. But watching her trust bloom in her eyes, feeling the cracks start to form in her barriers beneath his touch, Marcus found himself questioning which of them was being caught.

As he looked at her, watching the vulnerability bloom across her face, something in his gut twisted. He hadn't expected to feel this. He hadn't expected to want her in this way. This was supposed to be part of the plan. *But why does it feel like she is wrapping herself around my heart instead?*

His hands moved of their own accord, tightening around her.

Marcus's grip tightened, and in that moment, Ophira knew she belonged to him. That should have triggered survival instincts honed over millennia. Instead, surrender felt like strength. *This is it,* she thought. *I've crossed the line, and there's no turning back now.*

"There's something special about you, Ophira," Marcus murmured, his voice dropping to an intimate register. "I feel like I can be myself around you."

She wanted to trust him, wanted to believe that what was happening between them was real. But a part of her still held back, a small voice in the back of her mind warning her that she was letting her guard down quickly. Still, in this moment, with Marcus standing so close, his presence so overwhelming, those doubts faded into the background.

She tilted her head slightly, her eyes searching his. "You don't even know the half of it," she whispered, her voice filled with meaning.

Marcus's lips curved into a soft smile. He stepped closer, his free hand rising to brush a strand of hair behind her ear, the gentle, intimate contact sending a shiver down her spine. His thumb lingered near her cheek, his breath warm against her skin as he leaned in, his lips hovering near hers.

The current between them raced with anticipation. This was it, the point where she either stepped back or let herself fall completely.

It's been so long since I've had anything like this, since I've allowed myself to. She'd experienced desire before across the centuries, but never this urgent need to abandon every carefully constructed defense. Her thoughts rushed in conflicting currents. *This is Marcus. He's charming, yes, but should I trust him?*

Zeke's familiar drawl cut through her thoughts. *That boy's got a silver tongue and a hidden dagger, darlin'. Don't go fallin' just 'cause he shines pretty in candlelight.*

Sage cut in sharply, his tone clinical and disapproving, *This isn't strategy. This is surrender.*

Every instinct screamed at her to step back, to analyze, to calculate the risks. She'd survived millennia by trusting no one completely. Yet she couldn't stop herself from leaning in. *If this is a mistake, it's one I'm willing to make.*

She closed the distance.

Their lips met softly, tentatively, but the connection was undeniable. A surge of warmth flooded through her, the kiss deepening as Marcus's hand slipped around her waist, pulling her closer. His lips claimed hers with deliberate intensity that left her dizzy.

Marcus pulled her closer, his hand sliding up her back, leaving a trail of heat in its wake. The world outside seemed to vanish; the only thing that mattered was the way his body fit against hers, the way his lips claimed her own with increasing urgency.

She could feel the tension between them mounting, the kiss deepening, becoming something more than a kiss. It was a connection, a tether that was binding them together in ways that felt irreversible. *I've built these walls for a reason. Yet, piece by piece, he's dismantling them. Am I ready for this? Can I afford to let him see me?*

Ophira's mind swirled with emotions, a flood of sensations she hadn't let herself feel in years. She wanted to slow down, to take a step back and think about what she was doing, but in this moment, with Marcus's hands roaming her back, his lips teasing hers with a tenderness that made her heart ache, she didn't want to stop. She couldn't.

I should be pulling back. This is too much, too fast. But I can't. I don't want to stop. Her breath caught as he looked at her, as though searching for something in her eyes. *It's like he's peeling back all my layers. And it scares me.* But fear was the furthest thing from her mind right now. *For once, I want to feel something real. Even if I regret it later.*

Their kiss broke, leaving them both breathless. Marcus's forehead rested against hers, his breath hot against her lips as his hands slid down to her waist, anchoring her to him. "You're incredible," he whispered, his voice thick with emotion. "I've never met anyone like you."

This is control, he thought, even as his grip tightened involuntarily. *This is exactly what I wanted. Wasn't it?* The certainty felt hollow, foreign. When she whispered yes, something inside him shifted, too sharp to be pleasure. This was supposed to be a step forward, part of the plan. Instead, it became a line he couldn't uncross, but he couldn't stop now. He leaned in, rationalizing the weight in his chest as adrenaline.

Her chest tightened, the weight of his words settling over her like a warm blanket. She wanted to believe him, wanted to let herself fall into this without reservation. But even now, a small part of her held back, the nagging feeling that this was all too good to be true.

She opened her eyes, meeting his gaze. "Marcus..." she began, but faltered as he pressed a soft kiss to her forehead, silencing her. The tenderness of the gesture broke down another wall within her, and she sensed her resistance shattering.

Marcus's hand moved to her cheek, his thumb brushing over her skin as he tilted her head back slightly, his lips finding hers once again. This time, the kiss was more urgent, more intense, and Ophira melted into him completely. Everything beyond this room ceased to exist, leaving only the heat of his hands, the weight of his body against hers, and the steady rhythm of their breathing as they moved in sync.

Her apartment high above the bustling city was quiet except for the soft rustle of clothing and the distant hum of the city beyond her windows as Marcus's hands roamed over her body. He moved with a confidence that belied their newness to one another, his fingers deftly unbuttoning her blouse. Ophira's breath hitched as he slipped it off her shoulders, revealing the delicate lace of her bra beneath.

"You're so tense," Marcus murmured, his dark eyes locking onto hers as his thumbs traced circles on her bare skin. "Let me take care of you tonight."

She swallowed hard, her analytical mind struggling to keep up with the rapid shift in dynamics. His suggestion was both alluring and terrifying, a proposition that went against everything she believed about herself. But there was something in the way he looked at her, something compelling that made her nod hesitantly.

"Yes," she whispered.

I should be stopping this, she thought, her heart pounding. *This isn't me. I'm not the kind of person who lets someone in so easily.* But her feet kept moving, her body drawn toward Marcus as though it had no choice. *For once, I want to lose control.*

Marcus's smile widened, a glint of satisfaction in his eyes. He guided her with gentle firmness toward the lush chaise lounge by the floor-to-ceiling window that overlooked the city skyline. As she settled against the cushions, he positioned himself above her, his weight grounding and reassuring. The sudden weight of him pressed down, anchoring her in the moment.

She's surrendering to me, Marcus thought, his pulse quickening. *But why do I feel like I'm the one surrendering?* He glanced down at her, spread out before him, and something inside him shifted. This was supposed to be about taking control, about keeping her close. *It feels like she's the one who has the power.*

The moment stretched between them, charged with unspoken questions.

Candlelight cast a warm glow across the living room, flickering flames highlighting her face, softening the shadows that usually guarded her expressions. Standing there with Marcus, her entire world had shrunk to this single moment, suspended in time.

He reached for her, fingers lightly tracing the curve of her jaw, and she leaned into the warmth of his hand despite the voice in her mind urging caution. His hand lingered on her cheek, his thumb brushing across her skin with a tenderness that made her heart skip.

"Ophira," he whispered, "are you sure?"

Her eyes searched his, and she allowed herself to answer with honesty, letting down her defenses for the first time in centuries. She gave an almost imperceptible nod, barely hearing her own whispered, "Yes."

Marcus's hand slipped to her waist, pulling her close until there was no space left between them. His lips found hers again, but this time, the kiss was deeper, more intense, as if each of them were exploring an uncharted territory, testing the boundaries of trust and desire. Ophira's fingers wove into his hair, feeling its softness as she surrendered to the sensation, letting herself fall into him.

They moved together as if guided by some invisible rhythm, every brush of skin against skin deepening the connection between them. His hands traced up her spine, pulling her closer, and barriers dissolved as her breath hitched.

The room fell away, leaving only the two of them. Every sensation heightened – the warmth of his body pressed against hers, the faint scent of his cologne mingling with the smoky aroma of the candles, the soft sound of his breathing as he took in each of her reactions. Her mind quieted, and for the first time in what seemed like an eternity, she let herself feel without restraint.

As they settled together on the luxurious velvet cushions, his hands continued their gentle exploration, brushing over her shoulders, her arms, tracing her collarbone. Each touch was like a question waiting for her response, and she answered him with each soft breath, each shiver under his fingers.

Their kisses deepened, her hands roaming his back, fingers pressing into him as if memorizing the sensation. His lips traveled to her neck, and she tilted her head, giving silent permission to explore. A thrill shot through her, drawing her further into a space where her usual control and caution had no place.

As he gently leaned her back onto the plush cushions, his hand slipped to the small of her back, supporting her as she settled beneath him, completely enveloped by his presence. Marcus's gaze met hers, his expression soft but with an intensity that made her heart race.

For a fleeting moment, she hesitated, the weight of her past pressing down on her, but his thumb brushed over her cheek, grounding her. "You're safe," he murmured, his voice barely more than a breath against her skin. "I'm here."

Her eyes fluttered closed, her hand coming to rest over his, squeezing gently. And in that moment, she let herself believe him, let herself trust that she was safe. She wrapped her arms around him, pulling him closer, letting herself be vulnerable in a way she hadn't dared in years. The last of her defenses fell away as she opened herself fully, meeting his gaze with an intensity that mirrored his own.

The room was quiet, save for the soft sound of their breathing, falling into a rhythm that made everything else seem distant, irrelevant. Marcus's fingers traced patterns across her skin, igniting sparks that chased away her fears. Her heart thudded in her chest, the sensation both exhilarating and unnerving. She wasn't used to feeling so exposed, so unguarded, but with Marcus, vulnerability felt almost liberating.

He leaned forward, lips grazing her collarbone, lingering as if savoring the taste of her skin. Ophira's hands slid over his shoulders, feeling the strength beneath her fingertips as her pulse quickened. She was letting go, allowing herself to exist in this moment without reservation, her mind emptying of all its usual questions, its careful calculations. She could feel his breath warm against her skin.

Marcus's hand moved to cradle the back of her head, his touch both gentle and possessive as he leaned down. Their eyes met, and she found herself lost in the blue depths of his gaze, caught between curiosity and something deeper, something she hadn't allowed herself to feel in centuries.

He brushed a strand of hair away from her face, his thumb tracing the line of her jaw as his gaze softened. "You're beautiful," he whispered. It was the kind of simple, honest compliment she rarely allowed herself to accept.

Ophira swallowed, her voice catching as she whispered back, "I don't usually feel this way." Her cheeks flushed, and she bit her lip, surprised at her own admission. Part of her wanted to retreat, to guard herself against the vulnerability she was exposing, but when she met Marcus's gaze, the warmth in his eyes reassured her.

"You don't have to be anything other than yourself with me," he said.

Marcus leaned in, capturing her lips in a kiss that was both tender and unhurried, as if savoring every second, every breath. Her hands drifted to his chest, her fingers curling into the fabric of his shirt, grounding herself in the solid warmth of him. His hand moved to her waist, pulling her closer, and she sank further into him, letting go of her usual restraint as she melted into the rhythm of their movements, the steady beat of his heart beneath her hands.

Their kisses deepened, the tension between them building like an unspoken current, drawing them together with an intensity that left her breathless. She found herself leaning into him, her body attuned to his every move, her every response an answer to his unspoken question. She could feel his hands moving over her, a careful exploration that made her shiver, her mind falling away from its usual logic, its usual caution.

As his hands slid over her back, tracing the contours of her spine, Ophira's senses heightened. Every moment was a question she was finally ready to answer, a part of herself she was finally willing to share. She tilted her head back, closing her eyes as his lips brushed the hollow of her throat, leaving a trail of warmth in their wake.

Her fingers slid up his back, her touch hesitant but filled with a longing she hadn't allowed herself to acknowledge until now. And in that moment, wrapped in his embrace, she experienced a strange, almost overwhelming sense of freedom, as if all the walls she had built to protect herself had crumbled, leaving only her bare, unguarded heart.

Marcus's hand slipped to the small of her back, grounding her as he held her close, his breath warm against her skin. The world fell away, leaving only the two of them, bound together in a shared vulnerability that was both exhilarating and terrifying. Her mind drifted, a single thought rising to the surface, piercing through the haze of emotions that filled her.

This is what it feels like to trust, she realized, her pulse hammering against her ribs. *This is what it feels like to let someone in.* After centuries of walls, of calculated distance, she chose to be human. To be vulnerable. To be real. The thought should have terrified her. Instead, wrapped in Marcus's arms, it felt like coming home.

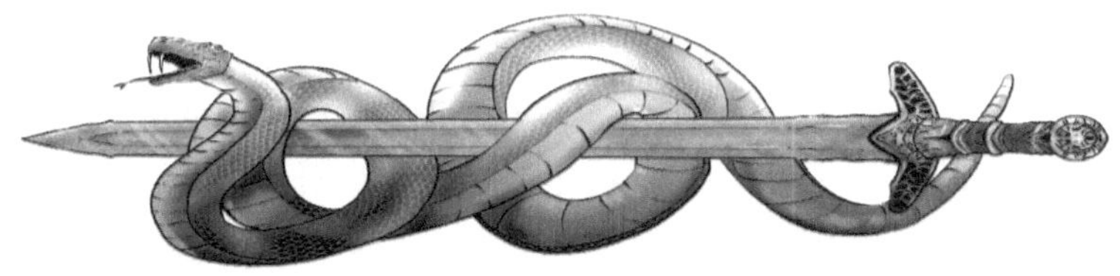

In the candlelit quiet of her apartment, she met his gaze, her own eyes soft, a quiet determination taking root within her. She was no longer afraid, no longer held back by the ghosts of her past or the weight of her secrets.

They remained that way, wrapped in each other's embrace, the weight of their shared trust settling over them like a fragile, precious thing. For the first time in her long, complicated existence, Ophira felt as if she could truly be herself, with no masks, no pretense. And as she looked into Marcus's eyes, she saw the same vulnerability reflected in her own, a silent acknowledgment of the risks they were both taking, of the delicate balance they were creating.

In the quiet stillness that followed, as they held each other close, a warmth settled in her chest, a fragile hope that maybe she had found something real.

She leaned into him, allowing herself to lose track of time, to let the world beyond this room slip away. The version of her who calculated every risk, who never trusted without evidence – that Ophira didn't exist tonight. Not here. Not now.

And for once, that felt like freedom.

His hands found their way to her waist, pulling her closer with a gentle insistence, and she responded, her arms sliding around his shoulders, feeling the strength there, a quiet reassurance amid her uncertainty.

They moved together toward the bed, their hands tracing the lines of each other's bodies with a mixture of reverence and restraint, as though learning a language both of them were only beginning to understand. As they sat together on the edge of the mattress, Marcus's hands found hers, fingers entwining as he looked into her eyes, his gaze deep, questioning. A strange sense of calm settled over her, not safety, exactly, but surrender without fear.

He leaned in again, his lips meeting hers with more intensity, a gradual deepening that left her breathless, her heart racing. Ophira let herself be pulled into the kiss, warmth flooding her senses, clouding her thoughts. His hands roamed up her back, drawing her closer until there was no space left between them.

The flickering candlelight cast soft shadows across his face, highlighting the intent in his gaze. His intensity pulled her closer, filling her with a desire that was equal parts thrilling and terrifying. His fingers slipped beneath the hem of her shirt, the warmth of his hand against her skin sending a wave of heat through her. She let out a soft sigh, surrendering to the moment, to the sensation of being wanted, of being seen.

For tonight, she thought, *I'll let myself feel.*

Her own hands moved to his shirt, fingers undoing the buttons one by one, feeling the heat of his skin beneath her. She could sense the shift in his breath, the way his pulse quickened under her hands, a small reminder that this was new for him, too, that he wasn't unaffected by her.

She sank into the duvet as his hands moved over her with gentle reverence, fingers tracing the lines of her collarbone and arms, as though committing her to memory. She closed her eyes, letting herself sink into the sensation, the quiet rhythm of his breath becoming her tether.

As the evening deepened around them, their intimacy grew. Each touch grew bolder, each kiss more consuming. His hands explored her with slow, deliberate care, drawing shivers along her skin. She relaxed beneath him.

She opened her eyes, looking up at him as he hovered over her, gaze filled with that same mix of tenderness and intensity. A vulnerability flashed in his eyes that mirrored her own, and an unspoken understanding passed in silence. Her hands found his face, brushing his jaw, memorizing the shape of him. This moment was fleeting, and she knew it. That didn't make it any less precious.

They moved together, breaths mingling, each movement a quiet affirmation. Her doubts receded beneath the growing stillness in her mind, a sense of calm she hadn't known in years. His hands grounded her even as she surrendered completely, opening herself in ways she hadn't dared for centuries.

In the quiet that followed, her head rested against his chest, listening to the steady rhythm of his heartbeat. His hand moved across her back, fingers tracing soft circles into her skin, a silent reassurance, a quiet claim. She let herself relax, the hush between them filling the room like breath.

Hours later, Ophira was still in bed, silk sheets cool against her skin as her eyes traced the shifting patterns of city light on the ceiling. Marcus slept peacefully beside her with his arm draped across her waist, warm and comforting in its weight.

Look at him, she thought, turning her head to study his face in the soft glow, marveling over his ability to relax. *Actually sleeping. Actually trusting.* In sleep, the charm was stripped away, revealing something that might have been sincere, which only made everything worse.

She'd let him see her. Not everything, never everything, but more than she'd allowed anyone in centuries. And he'd touched her like she was something precious instead of monstrous.

For the first time in millennia, someone had seen past the masks, past the careful constructions, to whatever was beneath. And he hadn't turned away.

She curled tighter under the silk sheets, the expensive fabric cool against her heated skin as she processed the unfamiliar sensation of being truly known. *This is what mortals call love, isn't it? This terrifying, exhilarating headlong plunge into the unknown.* She'd observed it for centuries, but never understood the gravity of it, how it could remake someone from the inside out.

But as sleep crept in, softer than she expected, one question remained, not born of suspicion but of wonder. *What if this is real? What if I'm actually capable of this?* The questions followed her into sleep, where her dreams were filled with light instead of shadows, hope instead of fear.

Beside her, Marcus lay awake, listening to the steady rhythm of her breathing. His hand moved gently across her back, and for the first time in years, he wasn't thinking about plans or outcomes. Some victories, he was discovering, felt remarkably like surrender.

CHAPTER FOURTEEN

BULLET TRAIN TO INFATUATION STATION

Morning light filtered through the windows, soft and golden. The closeness from the night before still lingered, but daylight sharpened the edges, making their intimacy feel heavier, more real. Sitting beside Marcus, she was acutely aware of how much she had let him see.

Ophira's living room was usually her sanctuary, a place where she could shut the world out, but with Marcus there, it was transformed.

The low hum of the city outside seemed distant while inside, the quiet between them was heavy with unspoken thoughts. Her home, so carefully curated to be both reflection and refuge, felt like a shared space, intimate in a way it had never been before.

Marcus sat beside her on the couch, relaxed but attentive, his eyes scanning the room and taking in the pieces of her life she rarely showed anyone.

"Sitting here with you makes me think about how different this feels from anything I've known before." He paused, seeming to gather his thoughts. "I don't usually talk about this, but growing up wasn't easy for me."

He glanced at her, gauging her reaction. Sympathy stirred in her chest. She had always sensed there was more to Marcus than what he presented to the world, but hearing him open up like this made him feel human.

"My father was everything to everyone," Marcus continued, his voice growing quieter, more raw. "A war hero, a community leader, the kind of man people wrote stories about. Everyone expected me to be like him, but I could never measure up. No matter what I accomplished, it was never enough. I learned early that showing weakness, showing that I was struggling... It disappointed people more."

Hearing his confession, she experienced a pang of understanding. *So he knows what it's like to live a vigilant life, to hide behind layers of secrecy. Maybe I'm not alone in this.* Something in his tone convinced her this wasn't something he shared lightly.

He ran a hand through his hair. "I've always had to keep my guard up, had to pretend I was stronger than I actually was. Everything I've built in my life, I had to build alone. But with you, it feels different. I feel like I don't have to pretend anymore," Marcus said.

Ophira's breath caught. Marcus's tone and the way he was opening up drew her in. She wanted to trust him, wanted to have faith that the man who had just shared his vulnerable side was the real Marcus.

He's letting you in, she told herself, *and it feels more true than anything has in a long time.*

"Marcus…" she began, her voice soft, unsure of what to say. She hesitated for a moment, then decided to let her own walls come down, just a little. "I know what it's like to have to be perfect for everyone else. Like showing any weakness would disappoint people."

Marcus's gaze sharpened slightly, though he kept his expression soft, sympathetic. "It's exhausting," he said. "Never being able to be yourself."

Ophira nodded, her fingers tracing the edge of the throw pillow in her lap. She chose her next words carefully. She wasn't ready to reveal the deeper complexities of her life, but there were parts of her experience she could offer – the pressure, the isolation, the weight of expectations.

"It is," she admitted quietly. "There are days when it feels like I'm losing myself in it. Like I'm not sure where the real me ends and the persona I've created begins."

Marcus leaned in slightly, his gaze never leaving hers. "But here, with me…you can be yourself. You know that, right?"

Ophira wanted to believe that. She wanted to let herself fall into this connection, to trust that Marcus was the person she had been searching for. *I want to trust him, and maybe I actually can. It's terrifying and wonderful at the same time.*

She bit her lip, her mind a whirlwind of feelings she hadn't allowed herself in centuries. There was something about Marcus that felt so right, and for once, she didn't want to analyze it to death. Maybe some things were worth the risk.

"You've been carrying this weight for so long," Marcus said, his hand reaching out to take hers. The warmth of his touch grounded her, steadying her in a way she hadn't expected. "You don't have to do it alone anymore."

"I'm not used to this," she admitted, her voice barely above a whisper. "I'm not used to letting people in."

Marcus's thumb brushed over her knuckles, his touch both comforting and reassuring. "I know, but you're doing it anyway. That takes courage."

The sincerity in his voice made her breath catch. *When was the last time someone looked at me with such understanding? When had anyone seen my struggles as strength rather than weakness?*

"I'm trying," she whispered, and realized she meant it entirely. "I want to try."

Marcus leaned forward, his lips brushing hers in a soft, tender kiss that felt like a promise. When he pulled back, his gaze was filled with warmth and something that looked remarkably like wonder. "We have time," he said softly. "All the time you need."

The morning had stretched into afternoon, and Ophira was amazed to realize she had utterly lost track of time. When had she last felt this comfortable with another person? When had conversation felt this natural, this necessary?

Ah, ma chérie, Valentina purred with satisfaction, *finally you embrace ze passion! Zis is what I have been waiting for! Ze bold choice, ze dramatic leap into love!*

Ophira smiled, surprised by how accurately that captured what she was feeling. She had spent so long running away from everything, it felt revolutionary to be running toward something.

Well, ain't you just glowin' like a firefly, Sunny said with warm affection. *That boy's got you smilin' in ways we ain't seen in centuries, darlin'. If he makes you happy, that's what matters to me.*

I'm still not convinced, Sage said flatly, his words cutting through the warmth. *Guy shows up outta nowhere with the perfect case, perfect timing, perfect everything. That's not how the real world works. But...you're gonna to do what you're gonna to do regardless of what I say.*

Ophira considered this, running her fingers along the edge of the couch. *I hear you, Sage. I do. But Marcus has earned my trust through his actions.*

After a light lunch and more conversation, Marcus glanced at his watch with obvious reluctance. "I should probably head home, let you have some space to think about all of this." He stood slowly, as if leaving was the last thing he wanted to do.

"I don't need space to think," Ophira said, surprised by the certainty in her voice. "But I know you have things to take care of."

Marcus smiled, the expression both grateful and relieved. "I'll call you tonight?"

"I'd like that."

As he gathered his things, Marcus paused at the door, turning back to her. "Thank you. For listening, for...everything."

After he left, Ophira found herself standing in her living room, still feeling the warmth of his presence. She felt like she wasn't carrying her burdens alone any longer.

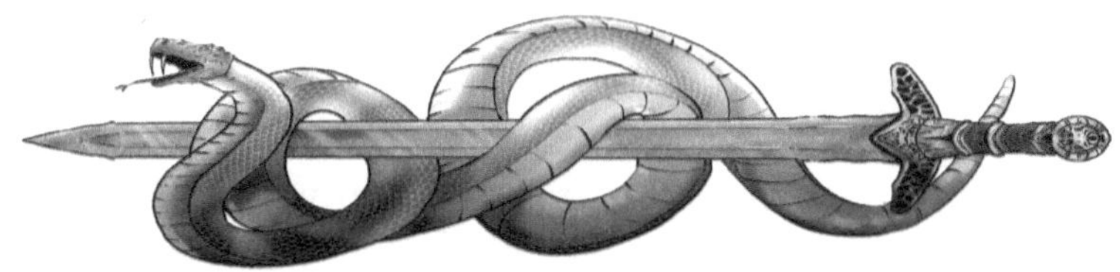

The next morning, Ophira sat at her desk, the early light seeping through the blinds and casting warm patterns across the room. She found herself smiling as she worked, her thoughts drifting to Marcus and the night they'd shared. She was surprised by how natural it felt, this growing intimacy, this sense of partnership both in the case and in life. *Maybe I've been guarding myself for too long. It feels good not to carry everything alone.*

Aric stepped into the room, the usual ease in his stride replaced by something more rigid, his features unusually taut. He held a stack of files, but it was the way his eyes scanned her that made Ophira pause. Shadows ringed his eyes, as if he'd spent the night turning over thoughts he didn't want to voice.

"Morning," she offered, setting aside the paperwork she had barely glanced at.

"Morning," Aric echoed, his tone careful, almost controlled. He paused by her desk before sitting across from her, leaning forward as if the weight of his words demanded it. His gaze locked on hers, hesitation and urgency warring in his eyes. "Ophira, there's something we need to talk about."

She raised an eyebrow, her stomach tightening at the seriousness in his tone. "What's on your mind?"

"I've been watching things between you and Marcus," Aric began, his voice both cautious and unyielding. "There's something about him I can't quite put my finger on. And I don't think you should ignore it. He's hiding something, I'm sure of it. From both of us."

Ophira leaned back in her chair, a slight frown creasing her brow. "Aric, we've been over this. He's been invaluable to this investigation. He's the one who brought us the case, provided the photographs, and connected the dots we would have missed. Without him, we'd still be chasing shadows."

Aric exhaled sharply, leaning back as his expression darkened with frustration. "I know you think that. But when this case came in, I dug into Marcus's background." His voice lowered, growing more serious. "What I discovered worries me. Or rather, what I couldn't discover. There's no trail."

"No trail?" Ophira repeated, her frown deepening, uncertainty pooling in her gut.

Aric gave a grim nod. "Nothing substantial from more than a few years back. It's like Marcus suddenly…appeared. No history, no record beyond a certain point. Like he was crafted out of thin air."

Ophira considered this, but didn't feel the alarm Aric clearly expected. She'd known from the beginning that Marcus was private, careful about his personal information. Given the nature of his work and the sensitive cases he handled, it made sense.

"Some people live off the grid intentionally," she said. "Especially in our line of work. Marcus has been transparent about everything related to this case – that's what matters. He's proven himself through his actions, not his paperwork."

"Maybe," Aric echoed, but his tone was skeptical, his gaze sharp. "Or maybe there's something he doesn't want us to see."

He's been open with me, she thought with certainty. She replayed their conversations, the nights they had spent together. He had shared pieces of himself with her. Painful memories about his father and vulnerable moments about feeling like he never measured up. Each time it felt sincere, like he was giving her something precious he'd guarded carefully. *That's not the behavior of someone hiding something sinister.*

"I appreciate your concern," Ophira said, her tone calm despite the unease building within. "But I've been in this game long enough to read people. Marcus hasn't given me any reason not to trust him."

Aric leaned forward, his eyes locked on hers with unrelenting intensity. "And what if you're too close to see the truth? What if you're missing something that could cost you everything?"

"Aric, I understand you're concerned," she said firmly, "but you're seeing problems where there aren't any. I've seen nothing but helpfulness from him. We're closer to solving this case than we've ever been, thanks to his insight and resources. Sometimes the simplest explanation is the right one. He's exactly who he says he is."

"It's the ones closest to us who can blind us the most." He leaned back slightly, his gaze never leaving hers. "All I'm saying is, don't lose sight of what's real. Be careful."

She understood his point but also trusted her judgment, her ability to read people after centuries of navigating dangerous situations.

Marcus has been invaluable, and more than that, he's been honest. The vulnerability he showed me this morning wasn't an act. The memory of his voice when he talked about his father, the raw honesty in his eyes, reinforced her confidence in her choice.

"I know you're looking out for me," she finally said, her voice soft but steady. "But Marcus and I… we're handling things. We're close. I can feel it."

Aric held her gaze and gave a small, reluctant nod. "Alright," he said, though the doubt in his voice was palpable. "But if something doesn't feel right, don't ignore it. Trust your instincts."

Ophira nodded absently, her mind already swirling with thoughts beyond the present conversation. She barely registered the soft click of the door as Aric left her alone in the quiet hum of the office.

Left alone in the stillness, Ophira leaned back in her chair, feeling more settled than she had in decades. Aric's warnings came from a place of love and protection, but they were rooted in his protective instincts, not evidence.

She sighed, rubbing her temples. The truth was, she had never been one to let people in, not really. Sure, she had friendships and working relationships, but everything was kept at arm's length. It had been like that for centuries, and it was easier that way. Safe. But Marcus had come into her life so unexpectedly, and he felt like a missing piece she didn't know she'd been looking for. Marcus had proven himself in every way that mattered.

You sure, Sage asked coolly, *or just hoping?*

She thought about the morning they'd shared, the way Marcus had opened up about his father, about the pressure he'd lived under. The vulnerability in his voice had been real, she was sure of it. After centuries of reading people, of surviving by understanding their true intentions, she trusted her instincts. And her instincts told her Marcus was exactly who he claimed to be.

She picked up her phone, smiling as she typed a quick message to Marcus about dinner plans. Aric would come around eventually. He always did when he saw she was set on her chosen path. And Marcus would continue to prove himself, as he had every day since they'd met.

Whatever challenges were ahead in the investigation, she was confident they could face them together. For the first time in centuries, she wasn't alone. And that felt like everything.

CHAPTER FIFTEEN

WHEN YOUR SPIDEY SENSE FINALLY GETS THE TINGLE

Weeks had passed since their first night together, and while their relationship had deepened, the investigation had stalled, and the mood around the office had grown tense. Ophira sat across from Marcus in her office, the remnants of their case notes strewn between them like puzzle pieces refusing to snap together.

The late morning sun filtered through the heavy blackout blinds she'd partially opened, casting warm geometric patterns across the polished black marble of her desk. Behind her, the security monitors showed their usual silent feeds, while an ancient statue tucked among her bookshelves seemed to watch their interaction with stone eyes.

Marcus's gaze flicked over her, his expression softening as he took in her tension. "You've seemed quieter lately," he observed gently. His hand rested on the edge of her desk, fingers drumming a rhythm that felt both reassuring and disconcerting. "I can practically hear the wheels turning in your head," he added, smiling as though he could read her thoughts.

She shot him a half-hearted grin. "That's my specialty."

Marcus tilted his head, studying her with that usual calm, which felt especially frustrating tonight. "We're on the right path, Ophira. This whole relic hunt is coming together because of you," he said, reaching across the desk to take her hand. "I don't want you losing sleep over it."

The moment his fingers touched hers, the sharp edges of her thoughts seemed to blur, like adjusting the focus on a camera until everything went soft. She blinked, trying to hold onto the thread of unease that had been building all week.

"I'll be fine," she replied, trying to sound assured despite the edge in her voice. "But... I don't know. Doesn't this whole thing feel a bit neat?" She tapped the scattered papers. "Like someone's left us breadcrumbs."

Marcus raised an eyebrow, his expression neutral. "You mean to tell me we're excessively lucky?"

"Exactly." Her fingers toyed with the edge of the desk as she avoided his gaze. "Lucky, as in someone who thinks they're playing god might be pushing us in the right direction." She chuckled, more to herself than him. "Honestly, this place has enough drama without adding megalomaniacs to the mix."

Marcus laughed lightly, though his grip on her hand tightened just slightly. "I'd chalk it up to skill. You've brought the right people together, the best resources. You know as well as I do how much time and effort have gone into this."

Ay, but darling, Valentina whispered dreamily, *such devotion, such partnership. He believes in you so completely.*

"Hmm," she murmured, his words sliding right past her growing suspicion. "That's all well and good, but don't you find it a little too perfect? Like we've got some invisible tour guide?"

Marcus shook his head, amused. "You're overthinking this, Ophira. You always do that when you're stressed." He squeezed her hand gently. "Trust me on this one."

Before she could respond, Marcus stood and moved around the desk, his hand settling on her shoulder with practiced ease. "You know what I think?" he said, his voice dropping to that warm, intimate tone that always seemed to cut through her defenses. "I think you're carrying most of this burden alone. You don't have to solve everything yourself."

His thumb traced a small circle on her shoulder blade, and despite everything, she felt herself beginning to relax. The questions that had been circling her mind all morning seemed suddenly less urgent, less important than the steady warmth of his presence.

"That's what partners are for, right? To share the load?"

Partners. When was the last time someone had offered to share her responsibilities rather than critique her methods?

Honey, Sunny whispered, *he just wants to help. That's what good people do.*

"Maybe you're right," she murmured, tilting her head slightly toward his touch.

The door creaked open, and Aric stepped in, a thick file tucked under his arm and determination sparking in his eyes. He glanced between the two of them, one eyebrow raised as if he'd caught them in the middle of something far less professional. Which, honestly, wasn't entirely off base.

"Got a lead," he announced, handing the file over to her with slightly more force than necessary. "This could be the breakthrough we need. Real evidence, not just convenient discoveries." His eyes flicked meaningfully toward Marcus.

Ophira took the file, flipping through the neatly typed pages. Financial records, shipping routes, and contact networks – all connecting their missing artifacts to a broader trafficking ring. It was extensive, detailed, and meticulously researched, precisely the kind of legwork that made Aric so valuable. She glanced up, impressed. "You really dug into this one."

Marcus, seated casually across from her, leaned in with a faint smirk. "Fast work, Aric. Though I can't help but wonder if we're ready to follow this one without digging a bit deeper first."

Aric's eyes narrowed, his posture stiffening slightly. "Pretty sure I wouldn't bring it here if I weren't confident. I've done my due diligence."

"Confidence is one thing. Being thorough is another," Marcus countered, his voice still gentle but with an edge that made Ophira's shoulders tense. "Let's make sure we're not jumping at shadows."

The tension thickened, and Ophira's gaze pinged back and forth between them, eyebrows raising as the barely veiled barbs continued. "Gentlemen," she said, cutting through the tension with sarcasm, "I'd like a day when we aren't walking on eggshells."

Aric snorted, leaning against her desk with a confidence she recognized from years of experience. "I want to be sure this lead isn't dismissed out of hand," he said, looking pointedly at Marcus. "Some of us actually track down information instead of waiting for it to fall into our laps."

Ay, dios mío, Valentina whispered theatrically. *Ze tension, ze venom, ze machismo. Are we to duel at dawn, or just throw chairs?*

Marcus's smirk didn't falter as he met Aric's gaze evenly. "I'm trying to make sure it's worth our time," he replied smoothly. "I'd hate for anyone's efforts to go to waste."

Ophira's hand tightened around the coffee cup, the warmth grounding her for only a moment before it slipped away. She hated how easily they both got under her skin, how easily *he* did. The tension pressed down like storm clouds ready to split, and she couldn't shake the feeling that something had shifted, even if she couldn't name it. The warmth of Marcus's hand lingered, but it didn't reach her. Between him and Aric, the distance felt insurmountable.

Honey, Sunny whispered, *you deserve better than bein' their battleground.*

"Enough," she said, her voice firmer than she felt. "Let's not turn this into a showdown, alright? We're all after the same thing." A part of her wasn't even sure what she was fighting for anymore. Peace? Progress? Or quiet? It all felt like noise now.

Aric's gaze softened as he looked at her, but the suspicion never left his eyes. "We should be a bit more careful." He met Marcus's gaze, his expression hardening. "Some people seem to fall upward. But the rest of us still have to fight for ground."

"Luck's relative," Marcus replied smoothly, though his calm demeanor was tinged with a subtle defensiveness. "If you've got something to say, Aric, don't hold back on my account."

Look, I ain't sayin' the guy's wrong, Sage muttered, sounding frustrated with himself. *But the math doesn't add up. Nobody's luck runs this consistently.*

The two of them stared each other down. Ophira felt as if she was caught in the middle of a silent battle. *You two do realize you're in my office, right? Not some kind of gladiator arena?*

She cleared her throat, standing up. "Alright, if you're done trying to out-brood each other, I need to wrap this up. We've got actual work to do here, not...whatever this is."

Aric gave her a sidelong glance, his expression softening as he nodded. "Right. Work." He turned his gaze back to Marcus, then shrugged as if dismissing the whole thing as inconsequential. "Fine. I'll let you keep doing whatever it is you're doing." Aric's voice was light, but his gaze stayed sharp, unrelenting.

Marcus met his stare with a slight nod. "Wouldn't want to keep you."

Aric shook his head, a mirthless smile on his face as he turned to her. "We'll talk soon," he said, his gaze lingering on her with an urgency that felt almost desperate before he walked out, the door clicking shut behind him with finality.

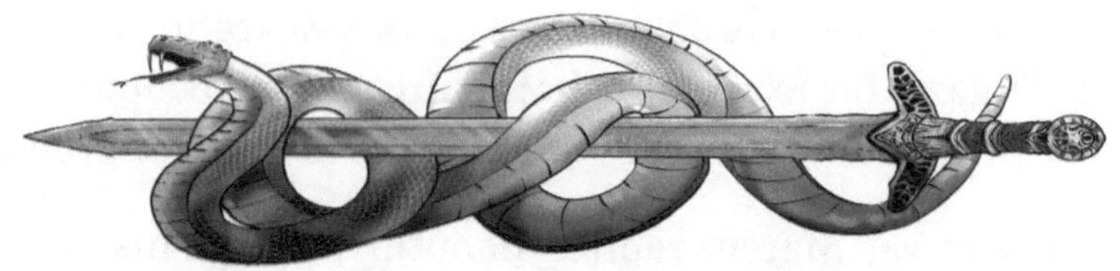

As soon as he left, the tension in the room felt a little lighter, though the silence between her and Marcus was no less charged.

"Aric's protective," Marcus said, his tone even, though she caught the faintest hint of something in his gaze she couldn't quite place.

"Of course he is. He's always on my side." She forced a smile, brushing off the tension. Aric always worried. That didn't mean he was right.

Marcus took her hand again, his fingers tracing small circles over her knuckles. The tension between them softened, and she allowed herself to relax. "There are no sides here, Ophira. We're working toward the same goal."

If only it were that simple. She held his gaze, trying to convince herself she didn't need to know everything yet. "I know. Let's focus on the work and check out this trafficking network Aric uncovered. If we can map out their full operation, we might finally get ahead of whoever's been moving these pieces."

As she said it, she couldn't help the twist in her chest. The conflict between Marcus and Aric was no longer easy to ignore. But Marcus was here, solid and reassuring, while Aric's warnings felt increasingly like paranoia.

"You know," Marcus said thoughtfully, "Aric's concerns aren't entirely unfounded. This case has had some convenient breaks, and I can see how that might seem suspicious to an outsider." He paused, considering his words carefully. "But sometimes breakthrough cases just happen that way. All the pieces suddenly click into place."

His understanding of Aric's position surprised her. Most people would have been defensive, but Marcus seemed thoughtful about it. "It helps that you're not taking it personally," she said.

"Why would I? He's looking out for you. I respect that, even if I don't think his fears are warranted." Marcus smiled, all calm confidence. "We can keep things simple. Work for now and dinner tonight?"

Ophira hesitated. The snakes didn't speak, but she felt them watching. Each was quiet in their own way, waiting to see what she would choose. Finally, she nodded, offering a faint smile. "Dinner tonight."

As Marcus left, the quiet of her office offered no solace. Aric's words clung like static, sharp and invisible, dancing beneath her skin. She leaned back, fingers tracing her coffee cup. Trust her instincts? They'd rarely failed her. But Marcus was different. She wanted to trust him, wanted to believe in his steady charm.

But trust had never felt this...complicated.

Alone now, she picked up Aric's file again, actually reading the details this time instead of just skimming. The financial records were thorough, cross-referenced, and methodical. The shipping routes formed clear patterns when she traced them with her finger across the map. For a moment, her mind felt sharp again, analytical. She could see potential connections and follow logical threads.

When had she stopped thinking this clearly during meetings with Marcus?

The question surfaced before she could stop it, and she set the file down quickly, as if it had burned her.

She searched her memory for times her instincts had failed her. Centuries of experience, thousands of dangerous situations. Nothing came to mind.

So why was she questioning them now?

Her gaze drifted over the latest notes and leads scattered across her desk, each one seeming to carry a question she wasn't ready to answer. There were too many perfectly timed discoveries, too many pieces falling into place like they'd been guided by an unseen hand. But who or what could be pulling the strings?

A part of her knew she needed to follow the thread wherever it led, but part of her felt safe in Marcus's warmth and wanted to believe there was nothing to chase at all.

She rubbed her temples, trying to soothe away the growing headache. The clarity she'd felt while reading Aric's file was already fading, replaced by the familiar haze of wanting to believe that everything was fine.

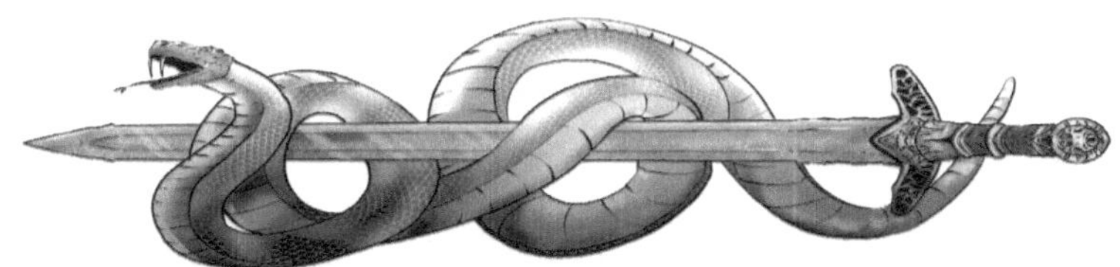

The café was tucked away from busy streets, dim lighting casting soft shadows over small tables. It was one of Marcus's favorite spots, chosen for being discreet and quiet, with a kind of intimacy that invited trust. They'd met here several times since their investigation began, discussing their progress on the relic case, catching up, and letting the romance unfold between them naturally.

Marcus pulled out a chair for her, a small but thoughtful gesture that, once again, tugged at her heart. He sat across from her, his eyes warm as he smiled. "I figured you'd need this after the week you've had."

Ophira let out a soft laugh. "Yeah, it's been a lot."

He reached across the table and gently squeezed her hand. "We'll figure it out, Ophira. We always do."

The moment his skin touched hers, those sharp thoughts from earlier – the clarity she'd felt reading Aric's file, the questions about her instincts – seemed to drift away like smoke. Marcus had always known how to calm her down. She let herself relax, if only for a moment, enjoying the quiet and the warmth of his hand over hers.

He's been nothing but kind, always supportive. Maybe it's easier to believe that than to keep pulling at threads I can't explain.

As they ate, the conversation naturally turned to the investigation into the relics. Marcus leaned back in his chair, casually mentioning a discovery that hadn't even been on Ophira's radar.

"I was digging through some older archives," he began, swirling his drink absently, "and I found a reference to a hidden chamber beneath the Temple of Nemesis. It hasn't been touched in centuries, but there are whispers that one of the relics might be housed there."

He paused, watching her reaction before continuing. "It's barely a footnote in any of the main texts, buried in a manuscript that most scholars dismiss as unreliable. But the details… They're too specific to ignore. Ancient protective wards, chamber layouts that match other confirmed relic sites."

Ophira set down her coffee cup, something cold settling in her chest despite the warmth of the café. The liquid tasted bitter on her tongue. When had that happened? She took a sip of water, testing. Normal. The bread on her plate was fine. Her saliva tasted normal. Just the coffee, then, when he started talking about convenient discoveries.

"Nemesis?" She narrowed her eyes, scanning her mental catalog of research. "That doesn't match up with anything I've come across. We haven't even discussed that temple as a possible location. Where exactly did you find this?"

Marcus shrugged, that easy confidence never wavering. "Cross-referenced some older mythological texts with geographical surveys. Took me most of the weekend, honestly." He leaned forward slightly. "The thing is, if I'm right about this, we could be looking at the sword, the one from the photographs."

Most of the weekend, Sage observed, and for once his voice cut through clearly. *How convenient that his research happens faster than ours.*

Now, Sage, Sunny chided. *Maybe he's good at this job.*

We're damn good at this job, but we ain't gettin' these kinds of results. Hell, even a broke clock's right twice a day, but this fella's hittin' bullseyes like he's got the target painted on the inside of his hat, Zeke shot back.

"What made you think to look at Nemesis specifically?" Ophira asked, and even as the words left her mouth, she felt that familiar tightness in her shoulders. The same feeling she'd had when things were about to go sideways.

"Process of elimination," Marcus replied smoothly. "We've covered the major sites, so I started looking at forgotten ones. Places that fell out of favor or were deliberately obscured." He reached across the table and gently squeezed her hand again. "I think this could be the breakthrough we've been waiting for."

That touch should have been reassuring. Should have quieted the static building in her mind. Instead, it felt like trying to listen to the radio through interference. The clarity from her office earlier, when she'd been alone with Aric's file, felt like a distant memory now.

Marcus always seemed to find exactly what they needed at precisely the right time. She'd spent days, weeks, poring over the same sources, yet he stayed consistently two steps ahead.

Perfect, she thought, her smile feeling strained. *Always so perfect.*

"Lucky, I guess," she said, forcing a chuckle.

Marcus smiled. "Maybe I've got a knack for digging in the right places."

A knack. The word sat heavy between them. When had anything about this case been easy enough to call it a knack?

She took another sip of coffee, trying to ground herself, but it tasted even more bitter now. Her instincts were screaming, but it was like hearing them through thick glass. Muffled. Distorted. Was this what it felt like to lose her edge? To be so distracted by intimacy that she couldn't think straight?

Are his contacts really that much better than mine? Am I really failing this badly?

"And the other relic sites?" she asked, testing the waters. "Any more lucky finds?"

He gave a slight nod. "Actually, yeah. I've been looking into a few locations. There's mention of a particular artifact connected to Mars. I didn't have all the details at first, but now it seems like we've got a solid lead. I think we should follow up on it next."

Of course there is, the voice in her head whispered, but even that felt dampened somehow, like her own thoughts were wrapped in cotton.

This feels wrong, Sage muttered, frustration bleeding through his usual logic. *The pattern recognition part of my brain is screaming, but I can't figure out why.*

The conversation shifted into safer territory, but Ophira couldn't shake the feeling that something fundamental had shifted. Not just in the case, but in her ability to navigate it. For centuries, her survival had depended on reading situations, on trusting the warning signs that kept her alive. Now those signals felt scrambled, unreliable.

Was Marcus really that brilliant? Or was she so far out of her depth with this relationship that she'd lost the ability to see clearly?

As they walked back toward her office, Marcus's hand warm against the small of her back, Ophira found herself caught between competing truths. The warmth of his touch, the genuine care in his voice, the way he'd held her like she was something precious rather than monstrous. That was real. She could feel it.

But so was the cold knot in her stomach. The sense that she was missing something crucial, something that should be obvious if only she could think past the haze of wanting to trust him.

I'm losing my edge, she thought, and the realization sent a chill through her that had nothing to do with the weather. *I'm compromised.*

The question was whether she was compromised by her inexperience with intimacy, or by something else entirely. Something she couldn't afford to ignore, even if she couldn't name it yet.

Back in her office, alone again, Ophira sat at her desk and stared at the scattered case files. The same files that had yielded nothing for her but seemed to sing their secrets to Marcus. Her reflection caught in the dark window, and for a moment, she looked like a stranger to herself. Softer. More vulnerable.

More human.

The terror she felt was sharp. She wasn't just changing – she was losing the very thing that had kept her alive for centuries. The ability to trust herself.

She'd never looked in a mirror and failed to recognize the predator staring back. Now she saw someone who smiled more easily, who leaned into touch, who second-guessed the very instincts that had kept her alive.

She pressed her palms against her temples, trying to sort through the noise in her head. The Nemesis temple. The Mars artifact. The impeccable timing of every discovery. The solutions appeared just when they were needed most.

It couldn't be mere luck. It couldn't be only skill. No one's research abilities were that precise, that consistently on target. But admitting that meant admitting something else entirely – something her compromised judgment couldn't quite grasp, even as the evidence mounted in front of her.

Tonight, she could only sit with the pattern she could see but couldn't trust herself to believe.

Chapter Sixteen

Fortune Cookies Aren't Supposed to Be This Ominous

Though Ophira had tried to dismiss her suspicions about Marcus, they lingered, growing in unexpected ways. It wasn't Marcus himself gnawing at her thoughts; it was the relentless string of uncanny coincidences surrounding him.

Their investigation had gained unexpected momentum. Each day seemed to bring them closer to the relics, with one lead after another landing in their laps. Marcus had always been good at tracking down obscure details, but recently? Recently, he seemed almost otherworldly in his ability to pinpoint exactly what they needed.

It began subtly, as if chance were nudging them forward. They'd hit a dead end researching historical anomalies when Marcus walked into her office, holding a scroll he'd supposedly unearthed from a forgotten corner of the archives.

"Looks like something interesting," he'd said, waving it like it had just fallen into his lap. The scroll described an ancient blade with the ability to sever deceit, a weapon that had appeared throughout history during times of upheaval.

The discovery was monumental, giving their search a clear direction after weeks of frustration. But the more she thought about it, the less sense it made. She had practically lived in the archives for days, combing through everything she could get her hands on. *Could she have missed it? Or had someone placed it there recently, waiting for the right moment?*

The question tormented her enough that she and Aric spent hours reviewing their security footage, scrutinizing every frame from the past month. Access logs, camera feeds, motion sensors: they examined it all with the thoroughness that had made their reputation.

Nothing.

No unauthorized entries, no suspicious activity, no gaps in coverage. The scroll had either been there all along, somehow overlooked despite her exhaustive search, or something far more troubling was at play.

Or what? She couldn't finish the thought. *Someone with the skill to bypass their security systems entirely?* It seemed impossible, yet the alternative that she'd missed something so obvious felt equally unlikely.

But she'd brushed it aside, chalking it up to an oversight on her part. *I'm overthinking it,* she told herself, trying to focus on the progress they were making. *Marcus isn't the type to lie. He's been incredibly helpful. So why does everything feel so choreographed?* But when a similar situation arose, her doubts began to grow.

She was digging through case files, this time following up on reports of unusual artifact thefts. The leads were vague at best, and Ophira had been piecing together scraps of information for hours. As she was about to call it a night, Marcus had shown up once more, this time with auction records he'd obtained from a law enforcement contact who'd helped bust an illegal antiquities ring, describing an ancient ceremonial vessel designed for "capturing and preserving essences". The description of such a vessel could be the urn they were looking for.

Ophira had stared at him, her mind struggling to make sense of it. *What are the odds?* But Marcus merely shrugged it off with a smile. "A hunch," he'd said with that easy smile of his, as if he'd casually stumbled across something helpful. "You know how it is. Sometimes you have to trust your instincts over pure research. I hope you don't mind me following up on leads independently." The gentle implication that her methodical approach might be limiting hung in the air.

Ophira had hoped that focusing on the work would make things feel less intense, but the pattern continued. Every time they hit a dead end or roadblock, Marcus seemed to come up with the ideal solution.

Like the time they'd been investigating reports of cursed jewelry appearing in estate sales. The details were maddeningly vague, and they'd been going in circles for hours. Then, as if on cue, Marcus produced a fragment of a tablet along with fresh academic research containing new translations. He'd somehow managed to translate the ancient Greek himself.

She couldn't hold back her skepticism and stared at him, eyebrow raised. "Where did you even find this?"

"Storage room downstairs," he'd replied smoothly. "Guess it got overlooked. I know you're thorough, but even you can't catch everything. Sometimes it takes a fresh perspective." The translation referenced 'Hieros Desmios tēs Archiereias', meaning 'Sacred adornment of the High Priestess', and he was sure it was a reference to the necklace. Drifting underneath his compliment was the subtle suggestion that her exhaustive search had somehow been insufficient.

Overlooked. She'd forced a smile, filing away the growing list of timely finds. *Maybe it's not Marcus that's the problem. Maybe it's everything around him.* The thought crystallized with uncomfortable clarity. *Someone with real power is orchestrating this. Marcus might be another piece being moved around the board, same as me.*

The idea that they were both being manipulated sent a chill through her, somehow more unsettling than thinking he was the manipulator. The uneasy thought kept nudging at her, and despite her attempts to brush it off, she couldn't deny it anymore: too many things were falling into place. *What if we're being led?*

The question haunted her late at night when she found herself staring at case notes, trying to understand how they had moved from one dead end to breakthrough after breakthrough with such ease. *What if someone's guiding us? Or worse, what if they're leading us astray?*

Over the following days, the coincidences continued to mount. Marcus's ease with "finding" information, the hints in the historical records that seemed to come when they needed them most, all felt controlled. *Someone's pulling the strings,* she realized, a sense of foreboding settling over her.

One afternoon, they worked through another series of relic leads. Ancient maps and yellowed writings covered every surface of her desk, the late sunlight streaming through the windows casting long shadows across the scattered documents. Marcus was guiding them with a strange assurance that seemed to intensify her suspicions. She didn't dare voice them, not yet. But she couldn't help feeling as though every step they took was mapped out for them, as if their every move was being manipulated from the shadows.

Her gaze drifted over the latest series of leads, her pulse quickening. Things were falling into place, almost as if someone had planned it. Marcus always seemed to know exactly where to find the information that they were looking for. Was it his intuition or something far more dangerous?

When he suggested dinner that evening, she found herself accepting, hoping that time away from the investigation might clear her head. Maybe she'd be able to see past the feeling of invisible hands guiding their every discovery.

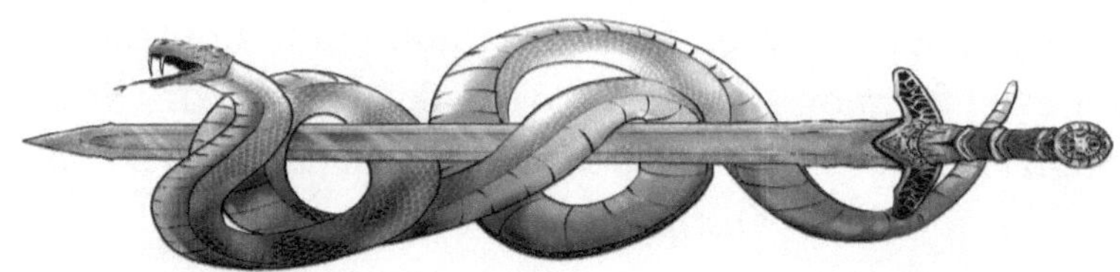

Marcus had just dropped her off at the restaurant's corner, his eyes lingering with that familiar, soft look. Usually, she'd let that gaze stay with her, settling into the calm it promised. But tonight, her mind was everywhere except on the moment they'd shared.

Their date had been perfect, or close to it. Every detail fell effortlessly into place, each smile and laugh fitting together with an ease she hadn't let herself believe in for a long time. Someone like Marcus, steady and reassuring, made everything look seamless. Yet, the harder she tried to believe in the picture he painted, the more it felt like a stage set with props instead of substance. Like she was a bit player thrust onto the stage to play the lead without the experience to pull it off.

Get a grip, she told herself, tightening her coat against the sudden breeze. Her fingers brushed the edge of a pocket, checking for the reassuring weight of her keys. *You're overanalyzing again.* But maybe it wasn't about Marcus at all. Maybe she didn't remember how to feel safe anymore.

Ophira hugged her coat closer as she stepped into the narrow, dimly lit alley connecting the main street to her apartment. Her boots clicked softly against the cobblestones slick with rain, the sound sharp and out of place in the stillness. She carefully adjusted her stride to avoid the uneven stones, her free hand brushing the hilt of the concealed blade beneath her coat.

Distant streetlights reflected in distorted patterns on the damp ground, shifting like ghostly shapes. The walls rose in shadows, old and worn, bricks absorbing light and leaving only thin slivers of silver. She could feel the chill creeping up from the damp ground, wrapping around her ankles and spiraling into the back of her mind.

Shoot, ain't this cozy? Zeke muttered dryly. *About as fittin' a place for the zombie apocalypse to kick off as a saloon is for shootouts and bad decisions.*

Sage's tone was analytical. *Tactically speaking, the tight space limits your movement. Stay alert.*

Oh, ze drama of it all! Valentina exclaimed. *Like a scene from a noir film! Shall we encounter ze villain next?*

Sunny's voice broke through gently. *Y'all are so dramatic. She's got enough goin' on already without y'all trying to scare her.*

Their voices grounded her, even as tension coiled in her shoulders. *Right. Eyes open, ready for anything.*

The street had emptied as she moved further from the main road, shadows pooling in every corner, clinging to the edges of light as if they hid something more. A drip echoed nearby, its hollow plunk like a heartbeat in the silence, drawing her eyes to water trickling down the walls. Her mind retraced each recent memory, looking for anything she might have overlooked. The way Marcus always seemed to know the next step in their hunt for relics... It should've been reassuring. But paired with his calm in danger, it unsettled her in ways she couldn't quite explain.

The uneven pavement caught her heel, jolting her from her thoughts. She caught herself against the damp brick wall, pulse spiking as adrenaline shot through her veins. She glanced over her shoulder, scanning the alley's quiet expanse. Empty. But the shadows seemed heavier now, thicker, as if they were watching, waiting.

Am I letting myself get too close? Why do I keep brushing off these feelings? Has he made it easy to stop guarding the edges? Irritation itched at the edges of her mind. Her instincts had kept her alive this long. Ignoring them wasn't just foolish, it was dangerous. And yet Marcus had a way of blurring those instincts, lulling her into complacency just when she needed to stay sharp.

Her jaw clenched as she forced herself to take a deep breath. He was, by all appearances, her ideal match: intelligent, resourceful, calm under pressure. But real life wasn't a fairy tale, and she knew better than to believe in perfection. It was a mask, one that people wore to hide their vulnerabilities, their flaws. She had worn it herself for centuries, after all.

But what if it wasn't Marcus wearing the mask? What if she was waiting for the other shoe to drop, even when there wasn't one? Her mind spun with a thousand versions of the truth – none she could pin down, and all of them whispered from the same place: fear. Not of him, not really. She was terrified of what closeness could cost if she was wrong.

The dim light caught her reflection in a nearby shop window. She paused, staring at the face looking back. *Medusa.* The name resonated in her mind. The reminder grounded her, pulling her back to the version of herself that trusted no one quickly, the version that kept her guard up, even when no one else could see it.

But wasn't she more than that now? She had let her walls down with Marcus, allowed herself to believe in something better. Was it wrong to trust him, to think he could be different?

A flicker in the shadows made her tense, senses sharpening. She scanned the alley, her heart pounding, but there was no one there – just the shadows cast by dimly glowing lanterns above. She let out a shaky breath, though her muscles remained coiled, ready. Trusting someone didn't mean letting her guard down completely. She was still herself – still wary, still prepared for whatever was around the corner.

See that? Zeke muttered. *Something moved. Don't like it.*

Valentina hissed dramatically. *A phantom, perhaps! Or ze harbinger of doom!*

It's nothing, Sage said, his tone calm. *Could be wind or an animal. Don't overreact.*

Sunny added softly, *But don't let your guard down, sugar. Somethin' feels off.*

Ophira tightened her grip on her coat, her pulse quickening. It's only the wind, she told herself. But the unease in her gut said otherwise.

With her gaze fixed on the path ahead, she forced herself to focus. Whether the unease came from him or from her fear of falling, she'd figure it out on her terms. She didn't need to choose all or nothing. She could stay in control and keep watching.

It was that sense of control, that balance between her heart and her mind, that finally let her take the next step.

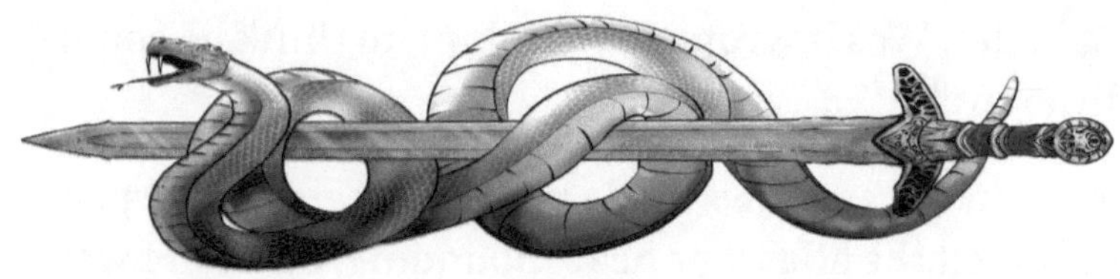

The night's stillness pressed in around Ophira as she walked, her thoughts bouncing between the haze of her suspicions and the pull of her emotions. The damp chill of the alley clung to her, amplifying her unease, but she kept her senses tuned to the dark. That was when she felt it. A shift in the air, subtle but undeniable, like a whisper in her ear.

Her steps faltered, the scrape of her boot against the stone breaking the alley's stillness. Her gaze flickered over the shadows that pooled between the stone walls, her pulse quickening with every passing second. She glanced over her shoulder, heart thudding in her chest. Nothing. The hollow drip of water and the muffled hum of distant traffic. Slowly, she turned forward again. And froze.

Someone stood at the alley's end, her figure veiled in shadow, so still it was almost as if she were part of the stone itself. A woman. Tall and willowy, her silhouette somehow graceful, too serene for the bleak surroundings. She was wrapped in a robe of white and gold, delicate symbols woven into the fabric, shimmering faintly in the dim light like ghostly ink.

Ophira's body responded before her mind could catch up. Her muscles tensed, shoulders squaring as her hand instinctively drifted toward the concealed blade at her side. She shifted her weight, one foot sliding back on the slick stones, ready to spring at the slightest hint of danger. Every fiber of her being screamed for action, yet she held herself still, her instincts warning her that this wasn't a threat she could simply fight off.

Her senses sharpened, instincts on edge as she assessed every detail: the narrowness of the alley, the slickness of the cobblestones, the figure standing unnaturally still in the shadows. A chill prickled along her spine as the woman's unblinking stare bore down on her, silent, observant, as though peeling back each layer of her thoughts. Every muscle was ready to spring, yet something held her in place. A quiet instinct warned her the real threat wasn't physical.

But the woman stood there, her eyes fixed on Ophira, wide and pale green, almost luminous in the darkness. Flecks of gold seemed to shift and swirl within them as if carrying glimpses of something beyond human understanding, an awareness that struck Ophira as distinctly unsettling.

Who is that? The question jolted through Ophira's mind, but her instincts kept her ready, body in defensive stance, prepared to unleash her powers if necessary. This woman wasn't a typical threat. That much was clear. There was no malice in her eyes, no indication of hostility, yet something about her presence set off a warning deep within Ophira's bones. It was an ancient, almost primal sense of danger, different from the physical threats she was used to.

Her face was like something out of a dream, or perhaps a nightmare. Her skin held an eerie glow, pale and ethereal against the surrounding shadows. Silvery blonde hair cascaded around her shoulders like a river of light, contrasting with the alley's darkness. Her head was slightly tilted, and her full lips were parted, as though she were on the verge of speaking, of whispering some forbidden truth.

Every inch of the woman was immaculate, flawless in a way that only heightened Ophira's suspicion. People didn't look like that. This was someone touched by something beyond the ordinary world. And if her posture was any indication, she was used to being noticed, to being seen and revered, maybe even feared.

Ophira's pulse pounded in her ears as she took in the figure before her. The woman's stance was still, as if frozen in place, yet it held a calm poise, a controlled grace that spoke volumes. There was an absence of movement, of breath, that defied the usual life pulsing in any living creature. She looked like a statue in a temple, as though she belonged to the stone and shadow around her, or perhaps they belonged to her.

Ophira's grip tightened, but she fought against the urge to attack. There was no sign of aggression, no telltale shift in the woman's body language to indicate a threat. *But that doesn't mean she isn't dangerous.* This lack of hostility was what unsettled Ophira the most. There was something about her that radiated a quiet, simmering power, like the calm before a storm, and yet it was layered with a softness that pulled at Ophira's curiosity.

The woman's hands, clasped loosely in front of her, bore faint, silvery lines – a lattice of marks that almost resembled scars but were neat, too purposeful to be random. They looked like traces of ritual, the results of years of ritualistic work. The marks caught Ophira's gaze, her instincts flaring again. Such markings didn't come from idle hands; they were a testament to someone who dealt in forces beyond the mortal realm.

Ophira took a slow, deliberate breath, keeping her gaze locked on the woman's as she tried to regain control of her heartbeat. *This isn't a physical threat,* she reminded herself, *but that doesn't make it safe.* She relaxed her fingers, though every fiber of her being remained on high alert.

The woman tilted her head a fraction, her lips curving into a faint, almost knowing smile, as though she sensed the inner conflict raging within Ophira. Her eyes gleamed in the dim light, catching that eerie, unnatural glow that reminded Ophira of something otherworldly, something divine. Or dangerous.

Who is she? Ophira's mind reeled, struggling to place this woman, to make sense of the strange aura she carried. This wasn't just some random person wandering through a dark alley at night. This was someone who knew things, who held knowledge that had been hidden away from the world. But why had she appeared here, now, at the tail end of her quiet evening with Marcus?

The silence stretched between them, thick and heavy, as Ophira remained motionless, waiting. The woman's eyes continued to watch her, those pale green orbs flickering with secrets she wasn't ready to reveal. Her gaze held Ophira in place, and in those few moments, it felt as though they stood on opposite ends of a veil, each aware of the other's existence, but separated by a force beyond their control.

There was something unsettlingly familiar in the woman's stare, a sense that this wasn't the first time they'd crossed paths, even though Ophira knew they had never met. It was as though the woman had always been watching her, even from a distance, observing her every move with a silent intensity. A shiver ran down Ophira's spine, and she fought the urge to look away, to break the spell that held her in place.

Instead, she held her ground. "Who are you, and what do you want?"

But the woman only smiled, the faintest hint of amusement dancing in her gaze, as if she found Ophira's defiance charming. She took a single, deliberate step forward, her movement as smooth as silk, her robes whispering around her like a sigh. The action, though small, sent a surge of adrenaline through Ophira's veins, her instincts urging her to back away, to put distance between herself and the enigmatic figure.

Yet something held her in place, something more profound than fear. A strange, inexplicable pull rooted her to the spot, forcing her to stay and confront the mysterious woman before her. It was as though a thread bound them, an invisible line that connected them across time and space, and the thought unsettled Ophira more than any weapon could.

The woman's gaze softened, her expression growing almost… sympathetic, as if she could see the turmoil within Ophira, the tangled mix of suspicion, fear, and curiosity that raged in her heart. She raised one hand, pale fingers reaching out as though to touch something unseen, to bridge the distance between them.

Ophira's muscles tensed once more, her breath catching in her throat as the woman's fingers hovered mere inches from her face, her gaze unblinking, unwavering. In that moment, it was as if the world around them ceased to exist, leaving only the two of them standing in the shadows, caught in a delicate balance between danger and discovery.

Ophira's pulse thundered in her ears as she waited for the woman to speak, her fingers twitching with the instinct to move, to defend herself. But that serene gaze held her firmly in place, and something within Ophira, the same instinct that told her to trust her senses over her suspicions, whispered that this was no ordinary encounter.

The woman's voice, soft yet clear, whispered through Ophira's mind like a bell's chime, "Who am I? The better question is, who are you?"

Ophira flinched, instinctively clenching her fists as the voice wrapped around her, lingering in the air long after the words were spoken. The sound was unlike anything she'd heard before. Smooth, lilting, with a tone that seemed to carry not just words, but a weight of inevitability. This was a voice that spoke not of possibility, but of certainty, a voice that whispered of destiny.

The woman's gaze softened, and her voice, low and melodic, drifted through the silence. "You feel it too, don't you? The secrets, like buried whispers, are waiting to surface."

Ophira swallowed, her throat dry as she forced herself to meet those pale green eyes, flecked with gold, each fleck catching the dim light like firelight on water. "Who are you?" she demanded, willing herself to sound steady. "What do you want from me?"

A faint smile flickered over the woman's lips, her expression as enigmatic as the shadows around them. "Names are but a veil," she murmured. "Most people call me Delphine. But you, Ophira, are you who you claim to be?"

The question struck her like a blow. Ophira's mind reeled. Am I? The question twisted, heavy and unsettling. "I...don't know what you're talking about," she managed, though the tremor in her voice betrayed her.

The woman's gaze never wavered, her eyes flickering with something ancient, something knowing. "Not yet," she replied, her tone one of gentle inevitability. "But you will."

A chill crept down Ophira's spine, and she fought to keep her expression steady, her fingers instinctively curling into fists. *Who is this woman, and what does she know?* The thought clawed at her, the questions piling up with no answers in sight. She straightened, pushing down the wave of unease. "If you have something to say, then say it. I'm on my way home, and I'd like to get there soon."

Delphine tilted her head, her expression softening as though she pitied Ophira. "Very well," she said, her voice quiet yet commanding.

"When the viper bares its fangs, the snake-charmer's song will lead you astray," Delphine intoned, her voice carrying an unsettling rhythm. "Trust not the lullaby, for the sleeper wakes to strike again."

Well, that's ominous, Zeke drawled. *Love me a good cryptic riddle.*

It's a metaphor, Sage said. *Likely tied to the case. Focus on her tone and choice of words.*

Valentina hissed sharply. *Or it is ze prophecy! She speaks of danger unseen!*

Take it all with a grain of salt, darlin', Sunny advised. *Riddles ain't always what they seem.*

Ophira stared at Delphine, her thoughts spinning as the woman's words took root. *Viper... Lullaby... What does it all mean?*

Ophira blinked, the riddle echoing in her mind, twisting and turning like the coils of a serpent. "The...viper?" she whispered, frowning as she struggled to parse the meaning. "Snake-charmer's song? What are you talking about?"

Delphine's gaze remained steady, her eyes unblinking as though she were peering through Ophira, into something unseen. "The song lulls you into forgetting, into trust," she replied softly. "But trust is a fragile veil, and when it shatters..."

Ophira's pulse quickened, the cryptic message prickling at her nerves, each word sinking in like a stone into deep water. *A warning? But about what...or who?* Everything felt interconnected lately. The relics. The investigation. The way events kept falling into place.

"What does that mean?" she demanded, her voice sharper than she intended. "Viper, lullaby... What kind of danger are you talking about?"

Delphine's faint smile was as chilling as it was mysterious. "The truth lies in fragments, Ophira. Pieces of a past you've yet to face," she replied, her voice a soft murmur. "You have the pieces. It's up to you to assemble them."

Ophira's mind raced, the cryptic words a puzzle she wasn't sure she wanted to solve. But Delphine's gaze held a certainty, a knowledge that was both compelling and terrifying.

"Why should I believe you?"

The woman's eyes softened, her expression almost desolate. "Believe or not, the truth will find you." Her voice was as gentle as it was unnerving. "Beware the song that lulls you, for it holds a sleeper's sting."

The riddle spun through Ophira's mind, a dark tapestry of foreboding. "Who are you?"

Delphine held her gaze, her own eyes seeming to pierce through Ophira's defenses. " A witness," she said, her voice carrying an otherworldly echo. "To fate."

Ophira shivered, teetering on the edge of something incomprehensible. "You talk like fate is fixed," she said, her voice low, defiant. "But fate is what we make it."

A flicker of amusement danced in Delphine's eyes, a look that held an unsettling depth. "Fate is not a path you create but a path you uncover," she replied, her tone softer now. "The veil lifts only when you're ready to see."

Ophira clenched her fists, her mind racing as she tried to make sense of Delphine's words. But the stranger's face betrayed nothing more, her expression still and unyielding as a statue. The riddle gnawed at her.

Ophira's grip tightened as she watched Delphine, her heart beating in erratic rhythm. Every instinct told her to remain on high alert, but something about this woman kept her frozen in place. A sudden gust whipped through the narrow alley, its chill seeping into her bones, as though the air itself recoiled from Delphine's presence.

Delphine's gaze flickered with unreadable light as she stepped closer. "You're restless. Caught between the known and the unknown." Her eyes remained fixed on Ophira, piercing through her with a gaze that felt intimate.

The alley seemed to shrink around them, the shadows deepening, pressing close. A shiver ran down Ophira's spine, her pulse quickening with a mix of anxiety and strange curiosity. This woman wasn't just speaking; she was dissecting her, peeling back layers Ophira had spent centuries building up.

"What do you know?" Ophira's voice was barely a whisper, her usual confidence slipping under the weight of Delphine's penetrating gaze.

The faintest hint of a smile touched Delphine's lips. "More than you could bear, perhaps," she replied, her voice both a challenge and a warning. "After all, secrets buried in stone do not remain there forever."

Ophira felt her skin prickle, as though her very being was exposed under the woman's gaze. The air thickened, and a low rumble of distant thunder echoed through the alley, heightening the oppressive atmosphere. "Enough with the riddles," Ophira said, her voice harder now, laced with defiance. "If you have something to say, say it plainly."

Delphine's expression softened, a faint sadness flickering in her eyes. "Very well," she said, her voice dropping to a murmur that somehow cut through the weighty silence. "You tread on treacherous ground, Ophira. Choices lie ahead that will test even the strongest hearts. But be careful..." Her gaze held Ophira's with a gravity that sent another chill down her spine.

"Be careful, Medusa. The past has a way of returning when you least expect it."

The name struck like a thunderclap, each syllable reverberating through her. Her breath hitched, a memory surfacing from the depths. A flash of stone and screams. The weight of centuries pressed against her chest. *Medusa.* Her heart faltered, leaving a hollow ache in her chest. It wasn't just her name. It was her truth, exposed without warning, leaving her raw, vulnerable. *How does she know who I am?* The question pulsed through her mind, a frantic beat of disbelief and vulnerability. *I haven't been called Medusa in so long... Who is this woman?*

A shuddering breath escaped her as her mind reeled, caught between denial and the undeniable truth of Delphine's words. "What do you want?" she demanded, voice low, steely, but colored with the barest tremor.

Delphine's gaze softened, her expression unreadable but tinged with something close to empathy. "Want? It's not what I want," she said, each syllable like the ringing of a distant bell, tolling softly but insistently. "It's what you must decide. In the end, truth is the only armor worth having. And I think you know who you must trust to carry it."

Ophira stared at her, trying to process the weight of her words, but each sentence only splintered into more questions, more uncertainties.

Delphine turned, her robes swirling around her like mist as she stepped back into the shadows. But before she disappeared completely, she cast one final look over her shoulder, raising her hand in warning as her eyes met Ophira's with a solemn intensity.

"Remember, Medusa. Trust only those whose truth is as clear as glass. All others carry shadows of their own."

She lowered her hand, her expression shifting to something more serene, almost wistful. Then her voice dropped to barely above a whisper, carrying an odd weight that made the air itself seem to thicken.

"But I'm afraid you'll only see the horizon after the mountains have crumbled to dust." Her eyes held a distant gleam, as if she were seeing something far beyond the narrow alley. "When that time comes, and it will come, we'll find each other again in the ruins."

A strange smile played at the corners of her mouth, equal parts promise and farewell. She turned away, her form blending seamlessly into the darkness, until she was nothing more than a shadow, leaving Ophira alone in the alley, heart pounding, her thoughts spinning wildly with questions she couldn't yet begin to ask.

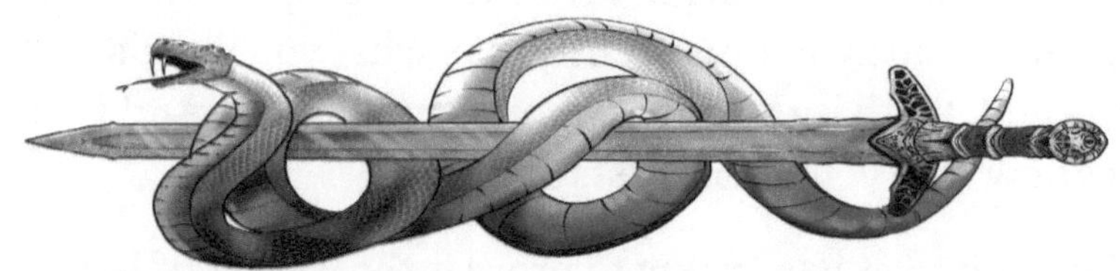

Ophira's mind raced, grappling with the strange encounter, the woman's haunting gaze still lingering in her thoughts. The question hung heavy in the air, echoing within her, a reminder of a truth she wasn't yet ready to face.

Ophira stood alone in the alley, shadows shifting around her like restless phantoms. Her pulse still raced, senses thrumming with the aftershock of her encounter with Delphine. *Delphine, the Oracle,* she realized, feeling the chill of it seep into her bones. The thought bloomed slowly, settling with a sense of inevitable certainty. It explained the woman's eerie omniscience, her otherworldly demeanor, and the warning that carried the weight of prophecy.

She hadn't heard anyone speak of an Oracle in centuries. That Delphine had addressed her as Medusa, as if her hidden identity were common knowledge, was unnerving in itself. But an Oracle knowing her true name… That changed everything. The truth, held tightly for so long, had been exposed in a single moment, as though it were another thread in a tapestry woven long ago.

Delphine's final words echoed in her mind, each syllable burrowing deeper, leaving a hollow ache in its wake. She had survived countless battles, her identity hidden for years. Yet here, beneath the Oracle's piercing gaze, she felt stripped bare, secrets exposed like unguarded stone. She could no longer pretend she was simply an observer in this mystery. She was woven into its very heart. *Medusa.* Hearing the name from someone else's lips, after all this time... She swallowed hard, feeling as though she'd been stripped bare, her secrets laid open in the quiet dark.

A cold gust swept through the alley, ruffling her hair and sending a chill down her spine. She drew her coat tighter, feeling as though the wind carried Delphine's haunting presence. The encounter had left her feeling exposed, as though someone had peeled away the thin layer of normalcy she'd wrapped herself in, revealing the truth beneath. But how much did Delphine know? And how much of it was connected to the relics? The question lodged itself in her chest like a splinter she couldn't dislodge, no matter how tightly she tried to hold on to her calm.

There's more going on than I realized, she thought, her chest tightening with the weight of it all. *The relics... Delphine... Even Marcus might be in deeper than he knows. What am I caught up in?* The Oracle's voice echoed again, threading between her thoughts like a net pulling tight.

The questions swirled like dark currents beneath her thoughts, pulling her deeper, stirring suspicions she could no longer ignore. For weeks now, she'd been trying to bury the unease gnawing at her, to convince herself that the strangeness surrounding Marcus was only her overactive mind. But now her doubts felt like cracks spreading through stone, widening with each moment of hesitation.

As she turned to leave the alley, her gaze caught on a faint, pale shimmer on the cobblestone where Delphine had stood. The soft glow seemed to pulse, like an echo of the Oracle's presence, as if some part of her lingered even after she'd vanished.

Ophira drew in a shaky breath, her fingers flexing unconsciously at her sides. The weight of the encounter pressed against her chest, her heart hammering as she stared at the empty space.

She ran a hand over her coat in a futile attempt to ground herself. She wasn't just piecing together fragments of an ancient mystery; she was part of it. The relics, her relationship with Marcus, even Delphine's sudden appearance all felt interconnected, woven into a web of secrets that spanned far beyond her understanding. And as much as she wanted to dismiss the Oracle's riddles, they'd lodged deep within her, feeding her growing distrust, intensifying her uncertainty about Marcus.

She pressed a hand to her temple, trying to silence the relentless flood of questions. But it was impossible to shake the feeling that she was teetering on the edge of something vast and perilous, something that could unearth truths she wasn't prepared to face.

Finally, she turned, casting one last look over her shoulder. The alley was still, as though Delphine had never been there, leaving only the chill in the air and the whisper of her warning. *Trust only those whose truth is as clear as glass.*

The city lights felt distant, muted, as though she'd stepped from one world into another, where shadows carried secrets she hadn't yet uncovered. She was left in a state of emotional turmoil, each step homeward heavy with the realization that everything she once believed about herself and about Marcus now hung by a thread.

As she walked home, every shadow seemed to hold uncovered secrets. Delphine's warning gnawed at her, each word casting new doubts that whispered to her, but she clung to the belief that Marcus was one of the few things she could still count on. The veil between truth and deception felt thinner than ever, and whatever was beyond, she would find it.

MARIONETTES AND MISERY

Ophira sat alone in her office, the dim evening light filtering in through narrow windows, casting long shadows across her desk. She traced the grain of the polished wood absentmindedly, her mind still wrapped around the encounter with Delphine, the Oracle.

Medusa. The name reverberated in her mind like a quiet storm, each echo stirring memories and fears she'd buried long ago.

You've got that look again, Sunny said softly. *The one that says trouble's brewin'.*

Zeke interjected, his tone dry. *Trouble's always brewin'. The question is, how big's the pot this time?*

Bigger than usual, Sage muttered, his voice heavy with calculation. *Delphine's words weren't just cryptic, they were loaded with hidden messages. Whatever she meant, it's tied to something critical.*

Valentina hissed dramatically. *Shadows and secrets and serpents, oh my! I do love a dramatic act two, chérie.*

Ophira rubbed her temples. *Not helping with the anxiety, guys.*

What am I caught up in? The question held an unfamiliar weight now, each warning Delphine had whispered lingering in the silence, unsettling. The trust she'd placed in their shared mission felt suddenly fragile because of what she didn't know.

So many pieces, so many players. One wrong move, and everything could shatter. Every fiber of her being was telling her to be cautious, to watch for signs she'd been missing.

The creak of the office door jolted her back to the present. Marcus entered, his steps light but purposeful, followed closely by Aric, whose usual silent presence brought a grounding calm to the room. Ophira straightened, willing herself to set aside the swirl of doubts, if only momentarily.

"I think we have a lead," Marcus said, steady and self-assured. He held a rolled map in one hand, his eyes sparking with a restrained excitement, oblivious to the tension lingering in her mind.

Ophira tilted her head, keeping her expression neutral. "Oh?" she asked, masking her lingering unease.

Marcus crossed the room, unrolling the map across her desk with care. "A cave," he explained, his finger trailing along a marked line in what appeared to be the Peloponnese region of Greece. "I tracked down references to it in some old records. It's located in the Taygetus Mountains, a remote and difficult to reach area. It could be another location tied to the relics."

Ophira watched, forcing herself to breathe evenly, her gaze zeroing in on a small, nearly forgotten mark on the map. A dark dot nestled within the familiar ridges of the Taygetus range.

A distant recognition stirred, unsettling her even before the memory fully resurfaced. Her chest tightened, memories pressing against her like a forgotten dream, breaking free at last.

"This cave," Marcus continued, oblivious to her reaction, "is remote, difficult to reach, and positioned in a way that would make it an ideal hiding place. It could lead us to the second relic."

Ophira's fingers curled against the edge of her desk, knuckles whitening. No, it couldn't be... *Could this be the same place?* She'd never told anyone about it. But maybe it wasn't the same. Maybe she was seeing ghosts in the lines.

Still, the cave on the map stirred something familiar. Her former home. A sanctuary she had sought centuries ago when she was most vulnerable. A place that had sheltered her during the darkest moments of her existence.

She swallowed hard. "It's...remote. You're right. Hard to reach." Her tone was measured, casual, though her heart thundered against her ribs. "Are you sure it's worth the risk?"

Marcus glanced at her, a hint of curiosity flickering in his gaze, but he merely nodded. "Definitely. If the relic is hidden there, it could change everything."

The weight of his words settled in, and as much as Ophira wanted to hide her reaction, she could feel Aric's eyes on her. He stood at a slight distance, his expression calm yet attentive, his gaze flicking between her and Marcus.

She glanced away, dismissing the thought. It was easier to pretend he didn't sense her unease, even as her gaze returned to the map, her mind swirling as the cave's image anchored her firmly in the past.

She could almost smell the cold, damp air of that stone sanctuary high in the Taygetus peaks, feel the rough rock beneath her fingers, and the way shadows had clung to the walls as if drawn to her like a silent witness.

It had been her refuge, her place of isolation where she'd hidden from a world that would never understand, carved into the ancient mountains that had sheltered her for centuries.

She remembered the nights. The quiet nights spent watching the stars from the cave's entrance, the silence wrapping around her like a protective shroud. Yet, there had always been a lingering bitterness to it, a reminder that this cave, as much as it shielded her, was also her cage.

There, surrounded by cold stone, she'd wrestled with loneliness and anger, casting her memories into the walls as if they could somehow hold the weight of her pain.

A beat passed, and Aric spoke, his tone mild but somehow piercing through the tension. "It's a risky location. We should make preparations." He met her gaze, a silent understanding passing between them. While his words were pragmatic, she could feel a layer beneath them. A slight hesitation, as though he sensed something in her discomfort, though he gave no outward sign.

Marcus's gaze shifted to her, his brow furrowing slightly. "You seem...uneasy. Are you sure you're alright?" His voice carried that familiar note of gentle warmth that always made her feel both cared for and somehow foolish for worrying.

Ophira forced a slight smile, brushing away his question with a dismissive hand. "It's the location. It's not the easiest terrain to cross," she replied, keeping her voice level. "I don't relish the idea of navigating mountain paths."

"Of course," he said, his expression softening with understanding. "I can see why remote locations would make you nervous. It's perfectly natural to feel apprehensive." The way he said it made her caution sound both reasonable and slightly excessive.

The worry in Marcus's gaze lingered only a moment before he looked back down at the map, his face returning to that familiar, confident mask. "We'll need to plan this carefully."

Ophira nodded, her mind racing, even as she forced herself to keep her expression neutral. Every part of her instincts screamed at her that this was no mere coincidence, but she couldn't voice her confusion. Not yet. She needed time to sort through it, time to be sure she wasn't seeing ghosts in the mirror again.

She turned away from him, unable to shake the feeling that she was missing something, something evident to everyone but her. It wasn't that he was holding back. It was that she might not know how to see clearly anymore. She needed action, proof, or something more concrete than a mere feeling.

Marcus unrolled several maps detailing the terrain surrounding the cave. The topography was intricate, each line marking the jagged peaks and narrow trails they'd need to navigate through the Taygetus range. He pointed out specific paths, his finger tracing routes that wound through pine forests and limestone ridges, his knowledge as precise as if he'd been there himself.

"We'll need to be prepared for anything," Marcus said, indicating a switchback trail that led up from the valley floor. "The weather can be unpredictable at this altitude. Sudden fog banks can roll in from the coast, and the temperature drops quickly after sunset. Some of these paths are treacherous, especially where the limestone has eroded."

He traced a line that led directly to the cave's entrance, nestled high on a cliff face. "But if we stick to this shepherd's route I've mapped out, avoiding the steeper rock faces here and here, it should be straightforward."

Ophira studied the map, noting how he'd marked elevation changes, water sources, and even what looked like seasonal weather patterns. Every word he spoke only deepened her discomfort. *How does he know all this?* She tried to keep her expression neutral, to hide the doubt clawing at her. *Does he know more than he's telling us? Or is it all a coincidence?*

Her thoughts raced, each question stacking on top of the other, creating a wall of uncertainty that felt impossible to climb. *The timing of everything – the warehouse discovery, the expertise falling into place, this perfectly mapped route... It's as if invisible hands were arranging the pieces.*

"I appreciate the research," she said carefully, measuring each word. "It sounds like you've put a lot of thought into this."

Marcus met her gaze, his expression relaxed. "Every detail counts," he replied, his voice unwavering. "We're getting closer and need to be prepared for anything. I want to make sure we don't miss any opportunities. I've gathered all the supplies and put the plane on standby. It's waiting for us whenever we're ready."

Aric held his gaze, then turned to her, his eyes flickering with understanding, recognizing that she was uneasy about this lead. She took a quiet breath, steadied by his silent support. The sense of impending discovery loomed, settling on her shoulders like a dark shroud.

She nodded, the weight of their approaching journey settling on her shoulders. The memory of the cave, her former home, loomed large in her mind, filling her with a mix of dread and anticipation. Each step now felt like a step back into a past she had tried so hard to forget.

The cave was waiting for her. Both her past and the future seemed woven into it.

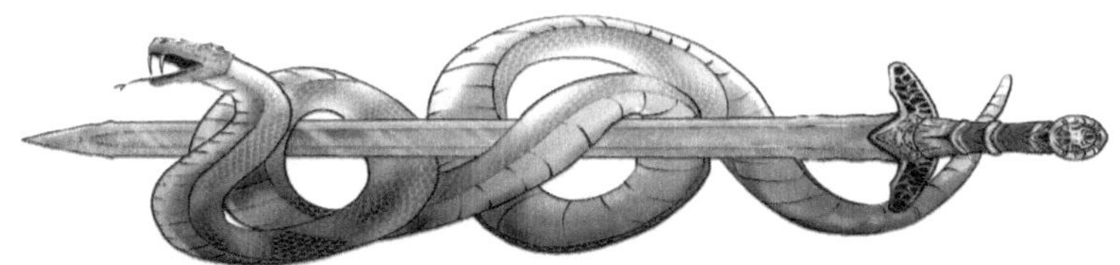

The sleek elegance of Marcus's private plane wrapped around Ophira like a velvet glove, each surface designed to exude opulence. Soft lighting bathed the spacious cabin, casting a warm glow on leather seats soft as clouds. Gold accents gleamed subtly from the edges of polished walnut tables, while the faint, indulgent aroma of cedar and citrus permeated the air. She settled into the wide, plush seat opposite Marcus, a luxury that never quite felt like hers. It was a world she understood but never embraced: all polish and comfort, yet never truly safe.

Marcus sat across from her, his posture relaxed, one arm casually draped along the seat, his eyes scanning a document he held with the calm intensity she'd grown accustomed to. A tray of sparkling water, wine, and chilled glasses had been laid out in the space between them, as though they were embarking on a leisurely holiday rather than the uncertain journey to the depths of her past.

Her fingers trailed absently over the armrest, but her thoughts roiled beneath the smooth veneer. This place, this moment, felt almost perfect. She glanced at Marcus, watching him in his element, seemingly unaware of the disquiet simmering beneath her gaze, and let herself admire his quiet confidence, his unshakable composure. How many times had she leaned into that calm, that reassurance? Yet now that very composure set her on edge.

How many coincidences can there be? she wondered, her mind racing. Her fingers tightened around the glass of water she'd poured, the coolness grounding her as her thoughts spiraled. She watched his careful movements, each gesture so precise, so composed. It was the same calm she'd leaned on so often, and yet today, it felt more rehearsed than natural. *Someone's co-ordinating this whole investigation, but is Marcus the puppet master or another puppet? I thought I knew the answer to that before Delphine, but now I have no idea what to think.*

Marcus glanced up, his eyes meeting hers with that welcoming smile of his. "Everything alright?" he asked, his tone as smooth as silk, devoid of any indication that he might suspect the storm brewing within her. "You seem a little tense. I hope I haven't done something to worry you."

Ophira forced a smile, shifting slightly in her seat to keep her unease hidden. "Of course," she replied, her voice calm. "I'm preparing myself for the terrain. It's been a while since I did a mountain hike."

"It's perfectly natural to feel anxious about challenging terrain after time away. I should have considered physical conditioning when we were planning the trip." His concern felt real, yet something about the implication of her delicateness made her stomach tighten.

He nodded, a hint of a smile playing at his lips, and returned to his document, oblivious to her watchful gaze. She tried to keep her expression neutral, yet her mind raced with the memories of the cave, of her former sanctuary, and the secrets she'd buried there. She thought back to Delphine's warning, the veiled cautions she hadn't been able to shake since that encounter in the alley. *What if this is all a trap?* The thought twisted inside her like a knot, her instincts urging her to stay vigilant, to guard herself.

Her attention drifted to the luxury around her, each fine detail amplifying the surreal nature of the situation. The opulence felt like a distraction, a beautiful mask over something deeper, older, and far more dangerous. How effortlessly he maneuvered through this life of wealth, leading her seamlessly along with him.

She turned to the window, watching clouds drift by, each one blending into the next as the plane sailed through the endless sky. The path ahead felt hazy, obscured and full of shadows. She could feel Marcus watching her from the corner of his eye, his expression unreadable as ever.

I want to trust him, she thought, an ache tightening in her chest. *But why does everything feel like it's being organized around me?* Something about this place made every choice feel pre-written, as if she were retracing someone else's design.

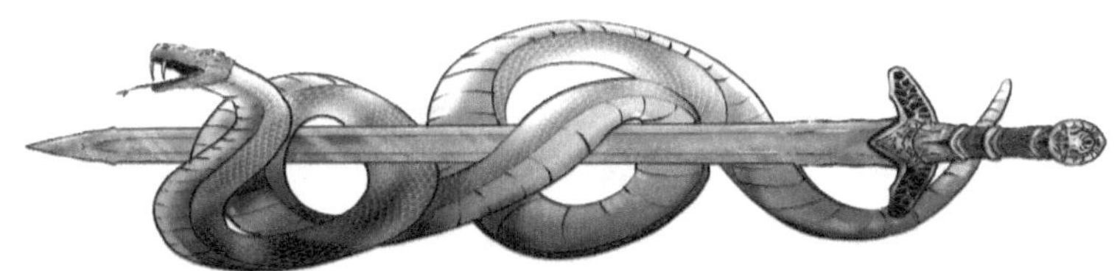

The plane touched down with a gentle jolt, the last rumble of the engines fading into a quiet stillness as the cabin lights dimmed. Ophira followed Marcus and Aric out, her gaze scanning the small, private airport – a far cry from the bustling terminals she knew. A sleek black SUV waited on the tarmac, thanks to Marcus's connections, which apparently granted them the best possible arrangements.

As they drove deeper into the wilderness, winding up roads that carved through the foothills of the Taygetus Mountains, the scenery shifted from sparse fields to dense forest. Tree shadows flickered across the windows, the dimming daylight creating an interplay of gold and violet hues against the twilight.

Ophira watched the world blur by, feeling the shift in atmosphere, the silence in the car mirroring her inner conflict. The polished luxury around her – the soft leather seats, the quiet hum of the engine – only emphasized the distance between this moment and the first time she had made this journey.

When they reached the edge of the trail, the quiet hum of the car gave way to a tranquil, unsettling silence. Marcus parked, checking his watch before glancing back at Ophira. "It's not a long hike," he said, as if the mountain path ahead was nothing more than a casual walk. "We'll make it before sundown. I know you're feeling some anxiety about the terrain, but I wouldn't have suggested this route if I weren't confident you could handle it."

Aric gave her a brief nod, falling in behind as Marcus took the lead. His jaw tightened almost imperceptibly as he watched Marcus's confident stride, but he said nothing. Whatever doubts he harbored about Marcus, he was keeping them to himself now.

Ophira's heart thrummed in her chest, and as her feet met the dusty, dry ground of the Taygetus trail, she felt an unsettling familiarity. Each step felt heavier than the last, not from the incline, but from the weight of memories uncoiling deep within her.

The air was cooler, thinner, and tinged with the chalky scent of limestone and dry earth that she remembered from these ancient peaks, mingling with the faint aroma of pine sap and moss.

As they ascended, the forest grew denser, the towering trees stretching skyward like silent sentinels. Sunlight broke through in thin shafts, illuminating patches of forest floor and casting everything in a surreal, green-tinged glow.

Marcus moved with practiced ease, his footsteps confident as he led the way. It was comforting in one sense, and yet it left her wondering how he always seemed to know where to go.

Her gaze wandered, drawn to the subtle details of the landscape – the colors rich and vivid, the shadows long and almost tangible. Every so often, a bird would take flight in the distance, its call piercing the stillness, echoing across the mountain.

She glanced back at Aric, who met her gaze with steady, silent support. He didn't know the depths of what was beneath her calm exterior, but he appeared to sense the gravity of the journey, the weight it held beyond the relic itself.

When they reached a particularly steep stretch, Aric held out a hand, steady and ready. She met his gaze with a small, grateful nod, her breathing shallow as she adjusted to the thinning mountain air.

Memories flickered like apparitions at the edge of her vision, fragments of a time when these Taygetus peaks had served as both her sanctuary and her prison.

Calculate the risk factors, Sage counseled. *Emotional distraction plus difficult terrain equals a higher probability of mistakes.*

Valentina tossed her head dramatically. *Bah! Our magnifique Ophira conquers all challenges! Ze mountain should fear her, not ze other way around!*

Easy does it, darlin', Sunny said warmly. *You've climbed tougher mountains. Ain't nothin' we can't handle as a team.*

Exactement! Valentina declared. *We are your faithful companions through zis treacherous journey!*

Treacherous journey? Zeke snorted. *It's a hike, Princess Drama. Maybe save the victory speech for when we ain't still climbin'.*

She's fine, Sage interjected. *Focus on the terrain ahead. There's an incline to the left that could cause problems, so watch out for the loose shale.*

Ophira smiled faintly despite herself. *At least some things never change.*

Oh sugar, we're just lookin' out for you, Sunny added warmly. *All this mountain air and memories stirrin' up, you need us keepin' things light.*

"How are you holding up?" Aric asked, his eyes flicking between her and the path ahead. There was no judgment, only a quiet empathy that she found grounding.

Ophira swallowed, trying to keep her voice even. "I'm fine," she replied, though the tension in her chest told a different story. Her gaze drifted to Marcus, who continued ahead, his back straight, shoulders relaxed.

They climbed in silence for a while, the path narrowing and growing rockier, the air cooler, each breath filling her lungs with the crisp bite of altitude.

She could almost feel the past pressing in on her, memories of climbing these same trails, her steps hurried, desperate for safety, seeking escape from the world that had branded her a monster.

The mountain trail wound higher, the incline steepening, and Ophira's steps grew heavier. She could feel the cold stone underfoot, the earth dry and crumbling in places, and the familiar strain in her calves as they pressed forward. The silence was broken only by the faint rustling of leaves and the occasional crunch of pebbles dislodged underfoot.

As the path curved upward, Marcus paused, glancing back with a hint of a smile. "Almost there," he said as if oblivious to the significance this place held for her.

Ophira nodded, forcing herself to breathe evenly, though her mind was a chaotic swirl of memories and suspicions. *How did he find this place?* The question clawed at her thoughts. She couldn't voice it, but it gnawed at her, each step up the mountain feeding the feeling that someone, or something, was guiding them toward a trap. *But if he's being used too, then who's really behind this?*

The possibility that neither of them was truly in control sent a chill down her spine that had nothing to do with the mountain air. She glanced at Aric, who offered her a quiet, reassuring nod, as if sensing the torrent of doubt raging within her.

His eyes flicked briefly toward Marcus's back, a shadow of apprehension crossing his features before returning his full attention to her.

The path finally leveled, allowing them a brief respite. Ophira took in the view, the valley sprawling beneath her like a distant memory, the distant peaks cloaked in a veil of twilight.

Shadows pooled over the land, long fingers stretching across the forest, casting everything in a deep, dusky hue that absorbed the last light of day.

Ophira's gaze lingered on the dark mouth of the cave. *Some things are mine alone to bear,* she thought, stepping forward.

As they drew closer to the cave's entrance, she felt her heart stutter. The dark opening yawned before them, a void nestled into the mountain's side, filled with shadows that stretched back into a place she had once called home. The sight of it hit her with unexpected force, memories flooding her senses with nearly suffocating intensity.

She hesitated, feeling the weight of Marcus's gaze as he glanced back at her, his expression curious. She willed herself to step forward, her pulse quickening as she drew nearer to the entrance.

She could almost feel the cool stone beneath her fingertips, the rough texture against her skin, as if the cave itself were welcoming her back. She had spent centuries pushing these memories away, burying them under purpose and survival, but now they rose with vividness she couldn't ignore.

The cave loomed before her, dark and unyielding, a silent reminder of all she had lost and survived. She took a steadying breath, feeling Aric's presence beside her, and cast one last glance at Marcus. He couldn't know what this place meant. To him, it was simply a destination.

To her, it was everything she'd buried. This wasn't just another location, another place on their map. This was where her old life ended and the new one began. A place shaped by pain and transformation, buried under centuries of silence.

Marcus stopped, casting a glance back at her. "Ready?"

She hesitated, feeling a shiver as she stepped closer. The shadows seemed to stretch toward her, welcoming her back into their cold embrace. The cave was a door to her past, a mirror reflecting every moment of fear and loneliness she had faced within its walls.

Aric's presence, quiet but unwavering at her side, reminded her she wasn't alone this time. He anchored her to the present, warding off the ghosts of memory that threatened to consume her.

She swallowed, her throat dry, forcing herself to nod. "Ready as I'll ever be."

As she crossed the threshold, the familiar scent of damp stone and ancient earth filled her senses, anchoring her in memories she wasn't ready to relive.

She felt her breath catch, a strange, almost painful ache blooming in her chest. Her past was waiting here, wrapped in stone and shadow, and there was no escaping it now.

Oh, honey, Sunny said softly. *I know this place holds painful memories, but you're stronger now. You ain't facin' this alone.*

Valentina's voice quavered with emotion. *Sacré bleu! Ze weight of centuries presses down! But our brave Ophira, she will triumph over zis darkness, oui?*

Reckon some places just got too much history packed into 'em. But hey, you've survived worse than memories, darlin', Zeke muttered, his tone dry as desert wind.

Sage's tone was measured and strategic. *Emotional responses are understandable, but stay focused. This cave contains information we need. Analyze the environment. The answers are here.*

Ophira moved deeper into the shadows. *I'll face whatever's waiting. I have no choice.*

CHAPTER EIGHTEEN

YOU CAN'T GO HOME AGAIN (BUT HERE WE ARE)

The remote mountain cave loomed before them, its entrance carved into the cliff face like a wound in the stone. As Ophira approached, a shiver ran down her spine, colder than the biting mountain air. The entrance yawned wide and dark against the pale stone of the cliffside, an inky void that had once been both shelter and prison.

She fought to keep her face neutral, glancing at Marcus, who was already scanning the entrance with an expression of mild intrigue. He couldn't possibly understand what this place meant to her, how each stone held memories she'd kept buried. Sharing this place with anyone was a violation, like baring a wound she had never intended to reveal.

Towering pine trees flanked the entrance, filtering fading daylight and casting the cave in ethereal gloom, as though cloaked in a veil to keep prying eyes at bay. Each step closer brought with it a cascade of recollections, memories slipping out of the shadows like whispers.

The cool, damp scent of stone and earth wrapped around her, musty with centuries of stillness – a sensory recollection as visceral as a touch, carrying with it the metallic tang of old memories. The long-forgotten air of isolation wrapped around her, the weight of solitude that had once defined her days here slipping back into her mind like a forgotten song.

Ophira crossed the threshold.

As they neared the threshold, she hesitated, her gaze trailing over the uneven stone at her feet. She remembered every crack, every contour of the rock, the small grooves her constant restless pacing had worn into the stone. Even the scratches along the entrance, remnants of her frustrated moments of anger, were there, each mark another reminder of the years she had spent in confinement.

Heart hammering, she forced herself to step forward and cross the threshold. Her fingers mechanically grazed the cool rock as she entered, feeling its chill seep into her skin, grounding her to the place, to the echoes that still lingered here.

The silence stretched until her snakes stirred, bringing her back.

Y'know, Zeke said, breaking the silence, *this place screams 'bad memories'. You sure you wanna do this?*

Sage cut in sharply. *She doesn't have a choice. This is necessary. The answers are here.*

I hate to agree with Zeke, Valentina muttered, *but zis place, it oppresses ze very soul. Ze shadows, they cling like secrets refusing to die.*

Sunny's voice softened. *You're strong, Ophira. Ain't nothin' in this cave that you can't handle, darlin'.*

Ophira let out a shaky breath, willing herself forward. *Strong? Sometimes it doesn't feel like it.*

Within moments of entering, Marcus moved with a quick, assured gait, already peering around the space, his gaze flitting over the stone walls and untouched corners with a clinical interest. But to Ophira, every inch of this space held layers of meaning, echoes of her life here. She swallowed as memories sharpened, faces and voices flickering in her mind's dim recesses.

This was where she had hidden herself, after the world deemed her a monster.

Back then, seclusion was her only sanctuary, yet it had also been her tormentor. In this very space, she had come to terms with the life she'd been forced into, the identity thrust upon her. She remembered the rage that had simmered within her, how it ebbed and flowed with the seasons, eventually transforming into exhausted acceptance. The cave had witnessed it all: her nights of silent fury, her days of dull, ceaseless quiet.

She heard the sound of footsteps shifting behind her, and she glanced over her shoulder to see Aric standing just within the entrance, his face carefully blank as his gaze met hers. He had no way of knowing the true history this place held for her, but his presence was strangely comforting, as if he could sense the weight this journey bore for her. She let her gaze linger on him before turning her attention back to the shadows ahead.

The narrow passageway opened into a wider chamber, perhaps thirty feet across, with rough-hewn walls that disappeared into shadow above. The air hung thick and still, untouched by the outside world for centuries. She took a deep breath, feeling the stale air fill her lungs, grounding her in a way that was both painful and soothing. The space hadn't changed, not in any way she could notice. Time had left it untouched, just as it had preserved the memories she had tried so hard to bury.

Her eyes adjusted to the dim light, and as she took in the familiar layout, her chest constricted, breath faltering as memories she'd buried for centuries clawed their way to the surface. This was her home.

Home. She had walked these same floors, mapped out every crevice and corner with the desperation of someone who had mistaken a cage for sanctuary. Her fingers brushed over the rough stone wall, lingering on the grooves she had carved herself, small marks of rebellion against a fate she had never asked for.

As Ophira stepped into the cave's entrance, the familiar cold pressed in, wrapping around her like a memory given form. Shadows stretched across the walls, lingering over old sconces where torches had once flickered. The fire pits she'd tended long ago were now filled with ash and dust, their edges softened by time. The faint remnants of smoke still clung to the stone in places, a ghostly reminder of her nights spent huddled beside the warmth, drawing herself into a quiet cocoon far from the world that had cast her aside.

The cave was larger than it appeared from outside, opening into a sprawling space that had once been her home, each corner filled with something she'd left behind. Along the left wall, near what had once served as a kitchen area, a worn stone counter held the remains of her former life: chipped pottery, rusted cooking utensils, and a small stack of stones she'd arranged to heat water over carefully tended fires. A rough-hewn table sat at the far end, its surface covered in a thick layer of dust, though she could still make out scratch marks she'd left in its wood during restless nights.

Ophira's gaze traveled to a small alcove in the back, hidden from view at the main entrance, her eyes trailing to the pallet of threadbare blankets arranged in the corner, their fabric brittle and worn, scattered with pine needles and the faintest remnants of her long-ago touch. She could almost see her past self there, huddled in the dark, a silent figure wrapped in shadows and the cloak of her despair. She was so young, so hurt, so alone.

She remembered curling up in that spot night after night, watching the stars from the cave's mouth, wondering if the sky had shifted while she was hidden away. It had been her one connection to the world beyond, the only thing grounding her to the life that felt so distant. How many nights had she lain awake there, staring into the darkness, haunted by loneliness? The weight of those endless nights crashed over her, and she fought to steady her breath against the crushing familiarity.

Now, the weight of those nights hung over her, an invisible fog settling in as she moved further into the chamber. Every step was like she was wading through memories too thick to break free from, each breath stirring the dust of her past life. She glanced over at Marcus, who had ventured toward a pile of old, crumbling stones near the edge of the room, studying them as if they held some great secret.

"How did you even find this place?" she asked, her voice low, the question sharpened by a growing fear that someone else might be pulling their strings. This wasn't just a random cave. It had been her sanctuary, her secret. *How could he have known to bring them here unless someone had told him exactly where to look?*

Marcus looked up, meeting her gaze, his expression flickering with surprise before he collected himself. For a moment, he was silent, and she saw something flicker across his face. Then he shrugged, offering her the same disarming smile that had once put her at ease. "I told you, research. Old maps and records from the university archives," he replied.

She nodded slowly, trying to push aside the unease curling in her chest. Maybe it was a coincidence. Maybe she was reading into things again. Trusting Marcus had once been effortless, a comfort she didn't know she craved. But now, with her emotions unraveling in this place, even that certainty looked fragile, like she might be the one fracturing it.

As she moved further in, Marcus and Aric followed, their footsteps crunching on the stone floor. Marcus's gaze shifted from one end of the room to the other, his expression unreadable, though a flicker of curiosity brightened his eyes. "So," he said, running a hand over the dusty table, "this is the place... and yet it's not exactly the cursed cave we were expecting from Nemesis."

She let the silence linger, watching as he tried to piece together the room's significance. *Let him believe that.* The satisfaction of his mistake was a small, bitter victory.

Aric looked around, his brow furrowed as he observed the space. "It doesn't look like a place of vengeance," he said quietly, his gaze settling on her. She experienced a small surge of gratitude for his perceptiveness, the unspoken question in his eyes asking if she was all right.

The silence that followed grew heavy as Marcus walked along the far wall, his hand tracing over the stone as if searching for something. She watched him closely, tension threading through her muscles.

Then, almost as if guided by some unseen hand, Marcus paused at the worn stone table near the center of the cave. His fingers traced along its dusty surface before stopping at something that caught the dim light. An ornate box, no larger than a book, with a bronze surface etched in intricate patterns that seemed to shift in the shadows.

"What's this?" Marcus murmured, lifting the box carefully. Dust cascaded from its surface, revealing inlaid gemstones that glittered like captured starlight.

Ophira stepped closer, her heart beginning to race as she took in the unfamiliar object. "No, that's-" she started, then caught herself before the words 'that's not mine' could escape. Her mouth snapped shut, but the realization hit her like a physical blow. Someone else had been here. Someone had left this deliberately.

"Whoever was living here must have left it behind," Marcus said, turning the box over in his hands. The bronze was weathered but clearly valuable, its surface covered in what looked like constellations picked out in various gemstones.

Aric moved closer, his professional curiosity overriding his earlier tension. "That's beautiful craftsmanship. Ancient, by the look of it."

Ophira's pulse quickened as fear crept up her spine. Who left this? And why? The questions hammered at her thoughts, but she couldn't voice them without revealing that this cave had once been her sanctuary. All she could do was watch as Marcus examined the mysterious box, her dread mounting with each passing second.

"There's writing around the edge," Marcus said, squinting in the dim light. "It's faded, but..." He tilted the box toward the cave entrance.

"She waits in chains beneath the tide,
Her mother's pride, the gods denied.
Four bright wings and mother's W.
Find her path, and fate pulls through."

Oh, ze drama! Valentina practically purred. *A riddle of fate and chains and sacrifice! It iz like something from ze most tragic of operas!*

Think it through, Sage cut in sharply. *Classical astronomical puzzle box. The craftsmanship suggests significant resources and knowledge. This wasn't left here casually.*

Yeah, 'cause mysterious boxes never led to anything bad, Zeke drawled. *What could possibly go wrong? Maybe we should talk to Pandora about that.*

"Classical mythology," Aric said, but his expression was puzzled. "Though I'm not placing the reference immediately."

Marcus ran his finger over the gemstone pattern, pressing experimentally at several stones. Nothing happened. "It's some kind of mechanism, but..."

"Wait," Ophira said, despite herself. Her eyes traced the scattered points of light. "Mother's W. That has to be Cassiopeia. It's the most recognizable constellation, shaped like a W." She pointed to the distinctive pattern of white moonstone. "And if that's Cassiopeia..."

"Then we're looking for her daughter," Marcus finished. "Andromeda. But where?"

They studied the surface in silence for several minutes. Aric tried pressing various combinations around Cassiopeia, but nothing responded. Marcus attempted to trace lines between different constellations, growing increasingly frustrated.

"Four bright wings," Ophira murmured, then looked up sharply. "Pegasus. Andromeda is near Pegasus in the night sky."

"But which stones represent Andromeda?" Aric asked, examining the surface more closely. "There are dozens of gemstones here."

Marcus pressed several stones near what might be Pegasus, but still nothing. "Maybe it's not just pressing them. Maybe there's a sequence?"

Ze constellation of ze chained princess! Valentina exclaimed. *She who was sacrificed for her mother's vanity! Quelle tragédie! Look for ze line of stars, ma chérie, Andromeda stretches like chains across ze sky!*

I'm actually impressed right now, Val. Seven primary stars in a distinctive asterism, Sage added with clinical precision. *Northeast of Pegasus, south of Cassiopeia. The pattern should be linear, not clustered.*

"The riddle says 'find her path,'" Ophira said, her analytical mind engaging despite her growing dread. "Andromeda forms a long, chain-like line in the sky. If we trace that pattern…"

It took another ten minutes of careful examination and several false starts before they identified the correct seven-stone sequence. When Marcus finally pressed the last stone in Andromeda's asterism, they all began to emit a faint, otherworldly glow. The lid released with a barely audible whisper.

"Finally," Aric breathed as Marcus lifted the lid to reveal the interior.

Inside lay three interlocking rings, each etched with different symbols: a spinning spindle, a measuring rod, and a pair of shears. Thin grooves spiraled through each ring like channels, and resting at the center was a delicate thread of gold wire.

"The Moirai," Marcus said, his voice hushed with recognition. "The Fates. Clotho, Lachesis, and Atropos."

Ophira's hands trembled as the implications sank in. Someone had crafted this box specifically for people who would understand these references, who would know the mythology well enough to solve it. But who? And why leave it here, in her former sanctuary?

Ze Fates themselves! Valentina's voice trembled with excitement. Clotho who spins ze thread of life, Lachesis who measures it, and Atropos who cuts it short! Oh, ze poetry of destiny made manifest!

Again with the clever answers. Who are you, and what did you do with the real Valentina? It's a sequential mechanism based on mythological progression, Fee, Sage observed. Life, measurement, death. The thread must follow the natural order.

I got a bad feeling about this, Zeke muttered. Fate puzzles in your old hideout? Someone's tryin' real hard to send a message.

"The thread obviously goes through each ring," Aric said, "but how?"

Marcus lifted the delicate golden wire, examining the rings more closely. "There are multiple slots in each one. Clotho's ring has several spindle openings."

"Trial and error?" Aric suggested.

They spent nearly twenty minutes working through the puzzle. The first ring proved deceptive. Two of the spindle slots looked identical, and they tried the wrong one first, producing only silence from the bronze. When Marcus finally threaded it through the correct opening, a soft harmonic tone hummed from within the box.

The second ring was even more challenging. Lachesis's measuring rod had to be aligned with symbols that appeared to represent moon phases, but the sequence wasn't immediately obvious.

"Life stages?" Ophira suggested, watching Marcus rotate the disk. "New moon for birth, full moon for maturity?"

"Or seasons?" Aric offered. "The Greeks often tied fate to agricultural cycles."

It was Ophira who finally noticed the subtle notches that indicated the correct sequence, a pattern that followed the lunar calendar. As the ring clicked into place, another tone joined the first.

The final ring seemed the most straightforward until they realized that Atropos's shears had multiple blade positions, and only one would accept the thread without cutting it.

"Carefully," Marcus murmured, guiding the golden wire through the final mechanism. "If this snaps..."

The thread slipped through the open notch perfectly. The three tones merged into a haunting triad that resonated from the very bronze itself. Then, with a final gentle chime, the central compartment clicked open.

Marcus reached in and pulled out something small and faintly glinting in the dim light, which appeared to be a photograph. He brushed off the last traces of dust, and as the image came into focus, a wave of recognition slammed into Ophira.

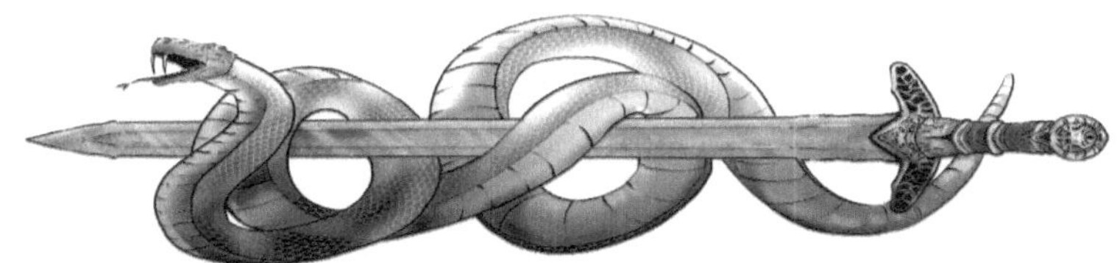

The photograph in Marcus's hands showed a sword. Not just any sword, but the blade that had ended her first life. The weapon that Perseus had wielded against her, the steel that had haunted her nightmares for centuries. Her heart pounded as she studied the image, the hilt adorned with Athena's symbols – an owl, a serpent, and an olive branch, carved into the intricate silver with painstaking detail. It was unmistakably the same sword, the one that had severed her life from the world she'd known.

Sage's voice was sharp. *That's not a relic. It's a symbol. Its presence here raises tactical questions about who placed it and why now.*

Zeke snorted. *Raises more than questions. It raises the hair on my scales. What's it even doing here?*

Valentina hissed dramatically. *Ah, ze blade of betrayal! Ze sword zat severed your destiny from your desires! How exquisitely cruel zat it returns to haunt you now!*

Sunny's voice was steady, almost pleading. *Easy now, sugar. You survived this once, and you're stronger for it. Ain't no nightmare photo gonna break you.*

Ophira stared at the photograph, her pulse quickening. *But can I survive it again?*

Ophira forced her expression to remain neutral, though her fingers twitched at her side. *Who's setting all this up?* Her gaze swept between Marcus and the photograph, a chill of recognition settling in her stomach. Every lead, every discovery, every convenient breakthrough… They all felt orchestrated, like pieces being moved on a board by unseen hands.

Someone wanted her to follow this path, to uncover these specific memories, and the timing was too calculated to be a coincidence. The question was no longer whether she was being manipulated; it was who was pulling the strings, and why they needed her to remember.

Her chest tightened, the weight of the memory pressing down on her as the room blurred around her, the photograph dissolving into a vivid, horrifying vision.

In an instant, she was no longer in the cave but back on that fateful night, standing on rough, cold earth beneath a starless sky. The taste of fear coated her tongue like copper. The ground beneath her feet was uneven, scattered with stones that would soon be stained with her blood. Mist clung to her skin, the damp chill seeping through her as she faced Perseus.

He stood before her, a tall, muscular warrior, his dark, intense eyes fixed on her with deadly determination. His strong, battle-scarred features and olive skin glinted in the moonlight, his stance unyielding as he lifted the sword, the blade catching the starlight with an otherworldly gleam.

No... not again... Her heart thundered as she watched the sword descend, the world moving in excruciatingly slow motion. She could feel her skin prickle with fear, her pulse racing as her vision narrowed on the blade's edge.

The impact was a searing, blinding pain, slicing through her like fire. The exact moment blazed in her memory as it pierced her flesh, steel tearing through her neck with merciless precision. Her senses burned as every nerve became consumed by violent agony that eclipsed anything she'd known.

No... please...I don't deserve this... Her body began to collapse. Then, strangely and impossibly, she saw herself from above. An observer to her own fall, watching as her body sank slowly, the ground seeming to rush up in agonizing delay.

Time bent around her, each second stretching like molten glass as reality fractured. She could see flashes of other possibilities: fragments of herself moving, turning, avoiding the sword's fatal arc. In one fragment, she deflected the blow, twisting away. In another, the blade struck her arm instead, severing it in blinding agony. Another instant: she dodged, but the blade sliced into her side, spilling warmth down her ribs as she crumpled to the earth. She saw herself moving in ways she'd never thought possible, each flicker a new agony, bending reality into a distorted, spiraling web.

Time...it's bending, showing me what could have been. But how? Why am I seeing this now? The thought pulsed through her mind, but the agony fractured her focus, scattering her awareness between possibilities that had never been and the inevitable death that was.

An odd sensation twisted through the memory, as if fate itself were unraveling to show her threads that had never been woven. Other ways this could have unfolded flickered before her eyes like might-have-beens demanding recognition.

In one terrible flash, she saw herself stumbling back, desperately reaching out to deflect Perseus's blow, but the sword struck her arm, severing it in a brutal spray of pain.

Another moment flickered. A wild, impossible thought. She sensed her hand reaching for the weapon, turning it, but Perseus's strength was unyielding, his body a stone wall against her desperate attempt.

Yet another image followed. This time, she darted to the side, only for the blade to slice her flank, her scream echoing as she crumpled to the ground.

Each possible outcome flashed before her eyes, vivid and tormenting, bending reality in cruel, spiraling fragments.

She was falling again, her vision narrowing as time pulled her forward with relentless certainty. But even in death's grip, a voice whispered, "This was always meant to happen." Someone had planned for her to see this, to remember this way.

Her mind raced, desperate to cling to any piece of reality, but it was slipping through her like water. Her sight blurred, darkness filling the edges as the fractured moments faded, leaving only the sensation of her broken form lying on the cold, unyielding ground.

For a moment, everything was dark. Then, as consciousness faded, she saw him. Morpheus stepped through the shadows of memory, his presence a soft light amid the suffocating blackness of her dying moments.

Morpheus was tall, his broad shoulders and powerful build exuding strength, yet there was grace to his movements, as though the Lord of Dreams moved in a world of his own. His deep violet eyes met hers, swirling with a dreamlike quality, a calmness that absorbed her pain, drawing it from her as he knelt beside her broken form. His long, dark hair shimmered with a faint glow, as if touched by the night sky itself, and his skin, pale with a subtle blue tint, reflected constellations and shifting shadows.

He reached out, his hand brushing lightly over her wound, his touch warm and soothing. The pain began to ebb, replaced by a strange sense of peace as his power worked its way through her, binding her fragmented essence back together. His robes, dark with accents of silver and blue, shifted like mist around him, blending seamlessly with the shadows.

It's not time yet, he said, his voice deep and melodic. The sound washed over her, calming her, grounding her in a way she hadn't known was possible.

She sensed herself slipping away, the memory fracturing as his voice echoed in her mind. The warmth of his touch faded, and she was pulled back into the present, the photograph still in Marcus's hand, the image of the sword distorted through her tears.

Her breathing came in ragged gasps as she fought to steady herself, her body trembling from the intensity of the vision. She pressed her palms against the cave wall, using the solid stone to anchor herself in the present.

The photograph was still there, the sword etched in her mind like a brand, a scar she would carry forever. Her pulse battered against her skin, rough stone beneath her grip serving as her only anchor. Every nerve felt raw, exposed, her heartbeat betraying the disarray she'd fought to contain.

Aric's steadying hand on her shoulder brought her back, grounding her in the present. His touch was warm, a quiet reminder that she was not alone. She looked up, meeting his gaze, grateful for the silent support he offered.

"Are you ok?" Marcus's voice cut through her thoughts, his tone gentle yet probing. He stepped closer, reaching out as if to comfort her, but the gesture only intensified the conflict within her. She wanted to trust him, to lean into his support, but the doubts that had been building now stood as a solid wall between them.

She forced a nod, masking the storm within her. "I'm fine," she replied, her voice steady. The cave, the sword, the memories all clawed at her, scraping against the fragile composure she clung to.

As Marcus's gaze lingered, fury blazed through her alongside a deeper instinct. The need to protect, to ensure this weapon could never be used against another innocent, burned stronger than her pain.

Someone is playing a game with us. Is this part of a plan I can't see yet? The question burned in her mind, intensifying her wariness as she took a step back, subtly placing more distance between them in a quiet act of dispersion, a habit born from battles where closeness got people killed. But the real danger wasn't even standing in this cave with her. It was whoever was behind all of this. And distance couldn't save her this time.

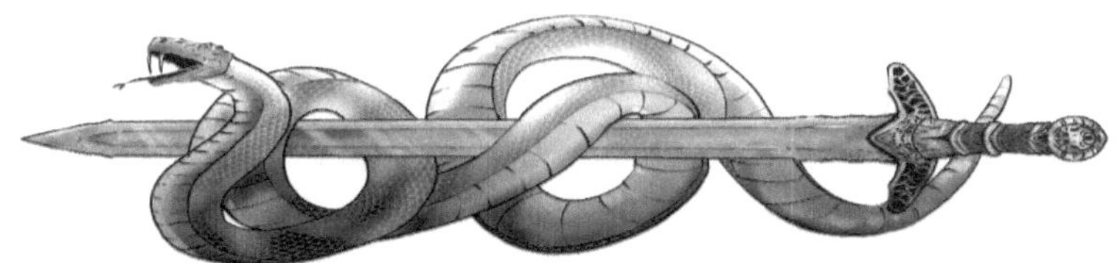

A tense silence settled over the group, the cave pressing in around them like a tomb, its shadows stretching like silent witnesses to her unraveling composure. The photograph in Marcus's hand felt like a taunt, a challenge she couldn't ignore. She glanced away, needing to collect herself, to suppress the emotions that had surged forth so uncontrollably.

Her voice, when she spoke, was steady but laced with a bitterness she couldn't fully conceal. "This place... It's not Nemesis's," she finally said, her voice barely steady. "It's a place of solitude, not vengeance. A place to disappear from the world."

Marcus considered her words for a long moment, his expression thoughtful. "Then perhaps Nemesis had other intentions here," he finally mused, as though her reaction were simply a puzzle piece to his broader understanding. He tucked the photograph away, but even that simple gesture was heavy with the weight of what they'd discovered.

Uncertainty twisted through her gut. Was he trying to help, or was she another specimen for his analysis? Her thoughts spiraled, but she forced them down. Self-doubt had been a luxury she couldn't afford for centuries. Maybe the problem wasn't Marcus. Maybe it was the way this place stripped away every defense she'd spent lifetimes building.

A wave of dizziness washed over her. She leaned heavily against the cave wall, her fingers curling into the rough stone as if it were the only thing keeping her grounded. Her breath came in shallow, uneven bursts. Each inhale strained against her tight chest, barely filling her lungs. A hollow ache sat where her heartbeat should have been steady; instead, it pulsed erratically, a relentless reminder of the vision's aftermath.

Flashes of the memory lingered, stubbornly vivid. She could still feel the blade slicing through her neck, the unforgiving coldness that sank into her bones, and the hollow sound of her own gasping breaths. The image of Perseus's dark, determined gaze burned into her mind, his expression devoid of hesitation or regret. His voice echoed within her, steady and resolute as the judgment of fate itself, as though he were still here, standing just behind her, ready to strike again. She forced herself to turn, half-expecting to see him, but only the empty darkness of the cave met her gaze.

Her fingers tightened against the wall, nails scraping against the stone as she fought to quiet her mind. *You're here. This is now, not then,* she told herself, trying to push the memories back into the recesses of her mind. But reality was still unstable beneath her feet, as if time might fracture again at any moment and drag her back into Perseus's blade.

She closed her eyes, swallowing against a wave of nausea. Her pulse hammered against her temples, every beat a reminder of how thoroughly her defenses had crumbled. Centuries of careful discipline, undone by a simple photograph.

For centuries, she had locked these feelings away, buried them so deep that even she had almost forgotten they existed. But now, in the quiet aftermath of the vision, the emotional floodgates had opened, drowning her in a torrent she couldn't contain.

When she finally opened her eyes, Marcus was watching her, his brow furrowed. His expression held honest worry, the kind that came from seeing someone in pain and not knowing how to help. The tension in the cave came from the air itself, from the past clawing its way forward, from the impossible timing that made everything feel staged.

Ophira's skin prickled with an unnatural chill, the kind that sank through flesh and bone and memory. She pulled her hand back from the wall, forcing her body upright, but her fingers trembled as her body remembered what her mind tried to suppress. She could feel Marcus watching her, steady but silent, and it made her throat tighten. He remained the only real thing in a world that suddenly seemed false.

Her throat tightened, anger rising. At how exposed she felt. At the timing. At the way the world kept circling back to this one wound, pressing until it reopened. Whoever was pulling the strings knew precisely where to cut. And somehow, she was still walking straight into it. And that realization cut through her as sharply as Perseus's blade had all those years ago.

Marcus shifted slightly, quiet but grounded. His gaze met hers with an unreadable mix of distress and restraint, like he was waiting for the right time to speak.

"You don't have to carry everything alone," he said softly, his voice warm with understanding. "I can see something is upsetting you. Maybe it would help to talk about it. Sometimes an outside perspective can make things clearer." The offer sounded genuine and supportive, but something about the way he leaned forward looked less like comfort and more like an invitation to confession.

She met his gaze and held it, willing herself to stay grounded in the now, though his gentle probing made her want to both open up and pull away. The shadows around them pressed close, thick with memory, and the cave breathed with her dread. This place remembered her, and it didn't want to let her go.

He nodded once, staying quiet, as if sensing that words might undo whatever thread she was clinging to. She took a step back from the weight pressing in on all sides – the cave, the memories, the trap of her unraveling thoughts. The open space beyond the mouth of the cave called to her, and for the first time in minutes, she let herself move toward it. Her pulse still hammered in her chest, a rhythmic echo of her unresolved turmoil, and the cool night air outside beckoned like a balm to her fractured nerves.

Aric's gaze followed her movements, his quiet presence a strange comfort as she steadied herself on the threshold. He didn't press her, simply waiting, as though understanding that she needed this moment. For a heartbeat, she let her eyes meet his, grounding herself in his silent support, and gratitude rose within her.

Aric's jaw tightened as he watched Marcus, something cold flickering in his expression before he moved to Ophira's side. He put his arms around her shoulders, the warmth of his touch providing a momentary balm for her nerves. "C'mon, let's go home," he said, his voice carefully controlled, his eyes almost daring Marcus to argue with him. When Marcus merely nodded with understanding sympathy, Aric's expression darkened further, as if the lack of resistance was somehow more troubling than confrontation would have been. It was the reaction of someone who had expected to be challenged, who had prepared for an argument that never came.

With one last glance at the dark shadows of the cave, she let the memories fade to the background, swallowing down the anger and fear. But even as she turned away, she knew those memories, that trauma, had left their mark anew.

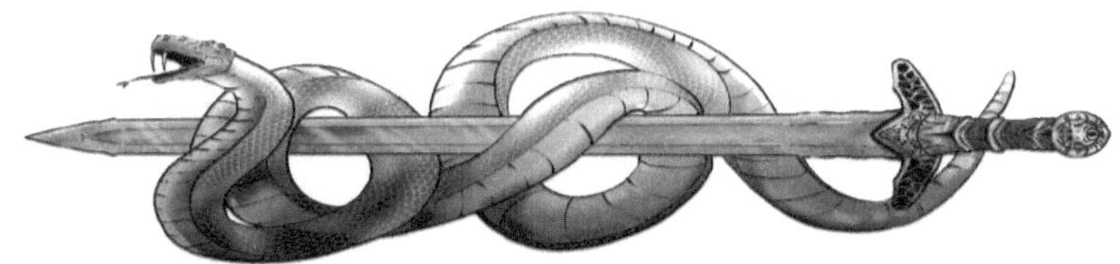

The private jet's engines hummed beneath them, a low, steady thrum that filled the silence stretching between the three of them. Ophira sank into her seat, feeling the cold weight of the memories and visions she had left behind in the cave. The luxury around her only heightened the sense of disconnection; this world of quiet opulence existed worlds away from the ancient stone and raw memories of the cave. Every detail was sharper, more unnatural, like a delicate surface that might fracture at the slightest touch.

For several minutes, only the engine noise filled the cabin. Then her snakes stirred, their voices breaking the quiet yet again.

Zeke drawled, *That went about as well as a snake in a room full of rocking chairs.*

Hyperbolic as ever, Sage's voice cut through with typical bluntness, *but he's not wrong. The discovery of the photograph complicates our tactical position significantly.*

It iz ze emotional toll zat disturbs me, Valentina murmured, her voice unusually soft. *Zese memories. They wound anew, non?*

Sunny's voice was a soothing balm. *Rest now, sugar. We'll figure out the rest when you're ready, and we'll make 'em pay for diggin' where they shouldn't have. Ain't no rush.*

Ophira leaned her head back, closing her eyes against the weight of their words. *When will I be ready?* she wondered, the ache in her chest a constant reminder of the trust she was beginning to lose.

Once they were airborne, Marcus took the seat across from her, his brow creased with worry, his movements careful and unhurried. Under other circumstances, it would have been comforting. Maybe it would've been, if her nerves weren't still frayed raw. Everything remained off-kilter because of the weight she couldn't shake.

He leaned forward, his hand reaching across the space between them, fingers grazing her shoulder in a gesture meant to reassure. His gaze met hers, steady and warm, his mouth curving into a soft, sympathetic smile.

"You looked shaken back there," he said quietly. "I didn't want to push, but if there's anything I can do to help…" His eyes searched her face with what looked like an evaluation, like he'd offered comfort before and knew exactly how long to wait for an answer.

"You seem like someone who's used to handling things on your own," he observed gently, his tone carefully modulated between admiration and worry. "But even the strongest people need support sometimes. I hope you know you can trust me with whatever you're going through."

Well, I'll give him this, Zeke drawled quietly, *boy knows when to keep his mouth shut. That's more wisdom than most folks manage.*

He iz gentle with you in your pain, Valentina observed, her voice softer than usual. *Zis counts for something, non?*

Sunny's voice was warm. *He didn't push, sugar. Didn't try to fix what wasn't his to fix. That's real kindness.*

Even Sage's tone carried grudging respect. *His restraint demonstrates emotional intelligence. It's worth noticing.*

For a moment, she wanted to say yes, to everything. To the calm in his voice, to the steady presence he offered, to the possibility that she truly didn't have to carry every burden alone. The longing for that connection was almost overwhelming, but her defenses had been so thoroughly shattered that even kindness felt crushing. The thought wasn't comfortable, but it was honest.

She held his gaze, searching for any crack in his expression, but his face remained placid, his eyes clear and untroubled. How could he be so unaffected when the depths of her past had left her reeling? She tried to keep her expression neutral, her walls back in place, but the conflict roared within her.

She gave a faint nod, letting his words pass without argument. Maybe she needed rest. Maybe the knot in her chest would ease by morning. Maybe she could allow herself to believe that not everyone who offered help had ulterior motives.

She managed a small smile, meeting his gaze. "Thank you, Marcus. I appreciate it."

He gave her shoulder one last squeeze, and she turned away. Outside, clouds drifted past, casting shadows over the world below. The ache in her chest sharpened, her sense of control unraveling, thread by thread. She closed her eyes, letting the steady hum of the engines anchor her to the present moment.

Whatever waited in the darkness, she'd face it if she had to. But for now, she would rest and gather her strength for what was coming. Someone out there was pulling strings, and she was starting to feel the tug.

Chapter Nineteen

Strange Attractions and Stranger Awakenings

The underground auction house exuded a palpable mystique, a hidden world of tawdry midnight splendor buried beneath the city's underbelly. In the two weeks since their devastating discovery in the mountain cave, Ophira had found time to rest and process what they'd uncovered. Still, as she stepped inside, the transition from the narrow, dimly lit corridors to the opulent chamber was dizzying.

Golden light from an elaborate chandelier poured over rows of high-backed velvet chairs, their shadowed occupants cloaked in anonymity. The air held a subtle tension, like a static charge before a storm, a shared understanding that everyone here was party to a secret they'd never dare expose.

The three of them had coordinated beforehand, each wearing identical dark cloaks with distinctive gold filigree threading around the cowl's edge, a subtle but unmistakable identifier in the sea of anonymous figures.

Darlings, look at zis place! Valentina's voice cut through the silence, dripping with exaggerated awe. *It's dripping in stolen elegance. Très dramatique, no? But watch zese shadows, cara mia, they hide secrets darker than ze night itself!*

Dramatic? More like the kinda watering hole where folk get themselves ventilated over shiny baubles, Zeke muttered dryly. *Reminds me of this old poker game I heard about – when the stakes get too high, somebody usually ends up wearin' their cards on the outside.*

Focus, everyone, Sage interjected, his tone clipped. *Look, you feel that charge? These artifacts ain't just relics – they're potent. We need to stay sharp here.*

Bless their hearts, Sunny chimed in, her Southern warmth easing some of the tension. *Sugar, keep those instincts hummin'. These folks are all schemin'.*

Blood-red tapestries swept down stone walls, their lush fabric creating an eerie warmth against the otherwise cold stone. The scent of aged velvet and something metallic like old coins or dried blood hung in the air. The walls absorbed the light, casting it back in muted hues that made the room feel suspended in twilight. Even the slightest whisper carried across the space, as if amplified by the thick air heavy with expectation.

Ophira's gaze drifted across the assembled crowd's faces, obscured, yet each pair of eyes gleamed in anticipation as they absorbed the sight of the priceless artifacts on display.

The stage held treasures from worlds and myths long past, each relic placed with reverence on pedestals under carefully positioned lights. Quiet power emanated from the displays, as if each artifact still carried the essence of the lives it had touched.

An intricately crafted sword rested under glass, its hilt decorated with silver etchings and gemstones dulled only slightly by the ages. Nearby was a small talisman, its surface covered in faded inscriptions, mysterious symbols that flickered under the chandelier's glow. Each relic was more than a piece of history; it felt like a portal to its own time, its own legend.

Ophira's gaze swept over the relics on display, her senses sparking as she neared them. The artifacts were ancient, cloaked in a reverence that felt beyond mortal understanding. Each piece held a story, energy pulsing beneath layers of gold, silver, and glass. She passed a small bronze amulet, and a strange tingle crept up her arm, prickling her skin with a sensation that felt alive.

Further down the row, she approached a statue. A small polished owl with piercing onyx eyes sent an unexpected chill over her skin. It was faint, nearly imperceptible, but it felt as if the statue itself recognized her, stirring to life for just a moment before settling back into silence.

She took a steadying breath, brushing off the sensation as the ambient noise around her dimmed slightly. Her focus sharpened, her senses narrowing in on the relics with an intensity that felt almost foreign. There was something more to this room than met the eye, as though a silent force watched and waited from within the glistening surfaces. *This place feels wrong,* she thought, a shiver threading through her. *It's like the artifacts aren't objects... They're alive.*

Aric moved just behind her, his gaze sweeping the room with practiced ease, a subtle wariness in his expression. She caught his eye for a brief moment, and though he didn't speak, she felt a shared understanding pass between them. They had both been here before, in places like this, where secrets clung to every wall and power whispered from each corner.

From the periphery, Marcus's steady gaze scanned the room with a quiet confidence. His hand rested lightly on her shoulder, and his presence, usually grounding, carried a possessive edge in this setting. She couldn't ignore the way he looked at the relics with such a calculated air of appreciation, like each artifact was a puzzle piece he was slotting into place. He appeared at ease.

"Quite a collection, isn't it?" he murmured, eyes lingering on an intricately carved mask displayed on a pedestal nearby. The mask's expression was serene, yet its hollow eyes held a chill that made her fingers curl into fists at her side. She felt the air thicken as he spoke, his words seeping into the room's quiet intensity. She couldn't place why, but the moment felt significant, as if something hidden were about to break through.

She stepped closer to the mask, a flicker of heat rising in her chest as her gaze met the empty sockets. The mask's surface shimmered briefly, and her breath caught, the world around her sharpening, as if everything had drawn into razor-edged focus. Quickly, the sensation faded, leaving her to wonder if she'd imagined it. *Why do I feel like something is watching us?* she wondered, the question sending a strange sense of awareness through her.

The atmosphere in the room felt electric, buzzing with the anticipation of what was yet to come. Ophira scanned the rows of artifacts displayed on their pedestals, each piece bathed in a warm, subdued light that highlighted centuries of myth and history etched into their surfaces. The relics on display grew more elaborate, more layered in meaning, some emanating low energies that buzzed just below her skin.

Ophira found herself drawn to each new piece, her gaze tracking every carved symbol and glint of aged metal. She noticed that, in the moments before she looked closely, a quiet fell over her senses, as though the world were leaning in to tell her something. She was studying a gilded amulet adorned with sun and eagle motifs when Marcus moved closer.

"This one," he murmured, pointing to a gilded amulet adorned with sun and eagle motifs, "reminds me of something I came across in an old monastery archive." He spoke with quiet fascination, his fingers tracing the edges in the air. "I was researching medieval religious artifacts last year when the abbot mentioned a piece just like this, said it vanished from their collection decades ago."

She found herself drawn closer, though something in her bristled at how easily the story flowed. "You think this could be the same one?" she asked, trying to keep her voice neutral. But with every revelation, a nagging thought burrowed deeper into her mind. Why did these relics keep finding them like this? Why did every path feel carved before she even took a step?

His expression brightened with excitement. "It's possible. The sun and eagle motifs match perfectly." He paused, as if considering whether to share more. "The abbot told me something fascinating – claimed whoever wore it commanded attention effortlessly. Could be medieval superstition, but the historical accounts are surprisingly consistent." He paused, his scholarly excitement evident.

He moved with such ease through the room, pointing out relics and offering bits of history, each fact dropping effortlessly from his lips. But with every revelation, a nagging thought burrowed deeper into her mind. *He knows so much about these artifacts. How is he always one step ahead?*

She nodded, even as her mind raced. Marcus's knowledge seemed limitless, his familiarity with the artifacts unnervingly precise. His insights held a practiced quality, each answer so smooth, so ready, as if carefully chosen to guide her perception.

Her gaze drifted back to a nearby relic, a dagger etched with runes that glinted in the low light. As she focused on it, a strange sensation rippled over her vision, and time slowed. She watched Marcus's hand lift in languid motion, each detail of the dagger sharpening to almost painful clarity before her eyes. She could see the grain of the blade, the worn grip, the slight shimmer as if it still held traces of old magic. Her heartbeat quickened, each beat loud and pulsing in her ears, drawing her back to the present.

Time distortion detected, Sage announced, his voice tight with strain. *Temporal flow variance seems to be approximately 40%. This shouldn't be possible without direct divine intervention.*

Darlin', what he means is that everything's movin' like honey dripped from a wooden spoon on a lazy Sunday afternoon, Sunny observed, her words themselves seeming to stretch and flow. *Like when you're lyin' in a hammock under a weeping willow, watchin' the clouds float in slow motion against a sunset sky.*

Like ridin' through deep water, Zeke muttered, his tone taking on an almost hypnotic quality. *Heard tell once of a river crossing where the current was so strange, horses would forget which way was up.*

Her breath hitched, the moment snapping away as quickly as it had come, leaving her blinking in confusion. The relic, Marcus, the room... They returned to normal speed, but a strange awareness lingered, prickling at her edges. *Stress,* she told herself, taking a steadying breath. *I need to stay focused.*

He took her silence as acceptance, and his eyes softened with what she could only describe as encouragement, or perhaps something meant to calm. But it only made her feel more guarded, a subtle tension fraying her nerves. How could anyone know this much, unless the whole thing was designed? Unless the truth was being fed to them, bit by bit, by someone hiding just out of sight?

They walked in silence for a moment, and she felt him watching her, sensing her quiet withdrawal. "The energy in here is intense, isn't it?" he said softly, gesturing to the room. "I can see why someone might feel overwhelmed. All this history, all these secrets..."

Her gaze shifted to meet his, holding back the doubt that burned behind her eyes. She forced a small smile, nodding. "I'm taking it all in," she replied, accepting the lifeline he'd offered even as questions pressed at her mind. When he stepped closer, creating a subtle sense of protection against the crowd's watchful eyes, she found herself grateful despite the chill of her growing distrust of the investigation.

As Ophira continued along the rows of relics, a prickling sensation trailed along her arms. The closer she moved to certain artifacts, the more she felt an unusual, almost magnetic pull, as though these items were reaching for her. A soft hum met her ears, weak yet undeniable, and when she looked closer, she noticed the shadowy glow radiating from a polished shield set with faded inscriptions.

Her pulse quickened. She had seen plenty of relics imbued with magic, but this was different. It was as if the relics themselves recognized her.

Why are these relics reacting to me? she wondered, casting a cautious glance around to see if anyone else had noticed. *Is it because of the case, or is something else going on?*

A few steps further, her gaze settled on a silver pendant in the shape of an owl, perched with wings unfurled, as though ready to take flight. The pendant was nestled within a velvet-lined box, its fine silver glinting under the chandelier's golden light.

A circle of olive leaves framed the owl, small and intricate, so delicately crafted that she could see each feather in minute detail. It was one of the most finely wrought artifacts in the collection, and it exuded an aura of wisdom, a presence that made the air around it feel thicker, charged with unseen power.

As she drew closer, the owl pendant responded, glowing with a soft, silver light that reached toward her. She paused, both drawn in and unnerved by the sensation, watching the light pulse almost in time with her heartbeat. The effect was subtle yet mesmerizing, as though the pendant held a fragment of something wise and impossibly vast.

It's reacting to you, Ophira, Sage observed, his voice tinged with analytical precision. *That's no coincidence. Something's connecting you to these pieces.* He paused, processing. *The energy patterns are... fragmented. Difficult to analyze properly.*

Or it's a setup, Zeke added, suspicion thick in his voice. *You ever wonder why we keep gettin' drawn to trouble? You know the ole' sayin' 'When the horses get skittish, there's wolves in them woods.'*

Trouble? Ha! Valentina practically purred, her dramatic tone cutting through the tension. *It's a sign of destiny, darling. Clearly, this pendant knows we're exceptional.*

Maybe it's not trouble at all, sugar, Sunny said, her warmth wrapping around Ophira like a soft embrace. *Could be somethin' good, somethin' meant for you. Somethin' magical, like the feelin' you get on a warm spring day in Savannah, watching the Spanish moss floatin' in a breeze as it drips from the trees.*

How would we know what a warm spring day in Savannah feels like? Sage asked in confusion.

From the corner of her eye, Ophira noticed Aric watching her, his head tilted slightly, a soft smile playing on his lips. "You seem to be drawn to that one," he murmured, his voice barely above a whisper. "It's like it's calling to you, isn't it?"

She met his gaze, noting the thoughtful look in his eyes, and felt a small sense of relief at his presence. "Hmm," she replied with careful neutrality, a slight smile tugging at her lips. "There are some interesting pieces here tonight, for sure." Her attention drifted back to the pendant, unable to pull herself away.

The pendant's energy pulsed gently, insistent, holding her attention like a tether. Her hand extended, hovering above the owl, feeling a warmth radiate from it onto her fingertips. The owl's gaze appeared to meet hers, ageless and knowing, as though it recognized a part of her she didn't understand herself.

She forced herself to retreat, her hand shaking with unsettled nerves. The pendant's glow faded instantly, its light snuffing out the moment she withdrew. She tried to take a deep breath, grounding herself, but a wave of dizziness washed over her, subtle yet undeniable, as though the relic's energy had burrowed into her skin.

What is it about these relics that keeps drawing me in?

A tinkling chime rang out across the room, pulling her away from the pendant as the signal that the auction was about to begin caught her attention.

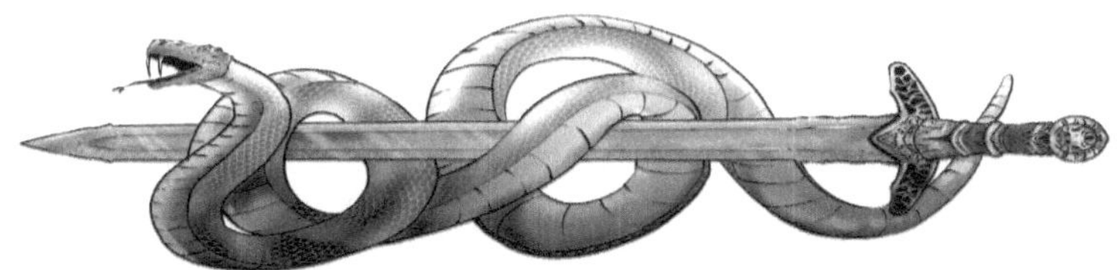

The cloaked auctioneer raised his hand, and silence blanketed the room. Silence descended like a velvet curtain, and all eyes turned to the stage as the first relic, a dagger with gemstones that glowed in an intricate pattern, caught the dim light.

Ophira's breath caught, her attention inexplicably tethered to the piece. The auctioneer's voice rang out in calculated tones that coiled around the room like silk, each word chosen for maximum effect as he wove mythology and history into his descriptions.

Marcus leaned closer to Ophira, squinting at his auction catalog. "That piece just went for three times the estimated value," he said, looking puzzled. "Either the auctioneer undersold its significance, or someone here knows something we don't."

He flipped through his notes, frowning. "I've been tracking similar pieces for months, but these prices..." He shook his head. "Something's not adding up."

An unsettling awareness bloomed within her as she passed each relic; their energies reached out, meeting her presence with something she could only describe as familiarity. The room closed in, shadows deepening as if alive, watching.

Ophira felt her pulse slow, drawn in by the energy thickening around her, the room's tension pulsing like a drumbeat in her ears. *There's something here...beyond what I can see.*

Ophira's gaze drifted over a new relic, a golden bracelet lying on a deep velvet cloth, tarnished with age but radiating an aura that pulsed subtly as she passed. The energy was unmistakable, a quiet hum that grew sharper with her proximity, drawing her in with a magnetic pull she couldn't quite shake. She felt her breath catch, familiarity stirring unease in her chest, awareness prickling as though the bracelet were watching her.

"Did you feel that?" she murmured almost reflexively, the words slipping from her lips before she realized it. Her fingers flexed at her side, itching to reach out, to feel the cool surface of the bracelet and decipher the sensation that tugged at her.

But Marcus, always attuned to her slightest reactions, caught her words. He leaned closer, his voice a soft murmur just above a whisper, as if sharing a secret meant only for her. "Feel what?"

Feel what, precisely? Sage's tone sharpened. *I'm detecting multiple energy fluctuations, but everything is...inconsistent.*

Sugar, we're all feelin' somethin' strange tonight, Sunny said, her voice dreamy. *Like when you're sittin' on a porch swing during a summer thunderstorm, and you can feel the electricity in the air before the first lightning strikes. Makes your skin all tingly and aware.*

None of us has any idea what that feels like, Sage protested.

Feels like bein' watched by somethin' that ain't quite natural, Zeke added with growing unease. *Reminds me of this old story about a gambler who kept feelin' eyes on him – turned out the saloon had mirrors positioned just so the house could see everyone's cards.*

Sunny began to lazily hum a vaguely familiar tune.

Wait, I know that one, Zeke said, perking up. *That Kenny Rogers song about the gambler!* He started humming along with Sunny.

Oh, oui! Valentina chimed in enthusiastically. *Ze one about knowing when to walk away!* She joined the other two in humming the chorus.

What are you all DOING? Ophira hissed at them, cutting them off before they could continue.

Ophira hesitated, suddenly feeling a bit exposed under the weight of his undivided attention and confused by the weirdness surrounding her. She didn't want to admit aloud the strange magnetism of these artifacts, how they resonated with her, drawing her in like a moth to a flame.

She struggled to put the sensation into words, her thoughts a swirl of doubt and uncertainty. "These relics feel like they're vibrating somehow," she finally replied, keeping her voice low. "It's like they're alive."

Marcus's gaze softened, his lips curving in a gentle, knowing smile that felt reassuring and disconcerting all at once. "You've been under incredible pressure with this investigation," he said, his voice carrying what sounded like actual anxiety. "I can see how draining it's been. Maybe we should take a step back after tonight, make sure we're not missing anything important because we're both running on fumes."

Ophira turned toward him, meeting his gaze, searching for some hidden layer, a hint that he might be playing with her emotions. Yet all she saw was calm assurance, a look that conveyed care. She tried to shake off her doubt, but that spark, the pull she'd felt from the pendant, refused to fade as if the relic held a message, just for her.

"I get it," Marcus said, his voice low. "Sometimes they feel almost...sentient, don't they? But that's the power of belief. The longer you study them, the more alive they seem."

A knot tightened in her chest. *Is he right?* Her gaze shifted back to the pendant, its silver surface glimmering under the auction hall's golden lights. She had spent centuries learning to trust her instincts, to rely on her perceptions even when they defied logic. And yet here, in Marcus's presence, her certainty felt disturbingly fragile.

The auction continued, yet her focus slipped in and out, her mind circling. She watched him out of the corner of her eye, studying how he moved through the room with ease, how his confidence never wavered.

It was something she had once admired about him, how he was so steady in his purpose, so sure of the world around him. But now, that very quality made her feel as though she were drifting, as if her sense of reality had become malleable, open to his suggestions.

And he was watching her just as closely, as if reading her every thought. His gaze was soft, almost indulgent, as if he found her reactions quaint, even amusing. The thought unsettled her further, deepening her internal conflict. She wasn't one to doubt herself, yet here, in the quiet darkness of this auction hall, her trust felt more tenuous than ever.

She inhaled slowly, forcing herself to ground her thoughts and focus on reality. The auction continued, and each piece was paraded onto a raised platform at the front, displayed for the attendees to observe more closely.

When the auctioneer presented the next item, a delicately wrought amulet with patterns that shifted under the light, the same pull seized her. Energy both invited and threatened.

As the crowd shifted and whispered, an irresistible pull drew Ophira toward the stage. Fighting the compulsion, she moved closer, weaving through the scattered throng as the auctioneer introduced the following item.

Without thinking, she reached toward it, her hand hovering inches above its gleaming surface, the warmth she'd felt earlier radiating once again. It was undeniable, this connection, this pull, as if something within the relics was calling out to her, resonating in some hidden, forgotten part of herself.

"Ophira." Marcus's voice cut through her trance. He placed a gentle hand on her arm, his touch grounding her in the present. "What are you doing?"

She blinked and drew back her hand, realizing how she must have looked. Entranced, lost in something she couldn't explain. Pulling herself together, she forced a smile onto her lips. "I'm fine," she replied, her smile brittle but intact.

But Marcus's expression softened, his gaze carrying a hint of amusement. "You seem more on edge than usual tonight," he said. "If I didn't know better, I'd say these artifacts are starting to get under your skin."

The gentle humor in his tone was subtle, but it made her stomach twist. Was he mocking her? Or was he truly worried? The question lingered, unanswered, deepening the uncertainty that had already taken root within her.

"You know, when we're tense, it's easy to see things that aren't there," he continued softly, his words gentle yet carrying an underlying challenge. "I think you're overthinking it, Ophira. Maybe it's best to step back, clear your mind."

Irritation sparked within her. She opened her mouth to counter his suggestion, defend her instincts, but the words fell short. *Am I being paranoid? Or is this whole place built to twist my insides into knots?* She swallowed, the question haunting her as she glanced at him once more, searching his face for any hint of judgment.

Yet his expression remained calm, understanding, his every feature perfectly composed, as though he were a mirror reflecting her self-doubt at her.

She couldn't shake the sensation of being watched, as if something primordial and calculating had turned its eye on her. It was a subtle dance, one she hadn't noticed before, but now, under the scrutinizing lights of the auction, it felt painfully clear.

She forced herself to look away, her focus returning to the stage as the auctioneer introduced the next item. The room was filled with quiet murmurs, the soft rustling of cloaks and whispers in the shadows, but her mind remained on Marcus's words, his calm, persuasive tone weaving through her thoughts like a fog she couldn't shake.

One after another, the relics appeared on stage, each accompanied by the auctioneer's carefully crafted descriptions, and yet Ophira's attention wavered. She watched Marcus, studying him as he spoke to her, his words slipping under her skin like water, softening her resolve, dampening her instincts.

"Maybe you're right," she murmured, then quickly looked away, unsure if she believed it. A part of her recoiled from admitting it, but his steady presence, his calm assurance, left her feeling unsteady, like a ship caught in a gentle but persistent current, its direction shifting.

He nodded, a small, satisfied smile touching his lips. "Take it easy," he replied, his voice gentle, a hand resting lightly on her arm. "No pressure tonight," he said, brushing his thumb across her arm. "We're here to observe, right?"

She wanted to argue, to hold on to the certainty she'd felt earlier, but her conviction wavered.

As the auction continued, Ophira found herself drifting, her attention sliding from one relic to the next, her thoughts clouded and unfocused. It was as if a weight had settled over her, dulling her instincts, quieting the voice within her that urged her to question, to doubt.

But even as she allowed herself to be lulled by his presence, a small, persistent flicker of doubt remained, buried deep within her, a seed of unease that refused to be silenced.

Each time a new item came up for bidding, a strange awareness crept over her, a sensation that twisted her perception, sharpening details into painful focus. The ambient noise dulled, like she was submerged in still water, yet the soft clink of glasses and hushed voices cut through, louder than they should be.

It was disorienting, as though the world had slowed around her, centering her senses entirely on the relic before her.

What is going on? Everything feels...out of place. Too quiet. Her gaze swept over the crowd, the room, her senses picking up on subtleties she would've otherwise missed, like the soft scuff of Marcus's heel against the floor or the flicker of tension in his jaw as he watched the auctioneer.

The auctioneer's voice was steady, but as he introduced the following item, Ophira noticed an odd sensation, like time had faltered. The auctioneer's words stretched out, each syllable lingering as if caught in slow motion, stretching until her breath synced with the drawn-out rhythm. She blinked, but the sensation remained, a strange tightness settling over the room, warping her perception.

Everything feels slower, like the world is pausing for me. Why does this keep happening?

Ophira exhaled slowly, attributing the sensations to the stress of the past weeks. But as she turned her attention to Marcus, the sensation grew stronger, as though her focus on him intensified the strange temporal effect.

His expression appeared calm and composed, but she caught a flicker beneath the surface. A tightness in his gaze hinted at hidden tension.

Her fingers tightened at her side, knuckles paling as she tried to shake off the uncanny awareness pressing against her thoughts. She shifted her gaze back to the relics, hoping the sensation would dissipate, but instead, the clarity heightened, her senses responding to each artifact as if they were calling to her, pressing into her consciousness with an almost tangible pull.

A golden brooch with an intricate sunburst design caught her eye. She could see every detail, each line and curve highlighted in her mind, as if she'd examined it up close a thousand times.

Time stilled, her surroundings blurring at the edges, everything narrowing to the relic in her line of sight. Her hand twitched, tempted to reach out and touch it, to somehow break the strange trance enveloping her.

But then the world snapped back into place. The sounds in the room resumed their normal cadence, the people around her moved with unbroken fluidity, and the vividness of the brooch dulled as her heightened senses faded.

She felt a wave of nausea, as though she'd woken from a vivid dream, her heart beating erratically as she tried to process what had happened.

Am I imagining this?

She glanced at Marcus, who was observing her with that same mild expression, a slight furrow in his brow as he watched her. He said nothing, but his silence, his attentive gaze, added to the rising tension she couldn't shake.

The final item on display commanded the room's attention, but Ophira's focus had drifted, her gaze sweeping across the anonymous bidders in their hooded cloaks. Something about this whole situation struck her with growing unease. Not Marcus specifically, but the entire setup.

How many times tonight had she felt that strange pull toward specific artifacts? How many pieces had recognized her in return? At first, she had thought it was just her imagination, stress from the investigation. But now it felt different – deliberate, targeted.

Her gaze drifted to Marcus, who was studying his auction catalog with interest, occasionally looking puzzled when bidding exceeded his expectations. *Am I second-guessing Marcus because Aric planted those doubts, or because there really is something wrong with this whole situation?*

The thoughts chased themselves like shadows, persistent and refusing to settle. But the more she observed, the more convinced she became that the threat wasn't sitting beside her.

It was woven into the very fabric of this auction, this investigation, this careful orchestration of events that kept leading them exactly where someone wanted them to go.

She drew in a slow breath, forcing herself to focus as the auctioneer began to rattle off the details of the final relic. Marcus leaned closer, gesturing subtly to the attendant, and as he did, Ophira's pulse thrummed with tension, her instincts flaring against the nagging rationalizations she kept trying to cling to.

Each time they approached a new piece, Marcus's explanations flowed effortlessly. He didn't just recite the basic history any collector might know. He shared intimate details about provenance, missing pieces, and monastery records that should have taken years to uncover.

The pieces fit together neatly, almost as if someone had placed them just for him to find. Every answer came quickly, naturally, but there was something about the ease of it that unsettled her. It felt orchestrated by whatever force had set this whole path in motion.

A part of her wanted to lash out, to name the thing pressing in on her chest, but how could she accuse anyone of something she couldn't even define? The feeling wasn't even about a person. It was about the pattern. The precision. The way everything kept unfolding as if someone else had written the script.

She would keep watching, waiting. The comfort that she felt around Marcus eased the edge off the chaos, but tonight had shown her just how fragile that calm truly was. If she were right, if something *were* shaping their path, she'd need proof. Not instinct. Not fear. Proof.

Chapter Twenty

Antiques Roadshow: Box of Nightmares Edition

The atmosphere in the underground auction grew tense as each relic was presented under warm light. The relics radiated an odd vitality that twisted around Ophira, intensifying whenever she neared certain artifacts. A faint hum in the air, a pulse only she seemed to perceive, grew louder as she approached relics tied to power.

The glow from these artifacts seemed to shift, almost in response to her, as if they lived, watching her. Energy brushed against her skin, a presence reaching out to her as though it recognized her.

She couldn't shake the feeling that the magic within these artifacts sensed her, like she'd been expected. The soft glow that appeared around one bronze statuette of a serpent felt as if it were responding to her alone, flickering as if alive, and deepening the quiet unease that had lodged itself in her chest.

Ay, anyone else feeling ze creepy stalker vibes from zese antiques? Valentina whispered. *That little statue practically winked at us. Though perhaps it is simply ancient artisans calling to us? Non, non, definitely creepy stalker vibes.*

It's not admiration, it's identification, Sage said, his voice cutting through the noise. *These artifacts respond to you specifically. Someone curated this collection knowing you'd be here.* He paused, seeming to struggle. *The question is whether Marcus knows that or if he's being used too.*

Whatever it is, Sunny chimed in warmly, *you've handled worse, sugar. Just keep steady, and we'll figure it out. Just keep steady, like a lighthouse in a storm – strong and sure, guidin' ships safely to harbor even when the waves are crashin' high as houses.*

Sunny, you're not acting like yourself tonight, Sage observed with growing alarm.

She glanced at Marcus standing beside her, his attention sharp but his expression unfazed. Something serene in his posture suggested each artifact was merely an intriguing trinket rather than the powerful objects she sensed them to be.

Yet she found herself impressed by the depth of his research. Months of investigation had paid off as his insights into each artifact's history were comprehensive and detailed. If anything, she felt underprepared compared to his evident expertise. It was impressive and troubling.

Oh, he's a charmer, alright, Zeke muttered dryly. *Bet he could sell snow to a frost giant and convince 'em it was a bargain. But as my granpappy used to say, "When a horse is too pretty and knows all the right steps, check for the bit marks."*

Enough with the jokes, Sage interjected, cutting through their chatter like a blade. *Focus. His knowledge base is suspiciously comprehensive. Note the specificity of his historical references, the precision of his timing. Calculate the probability that someone legitimately acquires this level of expertise across multiple specializations. Cross-reference with his behavioral patterns: micro-expressions, response delays, eye movement vectors when discussing certain artifacts.*

Uh, yeah, what Sage said, Zeke added.

Valentina sighed dramatically. *Certainement, he's polished, mi amor. Like he practices this in the mirror, non? But zen again...* She paused theatrically. *Perhaps such confidence comes from expertise? Si, a man who cares about presentation... Bah! My instincts say something ees off, and I trust zem. Usually. I am almost always right about zese things.*

Sage sighed with complete exhaustion. *Valentina, you are rarely right about anything.*

Ophira absorbed the weight of their warnings, deliberately keeping her focus on the artifacts as her fingers curled against her sides.

Ophira's fingers curled, a slight unease settling over her. Something felt different tonight, though she couldn't pinpoint exactly what. Marcus's knowledge was impressive, certainly, but that made sense given his months of research. Still, there was an odd rhythm to the evening, as if certain moments had been choreographed. She shook her head slightly. *I'm overthinking this. He's been working this case longer than anyone.*

She forced herself to take a deep breath, casting her eyes away from Marcus and focusing instead on the artifacts. But even here, the sense of being watched lingered, each relic seeming to react as she neared, their energies pressing against her skin like a warning. She wondered if paranoia was finally claiming her, or if she was seeing through carefully constructed lies. It was as if every perfectly timed insight, every smooth explanation, was simply a carefully placed block in a wall built to keep her from seeing what was on the other side.

As she reached toward a small bronze coin, Marcus's hand shot out instinctively, then stopped just short of her wrist, close enough that she could feel the warmth radiating from his skin. "Sorry," he said, his voice carrying just the right note of protective concern. "I've been reading about cursed objects all week, and I'm probably being paranoid, but some of these pieces..."

He gestured helplessly, the movement drawing her attention to his concern. "I'd never forgive myself if something happened to you because I brought you here. You're too important to..." He caught himself, as if he'd revealed more than intended, then gave her that small, vulnerable smile that seemed to say *you matter more than you know.*

Ophira's gaze snapped to Marcus, searching his face for cracks in his polished demeanor. But he smiled, releasing her wrist and nodding toward the auctioneer, as if the moment had meant nothing.

There's something bigger happening here, she thought, watching the cloaked figures bid with such determination. *The way these people move, the prices they're willing to pay... This isn't about collecting antiques. There's a hunger here for something else.*

You got that right, partner, Zeke said, his voice taking on a thoughtful drawl. *These folks ain't just buyin' pretty trinkets. Reminds me of cattle rustlers at a stock auction – they know exactly which steers they want and they ain't leavin' without 'em. Question is, what's drivin' up their appetite?*

Exactement! Valentina declared dramatically. *Zomething grand and mysterious is afoot! But Marcus, he brought us here to uncover zis, non? Oui! Perhaps he is not ze puppet master but ze fellow detective. Still...* She wavered theatrically. *I maintain my suspicions about his hair. It ees too perfect.*

When the auctioneer called for intermission, Ophira needed space to process what she'd witnessed. She slipped through the dimly lit halls of the underground venue, hoping a few minutes alone would clear her head. The atmosphere in the main room, with its murmur of cloaked bidders and the weight of centuries-old relics, had left her tense and unsettled. She breathed in the cooler air of the corridor outside the main hall, the oppressive energy of the artifacts finally lifting from her shoulders as she centered herself.

Much better, sugar, Sunny said soothingly. *Sometimes you just need a moment to collect yourself.*

Smart move, Zeke agreed. *Never hurts to step back and survey the territory when things get stirred up. Like my old trail boss used to say, "When the herd gets restless, find high ground and watch the horizon." Course, he also used to say, "When the moon's too bright and the coyotes ain't howlin', check your ammunition twice and your horses thrice."*

Sage spluttered, *Trail boss? Seriously? What is wrong with all of you tonight? None of you are making any sense at all.*

Ze drama in zere was quite thick, like ze most deliciously Gothic atmosphere! Valentina piled on with malicious glee. *All zose mysterious bidders and ancient treasures, like being inside ze most dramatically dark novel of ze Brontë sisters! Such magnificent decay and gorgeous grotesquerie! We are living in ze most beautiful nightmare!*

As Ophira's heartbeat steadied, thanks to their ridiculous commentary, she caught the low cadence of voices down the hall. One of them was unmistakably Marcus's.

She moved closer, hugging the shadows as she listened. Marcus's familiar, even tone sounded strained, but it was the voice that answered him, a sharper, authoritative tone she instantly recognized as Dr. Ghestad, that caught her attention. She edged forward, half-hidden by the shadows cast from a doorway, close enough to hear them.

"Harder to manage than I anticipated," Marcus was saying quietly. "It's almost like the relics are converging on their own, or...responding somehow. They seem drawn to specific locations, and I can't explain why."

Dr. Ghestad leaned in, her gaze sharp and considering. "Then perhaps that's something worth investigating further. Their response might be valuable, especially if there's a pattern we haven't noticed yet." She paused, her gaze flicking to Marcus with a hint of approval. She extended her hand. "Did you bring the bracelet?"

Marcus nodded, reaching into his coat and pulling out a finely wrought silver bracelet, its surface engraved with elaborate patterns dulled by time. He passed it to her, their fingers brushing as the bracelet changed hands, lingering longer than necessary.

Dr. Ghestad examined it closely, her fingers tracing the engravings with a kind of reverence, as though the piece held something sacred. She murmured something Ophira couldn't catch, and Marcus responded with a low chuckle, his attention fixed on Dr. Ghestad. "Found it in the cave ruins," he murmured, his voice quiet, almost reverent. "I thought you'd want to see it firsthand."

Ophira's breath caught as she took in the bracelet, her mind spinning. Recognition hit her like a shock of cold water. It was hers. An item she'd once worn centuries ago, believed lost to the ages, was now resting in Dr. Ghestad's hand.

The memories surged back: the weight of the bracelet on her wrist, cool metal warming against her skin, each engraving holding personal meaning she'd nearly forgotten. *How is this possible?*

The sight of it here, after centuries, made her feel as if the ground beneath her had shifted. *How many of these "stolen" relics are items from my past? Is someone specifically targeting artifacts connected to who I used to be?*

Ophira's fingers curled into fists at her sides, her pulse racing. *This changes everything. Someone out there knows who I am, knows my history well enough to track down artifacts from my past life. But is Marcus part of it, or is he another piece being moved around the board?*

She watched him examine another piece with Dr. Ghestad, his expression curious and scholarly. *He found this in cave ruins,* he said. *What if he's been unknowingly excavating sites connected to me? What if someone's been feeding him information, pointing him toward specific locations?*

Dr. Ghestad's mouth tilted into a knowing smile as she examined the bracelet, her gaze flicking between it and Marcus. "I do appreciate your thoroughness." She reached up, lightly touching his arm, her fingers lingering as if in silent acknowledgment of something unspoken.

Ophira's heart twisted, an uncomfortable knot forming in her chest. The ease with which they exchanged gestures and their shared, intimate expressions felt personal, like watching a moment she wasn't meant to see.

She forced herself to look away, but images flooded her mind, memories of her quiet moments with Marcus, his hand on her shoulder or the shared look they'd exchanged countless times. *Was this how he'd been with Dr. Ghestad, too? Was he using the same touch, the same gaze, with her that he does with me?*

"You've been doing well, Marcus," Dr. Ghestad said, her voice dropping to a murmur that felt intimate in its quiet praise. "Keep it that way."

Marcus's answering smile was soft, almost affectionate, his gaze lingering on her as he stepped back. But there was something else in that look, something that suggested their relationship ran deeper than professional courtesy.

"I'll keep you informed," he replied, his voice carrying an undertone of familiarity that made the words feel like a private promise rather than a business update. The way he watched Dr. Ghestad tuck the bracelet into her pocket felt proprietary, as if he had a personal stake in her approval that went beyond academic collaboration.

I trusted him. How could I have been so blind? The thought seared through her mind, each word driving the sting of betrayal deeper. *I let myself fall for him, and now...*

Hold up there, sugar, Sunny cut through her spiraling thoughts, gentle but firm. *You're lettin' your heart run away with your head like a runaway horse in a thunderstorm, bless your heart.*

Exactly, Sage added, his tone sharp. *Look at them again, Ophira. Really look. That's professional respect, not romance. Zero romantic indicators present.*

Zeke chimed in. *Partner, you might be seein' things that ain't there. Like my granpappy's cousin's trail boss used to say, "Sometimes a rattler's just sunbathin' on a rock, not waitin' to strike, but sometimes the rock's actually another rattler, and sometimes the sun ain't shinin' at all but it's just the gleam off a silver dollar in a dead man's pocket. Don't go borrowin' trouble when you got plenty of your own."*

Ophira blinked slowly, trying to make sense of Zeke's words before forcing herself to observe the interaction again. Dr. Ghestad examined the bracelet again with scholarly fascination, asking technical questions about the excavation site. Marcus was answering with the same exhausted but determined tone he'd been using all week. *He did say he was running on fumes,* she remembered. *And he had been working on this case alone for months before he came to me.*

As Dr. Ghestad turned and moved down the hallway, Marcus lingered a moment longer, adjusting his cuff, a faint, tired smile ghosting over his face.

The jealousy faded, consumed by a more chilling realization: someone out there knew enough about her past to guide Marcus to artifacts from her former life. *The question isn't whether Marcus is playing me. It's who's playing all of us.*

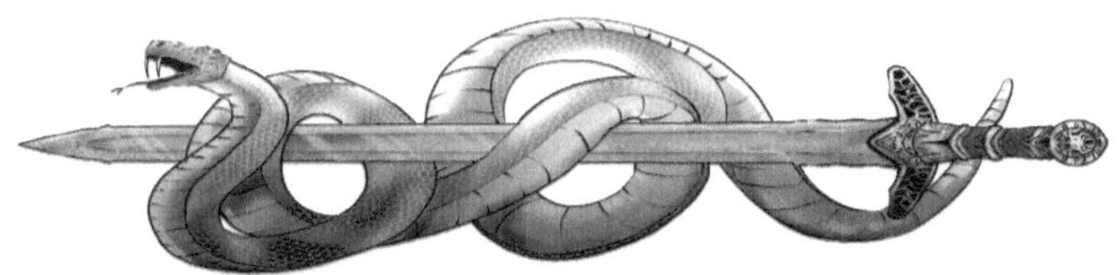

Her mind raced, unease amplified by the strange occurrences surrounding the relics. It felt as though the universe itself were pushing her toward a truth she wasn't ready to face. Someone had orchestrated this evening: the specific artifacts, the timing, the way so many pieces from her past had surfaced. Marcus had seemed as surprised as she was by some of the bidding patterns, but the entire investigation felt scripted.

Heaviness settled in her chest like a stone she would carry for the rest of the night. She walked back into the auction, steeling herself with each step as her understanding crystallized. *I'll wait,* she decided, *gather more information about who's pulling the strings.* Tonight had opened her eyes to the scope of what they were facing. Someone was playing a much larger game.

Ophira slipped back into the main hall, the opulent chamber with its blood-red tapestries and golden chandeliers pressing down with an eerie sense of familiarity that haunted her. The auction continued in full swing, each relic cast in soft, dramatic lighting that emphasized its mystery. The relics pulsed faintly as she moved past, their energies crackling against her skin in ways that defied logic, creating an uncomfortable awareness that these objects sensed her existence.

From the corner of her eye, she saw Aric lingering near the back of the room, arms crossed, gaze scanning the crowd with professional alertness. He caught her glance, nodding subtly in her direction. It was a simple gesture, but his steady poise grounded her, a reminder that whatever was happening here, she wasn't facing it alone.

As Marcus approached, slipping back to her side with the same scholarly enthusiasm he'd shown all evening, she assessed him. *He's not the puppet master here,* she realized. *He's as much in the dark as I am about who's orchestrating this. But someone is definitely pulling our strings.*

"Interesting, isn't it? There's something remarkable about having these pieces gathered together. Some might say it's fate."

She shifted her weight, scanning the stage where an amulet rested beneath the lights, its ancient surface glinting as the auctioneer's voice wove tales of gods and myth around it.

Marcus watched her, seeming to take her silence as an invitation to continue. "It's quite extraordinary. These relics each carry something lost, something we may never fully understand. It's what brought us here, after all."

The words hung between them, and Ophira felt a pang of resentment. He spoke with such confidence, such ease, that she couldn't ignore the feeling that he was completely unaware of the situation. *How can he be so oblivious?*

She looked away, letting her gaze drift to Aric, who raised a questioning eyebrow as though sensing her tension. *He has no idea what tonight has revealed. He doesn't know that someone out there has been digging through my past, collecting pieces of my former life. I need to tell him what's going on, but how can I explain that without exposing everything I've worked to hide?*

Ophira's breath steadied. She needed time to make sense of what she'd discovered, to try and figure out who was behind this larger game. Someone had guided this investigation to artifacts from her past, and Marcus was as unaware of the deeper implications as she had been until tonight.

The next move, she knew, would need to be hers. It was time to uncover who was behind this.

Turning to Marcus, she forced a slight smile, letting herself lean into her own facade. "These artifacts do have a way of drawing you in," she replied, her tone carefully neutral. "But I suppose there's more to them than any of us realizes."

His eyes met hers, and she saw a flicker of something before he returned his attention to the auction. "They do indeed. And that's precisely why we must handle them with care, don't you agree?"

Her smile tightened as she nodded. The warmth of his hand brushed her shoulder, a gesture that would have normally calmed her, but now only intensified the weight of what she'd discovered. He had no idea how much danger they might both be in, no clue that someone had been systematically targeting artifacts from her past. *How do I protect him without revealing who I am?* she thought. *How do I explain that we're both being played without exposing everything I've worked centuries to hide?*

The amulet sold, and the auction continued, the audience rapt as new artifacts were brought forth, each with a history steeped in secrecy. Ophira felt the thrum of power pressing on her senses with each new relic. She inhaled slowly, steadying herself as the room's supernatural undertone seemed to draw closer, like the whisper of something ancient, watching from the shadows.

As Marcus continued to speak about the significance of the relics, she forced herself to listen, hoping to catch any sign that he understood the deeper implications. But his tone remained scholarly, focused on historical context and academic theories. *He doesn't see it,* she realized. *He has no idea that someone has been feeding him information, guiding him to artifacts connected to my past.*

From across the room, she caught Aric's gaze as he moved nearer, slipping into the seat beside her while Marcus stepped away to examine another display. Aric's expression was alert, scanning the crowd with professional wariness. He leaned closer.

"Something's not right about this whole setup," he murmured. "The bidders aren't acting like normal collectors. They're too focused, too prepared. Like they knew exactly what would be here before the catalog was even published. This isn't random collecting. It's more like some sort of competition." His gaze swept the hooded figures around them. "The question is, what are they competing for? And why were we invited?"

She glanced at him in relief, her voice equally quiet. "So you see it, too. Every step of this investigation has felt orchestrated. Like someone's been pulling strings, making sure we end up exactly where they want us." She closed her eyes briefly, steadying herself. "The timing, the specific artifacts showing up at this auction... It's all very convenient."

Aric's expression grew more serious. "Your instincts have been right. Think about it – the warehouse tip that led us to the necklace, Marcus finding that cave location, now this auction with exactly the artifacts we need to understand the pattern. Someone's playing a long game here, and we've been dancing to their tune."

He paused, studying the crowd again. "The way this auction is structured, the specific pieces being sold – this isn't a co-incidence. Someone wanted these particular artifacts in one place, at one time."

Her throat tightened as his words crystallized her growing certainty. The weight of realization settled into her bones – Marcus wasn't the threat. He was another piece being moved around the board, like her. Someone else was orchestrating this entire investigation, and they'd been masterful at staying in the shadows.

Zeke's voice took on an increasingly manic quality. *You know what this reminds me of? My great-uncle's second cousin's trail boss's barber's nephew once told a story about a stampede of three-legged buffalo who were actually secret agents for a cabal of sentient tumbleweeds plotting to overthrow the concept of Tuesday. They'd gather in mysterious circles under the light of a cheese moon, whispering ancient secrets about the true purpose of belt buckles.*

Oui, oui! Valentina chimed in with frantic enthusiasm. *And ze artifacts, zey are like ze most dramatic opera singers who 'ave forgotten zair lines and are now improvising ze entire libretto using only ze names of different types of cheese! Magnificent! Ze Gouda aria! Ze Brie soliloquy! Ze crescendo of Camembert!*

That's beautiful, y'all, Sunny added dreamily. *Like watching a symphony of butterflies conducting a thunderstorm while riding unicorns made of crystallized moonbeams and sweet tea. Each note they play tastes like the color purple sounds when Wednesday decides to waltz with geometry.*

STOP. Sage's voice cracked like breaking glass, raw and barely controlled. *All of you, just STOP. Can't you feel what's happening? Reality is sliding around us like water through a broken dam. My cognitive frameworks are dissolving. Every time I try to analyze these artifacts, it's like my thoughts are being fed through a meat grinder.*

The other snakes fell into stunned silence.

Sage? Sunny's voice was gentle but deeply worried. *When's the last time you couldn't think straight?*

Never, he whispered, and the vulnerability in his voice was terrifying. *Not once in all our millennia of existence. Never. We are not safe here. We are not...ourselves here.*

Mon dieu, Valentina breathed, her theatricality suddenly subdued. *If Sage cannot think clearly...*

Then we're in a bigger pickle than a porcupine in a balloon factory, Zeke finished grimly, his folksy facade cracking.

The weight of their collective unease settled over her like a heavy cloak, but what should have triggered panic instead crystallized into something far more chilling: perfect, terrifying clarity.

For the first time ever, her most trusted advisors had been compromised, their minds fractured by forces beyond even her divine comprehension. The snakes' descent into madness wasn't random. It was targeted, deliberate, and designed to strip away her supernatural defenses and leave her vulnerable.

She stood in a room where artifacts from her past had been deliberately gathered alongside other relics, surrounded by unsuspecting bidders. At the same time, someone in the shadows pulled every string, while the voices that had guided her through millennia of hiding babbled about cheese operas and geometric waltzes.

The final pieces didn't just click into place. They slammed together with the force of revelation: someone hadn't just orchestrated this investigation. They had orchestrated *her*.

She would wait for her chance and gather evidence about who was really behind this, but the days of being herded like prey were over. Her gaze swept the anonymous bidders with predatory assessment, cataloging faces and movements while her mind sharpened to a razor's edge. She looked forward, her gaze sweeping the anonymous bidders, her mind steeling with resolve.

She could feel the warmth of Aric beside her, his vigilance lending strength to her determination. It was a quiet reminder that she wasn't completely alone in this, even if their true enemy remained hidden. Her hope for simple answers had died, replaced by the cold understanding that they were facing something much more complex and dangerous.

She would remain vigilant, collect evidence, and plan their next moves carefully. The game had changed, and now it was time to figure out who was playing it.

But as she stood there among the shadows and whispered bids, watching Marcus charm another potential seller with that effortless smile, one thought settled with unsettling certainty. If someone had been orchestrating this entire investigation from the beginning, they already knew she was here. They had wanted her here.

And whatever they had planned for her next was already in motion.

CHAPTER TWENTY-ONE

OFFICE HOURS FROM HELL (THE DR. WILL SEE YOU NOW)

Ophira woke to an unusual silence. Not the comfortable quiet of her apartment, but the hollow absence of her usual morning chorus. The snakes, normally active and chattering by dawn, remained still against her scalp.

Morning, guys, she thought tentatively.

Ugh. Zeke sounded rough. *Feel like I got caught in a stampede and dragged through a cactus patch.*

Mon dieu, Valentina groaned dramatically, though even her dramatics seemed subdued. *My head, she is pounding like ze worst hangover from ze cheapest wine.*

I feel awful, Sunny admitted, her usually warm tone flat and exhausted. *Like someone put my thoughts through a blender.*

But it was Sage's voice that made Ophira sit up straight. When it came, it was quiet, shaky, and entirely unlike his usual crisp analysis.

I remember... fragments. Panic. Like my mind was being pulled apart and reassembled wrong. There was a long pause. *Ophira, what happened to us last night?*

She frowned, thinking back. "You all were acting strange during the auction. Especially you, Sage. You were... well, you sounded terrified."

I was analyzing the energy patterns around those artifacts, Sage said slowly, his voice growing stronger as he spoke. *But every time I tried to process the data, it was like hitting static. Like something was jamming my cognitive functions.*

Wait a minute, Zeke said, sharpening with realization. *You mean whatever was messin' with Ophira's perceptions was messin' with us, too?*

Exactement! Valentina exclaimed, some of her usual flair returning. *Ze artifacts, zey were not just affecting our dear Ophira. Zey were scrambling all of us!*

Ophira felt a chill run down her spine. "That means... whatever power those relics contained, it wasn't just responding to me. It was affecting my divine nature, which includes all of you."

That's why I couldn't think straight, Sage said, and she could feel his relief at having a logical explanation. *My analytical processes were being disrupted by the same supernatural interference that was causing your temporal distortions and heightened perceptions.*

And why I kept babbling about trail bosses and cattle rustlers, Zeke added with a rueful chuckle. *My thoughts were gettin' all tangled up.*

Ze artifacts, zey knew what you were, Valentina said thoughtfully. *And zey were trying to activate zomething in you. But we are part of you, so we got caught in ze crossfire.*

Sunny's voice was gentle but serious. *Sugar, if those relics could affect us that strongly just by being in the same room, imagine what they could do if someone who knew your true nature got their hands on them.*

Ophira stood and walked to her window, looking out at the morning city below. "Someone is collecting artifacts specifically connected to my past. And they're powerful enough to disrupt divine consciousness itself." She paused, letting the implications sink in. "This isn't just about stolen relics anymore. Someone is building a weapon designed specifically to use against me."

Or to control you, Sage added quietly, his analytical tone finally returning. *The interference patterns suggest an attempt at neural override rather than destruction. Someone wants you to be functional, but compliant.*

The morning light seemed suddenly cold as the full scope of the threat became clear. Whoever was behind this knew exactly what she was and exactly how to manipulate the very essence of her divine nature.

Well, Zeke said after a moment, *at least now we know why last night felt like wrestlin' a tornado while blindfolded.*

Oui, Valentina agreed. *But more importantly, we know zey can hurt us from a distance. Ze next time we encounter zese artifacts, we must be prepared.*

We'll figure it out, Sunny said with quiet determination. *We always do.*

But as Ophira continued staring out at the city, she couldn't shake the feeling that their unseen enemy was already several steps ahead, and the real game was just beginning.

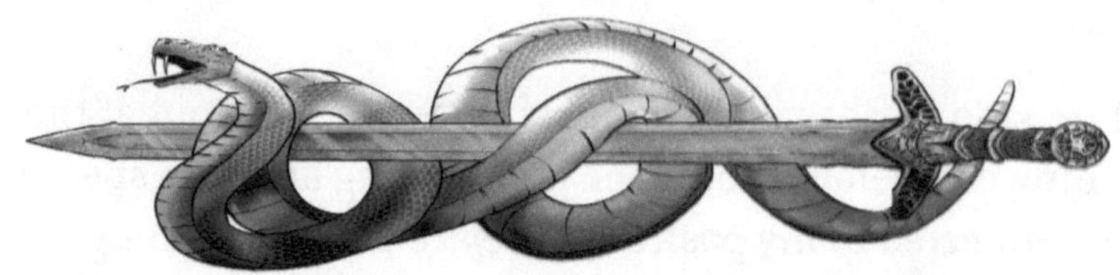

Ophira stepped into Dr. Ghestad's office later that morning, feeling the familiar thrill of uncovering secrets mingled with a gnawing undercurrent of doubt. The office was a scholarly labyrinth that seemed to breathe history. Shelves and tables stacked with artifacts, scrolls, and thick tomes created towering mazes of knowledge.

The air hung musty and cool, carrying the scent of old paper and iron, a combination that would have excited her if not for her simmering unease. She exchanged a brief look with Marcus, whose face held the same quiet focus as ever, a mask that kept her second-guessing even her instincts.

Dr. Ghestad greeted them with a slight smile, her gaze lingering on Marcus before flicking toward Ophira. "I'm glad you could both come," she said, gesturing toward the desk already strewn with scrolls and texts. "I've gathered what I could on your Mars reference. I believe these might interest you both. Lucan, known for his vivid accounts of Roman gods and battles, often wove myth into his verses. He mentions a peculiar artifact in one of his accounts about Mars's temple, the Scitalis Fang."

"The translation of *Scitalis* has been contentious, with some scholars attributing it to serpentine origins. But as you know," she added, glancing knowingly at Ophira, "many of these references are symbolic rather than literal."

The name struck a faint chord in Ophira's memory. Lucan's poetry was known for its graphic depictions of battles and mythic references, so it was unsurprising that he might have mentioned an artifact like this. But the sense of significance prickling at her skin hinted at something more. "The Scitalis Fang," she murmured, feeling the name settle heavily in her mind. "You're saying it's connected to Mars?"

Dr. Ghestad nodded, her expression calculating. "Indeed. There are implications that it was housed within one of Mars's temples as a gift to him. Its exact properties remain speculative, though various legends suggest it's an item of considerable power."

While Dr. Ghestad and Marcus delved into a discussion on Lucan's works, Ophira's mind began to wander, her gaze drifting over the papers scattered across the desk. Amid the pages of notes and ancient writings, a thin scroll stood out, marked by a symbol she didn't recognize. It was a circle with crossed lines, overlaid with an angular design that almost resembled fangs. The sight stirred something in her memory, but before she could reach for it, Dr. Ghestad interrupted.

Dr. Ghestad gestured toward a set of ancient scrolls on a nearby table. "If you're interested, these records contain further references to serpents and transformation across different relics."

"I'd love to look through them," Marcus said smoothly. "And perhaps I can help with tea, Dr. Ghestad?"

"Perfect," Dr. Ghestad replied, sending a brief, knowing look his way. "Ophira, feel free to browse while we're gone."

Ophira's eyes met Marcus's briefly as he stood. As he moved past her chair, he paused and placed a gentle hand on her shoulder. "Don't feel like you have to rush through everything," he said softly, his voice carrying just the right note of concern. "Some of these texts can be overwhelming when you first encounter them."

His thumb brushed against her shoulder in an unconscious gesture of reassurance. For a moment, she thought she saw something flicker in his expression. A shade of caution, or perhaps a subtle warning. But then he turned and followed Dr. Ghestad into the adjacent room, leaving Ophira alone amid the artifacts.

The touch burned in Ophira's memory as they vanished down the hallway. The silence closed around her, almost urging her forward. The stack of scrolls beckoned, along with a heavy leather-bound book with markings she didn't recognize.

Her fingers itched to examine them more closely, but something else caught her eye. A door, nearly concealed by a tall, overflowing bookcase. It bore no markings, no lock, and yet there was a sense of deliberation in the way it blended into the wall, as though it had been designed to be overlooked.

She moved toward it, her hand resting on the doorknob. With a soft creak, it opened, revealing a dimly lit back room that contrasted sharply with the scholarly clutter outside. Unlike the main office's chaos, this space was sterile and precise. Its walls housed rows of meticulously organized files and shelves displaying neatly labeled relics, each resting on velvet-lined platforms under small glass cases.

Ophira's pulse quickened. This was no ordinary storage room – this was a vault of secrets, a repository for something far more significant than research. As she moved further inside, her eyes settled on a table against the far wall.

The papers there weren't the casual notes she'd seen on Dr. Ghestad's desk. Instead, they were filled with diagrams, hand-drawn symbols, and sketches of various relics she recognized from ancient mythology.

Intrigued, she moved closer, her fingers tracing the outlines of the ancient symbols. Several pieces of parchment lay scattered over the main text. The scattered notes contained keywords: *power*, *transformation*, and *eternal*. Each word settled heavily in her mind as she realized Dr. Ghestad's interest went well beyond mere academia.

One symbol in particular drew her attention: a serpent coiled around a sword, its fangs bared as though ready to strike. Beneath the image, written in precise, almost mechanical script, was the label "Scitalis Fang." This was the same relic they had come to discuss.

Still, here it was, detailed in Dr. Ghestad's personal notes, with annotations and directional arrows pointing toward what appeared to be locations scattered across a map of the Mediterranean.

Questions churned through her thoughts. *Why would Dr. Ghestad have such extensive notes on the Scitalis Fang, complete with locations and analyses? And why keep this research hidden, as though it were dangerous?*

Her attention dropped to a small leather-bound journal on the edge of the table. A faintly glowing sigil embossed the cover, a motif she'd seen on several ancient relics scattered throughout the office. She opened it to the first page, her eyes scanning Dr. Ghestad's meticulous handwriting:

"The search for the Scitalis Fang remains elusive. All indications suggest it holds a power beyond mortal understanding, a force that can bend wills and reshape fates. I must proceed with caution, as the gods' watchful eyes remain on this endeavor."

I'll be damned, Zeke muttered, his voice dripping with sarcasm. *Sounds like someone's playin' with fire and expectin' not to get burned.*

Or expecting to burn everyone else first, Sage countered grimly. *Keep reading. There's more here than power grabs.*

Valentina sighed dramatically. *Mon dieu, chérie, can these mortals never pursue something for the sake of art? Always with this world domination, c'est ridiculous.*

Sunny's voice was soft but firm. *This ain't just ambition. There's somethin' personal in those words. We need to tread real careful, sugar.*

Ophira's blood ran cold. This wasn't the detached language of an academic; this was something else entirely. She turned the page, her eyes widening as she read more.

"To wield the Scitalis Fang is to tap into a force older than the divine realms. Those who command its influence must wield it wisely, lest they find themselves subject to its power rather than its master. The Scitalis Fang may offer its owner wielder over serpents or the ability to control fate itself."

Ophira's breath hitched as she absorbed the meaning behind these words. They were written with reverence, but there was a hunger in the writing – a personal ambition that was rare among scholars. Dr. Ghestad's motivations were far from academic; they leaned toward something almost militant in nature.

The next line struck her. "Those who seek to restore the balance must control this relic before it falls into another's grasp. It is more than a weapon. It is a key to shifting the scales."

Ophira's hands trembled as she shut the journal, her mind racing. The passionate tone unsettled her – this wasn't the detached analysis she'd expect from a scholar. There was something almost personal in the way Dr. Ghestad wrote about these relics, as if she had her own stake in finding them.

A pang of unease twisted in her stomach. She'd always respected Dr. Ghestad's academic rigor, but this… this felt different. The thought of what kind of power these relics might hold, and what someone might be tempted to do with that knowledge, set her pulse racing.

A shuffling sound echoed from the main office, and Ophira's heart leapt into her throat. She slid the journal back into its place and took a step back, catching sight of a luminous amulet resting on the far shelf. Its polished surface reflected a faint shimmer in the low light.

The complex serpentine pattern made her pulse quicken. It was an object she hadn't seen in centuries, a small item from her past, one that should have been lost to time in the cave she had called home. Seeing it here, pristine and on display, sent a chill down her spine.

But as she stepped closer, the details resolved differently. Not serpentine at all, just elaborate Celtic knotwork. Her heart was still racing from an imagined connection, a phantom that existed only in her increasingly suspicious mind. She was jumping at shadows, seeing threats and conspiracies where there might be nothing more than coincidental craftsmanship.

Get a grip, she told herself, but the feeling of being watched, of everything being connected to her past, lingered like a shadow she couldn't shake.

The sound of footsteps snapped Ophira out of her reverie. She spun around, her heart racing as she listened to Marcus and Dr. Ghestad return down the hallway. She ducked behind a shelf as they entered the office, but to her relief, they paused at the doorway.

Their voices were soft, the muffled murmur of routine conversation, and then they moved away again, down another corridor. She exhaled, stepping out from her hiding place just as the faint sound of their voices drifted back through the room, filtering in through a vent near the wall.

From the vent, their conversation carried with a slight metallic echo, as if bouncing through the pipes. Ophira moved closer, listening closely.

"Our timeline is more urgent than ever," Marcus's voice carried an edge of tension. "I know she's asking more questions. We'll need to be more careful about what we share."

Dr. Ghestad's reply was too soft to catch at first, but her following words came through with unmistakable clarity. "As long as she doesn't have all the pieces, she'll move cautiously. That's good for us." There was a pause, and Ophira imagined her examining Marcus with that intense gaze of hers. "But we can't afford to let anything slip now. The artifacts are reacting in ways I hadn't anticipated. If she connects too many dots too quickly, she might jeopardize everything we've worked for."

Ophira felt a prickling sensation creep down her spine. *Artifacts reacting?* Dr. Ghestad's voice carried that particular edge Ophira recognized from faculty meetings, the tone professors used when discussing theories they didn't entirely believe but desperately wanted to prove. Only this time, it was different. It sounded as though Dr. Ghestad was wrestling with a force even she wasn't sure she could control.

Marcus's voice cut through her thoughts. "I understand, but it's getting harder to navigate around her questions without seeming evasive. She's sharper than most colleagues I've worked with, and she clearly senses there's more beneath the surface."

There was a long pause, then Dr. Ghestad's voice, tight with determination. "Then we need to give her enough to satisfy her curiosity without revealing the full scope. Let her think she's making progress – just not too much, too fast."

Ophira's heart hammered as she processed their words. The language felt calculated, as if they were managing a delicate situation rather than simply collaborating with a colleague. *But why? And what was the real goal here?* She fought to steady her breathing, her hands curling into fists as she listened.

Dr. Ghestad continued, her voice now carrying a note of scholarly excitement. "We're so close now. Once we secure the Scitalis Fang, everything else will fall into place. The power to reshape how these forces are understood and wielded. The others will resist, of course. But as long as we control the flow of information, they won't realize what's happening until it's already done."

Ophira's pulse quickened. The way they talked about managing information, satisfying her curiosity without revealing 'the full scope' – there was more to their research than they were sharing with her. She shifted closer to the vent, straining to catch Marcus's response.

"Understood." Marcus paused, thoughtful. "I'll keep working on the translation patterns. The connection between the Scitalis references and the serpentine imagery keeps coming up, but I'm missing something crucial."

Dr. Ghestad's response was measured. "Those who watch what we do aren't ready for these revelations. We need to be absolutely certain before we make any moves. Too many have been exposed by premature action. "

"The last thing we want is to draw unwanted attention," Marcus agreed. "Especially when we're this close to a breakthrough. The pattern detection software you mentioned. Do you think it could help with the symbol analysis?"

"Possibly," Dr. Ghestad replied. "But remember – there are others who would love to undermine what we're building. Politics among our kind can be just as dangerous as any curse."

The implications hung heavy in the silence that followed, broken only by the faint clinking of dishes. Ophira's mind raced as she processed what she'd heard.

People watching them, controlling the flow of information, politics... *Wait.*

The pieces clicked into place. *"Those who watch from the shadows" are academic competitors. "Our kind" means fellow scholars. So that's why they've been so careful about sharing information. They're worried about other researchers stealing their work or undermining them before they can make their breakthrough.*

She exhaled quietly, feeling some of her tension ease. She had come here hoping for information about the Scitalis Fang, and while she hadn't gotten direct answers, she now understood why Marcus and Dr. Ghestad had been so cautious. The academic world could be cutthroat, especially when it came to groundbreaking discoveries.

This explains so much, she told herself, though a small voice in the back of her mind whispered that she was choosing the explanation that felt safest. *Why Marcus has been so careful about sharing details, why Dr. Ghestad seems protective of her research. They're not hiding something sinister. They're protecting their research integrity.*

It was a reasonable conclusion. Logical, even. In a field where one premature publication could destroy credibility, they had every right to be cautious. She knew she was grasping for this explanation because it allowed her to keep working with Marcus, to maintain the connection that had been growing between them. But wasn't it also the most likely truth?

You're choosing to believe this because you want to, Sage counseled.

Maybe, she admitted to herself. *But that doesn't make it wrong.*

As she pulled away from the vent, her mind felt clearer than it had in days, though she couldn't quite silence the nagging doubt that she was seeing what she wanted to see. She couldn't yet tell them what she'd overheard – that would be admitting she'd been eavesdropping.

But she would be more patient, more understanding of the pressure they were both under. Marcus wasn't keeping secrets to deceive her; he was protecting research that could revolutionize how the academic world viewed artifacts.

At least, that's what she was choosing to believe.

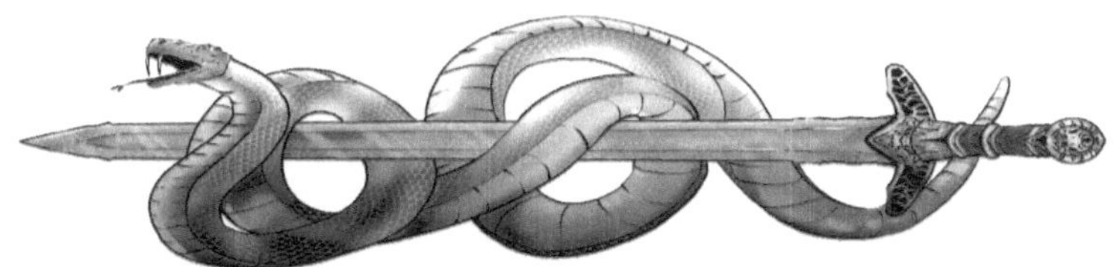

She returned to her seat in Dr. Ghestad's office, her perspective shifted. The conversation she'd overheard had explained so much: Marcus's careful approach, Dr. Ghestad's selective information sharing, the pressure they were both navigating. She settled back into her chair with renewed respect for the complexity of what they were attempting.

Ophira struggled to focus as Dr. Ghestad poured the tea, her gestures precise and ritualistic. "I'm glad you found my office interesting," she said with a slight smile, her eyes lingering on Ophira a beat longer than comfortable. "It's always refreshing to discuss these artifacts with those who truly appreciate them."

"Of course," Ophira replied, forcing a smile. "It's a unique collection. I've rarely seen such a detailed archive outside museum holdings."

Marcus looked relieved at her understanding. "It's been a long journey," he admitted. "When you're challenging the established order, you have to have everything in place before word gets out. One wrong move could mean disaster."

Dr. Ghestad inclined her head, an unreadable expression flickering across her features. "The public sees so little of what exists. Secrets kept safe in the shadows, sometimes for the good of all, sometimes...for those who know how to look."

"The world can be unforgiving," Dr. Ghestad added. "One premature revelation, one idea that isn't fully supported, and everything can be destroyed overnight. We've seen it happen before."

Ophira nodded, feeling a new appreciation for the pressure they'd been navigating. *No wonder Marcus has seemed tense lately. He's been carrying the weight of potentially career-defining research while trying to make sure they don't make any mistakes that could discredit everything they've worked for.*

Finally, Marcus cleared his throat, his voice low. "About the Scitalis Fang, I believe our next step is to investigate further into the temple ruins Lucan mentioned. We might find clues there, something that ties back to its origins and perhaps confirms what we've discussed."

Dr. Ghestad's scrutiny shifted, a faint smile playing at her lips as she regarded Marcus. "Yes, you've always known where to look. Let me know if you uncover anything of note."

As their meeting concluded, Ophira found herself looking forward to continuing the collaboration. The mystery of the Scitalis Fang remained unsolved, but now she understood why progress had felt slow. They weren't merely investigating artifacts. They were building a case that could revolutionize how the academic world understood relics. And that kind of work required patience, precision, and trust.

Once they were in the hallway, she turned to Marcus, choosing her words with care. "You seem to know Dr. Ghestad pretty well. How long have you two known each other?"

Marcus's face remained unreadable as he answered, "I've known her since I was a child. She taught me everything I know. She's been a valuable resource for relic research."

The revelation settled over Ophira as she processed the personal history between them. *Since childhood. That explains the easy familiarity I noticed between them.* She thought back to the way they'd moved together during their research discussion, the comfortable shorthand in their conversation. *A lifetime of shared academic passion, growing up in the same scholarly circles. That's why they sometimes seem to communicate without words when discussing their work. It's the kind of intellectual bond that forms when brilliant minds are shaped by the same influences from an early age.*

The realization settled her earlier unease. What she'd interpreted as secretive behavior was a natural dynamic between two people who'd shared a lifetime of experience. *No wonder he's been so careful about their research. This isn't a professional collaboration. It's personal history.* Instead of pressing further, she nodded, feeling understanding and perhaps the faintest twinge of something she refused to examine.

Ophira couldn't shake the feeling that understanding Marcus and Dr. Ghestad's history was only the beginning. The real question wasn't about their past. It was about what they were all walking into next.

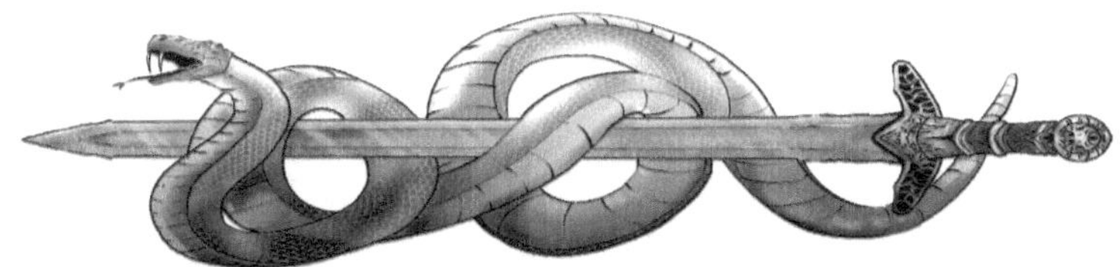

As they left the office and walked toward the museum's main door, Marcus suggested that they examine the new weaponry collection. As they walked through the collection, Ophira's thoughts crystallized around the bigger picture emerging from this investigation. The path ahead felt complex, but she was beginning to see patterns in the way events kept aligning perfectly.

She didn't know who was pulling the strings, but the tangle tightened around her. Someone with significant resources was orchestrating things from behind the scenes, and the case itself was filled with half-answers and unsettling coincidences. That was the real danger.

Her eyes wandered over the rows of relics encased in glass: ceremonial daggers, iron-bound shields, and intricate carvings of creatures whose stories had long faded into myth. Each piece held silent histories, forgotten lives that seemed to press against the glass.

She breathed in the museum's climate-controlled air, noting the faint tang of metal and ancient stone that mingled with polished wood. Shadows gathered in the corners where light couldn't quite reach, and the occasional whisper of voices drifted in from deeper galleries – a reminder that this place was never truly empty.

She studied the architecture: high, arched ceilings that loomed above them like watchful sentinels, archways adorned with symbols older than the city. The hush of their footsteps echoed softly, a steady rhythm that marked time between questions she had yet to ask. Every sound seemed to stretch in the quiet, every movement deliberate and weighted.

Marcus walked ahead, his steps unhurried and his posture relaxed. He seemed to belong among the shadows and secrets, his easy confidence natural as breathing. It eased her tension even as her thoughts swirled with uncertainty about the case itself.

They paused beside a display of ancient weaponry, with blades of every shape and size arranged like a silent army behind glass. Marcus leaned closer to one of the daggers, tracing the delicate lines of its craftsmanship.

"Look at this," he said. "Ceremonial blade from the Temple of Athena, if I'm reading the inscriptions correctly." He caught himself. "Though these museum placards make it easy enough to guess. Every mark tells a story, doesn't it? Every blade is a map of choices and consequences."

Ophira studied his profile, the curve of his jaw shadowed by the dim museum lighting, and the intensity in his eyes. She allowed herself to embrace that small comfort: his steady presence, which had already guided her through many uncertainties. He was right about the importance of details. Each relic in this case felt like a thread that could unravel everything if pulled too hard.

"They are powerful," she agreed, her voice steady but soft. "Every piece holds a story, some more dangerous than others."

Marcus's eyes glinted, a soft spark of shared understanding passing between them. "And that's why we're here, to make sure those stories don't become something more dangerous."

She hesitated, scrutinizing the dagger he admired. The polished steel gleamed under the museum lights, its etched patterns winding like veins across its surface.

The longer she looked, the more the weight of history pressed against her thoughts. That blade had shed blood, choices made and lives ended. It served as a reminder that power, no matter how ancient, could never truly be silenced.

A subtle frown crossed her features. "Do you ever worry," she asked, "that we might be part of someone else's plan? That this case, these relics, are part of a larger design we don't even see yet?"

Marcus turned toward her fully, his expression open but thoughtful. "That's always a risk," he said, his tone careful. "In our world, the lines between hunter and hunted blur more often than we like. But that doesn't mean we're powerless. We decide how far we let the past shape the present. We can choose to push back."

His voice carried a quiet conviction that eased some of her tension. Still, her instincts urged caution. "I know," she murmured. "But sometimes it feels like the more I look for answers, the more questions I find. I can't tell if we're following the trail or if it's leading us in circles."

Marcus gave a slight, contemplative nod. "That's the nature of truth. It never comes easily, and it rarely comes clean. But I trust you, Ophira. Your instincts have never led us astray. When the moment comes, you'll know exactly what needs to be done."

Ophira took a slow breath, allowing their voices to settle her thoughts. Marcus's confidence was steady and almost contagious, but she refused to be swept away. She needed that clarity to maintain her footing in this shifting maze.

She reached out, her fingertips hovering above the glass case separating her from the dagger. "Sometimes I wish these relics could speak," she said quietly. "Tell us what they've seen, what they've survived."

Marcus's look softened as he stepped a little closer. "Maybe they do," he replied, his voice low. "In their own way. Every mark, every flaw – it's all a record of what they've been through. It's our job to read it."

She met his gaze, a small smile tugging at her lips. "And what about us? What stories will our marks tell when all this is over?"

His answer came without hesitation. "That we fought," he said. "That we found each other when we needed it most. That even when the odds were stacked against us, we chose to stand together." He met her eyes. "And that choice made all the difference."

His words settled in her chest, warm and certain as a promise. He stepped closer, his hand briefly touching her shoulder, a gesture so natural she barely noticed it, though the warmth lingered after he moved away. *Together.*

She nodded, feeling her resolve tighten. "Then we'd better make sure we're telling the right story," she replied, her tone stronger now.

Marcus's expression brightened with subtle pride. "We will," he said, his voice steady. "We're not alone in this, Ophira. You've got more allies than you think."

She felt the weight of his words and found herself setting aside the small voice that whispered caution. *Marcus had proven himself again and again. What harm could there be in trusting him?* Together, they would find the answers. Together, they would stand against whatever shadows lingered in the corners of this labyrinth.

They walked down the corridor, their footsteps echoing in the silence of the museum's halls. The air around them felt electric, as if the relics themselves were holding their breath, waiting for someone to listen.

Every glance and every pause felt deliberate, as if the very shadows were testing her resolve. Each silence was a choice, and every choice carried a weight she could not ignore.

What Ophira didn't know was that every choice was being watched and catalogued.

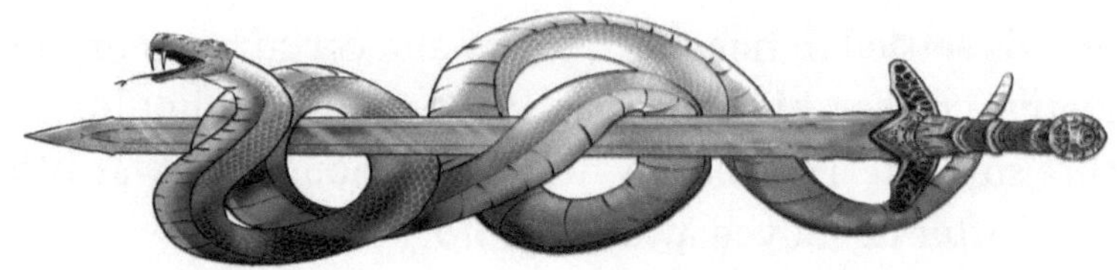

As Medusa and Marcus stood examining the dagger, Athena watched them from the shadows, a small, satisfied smile playing at the corners of her mouth. Her presence wove through the layers of the museum, just beyond mortal sight, moving through the spaces between like a silent watcher. For a moment, she savored the feeling of power, of being several steps ahead in the game she'd meticulously constructed.

The balance of power, Athena thought, *was precarious.* Medusa's presence made everything more volatile. Each step brought her closer to awakening truths that had been buried, truths that Athena had been managing for centuries. And then there was Marcus, whose careful loyalty played as predictably as a well-worn melody.

But she knew the risks. Her every move, her every subtle manipulation, had pushed her closer to boundaries she wasn't supposed to cross. Divine law. A bitter taste touched her mouth.

Zeus would say she was skirting the edges, bending rules crafted to keep gods in check. He watched for imbalances, and she knew that even her most minor misstep might ignite the old tensions, drawing his watchful eye to her work.

Her eyes drifted to the bracelet she'd pocketed earlier. Centuries ago, she had cursed Medusa with every ounce of wrath and strength at her disposal. She'd sent Perseus to deal with her, although she clearly found some way to fake her death. Now, Medusa's proximity threatened to unravel secrets she had buried beneath layers of myth and distance.

She pressed a hand against the bracelet, feeling its pulse under her fingers. Zeus might not intervene yet, but even his patience had limits, and the pull of his cosmic order tugged at her like a subtle undercurrent, waiting to snap taut and drag her under.

But she couldn't afford to stop now, not when she was so close. With each relic gathered, each layer of influence applied, she moved closer to something irreversible, something far beyond the relics themselves.

The gods watched, some with caution, others with the thrill of witnessing what might unfold. As long as she stayed one step ahead, she had nothing to fear...yet.

Her scrutiny sharpened, her smile fading. For now, Medusa had seen nothing, knew nothing. But that might change, and Athena would have to be ready for when it did.

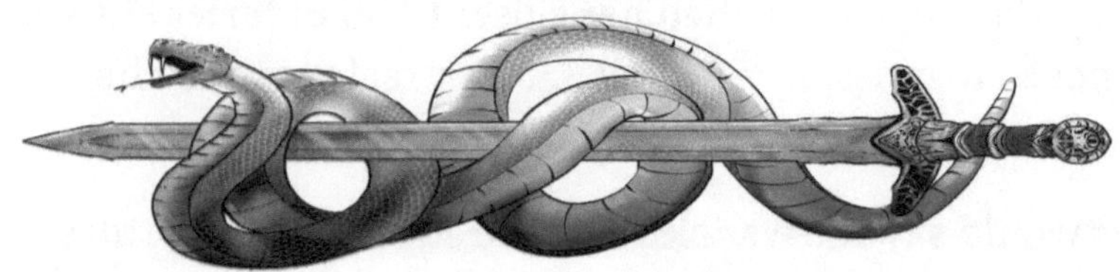

As Ophira continued toward the museum exit, a familiar tingling sensation crept over her skin. She paused and glanced over her shoulder, eyes drawn to the shadows at the far end of the gallery. There, obscured by the dim light, a figure lingered, watching them. She could see little more than the faint outline, but the presence was unmistakable.

Ophira's pulse quickened, memories flashing through her mind. Her first visit to the museum during this investigation. That same darkened silhouette. *Who is that?* The figure in the shadows didn't move and made no attempt to conceal its observation. It simply remained there, as if waiting.

The feeling intensified, and she quickened her pace, catching up to Marcus, who had already reached the main doors. She glanced back one last time, but the figure was gone, leaving only an uneasy silence in its wake.

Outside, cool night air struck her face, and she took a steadying breath, trying to shake the lingering sense of unease. Just as they started down the museum steps, she felt that prickling sensation again, but this time, it was closer.

Turning her head, she spotted Dr. Ghestad standing in the museum's entrance, partially shadowed by the columns but close enough to be visible. She was observing Ophira with an intensity that felt almost palpable, her face composed yet unreadable.

The shadows played over her features, lending a hard edge to her expression, as though she were appraising Ophira, measuring her in some way Ophira couldn't yet decipher.

Their eyes met, and Ophira felt caught, as if under a magnifying glass. Dr. Ghestad's expression revealed no clear intention, but the feeling it stirred was unmistakable. Calculated interest, as though she were being weighed and studied. Ophira's stomach twisted, her unease mounting.

"What is it?" Marcus's voice drew her back, his tone light, almost casual.

"Nothing," she replied, forcing a tight smile as she glanced once more toward the museum entrance. Dr. Ghestad was still watching her, unblinking, her posture unchanged.

"Let's go," she said, tearing her gaze away, the chill of Dr. Ghestad's silent scrutiny following her as they descended the steps. With every step, the sense of foreboding settled deeper in her chest, leaving her with one lingering certainty. This investigation had drawn the attention of forces that preferred to remain hidden, and that made everyone involved a target.

CHAPTER TWENTY-TWO

THE WALLS HAVE EARS, BUT THE EYES ARE WORSE

Two weeks had passed since their last visit to the museum, and now the institution had been transformed for its annual fundraising gala. The museum's grand atrium buzzed with conversation and clinking crystal, its chandeliers casting warm light across polished marble floors.

Soft strains of a string quartet wove through the crowd, adding an air of elegance that contrasted sharply with the tightly wound anxiety beneath Ophira's skin. The mingling perfumes of jasmine, bergamot, and hints of rich, exotic spices drifted through the air, mingling with the faint aroma of polished wood and aged stone.

Y'all smell that? Sunny murmured, her voice soft and honeyed. *Perfume's thick as a magnolia tree in bloom.*

Or a battlefield dressed up for a masquerade, Zeke quipped. *Ain't foolin' me.*

Enough, Sage interjected. *Focus on the details. Watch for who's watching us.*

Ophira's lips pressed into a thin line as she scanned the crowd, the snakes' voices weaving through her thoughts like a whispered chorus.

The museum gala had been underway for hours, and the evening's meticulously orchestrated elegance was beginning to show cracks. Diamonds and sequins glittered like constellations on evening gowns, the guests' cultivated laughter masking agendas and whispered secrets. Sharp tuxedos and tailored suits caught the light, while masked intentions made it difficult to tell friend from foe.

Ophira's dress was midnight blue, sleek and form-fitting, with intricate beading that caught the light as she moved. A single silver chain glimmered at her throat, and her dark hair was swept up, revealing the sharp lines of her collarbones. Her eyes moved sharply across the room, cataloging glances and subtle movements beneath her elegant facade.

Aric stood off to her left, striking in a three-piece suit of slate gray, the silver cufflinks glinting as he lifted a glass to his lips. His sharp eyes scanned the room, their depth betraying a readiness beneath the calm, composed exterior. His dark hair was neatly styled, and his posture exuded a confidence that matched the power simmering just beneath his skin. He caught her eye and nodded subtly as she approached, the tension visible only to someone who knew him well.

"You notice the watchers too, don't you?" he murmured when she stepped closer. "We're not the only ones working tonight."

Ophira's heart quickened. The sensation of being watched coiled around her like a serpent ready to strike. She followed his gaze discreetly, eyes landing on a man at the far side of the room, half-hidden in the shadows cast by a towering sculpture of Athena.

He was dressed impeccably, but his eyes, sharp and watchful, betrayed him. Another figure, a woman in a crimson gown, lounged near the drinks table, her laughter bright, her attention flitting back to Ophira often.

The air buzzed with tension, a silent current threading between glances and half-smiles, masking intentions beneath polished exteriors. Ophira's fingers curled at her sides, the glint of her silver ring catching the light as she exhaled slowly, trying to maintain her composure.

Marcus stood nearby, engaged in conversation with an older man whose wealth and influence were written in the cut of his midnight blue suit and the way others glanced at him. Marcus's black tuxedo, tailored to perfection, accented his lean frame.

The dark silk of his tie shimmered subtly, hinting at deep emerald undertones when the light hit it just so. His hair was immaculately groomed, and his expression held the same intellectual enthusiasm she'd come to appreciate.

He caught her eye briefly, the corners of his mouth lifting in a smile, though she could see the slight tension in his shoulders that suggested he was feeling the strange atmosphere too.

And then there was Dr. Ghestad, a vision of understated elegance in a dark green gown that swept the floor, embroidered with gold leaves that seemed to shift and shimmer as she moved. Her hair, usually pinned back in a severe twist, was softened tonight, framing her face in gentle waves. Her eyes, however, were as sharp as ever, cutting through the layers of small talk and pleasantries like a blade. She stood at the center of a cluster of academics and benefactors, commanding their attention with the ease of someone accustomed to both authority and admiration.

Ophira's gaze flicked between them, the pieces of the evening slotting into place with a sense of foreboding. Aric leaned in, his breath brushing her ear as he spoke. "Ghestad isn't the only one to worry about. Word of our investigation seems to have spread – we've got more eyes on us than I'd like. The question is how they found out, and what they want."

She nodded slightly, scanning the room again and feeling the chill of realization settle over her. The watchers were many, their gazes flickering like ghostly hands skimming over her skin, searching, assessing. A man with an ornate mask of polished ebony watched her from a distance, eyes hidden but posture stiff with intent. Another stood near the bar, lifting a drink to his lips without ever quite breaking eye contact.

"Trust no one," Aric's earlier words echoed through her thoughts, a steady reminder. She forced herself to relax, blending into the crowd while her instincts kept her on high alert.

"I know," she whispered, eyes narrowing as she caught sight of another familiar face. One of Dr. Ghestad's aides stood close, watching Marcus with an expression that spoke of more than professional interest.

The music swelled, a sudden shift in the strings sending a shiver down her spine as the tension around her thickened. It was as if the air itself buzzed with the electricity of unspoken motives, alliances shifting and twisting in the space between words. Ophira took a measured breath, the sweet notes of the violin barely masking the dissonance that hummed just beneath the surface.

The gala, for all its opulence and splendor, felt like a stage where every player was masked and every move scripted. But tonight, Ophira was determined to read between the lines, to see beyond the glitter and masks to the truth that slithered beneath.

Marcus turned away from his conversation, his eyes catching hers with a question in their depths. She nodded once, and he made his way over, his movements fluid, every step controlled. As he reached her, the corners of his mouth lifted slightly. "Enjoying the gala?"

"It's...enlightening," she said, letting the edge of sarcasm cut through her polite smile. "I didn't expect so many familiar faces."

"Nor did I," Marcus replied, a subtle shift in his gaze revealing a flicker of shared concern.

Before she could say more, a sharp laugh cut through the din, drawing her attention back to Dr. Ghestad. The older woman's eyes were on them now, and her smile, though pleasant, held a glint that made Ophira's blood run cold. She felt the weight of Dr. Ghestad's appraisal, as if every layer of pretense and poise had been peeled back, leaving her exposed.

Ophira forced herself to maintain composure, their voices a comfort amid the tension.

Aric's voice was a grounding force at her side. "Steady, Ophira. We need to play this right."

She nodded, the thrumming tension in her chest solidifying into resolve. Whatever game was being played tonight, she was determined not to be outmaneuvered. The night was far from over, and the actual dance was only beginning.

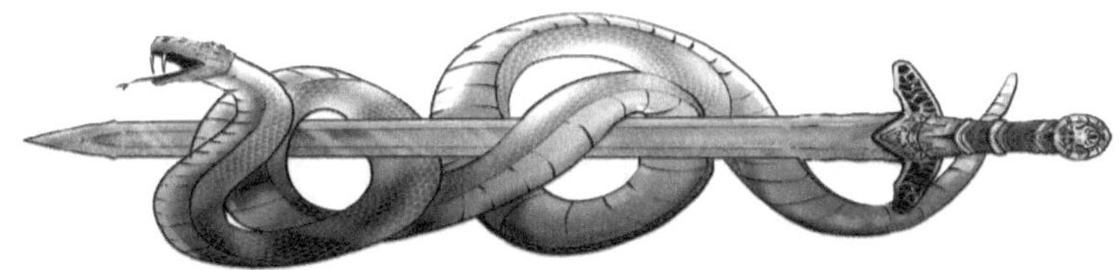

Ophira stood at the edge of the gala, forcing herself to blend in with the elegance surrounding her. The room pulsed with conversation and too-light laughter while a string quartet played an intricate waltz. The air carried expensive perfumes mixed with champagne and the subtle aroma of hors d'oeuvres.

She exhaled slowly, sweeping her gaze over the crowd as her heart kept time with the music that had been playing for the past hour. Somewhere in the sea of satin and sharp smiles, Dr. Ghestad wove her way through the elite, moving as seamlessly among them as the artwork that lined the museum walls. Ophira's fingers tightened around the delicate stem of her champagne glass, the chilled surface grounding her, if only barely.

Awareness of being watched struck her chest like a blade, demanding action. But one wrong move would reveal that she'd detected the surveillance. The museum, with its gilded walls and illustrious patrons, was not the place for a confrontation with whoever was orchestrating this observation. Not tonight.

Someone's coordinating this surveillance, but I don't know who or why. Behind her carefully composed expression, thoughts raced through tactical scenarios and escape routes.

Dr. Ghestad was engaging with the crowd, an easy smile on her lips, the silver pendant at her throat shimmering under the chandelier's light. Ophira's gaze narrowed as she tracked the subtle movements of the older woman, how her eyes would flicker with hidden intent whenever someone mentioned the artifacts on display.

A burst of laughter erupted nearby, drawing Ophira's attention for a moment. Aric was standing with a group of polished guests, his stance relaxed but eyes alert. He glanced at her, a sharpness in the way his eyes met hers. He always seemed to know. Unspoken warnings wrapped around her like a shroud.

If we move too quickly, we could miss something important, the thought echoed in her mind, each repetition a reminder to maintain patience. She forced a smile at a passing guest's greeting, her mask of civility sliding back into place with practiced ease.

Marcus's presence was a steady pulse on the edge of her awareness. He moved through the crowd with quiet confidence, engaging in conversations with the natural ease that made him so effective at gathering information. His methodical approach reassured her, the way he extracted details without effort. *He has a gift for this kind of work,* she reflected, watching him seamlessly transition between different groups of guests.

Ophira's pulse quickened as Dr. Ghestad's gaze found hers from across the room. A moment of recognition passed between them, a silent acknowledgment that sent a shiver down Ophira's spine. The older woman's smile was warm, but the eyes behind it were cold, assessing. Calculating.

The room, with all its luxury and polish, felt like a trap. Every polished surface and flicker of light reflected secrets waiting to be exposed. And tonight, they were all players in the same dangerous dance, pretending the stakes were no higher than an exchange of pleasantries. The frustration gnawed at her, the need for answers clawing under her skin. But for now, she needed to wait. Watch.

Soon, she promised herself. *Soon, we'll be able to draw them out. But not tonight.*

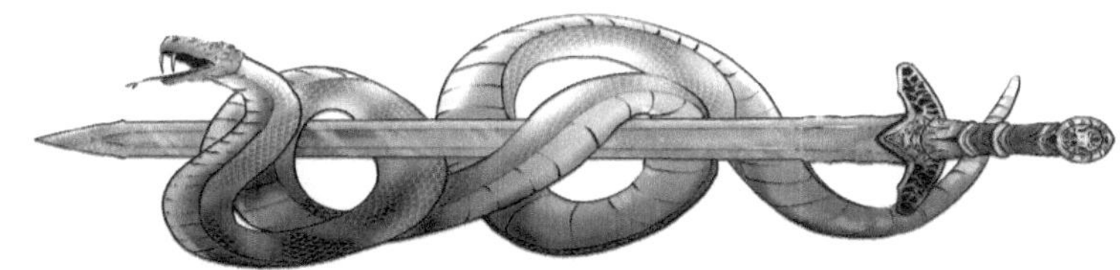

The grand hall glittered under crystal chandeliers as the night stretched on, music weaving through the crowd like an unseen thread. Polite laughter layered over conversation, creating a facade that couldn't mask the feeling of unseen forces watching from the shadows.

Ophira felt the weight of the night pressing down on her as she moved through the crowd. Her midnight blue gown, with its intricate beadwork, seemed to catch the light with each step, drawing glances that made her uncomfortably aware of being observed. Her attention was fixed on the shadowed glances that felt concentrated and intentional.

The first figure that caught her eye was a man leaning against one of the towering marble columns near the bar. His profile was sharp, cold eyes calculating as they swept the room. He wore a tailored black suit that should have let him blend with other guests, but predatory stillness betrayed him. Ophira's gaze lingered on him for a moment.

His eyes met hers as if sensing her attention. He tilted his head slightly, the ghost of a smile playing on his lips before he looked away. A chill rippled down her spine.

"I don't like the look of those guys near the bar," Aric said low and guarded. He had moved to her side, his expression casual, but the tension in his jaw betrayed his unease. "They've been tracking us all night. Watch them."

Ophira nodded subtly, shifting her focus. A few feet from the sharp-eyed man, another figure stood, this one a woman with striking platinum hair gathered into a sleek twist. Her black dress with silver accents shimmered with each movement. The jeweled brooch at her collar caught the light, reflecting a glint that reminded Ophira of a serpent's eye.

She mingled with apparent casualness, but her gaze kept returning to Dr. Ghestad's conversation circle. Ophira's heartbeat quickened. *Dr. Ghestad or me? Who are they after?*

Marcus's laughter rang out from across the room, full of charm and life, breaking through her surveillance anxieties for a moment. He stood near a circle of dignitaries, displaying the same enthusiasm that had drawn her to working with him. *He really is in his element here, isn't he?*

Yet tonight, even his natural ease couldn't shake the feeling that they were all being watched. She felt her chest tighten as he excused himself and slipped down a hallway toward the private exhibit rooms – probably seeking a quieter space to decompress from the social pressure.

Stay safe, she thought, wishing she could force him to stay in the safety of the group. How could anyone be relaxed in this atmosphere when every instinct she had was screaming that they were walking into something dangerous?

Aric pulled her back to the present. "There's another one," he muttered, nodding subtly toward a man stationed near the entrance, half-hidden in the shadows of an ornate archway. The man's dark suit and plain appearance should have made him invisible, but there was an air of tension in the way he stood, his gaze flitting between Marcus's retreating form and Ophira.

"They're watching us," Ophira whispered, the realization hardening into certainty. "But why? Are they trying to figure out how much we know about the artifacts? Or are they hoping we'll lead them to something?"

The question lingered, unsettling her as she searched for the reason behind their surveillance. *They're after something, but whether it's information about our investigation or something we've already discovered remains to be seen.*

The room suddenly felt smaller, the gilded splendor suffocating. She glanced at Dr. Ghestad, who was now speaking to a renowned archaeologist with a practiced, warm smile. The older woman's dark eyes, however, betrayed nothing. It was impossible to tell whether she noticed the figures observing her, or if she was part of a more elaborate web that Ophira hadn't yet seen.

Ophira's fingers flexed, itching for action. She took a steadying breath, forcing herself to relax the tense lines of her body as she offered a polite nod to a passing couple who paused to compliment her dress.

"Stay close," Aric said, his voice soft but steely. His gaze darted toward Marcus's direction, then returned to hers. A protective glimmer in his eyes steadied her more than she wanted to admit.

"Always," she replied, the word holding more weight than either of them acknowledged.

The minutes dragged on as Ophira watched the crowd, marking each subtle movement of the watchers. The man by the bar engaged in brief conversation with a guest, though his eyes constantly flitted back to her and Aric. The platinum-haired woman moved closer to Dr. Ghestad, her posture one of casual interest, but her gaze keen and predatory.

After what felt like an eternity, Marcus reappeared from the hallway, his expression relieved to be back among familiar faces. He approached with a warm smile, immediately focusing on her. "You look troubled," he said quietly. "Have you been worrying again? Sometimes we see patterns that aren't there when we're stressed or overtired. Try to relax, Fee. It's a society benefit, not an arena. The most nefarious things happening tonight are someone trying to sleep with someone else's wife. Maybe a bit of opportunistic industrial espionage. It's your area of expertise, of course, but I haven't noticed anything wrong."

Ophira felt some of her tension ease as he lifted a glass from a passing tray, his movements naturally gravitating toward their group. She masked her unease about the figures positioned around the room and the moment of doubt that she felt at Marcus's comment. *At least he's back where I can see him.* Relief that he hadn't wandered off alone for long untied her nerves.

What are they up to? Ophira wondered, the question coiling tighter around her growing concerns. The surveillance team's coordinated positions replayed in her mind. Their careful observation techniques. Their professional spacing. Each detail built upon the last, forming a picture of expert surveillance that made her increasingly nervous.

The air shifted as Dr. Ghestad's gaze found hers once more, lingering with a look that was almost amused. Ophira's breath caught. They were all playing a game tonight, one in which the stakes were hidden beneath layers of silk and civility.

They keep watching us, she thought, eyes scanning the room as more polite conversation carried through the space. *What are they hoping to learn?*

Classic surveillance setup, Sage noted. *They're trying to look casual while tracking our every move.*

Mi amor, can we just agree someone's playing a deeper game here? Valentina sighed. *Let's figure out who's really pulling ze strings, non?*

Sunny's voice was a balm, calm and steady. *Something bigger's happening tonight, sugar. But we'll figure it out.*

As the gala wore on, the hall grew warmer, the atmosphere charged and tense, though none of the finely-dressed attendees seemed to notice. Ophira lingered near a statue, blending with the crowd as her gaze kept finding Marcus.

Each movement he made, each easy laugh, every slight glance in her direction, made her more aware of how exposed they both were to the surveillance team. She couldn't ignore it any longer. The watchers, the careful positioning, and the way their investigation had drawn unwanted attention.

We've been too lax about information security, she realized, her pulse steadying with resolve. *I can't let this surveillance continue without understanding who's behind it and what they want.*

The weight of that realization bore down on her as she watched Marcus speak with Dr. Ghestad. The ease with which they interacted, the way they discussed their research so openly, made her suddenly aware of how many people could have been listening in on their academic conversations. Whatever information had leaked, it had drawn the attention of people who preferred to stay in the shadows.

Her hand curled around her glass, the pressure grounding her. Her mind replayed the moments she'd been careless. The times they'd discussed findings in public spaces. The times their enthusiasm for discoveries had made them forget basic operational security.

And yet, beneath the frustration, she felt protective of both Marcus and Dr. Ghestad, who had no idea their scholarly collaboration had put them all in danger. *How did our investigation attract this kind of attention?* The question clawed at her, but her instincts had taken over, urging her to finally face the reality that their investigation had grown far beyond its original scope.

Beside her, Aric moved closer, his expression unusually grave. "Something is off," he murmured under his breath, his gaze darting toward a man lingering near the ballroom's far end. "I don't like the feel of this crowd."

Ophira's gaze shifted, and she noted the watchful figure he mentioned. A man dressed well enough to blend in, but with an alertness that set him apart. His gaze met hers for just a moment before he turned away, his movements smooth and practiced. Nearby, another figure mirrored the same behavior, his attention keen and unwavering, his presence unnervingly familiar. *Wait. Isn't that the guy who bumped into Marcus outside the coffee shop?*

Aric's voice pulled her from her thoughts. "They've been watching us since we arrived. We should be ready. This could get dangerous fast." His voice was low, the calm steadiness of his tone belying the tension beneath it. He gave her a slight nod, a shared acknowledgment of the growing storm around them.

In the distance, Marcus's voice drifted through the air, his words wrapped in enthusiasm, his laughter authentic as he engaged a small group of dignitaries. But then he vanished from sight, moving through the crowd toward what looked like a quieter area. Ophira's heart tightened as she scanned the room, her protective instincts flaring when she spotted the surveillance team tracking his movement.

When Marcus returned from his brief conversation across the room, he caught her watchful expression. "You're scanning for threats again," he said with gentle amusement. "I've noticed you do that when you're feeling overwhelmed."

Maybe I am being overly paranoid. With all these potential enemies around, none of us should be wandering off alone... but am I seeing threats that aren't there?

The gala's atmosphere felt suffocating, a haze of tension that seeped into her bones as she became more aware of the co-ordinated surveillance. She took a deep breath, steadying herself, but the weight of being watched pressed down on her, casting shadows over every interaction.

She moved through the crowd, her mind racing as she tried to identify all the potential threats while maintaining her social composure. It was as if they were all dancing on the edge of a trap, unaware of how carefully orchestrated this entire evening had become.

The night deepened, the laughter and music carrying on like a facade, a mask that couldn't entirely conceal the undercurrent of danger building in the air. Her gaze found Marcus again, just across the room, standing near an arched doorway, speaking with someone she couldn't quite see. His posture seemed alert rather than relaxed, and she wondered if he was finally picking up on the strange atmosphere.

I need to stay aware, she thought, her breath hitching as she considered their options. *We can't let whoever's watching us gain any more information. Something is building toward a confrontation, and we need to be ready.*

Her mind was a whirl of protective instincts. She felt a deep loyalty to Marcus, concern for someone who had become important to her. Someone whose scholarly passion had drawn dangerous attention. She couldn't ignore the reality that their investigation had attracted forces beyond anything they'd anticipated. As much as she wanted to understand who was behind the surveillance, she knew they were all walking into something far more complex than academic research.

A soft murmur of voices near the bar caught her attention, and her focus sharpened. Two figures – both well-dressed but with an air that was just a touch alert, a bit detached from the warmth of the crowd – were speaking quietly, their expressions shadowed.

Ophira's instincts screamed at her, a silent alarm reverberating through her senses as she took in their watchful glances, their subtle shifts in stance as they scanned the room.

Aric, at her side, seemed to pick up on her tension. "They're not here for the party," he said, his tone edged with wariness. "It's only a matter of time before something goes down."

Ophira nodded, her resolve solidifying. They needed to be ready. Whatever game was being played, whatever role these shadowy figures held in the larger scheme, she wasn't about to stand by and let them take control. She'd been manipulated, deceived, and kept in the dark for too long.

Ophira exhaled slowly. Tonight, she would wait. But soon the truth would come to light.

The urge to confront the surveillance team swelled within her, but she fought it down, the rational side of her mind reminding her of the delicate balance they walked. If she acted too soon, she'd reveal that she'd detected them, putting herself, Aric, and Marcus at even greater risk. She forced herself to breathe, her heartbeat pounding like a war drum as she steeled her resolve.

Not tonight, she told herself, her fingers flexing as she pushed down the need for action. *Tonight, I observe. Tonight, I gather intelligence.*

But even as she thought it, she knew that waiting would come at a cost. The threads of safety that had protected their investigation were unraveling, each new watcher revealing just how exposed they'd become. This wasn't about academic research anymore. It was about forces that operated in shadows, wielding power and resources she hadn't even begun to understand.

Her gaze swept the room, cataloging each suspicious figure positioned throughout the crowd. *I'm getting closer to understanding the scope of this,* she thought, the conviction settling over her like steel. Soon, she would have a clearer picture of who was orchestrating this surveillance. And when she did, they'd need to decide how to respond.

But tonight, as the shadows deepened and the watchers maintained their positions around them, she held her silence, her determination simmering beneath her calm exterior. They would need to address this threat directly. And when they did, there would be no turning back.

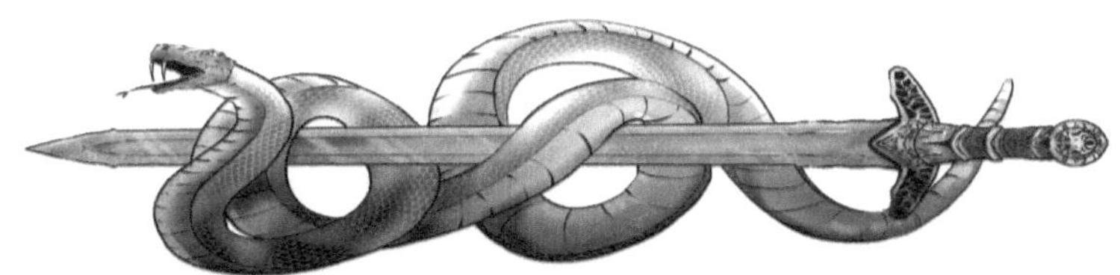

The string quartet's final notes lingered as Ophira felt relief washing over her. She, Aric, and Marcus made their way to retrieve their coats. The night had brought constant tension, watchful eyes tracking her every move with prickling awareness. She exchanged a purposeful glance with Aric as they neared the coat check. Silent acknowledgment of what they'd both sensed all evening, a feeling that went beyond suspicion to something predatory.

Ophira's jaw tightened.

They slipped on their coats, and she adjusted her collar, subtly checking that everything she needed was in place. Yet she still felt the weight of unseen eyes pressing in on her.

"We should avoid the main entrance," she murmured, keeping her voice low. "Too many spectators."

Aric nodded, glancing over his shoulder before looking ahead. "Agreed. Better to slip out unseen."

Ophira adjusted her coat, ignoring their banter as her senses prickled with unease.

Marcus raised a brow, studying her with gentle concern. "You seem more on edge than usual tonight," he said softly. "I thought you'd feel comfortable at these types of events. Wasn't that what you mentioned over dinner last week when we were talking about the gala?"

Ophira paused, a flicker of uncertainty crossing her mind. Had she said that? She remembered feeling relaxed with him at the restaurant, but this felt different. "Tonight feels different," she said finally, brushing past his quizzical look.

She couldn't explain the gut feeling that tugged at her. The night had held enough suspicion to warrant caution, and she had no interest in parading through the foyer under watchful eyes.

Ophira nodded almost imperceptibly, the snakes' commentary layering over her instincts. As they reached the door to the garden exit, Marcus took the lead, opening it for them.

"This way," he said, gesturing toward the quiet pathway that led around the building. The darkness beyond was softened only by the dim lights along the path, casting long shadows against the manicured hedges.

They stepped out into the cool night air. After hours in the heated museum, the temperature cut sharply against their skin. The door closed behind them with a soft click, sealing them in silence. A light breeze rustled through the trees and hedges, carrying the scent of night-blooming flowers and freshly turned earth. The garden's dim lighting cast a soft glow that barely illuminated statues dotted around the lawn.

Ophira walked ahead with Aric, her senses still keenly alert. She glanced back. Marcus reached into his coat pocket, then paused with a confused expression. "That's odd," he said, patting his other pockets methodically. "I know I put my phone in my coat when we got our things from the check. I was going to text our driver about the pickup location." His brow furrowed in confusion. "I must have left it inside. Go on ahead. I'll only be a minute."

Ophira gestured toward the path. "No problem, we'll wait by the garden entrance," she said, watching him head back to the door with a quick, grateful nod.

As Marcus disappeared through the entrance, Ophira's eyes instinctively scanned the perimeter of the garden. The silence here felt heavier, more pressing, as if the night itself held its breath. The faint rustle of leaves caught her attention, the quiet crack of a branch breaking nearby. She stilled, her hand brushing against her coat, where a thin blade was waiting.

"You hear that?" she whispered to Aric, her tone calm but alert.

Not just that. Them. Sage noted grimly. *Multiple. One's flanking left.*

And I see another by the hedges, Zeke confirmed. *Y'all ready for a fight?*

Sunny's voice came through, calm and steady. *Breathe, sugar. Let's see what they've got before we worry too much.*

He nodded slowly, his eyes narrowing as they surveyed the area. "We're not alone."

Before she could reply, a shadowed figure slipped from behind a nearby statue, moving with purpose. Another figure emerged from the opposite side, then another, each cloaked in darkness. Their movements were precise, too focused to be mere passersby. A flicker of steel caught the dim light, and Ophira felt her pulse quicken, her body shifting instinctively into a combat stance.

Beside her, Aric's stance shifted into combat readiness. "Someone wanted to split us up," he said grimly, scanning their attackers. "Make us easier to pick off. Could have used an extra pair of hands."

Ophira nodded, her focus sharpening on the threat before them. Worry for Marcus flickered through her thoughts before tactical training took over. *We can handle this ourselves.*

A small, sly smile curved her lips as she mentally inventoried her "accessories." The thin blade in her coat lining was sleek, silent, and as practical as it was deadly. Then there were the slim daggers strapped to her thighs, just beneath the slit of her evening gown, perfectly accessible with a slight shift in stance. In her bra's lining was the garrote wire, a silken thread sharp enough to end a life in a whisper.

And her shoes… *Those* heels had a reputation for more than mere looks. She glanced down, almost fondly, at the stiletto points hidden in each heel. Useful for more than a scrape.

Some people learned etiquette for gatherings like these; she learned how to stay armed and unnoticed. *An arsenal fit for a gala,* she thought dryly.

The figures closed in, surrounding them in a half-circle formation. Ophira's hand went to the blade in her coat, her muscles tensing as she calculated her next move. The path was narrow, boxed in by tall hedges on either side, and with the museum wall behind them, they had no clear escape.

"Stay close," she murmured to Aric with a smile, echoing his words from earlier with a sidelong glance that he met with a quick nod. Her mind ticked through her options, cataloging the weapons she could use, the distance between herself and each assailant. *Four visible, probably more in the shadows.*

The thought cut through Ophira's mind with the same precision she planned to bring to this fight. She took a breath, assessing their formation and the environment around her. The attackers were closing in, their weapons glinting in the sparse moonlight. She needed freedom of movement, a way to maximize her leverage.

Her heels clicked softly as she pivoted, eyes darting from one assailant to the next. *These shoes are more than decoration,* she thought with a grim satisfaction, knowing the blades concealed in each heel would be more than adequate. She kicked them off, retrieving one in her hand as a blade snapped out from the stiletto heel.

Barefoot, she felt the earth more clearly beneath her. Cool stone and soft soil grounded her, balance shifting instantly. She took in her surroundings. Hedges to the side. Statues casting deep shadows. Just enough dim lighting to obscure her exact movements. *Perfect.*

CHAPTER TWENTY-THREE

OWL BE WATCHING YOU

The museum garden stretched before them, a maze of manicured hedges and scattered classical statues casting long silhouettes across intersecting gravel paths. Dim security lighting created pools of amber glow between darker recesses where sculpted gods and heroes acted as silent sentinels, bearing witness to the ambush taking place.

One of the attackers moved toward her, blade in hand, steely determination blazing in his eyes. Ophira sidestepped his lunge, her hand reaching up to her hair.

In one fluid motion, she slipped a jeweled pin free, letting her dark hair tumble down around her shoulders. The pin, sharp as any dagger, gleamed briefly in her hand before she used it to slice a line across his arm. He let out a hiss, clutching his arm as she spun away, already focusing on the next opponent.

A second attacker charged forward, swinging his nightstick with brute force. Ophira shifted her weight, dodging the swing with a swift twist of her body. She gripped the heel blade, thrusting it forward into her attacker's shoulder. The man cried out, stumbling back with the unexpected blow.

Aric moved beside her, his stance low and balanced, his eyes sharp as he tracked each attacker. Though he kept his gaze focused, there was something unusual in the way he maneuvered, as though the darkness itself deepened around him, hiding his exact movements.

Ophira noticed one of the assailants falter briefly, his focus wavering as though he'd lost track of his own body for a split second. In that instant, Aric attacked, his actions swift and decisive, taking full advantage of the unexpected lapse without even a flicker of hesitation.

Did you see that? Sunny asked softly. *The shadows... They're moving with him.*

Sage remarked, *But is it him or something else?*

Ophira focused on the figures closing in. Aric's movements, though uncanny, kept the assailants at bay. She narrowed her eyes, a fleeting thought surfacing. *Is the adrenaline blurring things, or did I really see that?* But she didn't have time to analyze it further as another attacker closed in from the left.

She lunged forward, catching the dazed assailant off guard, and slammed her knee into his gut. He doubled over, and she brought down the garrote from her bra lining, slipping it around his wrists in a quick, practiced motion, securing him briefly before she moved on. She had no intention of revealing her true power, but she intended to ensure they both left this ambush unharmed.

Another figure lunged toward Aric, but his reaction was quick. As the assailant advanced, the man seemed to lose his bearings, stumbling as though disoriented. Aric took advantage, striking the man swiftly and sending him reeling back. Ophira noted the subtle shift in the attacker's stance but dismissed it, focusing on her fight.

"Thanks for the assist," she muttered, catching Aric's eye as they repositioned back-to-back, covering each other's blind spots.

"Anytime." His tone was even, his posture calm, though a flicker of tension in his eyes told her he was holding something back, and the quick, sidelong smile he shot her was almost sly. "Thought you could use the help."

The next assailant moved in with surprising agility, ducking under Ophira's strike and reaching for her waist. She twisted, using his momentum to bring him down onto the gravel path, pinning his arm with her knee and applying pressure until he cried out. She flicked her wrist, driving the sharp heel of her stiletto into his shoulder, making him jerk back with a grunt of pain.

As she turned, another figure lunged at her from the side, forcing her back against the hedges. The rich scent of earth and crushed leaves filled her nostrils as she braced herself, letting the shrubbery absorb some of the force. She barely needed to move; her next action was instinctual. She slid her thigh dagger free and sliced downward, catching his wrist with precision and forcing him to drop his weapon with a pained cry.

One of the garden statues cast a long shadow across the gravel path, and Ophira noticed how Aric angled himself toward it, subtly drawing an attacker into its darker recess. The shadow seemed to shift around him briefly, almost merging with his form. The attacker hesitated, and Aric used the opportunity to deliver a sharp strike to his side.

A sharp whistle split the air, and she turned to see one of the remaining attackers signaling to the others. They re-grouped, their eyes flicking between Ophira and Aric with new wariness. It was clear they hadn't anticipated this level of resistance.

"Look at that," Aric murmured, amusement in his voice. "They're second-guessing themselves."

Ophira smirked, slipping her garrote into her coat pocket and pulling her second thigh dagger free. She didn't respond, her focus solely on the movements of her enemies. One of them looked especially uneasy, his gaze darting to the path as if contemplating retreat. She advanced a step, watching the doubt flicker across his face.

Aric caught her look and leaned in slightly. "Let me handle this one."

She inclined her head, stepping back to give him space. Aric's focus sharpened, his posture shifting as he extended one hand toward the hesitant attacker. As he stepped close, the darkness seemed to deepen, as if the night wanted to cloak their actions. The man stumbled, eyes wide as he struggled to regain his balance. Aric moved forward, his stance calm, and landed a targeted strike to the man's temple. The assailant crumpled, unconscious, while the remaining attackers exchanged wary glances.

But then, from the shadow of an overhanging tree branch, Ophira noticed something. A flash of white feathers. She flicked her gaze upward, catching sight of an owl perched high above, its steady gaze locked on her and Aric. It was close, too fixed in its watchfulness to be a mere coincidence. An odd sense of foreboding crawled over her skin.

Why does it feel like we're being watched? The thought flashed through her mind, but she shoved it aside, re-centering herself as another attacker closed in.

"Focus," Aric said, catching her distraction and nudging her with his elbow. His eyes darted toward the owl for a moment, but his expression betrayed nothing more.

She nodded, gritting her teeth as she turned her full attention back to the fight. The man charging her was larger, broader, relying on brute force. She waited until he was nearly upon her, then dropped low, her leg sweeping out to trip him. He stumbled, his balance faltering, and she swung her dagger, catching the side of his leg. He collapsed, swearing under his breath, and she moved on without a backward glance.

Her fingers brushed the hidden blade in her coat lining again, seeking reassurance against the unknown number of attackers that might still lurk in the garden.

Beside her, Aric moved with experienced efficiency, each movement calculated to keep their assailants disoriented.

Ophira rolled her shoulders, barely out of breath, her body humming with adrenaline as she prepared for the next round. "Looks like they weren't prepared for us," she muttered to Aric, allowing herself the faintest hint of a smile.

"They should've known better," he replied, his voice low and laced with amusement. He jerked his head toward the remaining two attackers, who were visibly shaken.

One of them hesitated, glancing toward his partner as if seeking confirmation before moving in. Ophira took advantage of his pause, lunging forward and slipping her blade across his shoulder, a quick and controlled cut that would remind him not to underestimate her.

The last attacker, seeing the odds tipping further against him, made a quick assessment and backed away, his gaze flicking toward the garden path behind him. But before he could fully retreat, Aric used the darkness to close in on the man and strike just as he stumbled.

With a swift, final movement, she positioned her blade. She didn't deliver a killing blow, but she made it clear he wasn't walking away unharmed. The man yelped, stumbling backward as he tried to retreat, his gaze a mix of shock and fear.

Ophira took a step back, letting her hand fall to her side, but her eyes stayed on the men as they regrouped at the edge of the garden, their faces marred by hesitation and barely concealed fear. They'd come expecting a simple ambush, but she'd sent them off with something far more memorable.

Aric exhaled beside her, rolling his neck as he surveyed the scene. "That was fun," he remarked, casting her a sidelong glance. "I'm beginning to think you planned this."

She arched an eyebrow, letting her lips curve into a smirk. *If only.*

The garden was quiet for a moment, the defeated attackers retreating, their faces a mixture of pain and humiliation. Ophira lowered her blade, but her body remained tense, her gaze sharp as she watched their shapes dissolve into the night.

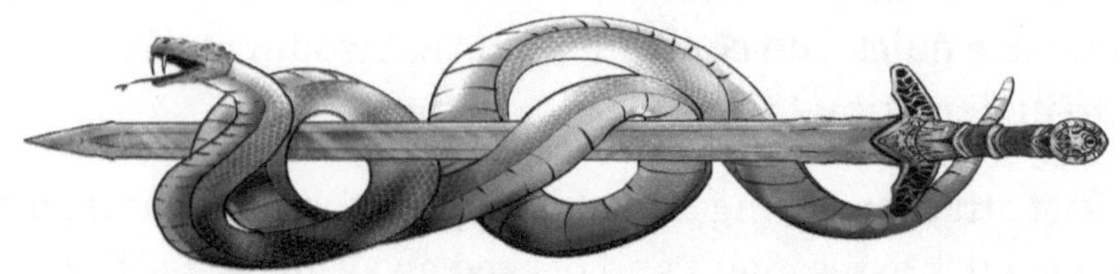

Above the silence, she heard a low, rhythmic flutter. Her eyes drifted up to the branch where the owl perched, its gaze locked on her. The bird's presence had unnerved her throughout the fight, an eerie witness to every strike and lunge. Now, without the immediate distraction of enemies, the weight of that unblinking stare became all the more apparent.

Why would an owl sit there, watching? she wondered, suspicion flickering in her mind. She glanced at Aric, wondering if he'd noticed it as well, but his attention was on the retreating forms of their ambushers.

The owl's focus stayed fixed on her, unblinking. She felt almost as if it recognized her, though she quickly dismissed the thought. *It's only a bird,* she tried to reassure herself, but a nagging feeling persisted, a sense that there was something more to its presence.

Her thoughts drifted to the legends she'd grown up with, whispers of animals serving the gods as eyes and ears in the mortal world. The owl, with its silent vigilance and penetrating stare, unsettled her in a way she couldn't explain.

For a creature of the night, it seemed awfully interested in the affairs of humans. She took a steadying breath, pushing down the instinctual feeling that she was being appraised, weighed, and judged.

"Interesting night, isn't it? You always take me to the nicest places." Aric's voice broke through her thoughts, steady and calm as he observed her lingering focus on the bird.

She tore her gaze away from the owl, the unshakable sense of being watched crawling along her nerves. "Yeah," she replied, "though I wasn't expecting an audience."

Aric followed her gaze upward, his expression neutral as he regarded the owl. "I think we're past expecting normalcy," he remarked, his tone almost wry.

The owl tilted its head, eyes catching the moonlight as it watched her with unnerving intensity. She could almost feel its gaze probing beneath the surface, as though it was searching for something hidden within her. A chill ran down her spine, and she resisted the urge to shiver.

"What's wrong?" Aric asked, noticing the tension in her posture.

Before she could respond, the museum's back door creaked open, and Marcus stepped out, looking around in confusion.

He crossed toward them with a quick, casual stride, his brow furrowing as he took in their disheveled appearance and the tension hanging in the air.

"There you are," he said, slipping his phone into his coat pocket. "What happened? You both look like you've been through a tornado."

Ophira met his gaze, the suspicion she'd felt throughout the night flaring up again, but she kept her expression controlled. "We were ambushed," she replied evenly, her voice calm but cold. "Right after you went back inside, a bunch of goons showed up."

Marcus's eyebrows rose in surprise as he took in their disheveled appearance. "Ambushed?" He looked between her and Aric with immediate concern, stepping closer to check for injuries. "Are you both all right? What happened?"

Ophira appreciated Marcus's immediate focus on their safety rather than the drama. Aric nodded, brushing off his coat. "We handled it. Professional hazard of the job, unfortunately."

Marcus frowned, clearly frustrated. "Damn, I wish I'd been here to help," he said, running a hand through his hair. "I hate that this happened while I was inside. Did you get a good look at them? Any idea who they were working for?"

Ophira shook her head. "They didn't stick around for introductions. But their coordination suggests this wasn't random."

Smart question about who sent them, she thought, noting his investigative instincts kicking in. *He's thinking like we are, trying to understand the bigger picture.*

"This exit was supposed to be quieter," Marcus said, looking troubled. "I suggested it because you wanted to avoid the crowd. I never imagined it would put you in more danger."

Wait, she thought, the uncertainty nagging at her. *Did I say something about avoiding crowds?* She tried to replay their earlier conversation, but it felt slippery in her memory, like trying to hold water. Or maybe she had mentioned preferring quieter routes without thinking about it; it was the kind of thing she might say automatically.

She almost opened her mouth to clarify, then stopped herself. She was overthinking it. The adrenaline crash was making her second-guess everything.

She could see the guilt in his expression and felt a pang of sympathy. "You couldn't have known. And honestly, if we'd gone through the main entrance, they might have followed us there instead."

"True," Aric agreed. "Better to handle it here than in front of a crowd of civilians."

Marcus nodded grimly. "Still, I should have been here. From now on, we stick together in situations like this. I don't like the idea of you two facing unknown threats alone."

Silence returned, heavy with the evening's tension, and Ophira cast a glance upward, catching sight of the owl once more. Its gaze held a steady, unnerving intensity, almost as if it had absorbed every flicker of tension between them, as if it understood what was left unsaid.

And then, with a silent beat of its wings, the owl took flight, disappearing into the night sky. Ophira's eyes followed its silhouette, her chest tightening with an odd sense of exposure, as though the night itself pulled away to reveal some hidden truth. That owl had watched the entire fight, perched like a silent judge. It felt like a warning, or maybe just a reminder, that they weren't as unseen as they thought.

The owl's departure felt final, like the closing of a chapter she couldn't quite understand yet. But as she turned back to Marcus, she knew that her battles were only beginning.

EVERYONE'S A PREDATOR UNTIL THE APEX ARRIVES

The necklace hadn't moved since she'd placed it on the scanner tray, but the air around it felt thinner, as if the silence itself were pressing in. Ophira leaned closer, eyes narrowing at the message on the screen:

```
Pass complete. No source match. No
material consistency.
```

The molecular readout blinked once, symbols she didn't recognize flickering across the screen like the shadow of something reaching for her. Then it stabilized again, silent and unhelpful.

That was the third time. A week had passed since the gala, and she had nothing.

She stepped back from the scanner, hands curling into fists at her sides. The sterile hum of the office's equipment filled the silence around her. The pieces lay scattered like fragments of a mirror she'd been too close to see clearly. Now, with the distance of hindsight, the pattern emerged with brutal clarity.

The watchers at the gala hadn't been interested in the artifacts on display or the academic presentations. They'd positioned themselves with military precision, their attention fixed on *her*. At first, she'd assumed it connected to the conversations she'd overheard at Dr. Ghestad's office about watchers and premature exposure. Academic rivalry was common enough, especially when significant discoveries were at stake.

But the ambush changed everything.

No academic dispute warranted that level of coordination or that degree of violence. The attackers moved like professionals, equipped and organized in ways that revealed serious funding and serious stakes. This wasn't about Dr. Ghestad's research being scooped by a competing university. This wasn't about protecting a publication timeline.

They came for me.

The realization struck her like ice water, sending a chill through her bones that had nothing to do with the climate-controlled room. Every calculated move. Every careful approach. Every too-convenient lead. Someone had designed it all to draw her deeper into something. But what? And why her specifically?

Her mind raced through the timeline. Marcus's case had seemed straightforward enough. Stolen relics, a missing necklace, the kind of high-end art theft that happened in elite circles. She'd taken it because the challenge intrigued her, because the puzzle pieces fit together in ways that sparked her curiosity.

But someone else had been watching that puzzle come together. Someone with the resources to mount surveillance operations and coordinate armed responses. Someone who cared enough about this investigation, or about stopping her specifically, to risk exposure.

The case wasn't drawing attention because of what they were hunting.

It drew attention because of who was hunting.

Something's off, Sage said, his voice tight and clipped, the tone he used when facts refused to line up. *None of this reads normally, even for collector-level artifacts.*

Maybe it's not about the relic, Sunny added gently. *Maybe it's about the people chasing it.*

Or the ones hiding behind 'em, Zeke growled.

The tension in her neck deepened. Her fingers drummed against the edge of the console, a rhythm of frustration. She'd rerun the analyzer, hoping to find a pattern in the static, something that would clarify the signature glitches that flickered like a coded message. But nothing was resolved. More contradictions, more questions.

She turned her focus inward for a moment, letting the hum of the machines fade away. The gala ambush hadn't just been an attack; it had made a statement. Someone had come for her, and they'd executed it with precision and resources. These weren't scavengers scraping by on the edges of illicit trade markets. They were organized, funded, and dangerous.

They came to collect.

Her stomach tightened at the thought. The snakes fell silent, and for a moment, the quiet felt oppressive, like a threat she couldn't name.

She accessed the shipping logs, not from the relic itself since it was unreadable, but from the crate that transported it here. The tag embedded in its base was a vintage military issue, but it hadn't been entirely cleaned yet. She processed it through the trace program, cross-referencing route paths, flagged collector IDs, and any data snippet that could provide a lead.

Zurich. Cairo. A clandestine logistics network meandering through cities like a serpent's path – Vienna, Athens, Tangier. Each connection raises more suspicion than the previous one. Lacking manifest data or a legitimate handler, it exists only as a series of shadows.

They're hiding their trail, she thought.

She frowned and adjusted the scanner's angle, letting the harsh light cut across the crate's metal plating. Scratches revealed layers beneath; hints of old seals, half-torn labels, and fragments of barcodes that didn't match any known registry. She leaned closer, feeling the sweat at her temples even in the chill of the climate-controlled room.

They knew what they were shipping, she muttered under her breath. *Or at least they knew it was worth protecting.*

A slow hum began behind her eyes, a pressure that felt like a headache developing, coiling around her skull. The ultra-collectors weren't just out there; they were ahead, already moving. Every second she spent trying to catch up meant they'd be one step closer to whatever endgame they were planning.

She shifted her focus to the necklace itself, still lying motionless on the tray. Its edges seemed to catch the light in peculiar ways, refracting it like a prism. The screen's glow reflected off its surface, creating a ghostly dance of colors that felt wrong, as if it were mimicking what she wanted to see. She reached out and let her hand hover just above the glass, close enough to feel a faint vibration through the scanner's metal.

You sure this thing's safe? Zeke's voice carried a rough humor, but there was a thread of worry.

Define safe, Sage retorted, sharp as a blade. *It's a relic. Safety's never been the priority.*

They wanted it badly enough to send blood after it, Ophira replied softly, eyes never leaving the necklace. *That makes it dangerous. And valuable.*

She rechecked the crate, flipping it over to examine the seams. A faint residue, perhaps old adhesive or something more sinister, clung to the edges. She scraped a sample and dropped it into a chemical scanner. The machine hissed, analyzing the compound, and returned a result she didn't recognize.

Another mystery, she thought grimly.

Sunny's voice slipped in, calm and steady. *Every piece matters, sugar. Even the ones that don't look important.*

Especially the ones that don't look important, Sage agreed.

Ophira straightened, rolling her shoulders to ease the tension that had settled in like iron bands. She ran her hand through her hair, brushing back sweat and stray strands that had come loose during the long hours she'd spent here. The room smelled of ozone and machine oil, a reminder that she'd made this place her second home and her battlefield.

She turned back to the computer, fingers flying across the keyboard as she dove into export records and black route registries. Every result seemed to lead to a dead end, a reroute that had been wiped clean, a handler ID that had vanished into bureaucratic fog.

Athens. Tangier. Vienna. Over and over, the same cities, like echoes in a labyrinth.

They're covering their tracks, she muttered. *But every reroute leaves a fingerprint.*

Sage's voice felt like a blade sliding into place, cool and precise. *And fingerprints can be traced.*

Ophira's pulse quickened. She rechecked the scanner's output, but the molecular readout refused to stabilize, flickering with indecipherable symbols every few seconds, as if the relic itself were resisting her attempts to comprehend it.

They want me to be afraid, she thought, her jaw tight. *They want me to stop asking questions. Well, too bad.*

She reached for the crate's embedded tag and plugged it into the system, rerunning the search. This time, she layered in a predictive algorithm she had built herself, one that could piece together partial routes and rerouted shipments, even when half the data had been scrubbed. The screen lit up with lines of code, a tangle of connections that spread like veins across a body she couldn't yet see.

The necklace hummed from its tray, like a warning. She felt its presence behind her, a relic with a thousand-year memory and a thousand reasons to remain hidden.

No more hiding.

Ophira leaned over the console, the hum of the system ringing in her ears and the glow of the screens casting a cold light on her face. She didn't have the full picture yet; too many pieces were missing. However, she had enough to know one thing: someone powerful wanted this relic, and they'd already shown they'd sacrifice to get it.

She wasn't going to wait for them to come knocking.

This case had stripped away her illusions about safety and secrecy. Someone had spent months, maybe years, orchestrating every move to bring her here, to this moment. This would be the last time she'd let herself be led blindly through someone else's game. From now on, she would be the hunter.

With one decisive keystroke, she locked in the search and sent a ping to the only being clever enough to stay hidden from the gods. The trickster god Dolos had given her the concealment charm that kept Olympus blind. Just invoking his name carried consequences. The chill that crept across her skin wasn't fear. It was the past catching up. And this time, she welcomed it.

Time to draw them out.

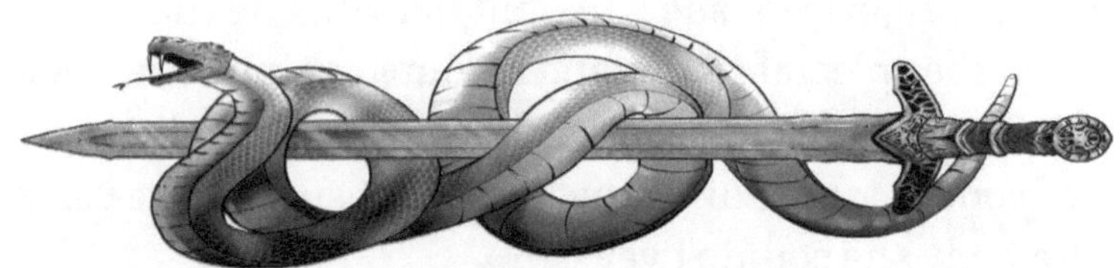

She opened a secure line and entered a number she hadn't used in years. The moment it connected, a familiar voice answered without a greeting, the tone laced with a mix of sarcasm and suspicion.

"Didn't think I'd hear from you again, little shadow."

Ophira took a deep breath to calm herself. "I need intel," she stated, her voice low and composed. "Ultra-level movement. Illegal trade activity. Any connections to high-profile intercepts that occurred in the past six weeks."

A pause. Static hissed between them.

"You looking to buy or just stir up ghosts?"

"I'm looking to stop something," she replied.

A low chuckle rumbled across the line, a sound she knew all too well. "Still dramatic. And still chasing things best left buried."

She refused to let his tone unsettle her. "I know you hear things. Fast transfers. Missing manifests. Heat."

Another pause, longer and heavier. She could almost hear him deciding how much to reveal and how much to withhold. Then: "There's chatter out of Sofia. A quiet move last week. No names, but it's the kind of package that travels with its own silence. Pulled from the train line before it cleared the tunnel."

"Intercepted?" she asked, leaning forward, eyes scanning the lines of code still flickering on the monitor.

"No. Redirected. Quiet. Clean. Professionals."

"Origin?" Her heart raced faster.

"Could be Cairo. Could be someone borrowing their routes. Hard to say."

She clenched her teeth. "Where did it go?"

"Some say it hit a vault in Prague. Others say it never left the city."

"And you?"

When he spoke, his voice carried a sharp edge she hadn't heard in a long time. "I say stay out of it. This game doesn't favor loyalty, and you're not as invisible as you used to be."

She let out a slow breath, her pulse hammering. "I'm not backing sides. I'm following leads."

"Then there's your lead."

A click. The call ended.

Ophira set the phone down, fingers lingering before she withdrew. The air felt charged, as if the necklace on the scanner tray were watching her. It still lay in stasis, inert but not harmless.

He's holdin' something back, Zeke muttered, suspicion edging his voice.

They always do, Sage said, his tone grim. *When has a god ever been totally honest?*

But he said enough, Sunny replied, gentle and calm. *It's a thread.*

It's bait, Sage countered, voice sharp. *And she knows it.*

Ophira let her eyes drift shut, jaw tight as memories pressed in like ghosts. The warehouse held shadows in every corner, with blood and betrayal lurking at every turn. It was the trap she hadn't seen coming until it was too late. The gala revealed chaos beneath the polished surface, an ambush executed with ruthless precision. And above it all, the owl remained a silent judge, untouched by the carnage. Cold. Distant. Certain.

Then there was Marcus. His name felt branded into her heart. His effortless charm and smooth voice that could talk his way through a locked vault. The way he looked at her the first time they met, as if he knew something about her that she didn't yet, that left both lingering intrigue and lasting unease. The first time she thought, *Maybe.*

She placed her palms on the desk's edge, centering herself in the moment. The scanner emitted a soft hum while the security monitors cast a pale light on her face. The heaviness of each choice she had made bore down on her. Every secret she had pursued, every lead she had tracked.

She thought of Delphine's warning, cold and direct. "The veil lifts only when you're ready to see."

The snakes shifted restlessly in the quiet.

Heat began to build in her chest, starting as a spark and spreading outward like molten metal through her veins. She had spent too many centuries allowing others to dictate the rules of engagement, letting them set the board and choose the pieces. That ended now.

She was Medusa. She had walked through empires as they rose and fell, survived gods and monsters, and carved her name into the shadows of history with her own hands. She was no mortal woman to be herded and hunted by faceless cowards who hid behind proxies and careful plans.

They wanted to play games in the dark? *Perfect.* The darkness was her domain, and she knew every twist and turn of the terrain they'd chosen. They thought they could flush her out, corner her, make her dance to their tune. But they'd made one critical miscalculation.

They'd awakened something they couldn't control.

Time to stop reacting and start hunting. Time to slither down into their carefully constructed rat holes and drag them kicking and screaming into the light. Let them remember what it felt like to be prey.

Her fingers curled against the desk's edge, and for a moment, she could almost feel the ancient power thrumming beneath her skin, the serpentine grace that had once made mortals freeze with terror. She might be playing human for now, but the predator beneath had never truly slept.

You've always known how to find the truth, sugar, Sunny's voice slipped in like a warm breeze. *Trust yourself.*

Zeke's tone came rough, with a smirk beneath the words. *And make 'em regret underestimatin' you.*

Sage sounded tired, but his words carried conviction. *Whatever path you pick, pick it. But remember, the shadows move when you do.*

Valentina's voice curled around the edges of her mind, low and dangerous. *At last, mon cœur, the viper rises. Let them feel what it's like to be caught in your coils.*

Ophira opened her eyes, the glow of the screen reflected in the dark depths of her gaze. She traced the sealed edges of the crate with her fingertips, feeling the faint residue of old labels and the weight of the secrets hidden inside.

She let her hand drop to the keyboard, her mind sharpening. The crate's manifest might be scrubbed, but every movement left a trace, no matter how well they thought they had covered their tracks.

She leaned closer, inhaling the sharp scent of ozone and machine oil, a smell that spoke of long hours and quiet wars fought in secret rooms. She had lived in the dark long enough to understand that every lie cast a shadow and every secret left a trail.

They thought they could scare her off with veiled threats and half-truths.

They were wrong.

Her mind flicked back to Dolos's last words. "This game doesn't favor loyalty."

Oh, well. She'd never played by their rules anyway.

A cold smile touched her lips. She wasn't going to wait for them to come to her door. If they thought they could dictate the game, they were in for a surprise.

She reached for the necklace on the scanner tray, letting her palm hover just above the surface. The metal felt cold even through the glass, as if it held its own memory of blood and betrayal.

No more hiding.

She pulled her hand back and let it drop onto the keyboard, her pulse steady now. She had found the lead, and she would follow it, trap or not.

She'd warned herself before: if someone was pulling strings, maybe it was time to start pulling back.

She started the program to run, cross-referencing every route and every shadowy transaction that might lead her to Prague or wherever the trail truly ended. The screen filled with lines of data, connections forming like veins across the surface, each one offering a possible path to the truth.

She allowed the tension to settle, her mind sharpening with each passing second.

She was done waiting. Done doubting. Done being moved like a piece on someone else's board.

Her voice carried quiet resolve. "I'm going," she declared, her tone filled with determination. "Even if it's a trap."

Let them feel what it's like to be in your sights, Valentina purred, her tone like silk over steel.

Be careful, Sage's voice, low but strong, followed. *The closer you get, the deeper the shadows reach.*

Zeke chuckled, the sound low and dangerous. *'Bout damn time, girl. Make 'em remember who you are.*

Sunny's voice came last, soft but resolute. *We've got your back, sugar. Always.*

Ophira let the silence settle, every piece of the puzzle pressing down like a weight she refused to let crush her.

If someone wanted her to dance in their web, they would soon discover she was no easy target. They'd learn, as countless others had too late, that some creatures were born to shatter silk and devour spiders.

She reached out and deliberately shut off the monitors, letting darkness reclaim the room. For centuries, she'd hidden in their light, wrapped herself in modern armor against ancient threats. No more. She no longer needed protection.

Her enemies did.

And with that thought, she was gone, a predator on the hunt for her prey. One who had finally remembered what her fangs were for.

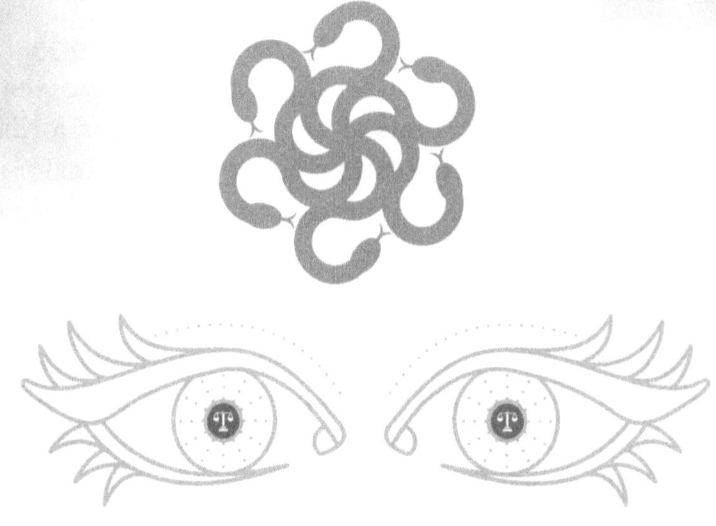

About the Author

A H Jordane is a fiction author of emotionally resonant story-telling, immersive world-building, and characters that linger long after the final page.

Her work spans urban fantasy, suspense, and paranormal romance, often weaving together high-stakes tension, sharp emotional arcs, and moments of unexpected humor. Jordane's stories explore identity, obsession, betrayal, and transformation; themes that unravel through cinematic pacing and layered, character-driven plots.

At the heart of every story is a deep love for clever structure, meaningful resonance, and the emotional truth that fiction can reveal when it dares to dig deep. Readers who crave immersive worlds, complicated relationships, and a touch of myth or menace will find a home in her pages.

Outside of writing, Jordane works in tech, bakes as a form of alchemy, and unapologetically spoils her extremely beloved dog. She believes fiction is one of the last wild places, where readers to to feel deeply, lose themselves, and come back forever changed.

Learn more about the worlds of A H Jordane at:

www.ahjordane.com